# LUBELIA
# ALYCEA

## One Hundred Years

# J.E. SPINA

# PUBLISHED BY J.E. SPINA

# COPYRIGHT 2021
# J.E. SPINA/JANICE SPINA

# COVER BY JOHN SPINA

# ALL RIGHTS RESERVED

# ISBN 978-1-7361673-2-8 (paperback)

# LCCN 2021906394

# DEDICATION

This book is dedicated to the memory of my Avoa (grandmother)
who lived for 100 years and five months.
She was loved for her feistiness and strength. She
was my inspiration to write this fictitious story about
a woman of her time.

# ACKNOWLEDGEMENTS

A very special thank you to my wonderful beta readers, Patricia Bradley, Michele Rolfe, and Frances Stewart for working tirelessly to read and review my work and for their helpful input. Their assistance is invaluable and appreciated.

Thank you to my husband, John, for the beautiful cover and for all the dinners he cooked that made it possible for me to write.

# Table of Contents

# CHAPTER 1

As they arrived at the restaurant, Jasmine and her husband, Giovanni, could see all the family getting out of their cars and heading into the big party. Avoa, (grandmother in Portuguese), would be coming shortly. They had to tell her ahead of time because of her age. She had turned 100 years old a week before. She was excited about her party, they had heard. Thankfully she was still in full charge of her faculties. That, in itself, was quite an amazing feat!

They rushed in and greeted everyone. There were so many of them now. Jasmine had lost count of how many relatives there were and the family kept on growing.

Before long Avoa was brought in by one of her grandsons. She was all dressed up with her navy blue dress, pearl necklace, earrings, and her two inch heels as always. They settled her down into a comfortable chair so that they could greet her with kisses, hugs and birthday wishes. She smiled at each in turn. She was a little hard of hearing now and one eye was not too clear, her vision dimming from detached retinas. She was still the feisty grandmother they had always known. She couldn't remember all of their names now, just the oldest ones. There were too many new great, great grandchildren to remember. Jasmine didn't know all of the many cousins' children by name either.

Jasmine observed her grandmother sitting with her aunt as she opened her gifts. Avoa watched the slide show of her life, blew out her candles and made a wish. What could she be wishing for now? She had it all, Jasmine wondered.

Jasmine had watched her grandmother open the present that she and her husband, children, spouses, and grandchildren had given to her. It was a pictorial book of Avoa's life as they knew it. Jasmine had written a short story and a poem of Avoa's life to put into the book. Her daughter-in-law Marianne, Timothy's wife, talented in scrapbooking and such, had put family photos and other mementos together and then added Jasmine's story and poem to the book. It was a beautiful testament to their grandmother's life and legacy.

Jasmine wanted to put Avoa's life into a novel to go along with the pictorial. She hoped to have it complete to show Avoa before she left this world. Time was passing too quickly now and who knew but God how long Avoa had left to tell her life story so it could be immortalized. Jasmine decided that today was a good time to get to know more about her grandmother's life and any secrets she may want to share with her. She had heard bits and pieces of her life through her mother and aunt over the years but it would be even better to hear these stories first hand from the source.

Jasmine walked over to her grandmother to ask, "Avoa, are you happy with your life? Is there anything you regret that you did or did not do? Would you like to share the story of your life with me?"

Avoa looked at Jasmine and smiled, a faraway look coming into her rheumy eyes. She sighed and said, "Yes," in a whisper."

She began the tale of her adventurous life...

# CHAPTER 2

One summer day in 1918 Lubelia was heading home from school with her twin brother, Antonio, lagging behind her skipping through the fields. She saw two men coming out of their house with a body on a board draped with a sheet. Tears filled Lubelia's eyes as she watched the men carry the body to the horse-drawn cart which was laden down with other bodies. She never looked away as they drove down the street. She continued to stare in that direction until the cart had disappeared.

My family! Could it be one of my family? Oh God, was it my father? She knew he hadn't been feeling well lately. What happened? She choked up at the thought. She grabbed hold of Antonio's sleeve and dragged him along to find out.

She ran into the house with Antonio in her shadow. Her mother, Filomena, and Lubelia's older brother, Manuel, were there to meet them with tears in their eyes and frightened faces. Her mother pulled them both into her arms and held them tightly. She then took Lubelia aside and sent Antonio to his room. She sat Lubelia on the edge of her bed. With a sad look in her eyes she told her what had happened to her father.

"Lubelia, you know your father was sick. I didn't tell you or your brothers that he was dying. I called the doctor. He examined him and called the undertaker. They took your father away. They said, 'He has Influenza and will not get better and that he will put everyone in danger of getting sick. He had to be removed immediately.' I'm sorry, mia filha. He did not make it. You know he loved all of us and would want us to be safe. You must do as I tell you. It would be what your father wanted. We have to be strong for him.

We need to pack our things and leave now. They will be back to take all of us away. They fear that we have been tainted with Influenza too and that we will spread it. Pack up only what you absolutely need for we have a long trip ahead of us. I will pack up some bread, cheese, fruit and water to take with us. It will only be enough for a few days. We need to get to the boat and leave our beloved island of Madeira."

"But Mae, where are we going? Will we ever come back to our home?" The words got stuck in Lubelia's throat as the tears ran multiple tracks on her face.

"This, I do not know, mia filha. You must be strong even if you are only eight years old. Go help your brother Antonio pack. He's slow and needs to be prodded along. You are stronger than he is, even though he is your twin.

Lubelia, before you go, please listen to me now. This is extremely important. Once you are finished packing you must go with your brother Manuel. Take your packs and run out to the fields and lay low. Do not let anyone see you. You must wait there for me. I need to take your brother, Antonio, to my cousin, Grinalda's house. Wait for me in the fields, do you understand, Lubelia?"

"But Mae, why are you taking Antonio to Grinalda's house? Why isn't he coming with us?"

"I will explain this to you in time, mia filha, my daughter, but now I must hurry and get him there safely. Hurry Antonio along now. Quickly, Lubelia!"

Lubelia went into the adjoining bedroom that she shared with her twin brother and told him to hurry up. He was sitting on the bed reading a book. He looked up to see her standing in the doorway with tears running down her face.

"Lubelia, what's wrong? Father will be okay. He will be coming home after he is better. Don't worry."

He is such a sweet little boy, Lubelia thought, and not nearly as tough as I am. She didn't have the heart to tell Antonio that it wasn't her father she was worried about but him, for he would not be going with them. As she looked at him with tenderness, she sighed and said, "Antonio, you must hurry. Mother said we have to pack up only what we need and wait for her. It is not safe here now."

"What do you mean, Lubelia? Why are we not safe here? We can't leave. Father will not know how to find us if we leave."

"Oh Antonio, father will not be coming back. He is...dead." Lubelia looked at her brother's grief stricken face as he started to cry.

Lubelia rushed over to the bed and grabbed Antonio's arm, pulled him up and hugged him tightly. She picked up his backpack, tenderly pushed him towards his bureau and instructed him on what to pack.

He looked at her with confusion; a hurt expression clouded his once bright, innocent, and happy face. Alycea wiped his tears and patted him on the arm. He resigned himself to packing and just shrugged his shoulders when she urged him to hurry up once again. He stuffed underwear, socks, pants and shirts and then put his favorite book, drawing pad and stuffed lion, Simmy, into his backpack as he was pulled from the room by his sister.

Their mother was waiting outside their room. She took Antonio by the hand and led him out of the house. He turned to look at Lubelia with a sad little smile and wave and went along with his mother, tears still brimming in his eyes.

Lubelia grabbed her backpack and choked back her own tears as she ran out of the room to meet her older brother, Manuel. She didn't understand why Antonio couldn't come with them. She didn't think she could leave without him. He was her other half, her twin.

Lubelia looked into the kitchen and saw Manuel standing there with his backpack, looking forlorn. She raised her hand to wave at him and he winked, smiled and threw her a kiss. His eyes did not reflect his smile but he nodded and beckoned for her to hurry and join him. They needed to hurry to the fields to wait for their mother.

They crossed the road from their house and ran into the fields of hay with their packs bouncing along on their backs. Once they reached the fields, Manuel told Lubelia to lie down and put her backpack next to her. He told her that she must lie still and be quiet. As he finished up his instructions and laid down next to her, he heard the clip clop of a horse-drawn cart coming up the dirt road.

# CHAPTER 3

Lubelia was the older of the twins, being born a few minutes sooner than Antonio. She was always the louder one when she cried, complained more when she was hungry, and caused more trouble when she did not get her way. She grew into a little girl who had a stubborn streak and a mind of her own. She was determined to do what she wanted and do it on her own terms. 'No' was not a word she would accept from anyone. Her parents loved her but didn't know what to do with her at times. She was not like either of them.

She had amber colored eyes and luxurious dark brown hair that waved and curled at will. As she got older it was more beautiful and so was she.

Antonio, on the other hand, was a complacent, sweet, happy and contented baby who became more so as he grew older. He only wanted to please everyone. He was attractive and had thick, curly, dark brown hair, the kindest and softest brown eyes you could ever hope to see. He loved reading, painting and walking in the sun by the shore. He favored his mother in looks and temperament. He was his mother's favorite son.

Manuel was Lubelia's older brother by five years. He was an adventurous boy with a free spirit. He never was serious about anything, whether it was school or chores. He slacked off with as much as he could. His parents never got angry with him since he was handsome and could charm his way out of any situation with his bright smile. His beautiful hazel eyes would sparkle when he knew he was in trouble. His hair was lighter brown than his siblings and was unruly, coarse and wavy; persistently falling into his eyes.

He always had something up his sleeve. His loves were the sea and girls, in that order. He had many girls following him around, in love with him daily. Manuel was his father's favorite son since he was so much like his father in every way.

Their mother, Filomena, was a lovely, sweet, caring and kind woman who possessed great strength of character. She was always putting others before herself. She took in anyone who came to her door and shared what she could of their meager supper with them. No one who came to her for help was ever turned away. She could be considered a saint by the Catholic Church for sure. She loved her family and took inordinate care to feed and clothe them. She was especially talented in needlepoint and sewing. She was also known to be an excellent cook, making many delicious Portuguese fish and seafood dishes.

Lubelia's father, Aurelio, was a charmer. He swept Filomena off her feet. Filomena was lovely as a young woman when they first met and he fell instantly in love with her beauty, lovely green eyes, light brown curly hair and her sweet nature.

Aurelio was a dashingly, handsome young man and had a dazzling smile and luminous light brown eyes. All the girls swooned when he walked by. But, he only had eyes for his Filomena. His loves, besides Filomena, were the sea, fishing and sailing.

Lubelia's parents did not finish school, each having to quit at the age of thirteen to help their families at home. But Aurelio had escaped working with his family in the fields after a short time by becoming a Merchant Marine at the tender age of thirteen hiding away on a ship that had docked at the port. He always had dreams of faraway ports and adventures, reading stories of buccaneers and pirates. He longed for excitement and loved the feel of the salty sea spray on his face as he sailed.

While he was a Merchant Marine, he had sailed for months at a time traveling to many ports. He returned home to see his family as often as he could.

Filomena and Aurelio both came from large families. Filomena had four sisters and three brothers. Aurelio had five sisters and three brothers.

Their families had farmed all their vegetables and raised chickens and cows. Back in 1890 life was hard and every member of the family had to pull their weight. As soon as each child reached the tender age of four they had chores to do. The children were taught how to feed the animals, clean out their stalls, milk the cows, gather eggs, and pick the vegetables from the gardens.

The younger ones were always watched closely by an older sibling to make sure they did not eat the animal feed or raw vegetables that they picked. Every item picked was used and nothing was thrown away or wasted. Food was scarce and precious. Life was difficult.

They married when Filomena was 15 and Aurelio was 18. Back then if a woman was not married by the time she was 15 she was considered an old maid.

Filomena and Aurelio gave up farming and moved away from their families to their own home. Their house was small but adequate for their needs. Their home had once been a small barn which they renovated on their own. They were determined that once they had a family, their children would have a better life and not have to work at the age of four as they had.

They had their first son, Manuel, within a year after they were married. Filomena had two miscarriages then a daughter,

Constanzia, or Constance. Constance died when she was only three from pneumonia. Once the twins were born two years after Constance, Aurelio left the Merchant Marines and returned home for good to help out. He took up fishing for his livelihood. Filomena's deliveries were long and painful and she nearly died birthing the twins. She could not have any more children after that. It was a blessing for her, for having another would have surely killed her.

Filomena Theresa always took time out of her busy, chore-filled days to pray to her favorite saint, St. Theresa, whom she was named after. It certainly had helped her spirits while Aurelio had been away at sea.

She kept St. Theresa's picture and statue in her bedroom and recited her prayer twice a day. She was never disappointed for St. Theresa showered her with blessings in many forms. She often smelled the scent of roses as she passed by St. Theresa's statue. The roses in her garden flowered even in the snow one year. She was thankful for she had been blessed with a good husband and three beautiful children.

She petitioned for good health for her family and was rewarded up until the day her husband fell ill. She trusted God to have a reason for his illness and subsequent death. She was to be given this task of keeping her family safe to prove herself worthy. She would not fail this task and would succeed in bringing her family to a safe haven. That safe haven would be America.

The day she was leaving her beloved Madeira, she prayed to St. Theresa for guidance, that through her intercessions with Christ, she would stay strong for her children and make a good life for them.

Aurelio had told her, when he had taken ill, that he was not going to make it. He wanted to make sure that his family was taken care of and safe. He told Filomena to take their savings and buy passage on the first boat out of there for herself and their children. Aurelio feared that they would all succumb to the same illness and not survive if they stayed with him. A few days later they came to take him. She only got to hold his hand a second, giving it a reassuring squeeze, before they whisked him away. He mouthed to her his last words, 'I love you. Do what I told you, Filomena,' and then he had passed.

She could not afford to pay for passage on the boat to America for all four of them. They had only saved up enough to pay for three. Her husband was taken ill too soon before he could earn enough to help her. She had used some of his earnings just to live and take care of him when he took ill. Her sewing and needlepoint were not bringing in enough revenue and she couldn't wait any longer to reach the amount she had needed for another passage.

She had to make a heartwrenching decision, no mother ever wants to make - to leave one child behind as she and her two other children fled the country of their births. She had decided to leave her youngest son, Antonio, with her cousin's family since her and her husband's siblings (the few that were still alive) were spread out all over Portugal and couldn't be reached as easily. She prayed that her son would forgive her for leaving him behind. He was not as strong as the other two children. She felt he would not survive the rough trip ahead by boat.

Her cousin had assured Filomena that her son would be well taken care of by her and her family. Once Filomena had a job in America she could send money to her cousin for his passage. She hoped to have all her children together in less than a year. After all, she had heard about America being the land of hope, opportunity and great fortune.

So, to America she would take her family to find this good fortune with the help of God.

# CHAPTER 4

Lubelia was careful as she peeked through the tall grass in the field at the horsedrawn cart that had just pulled up at their house. Two men had gotten out and had walked up to their door. They stood there a minute after knocking. When they realized no one was coming to open the door, they broke in.

Filomena was running towards her children now, but also keeping a watchful eye on the men as they went into her house. She took this as a sign to run to get Lubelia and Manuel and take them to the dock to buy their passages on the boat to America. Lubelia's parents had some friends who lived in America and they had told her they would sponsor her whenever she decided to take the family there.

Manuel was fast and strong but Lubelia's legs were shorter. She had a harder time keeping up with him and Filomena. They had to pull her along between them so they could get out of the fields and head toward the docks. Once they got there, the men would not be able to find them. The docks were always bustling with fishermen selling their catch and many men and women buying from them.

Filomena went to the window to buy their passage as the children watched in awe all the boats and the fishermen pulling in their catch. There were large tubs filled with blue and white marlin, bonito, wahoo, yellowfin tuna, cod, squid, shrimp and other fish they had never seen before. The air had the distinct smell of fish and blood mingling with the sweat of the fishermen. The children looked around at the beauty that was Madeira – the mountains, greenery, flowers and the sparkling ocean that offered them an escape.

Lubelia turned toward Manuel and said, "I remember the stories Pai told us about his life on the seas as a Merchant Marine. He loved these smells. I can see why. I feel them inside me and they are stirring me to want to go to sea too. I can't wait to get on the boat. It will be an adventure for us, Manuel. Can't you just see it now? We are going to America. They have a lot of stores there and food to eat, Pai said. He said he once went to Boston and New York. I hope we can go to those places too!"

Manuel just smiled and nodded at Lubelia. He seemed at a loss for words. But she knew that he loved it all too. He didn't need to say a word. She knew he understood and agreed with her. Lubelia could see the excitement in his eyes. She only wished her brother Antonio was with them to share this experience.

Manuel put his arm around Lubelia when he saw a tear run down her face. He patted her on the arm and placed a kiss on her cheek. He whispered in her ear, "You shouldn't cry and worry about Antonio. He will be fine. He will be joining us as soon as we can save up enough money in America to send for him. I promise I will do all I can to make that happen. I will even get a job."

At that thought Lubelia had to smile. It wasn't likely that Manuel could hold onto a job for long. The idea of it made her laugh. He had a good heart and meant well but was not dependable. He was just too free spirited to stay in one place for long.

Filomena tapped Lubelia on the shoulder and told her that they were ready to board now. She took Lubelia's hand while Lubelia grabbed onto Manuel's too as they headed up the gangplank to board.

They were about to embark on an adventure of a lifetime - one Lubelia was sure none of them would ever forget. She looked forward to a new life of excitement and sights that would be unforgettable.

***

The boat was swaying and dipping with each new three-foot wave and swell. The three of them were down below in their bunks stacked closely together.

Thank God the weather was still fairly warm. They were bundled up with a lot of their clothes on their backs that they had not been able to fit into their packs. This extra padding helped when each time the boat dipped with the waves they fell out of their beds, rolled into each other and bounced around the cabin.

Some passengers were in other cabins on top of their bunks holding their stomachs and bent over in pain, throwing up on one another, moaning and groaning for the swaying to stop. Others were deadly quiet – too quiet. Some would not survive the trip.

Their mother held onto both of them, swaying with the boat. All the time she was singing and praying to St. Theresa to keep them well and deliver them safely to their new home. She had brought a small statue of St. Theresa which she kept in her bag with the rest of her belongings.

Manuel and Lubelia were not as severely affected by the rocky movement of the boat. In fact, they both thought of it as an adventure, like riding on a wild horse. It was nice though to have their mother holding them tightly. They knew that she needed this comfort even more than they did. They feared for her health, for she was deathly pale.

They finished all their food in the first three nights. There was little food on board to go around. Right now that was okay since no one seemed to want to eat and probably wouldn't be able to keep anything down anyway. They rationed the water too, coming around once a day to give them all a sip from a bucket.

Lubelia started to pick up the singing and praying to St. Theresa that their mother had started. She felt that it couldn't hurt. Maybe St. Theresa couldn't hear her mother's voice alone and having one more voice might help St. Theresa hear them, Lubelia thought.

She poked Manuel and he started singing too. Before they knew it there were more voices joining them in prayer and song from the other cabins. They had been listening so long that now they knew the words too.

As their voices rose louder and stronger Lubelia detected a slowing of the swaying of the boat and she no longer heard the slap of the waves on its bow. There were others who were noticing this too and they softened their voices to listen.

Suddenly in the lull, they heard a cry from one of the hands above deck. He was yelling 'man overboard.' There was a scurrying sound as many other feet were heard overhead rushing to the rescue of the person who fell overboard. They threw a line to the man in the water but he couldn't reach it. After many more attempts to rescue him they could no longer see him in the water. They were finally resigned to the fact that they had lost him.

A scream went up from a woman in the next cabin across the corridor, who couldn't find her husband. She ran up on deck to find out if the man that had fallen overboard was her husband. She knew that he had gone on deck to get some fresh air earlier and had not returned.

One of the deck hands ran over to keep her from jumping overboard once she heard that it was her husband. The deck hand brought her below deck and she crumbled onto the floor, pulling at her clothes and hair, all the while calling out her husband's name – Manuel!

Filomena turned toward the sound of the woman's distressed cries and told her children to sit still and don't move, that she would be right back. They watched from the doorway of their cabin as their mother went to the woman, wrapped her arms around her and rocked her back and forth. She started a song that she had always sung to her children to help them go to sleep when they were babies.

The woman, Rosa Freitas, immediately calmed down and in turn hugged their mother back, all the while crying and thanking her. She asked Filomena, "What am I going to do when I get to America? I have no one, now that my husband is gone."

Filomena told her, "Please don't worry, Rosa. I will help you find a place to live." Other people hearing this also offered to help Rosa. Rosa praised God for all her new friends.

Mother certainly has a special way with people because she is so caring and compassionate, Lubelia thought. These were qualities Lubelia did not have but her brothers did. They were compassionate, caring and kind just like their mother. Her father was a good man too. She didn't know who she took after, thought Lubelia. She knew that she was strong, tough and stubborn. She had been told this often enough by her parents.

This strength, toughness and stubborn streak would serve her well over the years with the many trials she would have to bear.

# CHAPTER 5

It seemed like it had been a lifetime that they had been on this boat. Lubelia was tired of lying, sitting and walking around in circles.

It was an adventure at first but now it was sheer drudgery. She wanted so much to run free on land, smell flowers, see bees, birds and feel grass between her toes. She knew her brother Manuel felt restless and itchy too. He loved the sea but wanted to see America and was anxious about what they would find there.

He planned to get a job along with their mother while Lubelia would have to go to school. Lubelia told her mother that she could get a job too, but Filomena wouldn't even discuss it with her.

Filomena said, "Lubelia, you must finish school first. There will be plenty of time for you to work when you are old enough."

Lubelia fell asleep and dreamt of what she would do and become in America. She saw herself growing up and going out dancing with American men and to fancy restaurants to enjoy all the good food. One day she would meet a handsome man and get married and have children. Her children would have much more than she had and would grow up to become prosperous.

She woke up excited with her head full of wondrous things. She wanted to grow up to do all those things. She told Manuel what she wanted to do when they got to their new home. He said he had many things that he planned to do also. But he must first get a job, hence he would have some money. He wanted to meet the beautiful American girls and maybe settle down one day with one of them. He had many girlfriends in Madeira. Lubelia didn't know why they loved him so much. Well, he was handsome, after all, and had a nice way about him. Also, she couldn't forget that dazzling smile and his kind heart. She loved him deeply too!

She found herself leaning on him a little more because she missed Antonio intensely! She and her twin had been inseparable growing up. She wondered what Antonio was doing right now. Was he thinking of her too? She would have to write to him once they got to America and tell him all about everything she had seen and done.

She was feeling a little sad and homesick for Antonio and their beautiful island of Madeira. It was lush and green, had clear blue skies and beautiful views of the sparkling Atlantic Ocean all around and rugged mountains. She thought of the ships and the smell of the salt and fish that she loved. Her Madeira was famous for wine, gastronomy, historical and cultural value, flora and fauna, landscapes and embroidery artisans.

Manuel saw the look of sadness in Lubelia's eyes and promised to find work and send some of his pay to cousin Grinalda for Antonio's passage to America. He missed Antonio too even if he had teased him a lot about being small. Antonio loved Manuel dearly and looked up to his big brother.

No one could get angry with Manuel, no matter what he did. Their parents would scold him for teasing Antonio but they always had a twinkle in their eyes when they did it. They knew he really didn't mean it. His heart was too good.

As they were reminiscing, the boat was slowing down and most of the passengers were poking their heads out of their cabins to see what was happening. Manuel and Lubelia ran out into the corridor and up the stairs to the top deck. The sun had already risen and the sky was getting brighter and clearer. As they looked over the rail, they could just make out a tall figure holding something up.

More and more people were coming out on deck shielding their eyes from the bright sun. They, too, were looking in the direction of the figure. There was an audible buzz in the air as more and more passengers looked toward the horizon with mouths agape and eyes wide.

The children ran over to one of the deck hands and asked him what it was. He replied, "It's the Statue of Liberty. It is a great lady holding a torch to light the way for everyone who comes to America."

Lubelia couldn't contain her excitement and wonder at the statute. "Who made this lady?"

"She was built by a Frenchman named Frederic-Auguste Bartholdi," the deck hand replied with a smile of amusement on his face at Lubelia's question and intense interest.

"Why did this Frenchman built this for America?" Lubelia asked completely puzzled by what he told her.

He replied, "The people of France gave the Statue to the people of the United States in 1886 in recognition of the friendship established during the American Revolution. The Statue symbolized freedom and democracy as well as international friendship."

Lubelia looked at the Lady with great awe. She was truly beautiful holding that torch that lit the way for her, her family and many others to come to their new homeland.

She felt hope and promise growing inside her. Lubelia was feeling homesick for Madeira but now she felt that their new home would be wonderful too. She found a fluttering of excitement in the pit of her stomach. It could also be due somewhat to her growing hunger. It wouldn't be long now; they were getting closer to the Lady who was growing larger all the time.

Lubelia found herself straining to look up at the Lady's face. The Lady stood so tall, she blocked out the sun's rays as they got closer to her.

Lubelia asked the deck hand excitedly, "How tall is the Lady?" He smiled at her when he saw her eyes bright with anticipation and answered, "The Lady stands 305 feet tall from the ground to the tip of her torch."

"Can I go inside her and look out at the boats when we get there?"

He chuckled as he watched her excitedly jumping up and down. "Once you are processed you may go there. But don't expect it too soon. There are many, many more people ahead of you to be processed at Ellis Island," he added with dismay as she frowned at him.

Lubelia looked at him with a furrowed brow as she asked, "What is Ellis Island?"

"You are an inquisitive one, full of questions. Just keep your eye on the Lady and you will see the Island around her. We will be docking shortly. But as you can see there are many other boats ahead of us. We must wait our turn."

She looked at the Lady as he had instructed and saw the land around her take shape. She also noticed all the boats situated ahead, around and behind them. It seemed as if everyone was coming to America at the same time.

It would be many hours before they would step onto land for the first time in several weeks.

The lines were long and families were trying to stay together by tightly holding onto one another's hands. There were men stationed at each line coaxing them along through cordoned off areas. As they reached the desks they were asked their names, where they came from and the name of their sponsor. There were several men writing in large books their names, places of origin and sponsors. Those who did not have a sponsor were put into another long line.

It was now their turn and their mother stepped forward to give her name. She told the man her name, Filomena Ataide from Madeira Island, Portugal and that Marion De Sousa was their sponsor. He wrote Filomena's name on a card attached to a string and put this card over her head and around her neck to hang against her chest.

Lubelia and her brother stepped forward at their mother's urging and each in turn told the man his/her name. When she said Lubelia Alycea Ataide, the man wrote Alycea Ataide and another man placed the card over her head. Lubelia tried to correct him but she was already being pushed along by other attendants.

Her brother raced up behind her with his card resting against his chest. Lubelia strained to look at it and noticed that his card stated Manuel Ataide not Manuel Antonio Ataide. He gave Lubelia, now Alycea, his usual comical expression, winked at her and took her hand as they walked forward to catch up to their mother.

Alycea poked her mother in the ribs to try to get her attention. She tried to tell her about her name being changed but Filomena just pulled Alycea along and didn't look down at her. She was looking forward at the masses of people in this large room waiting to be processed.

It was quite noisy in the room as they got into the lines to go to the next desk where men and women were in white uniforms. Some of them had funny things hanging from around their necks. They used these things on each person as the reached the front of the line. Alycea found out from the man, the doctor, as she reached him that it was called a stethoscope. He said he was checking her heart and lungs to make sure she was healthy. He did the same to Manuel and Filomena and pushed them along the line to the next person.

At this junction their eyes were checked for jaundice (sickness) and their hair for something they called lice (bugs) by women in white. These women were nurses, Alycea was told.

They were okay she guessed because they were again pushed along to get into another line. This line seemed to be endless. They couldn't see where it was going. People were no longer in single file but families were gathered together. Alycea heard from people talking around them that they were preparing to get onto boats again to go to the mainland.

There were many languages being spoken, most of which she couldn't understand. Alycea heard Portuguese which she could understand and some English which she had learned in school and planned to learn more extensively once they got settled. Surprisingly Alycea's English was much better than her parents' and her brothers' because she had practiced it each night in hopes of one day going to America.

There were several boats waiting to be filled and they had a long wait because of all the people ahead of them. As Alycea looked around them she saw men, women and children of all ages clustered together. Some of the young children were asleep in their parents' arms while the older ones were running in circles around their parents. Since it was so crowded they couldn't run too far away. They were more like pushing one another around.

Alycea was itching, at this time herself, to run to one of the boats and jump on. She couldn't wait to get to the mainland and see America. Her mother was holding onto her hand tightly so she couldn't get away. Filomena told them that they must not get separated since it was much too crowded and she would not be able to find them easily.

She and her brother held onto their backpacks and stayed close to their mother as she had sternly instructed. They didn't disobey her unless they wanted to pay for it later.

Alycea, looked up to her mother and saw her face was tired and lined with stress. Even as a child of eight she could see the strain plainly on her mother's face.

She missed their father and their brother, Antonio. Alycea squeezed her mother's hand. Filomena looked down at her daughter with such a loving and kind expression that it brought tears to Alycea's eyes.

Alycea asked her mother, "Can I go visit the Lady and climb inside to look out one of the windows at the boats and the mainland?"

Filomena said, "Not today, mia filha." Alycea just nodded, sniffled and dabbed the tears away with her sleeve.

Filomena saw Alycea wiping her eyes and said sweetly, "Don't fret, my little one. We have much to see and do first and there will be time later to come back to see The Lady."

Manuel Antonio or Manuel, the name under which he would now be known, was excitedly looking around and busily checking out the pretty girls who were chattering close by. They were giving him the eye too.

These girls were being silly, thought Alycea. I don't want to be like that. I don't even like boys! I am definitely not going to act like that! Alycea said with conviction.

The line began to move and now they could see the boats up ahead. Their mother leaned over to them and whispered that they must stay together and get on the same boat. People behind them were pushing them forward and there was nowhere else to go but with the crowd. As they got closer there were several men standing behind ropes keeping them back and only letting a few people at a time onto the boats. You could hear the anxiety in the voices of parents trying to keep their children together to get onto the same boats.

Names were being called out and as they heard their names, they stepped forward to enter a large boat. A man helped them step down into the boat and directed them to seats at the bow or the stern.

Alycea felt such excitement. This was the beginning of their adventure to their new home. The water was clear and sparkling as she looked over the rail. She tried to lean further over to touch the water but her mother pulled her back from leaning over too far. She was afraid that Alycea would fall. Alycea kept trying to lean over and trail her hand into the water when her mother wasn't looking. At one point she was saved from falling in by her brother who happened to look away from his female admirers and caught his sister just in time before she fell head first.

Manuel was talking to one of the girls who was making eyes at him earlier in the line. She was already in love with him. She had that goofy look on her face as she absorbed his every word. Alycea looked away, and couldn't stand to watch him in action. He never stopped.

She thought, he likes girls more than anything in this world. You would think he would be more excited about getting to our new home. Oh well, I am excited enough for both of us, she mused.

As each person got onto the boat, it rocked and dipped in the water. Soon the boat had reached its passenger limit. They were underway as the boat pulled away from the dock at the Island. Alycea leaned on the rail and watched the water as the boat cut a smooth, graceful path through its glistening wake. She saw the land ahead. It looked crowded and small and they said it was an island too, Manhattan Island.

It certainly didn't look like an island. Their island of Madeira looked much greener and had no high buildings on it. This place had more buildings than land.

It would be different for them but Alycea was sure they would be happy and adjust. She was looking forward to many new adventures.

Little did she know how different it would all be.

# CHAPTER 6

Filomena grabbed Alycea's hand, and held on tightly to her as they were getting off the boat. She called to Manuel behind them to hurry and catch up.

"We are going to the Office of the Housing Authority as they told us to do at Ellis Island. They said we would be given a place to stay as long as we could pay the first months' rent. They would also direct us where to find a job," Filomena announced to her children.

It had been difficult understanding the Americans because Filomena did not speak English well until a kind man came forward who could translate the English into Portuguese for her and vice versa. Alycea was too young to interpret what they were trying to tell her mother. It was all far beyond her comprehension.

Alycea was glad to hear the part about a place to stay which would mean food because she was starving. All that fresh air and travel had made her famished. They really didn't have much to eat on the boat during their travels. Their mother had always made sure that they got a bigger portion of the food than she took. That was probably why she looked extremely tired and pale.

They walked a few blocks and finally found the building of the Housing Authority. They found a long line snaking around the building which was not surprising since all the people who were at Ellis Island ahead of them were now in line. They got in the back of the line and sat down on the pavement too tired to stand any longer. Filomena assured them it would not be long before they would have a nice place in which to eat and sleep tonight. Looking at all the people in line ahead of them, Alycea began to doubt if that was at all possible.

She now feared that they would have to sleep out in the streets because the Housing Authority would run out of available places to stay before they could get in the building.

This adventure was turning into anything but fun, Alycea thought to herself. She hated the long lines and the waiting. She didn't know it would be like this. She thought they would get off the boat and go right into a place of their own and have something to eat and a nice place to sleep. She began to wish she had never left Madeira.

Just as she was moaning and groaning about their situation and settling down on the pavement, the line began to move. Filomena urged them both up and moved them along. She smiled at Alycea to encourage her to stay strong and be a big girl. Alycea felt anything but strong. She just wanted something to eat and a place to sleep. She felt she could sleep for a month; she was exhausted.

Filomena patted Alycea on the head, hugged her to her side and placed a kiss on the top of her head. She could see Alycea's face and knew how she felt. But Filomena would never let on that she felt the same. She was resilient and would persevere. She intended to keep them together as a family and would do whatever it took to make sure they were fed, clothed and loved. Alycea didn't doubt the love part but she wondered about the fed and clothed part.

They finally reached the door of the building and were directed to a desk and requested to take a seat. They were asked their names, places of origin and date they arrived in America. Her mother did all the talking for them struggling in her Portuguese accented version of broken English mixed with more Portuguese as Alycea sat or slouched in the chair and rubbed her tired eyes and yawned. It was becoming too difficult to explain things to Filomena who clearly did not have a command of the English language.

The man looked at Alycea with a kind smile and reached into his desk drawer and pulled out a lollipop which he then handed to her. She took it, but not before her mother gave her a stern look. Alycea realized what she expected from her and promptly said, "Obrigado, thank you, sir."

Her mother smiled at her and nodded. He offered the same to Manuel but he felt he was too grown up to accept. But Alycea noticed the longing in her brother's eyes. He really did want to take it but was torn between being grown up and being a child. The man saw this also and told Manuel he would feel badly if he didn't accept it. Manuel reached quickly for the pop before the man changed his mind. He also was given that look from his mother, and he, in turn, mumbled, "Abrigado."

Now that they were both busy sucking noisily on their pops, the man leaned forward to discuss their housing situation. He called over one of the translators in the office for assistance who knew Portuguese, in relaying the information to Filomena. The translator told their mother that there was a place for them in a large building. Each family would have two rooms, a kitchenette and a bedroom with two beds. They could have a cot if they needed one. He said that there was one bathroom on each floor to be shared by three or more families. He stressed that this was temporary housing only and that they would be required to pay a month's rent or be evicted. Filomena promised to pay and be out in less than a month once she reached her sponsor. The man nodded his approval.

He asked Manuel, "Are you old enough to work?" Filomena replied for him, "He is thirteen years old."

The man said, "I'm sorry but he cannot work in the factories yet until he is sixteen but he could find other work in the grocer or apothecary as a sweeper."

Hearing this Manuel curled his lip in disgust. He felt that he was grown up enough to do the job of a man not a menial job as a sweeper. His mother tousled his hair and told him, "Don't worry, Manuel. I will find something for you to do to keep you busy."

The man explained, "You must give me $10 for the first month's rent."

Filomena nodded as she pulled out a $10 bill out of her pocket and placed it in the man's outstretched hand. He handed Filomena an envelope and a set of keys and gave her the address and directions to get to their new place.They all jumped up and quickly left the building now that they knew they had a destination and would soon have something to eat.

They found the address and entered the building to see a crowd of people waiting to get into the rooms. It seemed that there were more people than rooms available.

They pushed their way through the crowd and found their room. They were lucky there was no one already in the room like some of the others who had to share an apartment with another family.

The kitchen was a sparse room with a small cast iron stove, ice box and sink on one end of the room and on the other end was a small sitting area with a loveseat, chair and coffee table. There was a set of four dishes and glasses on the counter with utensils. There was also a square table and four chairs.

The adjacent room held two beds; one was a twin and the other a regular bed. Sheets, blankets, pillows and quilts were piled high on each bed. They would have to make up the beds before they could sleep.

Filomena told them to make up the beds the best they could while she went to find a store to buy them something for supper with her meager savings. She would be back as soon as she could.

Manuel and Alycea started with the twin bed and tossed around the sheets and blankets onto the bed and hit each other with the pillows. The bed didn't look much better made than it did before it was made.

After looking over the mess they had made of the bed, Alycea said, "Manuel, we had better fix the beds up a bit or Mae will be unhappy with us."

"Yes, I think we better," he finally agreed and they made it look a little neater and smoothed out the quilts to put the finishing touches to each bed. It was decided that Manuel would sleep in the twin bed. Mae and Alycea could share the larger bed. She soundly agreed. She liked having a bigger bed than her brother had. Manuel smirked at her and with his usual dazzling smile and wink, he plopped onto the small bed and closed his eyes. He was soon snoring loudly.

Alycea felt weary and couldn't keep her head up any longer either. She dropped down onto the bed she would share with her mother and curled up under the covers and soon fell asleep too.

They both jumped up at the same time with a start when they heard a loud rapping at the door. Manuel shushed Alycea and rushed to the door to see who it was. He inquired through the door and heard his mother's tired voice. "Manuel, for goodness sake, abbrir porta; open the door."

"I am sorry, Mae, but I didn't know it was you," he said with a sleepy look on his handsome face.

"Well, who did you think it was? Listen, dear. I am also a little tired and want to get settled and prepare supper for you both. I have some nice sausages and bread and cheese. I even bought you some milk. I had to pick up a small block of ice which I am afraid melted a little during the walk back here. We must keep the milk on ice so it will not spoil. Please put this ice and milk into the ice box quickly, Manuel," Filomena said with exhaustion visible in her voice and manner.

"I have to get the stove going with the wood and paper. I will cook up the sausages, cut up the bread and cheese. Then we can sit down and eat. Lubelia, or should we call you by your new name. Alycea, please set the table."

Manuel made a face at his sister and chuckled. Alycea stuck her tongue out at him when Mae wasn't looking. Alycea frowned but did as she was told. She was not yet sure if she liked her middle name as her given name but she guessed she would get used to it. She hurriedly set the table because her stomach was rumbling its discontent.

After they had eaten all their stomachs could hold, Alycea helped Mae clean up and excused herself to use the communal bathroom. Mae handed Alycea a towel and soap with which to wash up and her toothbrush.

Alycea was lucky enough to reach the bathroom with only one other person in line ahead of her. Once she got inside, she saw that the bathroom had a new toilet and claw foot tub and sink. She rushed in and out to do everything she could as quickly as possible because people kept knocking on the door who wanted to use the bathroom too. There evidently were a dozen or more people who used this same bathroom. They were standing in a line with their towels, a toothbrush and soap in hand as she exited the room. They were all wearing tired frowns on their fatigued faces.

She rushed back to their rooms to tell Mae and Manuel about the new bathroom and the lines of people waiting to use it. Manuel said that since he was a man, all he has to do was use a pot. He did not want to wait in line to do that. Mae heard him and told him to get a towel and his toothbrush and get cleaned up. He went over to the kitchen sink. He brushed his teeth, wet his towel with some soap and water and ran it over his face, hands and chest.

He turned around after brushing with some baking soda, and showed off his clean white teeth in a bright smile. He kissed his mother and sister lightly on their cheeks and retired to his bed but not before he thanked his mother for the delicious supper. She told him to say his prayers to God and give Him thanks for all they had. He then found an old pot, relieved himself and walked outside to dump the waste into the gutter before his mother could yell at him.

When he came back in, he promised to say his prayers and soon was fast asleep on his bed. Alycea leaned over his bed, kissed him soundly on his cheek and covered him with the blanket and quilt.

She kissed Mae and wished her good night and lay down on their bed. Before she knew it, Alycea, too, was sound asleep. She felt the covers being brought up around her and tucked under the mattress after which Mae herself slipped into the bed next to Alycea.

Alycea found herself dreaming of their boat trip with the waves rocking and rolling. She felt a little queasiness coming over her and was sweating, tossing and turning.

Mae leaned across the bed to touch Alycea's head and asked her, "Are you all right, mia fihla?

Alycea mumbled, "I'm okay."

Filomena arose from bed to get a wet cloth and put it on Alycea's forehead and smoothed her hair in a gentle loving motion. Alycea moaned and went back to sleep feeling a little cooler and less queasy.

Filomena knew what a traumatic voyage it had been for her young daughter. Filomena sighed heavily and prayed to St. Theresa that she would have the strength and courage to take care of her family. She closed her tired eyes and fell asleep knowing that her patron saint would not forsake her in this time of need.

# CHAPTER 7

"Manuel and Alycea! Please get up. It's already 6:30 am. I need to register you in school, Alycea. Manuel, you and I need to find jobs to pay for the rent and food. I have breakfast on the table already. We have bread and cheese. Hurry up, dress and come out here and eat."

Alycea opened her eyes reluctantly and groaned her displeasure but it didn't do any good. Mae came into the room and pulled the covers off of both of them and gave them each a shake and pat on their behinds to get them moving.

Manuel jumped up and put his clothes on first and ran to the bathroom to beat Alycea. She pulled her clothes on in slow motion and dragged herself out to the kitchen table where Mae had set out their breakfast. Alycea mechanically ate and yawned in between washing down the bread and cheese with a glass of milk.

By this time, Manuel had arrived back from the bathroom to gobble down his breakfast. With his usual wink and smile at his sister, he ran out the door to go job hunting. Mae yelled after him, "Manuel, please make sure you check out the local shops first for a job."

After they finished breakfast and cleaned up the dishes, they headed out the door to the local school which was a block and a half away. The fresh air from the short walk revived them a little so that Alycea was not groggy anymore. She was anxious about starting a new school. She was not the best student because she tended to daydream a lot.

The school was a large brick building with three floors. They entered by the massive front doors and followed signs to the office. There was a chubby-faced young woman filing in the corner and an older gray-haired woman with a sweet smiling face sitting at the large desk. She asked them in a soft, lilting voice, "How may I help you?"

Mae stepped right up to the desk and presented Alycea's paperwork from her school in Madeira. "My daughter to start school…um." Alycea didn't even realize her mother had brought her papers with her. They had left in such a rush.

The woman looked it over and handed Mae a sheet of paper and a pen so that she could fill it out with Alycea's information. They sat together on a bench while her mother completed the form.

The gray-haired woman looked at Alycea with kind eyes and asked, "Do you speak English?" The secretary wasn't sure if Alycea spoke English at all because of her mother's strong accent and broken English. Alycea surprised her by answering clearly in English with barely an accent.

Alycea responded softly, "I learned English in school in Madeira, Portugal and practiced with my brother, Antonio. We both hoped to travel one day to America and wanted to speak and understand English. I am, une pequiana, a little excited about going to school."

"That's good to hear. You will love this school and your teacher."

She then asked Alycea, "Is your brother coming here? Any sisters going to school here too?"

She noticed the sad look in Alycea's eyes and the way she hesitated before answering the question.

"I have two brothers, no sisters. My older brother is looking for work and the other one is not going to school here. He is in Madeira," Alycea answered much too abruptly, clearly trying to keep her emotions in check.

Alycea could see that the kind lady wanted to ask why, but Alycea's face and eyes, misty with tears, stopped her.

Filomena handed the paper back to the secretary and they followed her out to Alycea's classroom down the hall. The teacher opened the door as soon as they got there and took Alycea by the hand to guide her to a desk saying, "Hi Alycea. I am Miss Hanley, your teacher, and this is your new third grade classroom."

She returned to shake Filomena's hand upon introductions by the secretary and turned her attention once again to Alycea. She introduced her to the class and asked the class to say a special 'hello' to Alycea to make her feel welcome.

Alycea looked around at all the eager, inquisitive faces looking back at her. She spotted one girl who smiled and waved and mouthed her own name – "Mary." Alycea waved back.

Once seated at her desk, behind her a boy tapped her on the shoulder and said, "Hi, my name is Arnold."

Alycea smiled at Arnold and said 'hi' to him. He sat up straighter in his seat and grinned back at her.

Filomena waved goodbye to Alycea as she turned to face the front of the classroom and said that she would be back to pick her up at the end of school. Alycea looked at her mother and smiled so that her mother could relax. Her mother appeared anxious but relaxed a little when she did this. Filomena turned and closed the door behind her after thanking the teacher.

Miss Hanley was sweet and kind. She was always patient with everyone. In no time, Alycea felt at home and a part of the class. They recited the Pledge of Allegiance which Alycea did not know yet but would soon learn. She planned on practicing every night. Then they said their daily prayer bowing their heads. They also sang the song, 'My Country 'Tis of Thee.'

Miss Hanley gave the students some lessons on arithmetic and spelling and geography and then they had lunch. Mae had given Alycea a slice of bread and cheese to keep in her pocket for lunch. She was glad to have it because, all of a sudden, she was starving.

At the end of the day Miss Hanley gave them homework and they filed out of the class to wait outside for their parents to pick them up. Some students were walking home in groups or pairs. Alycea waited patiently looking up and down the street for any sign of her mother. She had a lot to tell her and was excited about her first day in an American school.

***

After dropping off Alycea at her school Filomena walked briskly to the mills two blocks away to meet with the foreman. She went from mill to mill waiting in each line to see if there was any work available. There were many people waiting for the same jobs. She feared that she would not find one.

The last office she was directed to was for the material handlers and stitchers. They were making different items of clothing such as dresses, blouses, pants, shirts.

After waiting for a few hours in this department the foreman told her, "There are only a few openings left as a stitcher but you have to be able to work long days at times as long as 10-12 hours a day." Filomena said with as much conviction and in broken English, "I will work….hard and do things…that is…you want of me."

43

He said she could start right away and assigned her to a sewing machine at the back of the large room. It was an expansive room with spacious, high ceilings – probably 30-40 feet high. It almost felt like being in a church except it was anything but quiet, multiple squeaking sounds of sewing machine floor pedals being manipulated by the feet of many workers. At times the pace of the workers, rushing to and fro bringing material to the stitchers, was frenetic.

She settled herself down and was given quick instructions of what to do with the sewing machine, pattern and material and then left on her own. Luckily she already knew how to sew by hand but using the machine was a little tricky at first. Before long she was working in her own smooth pace and keeping up with the workload. It was quite warm in the place and soon her hair was wet and tendrils were hanging around her face. She wiped away the sweat with the back of her arm and continued working.

The women on either side of her lifted their eyes up and smiled over at her. They talked over the noisy din introducing themselves as Antonneta and Tatiana. They said they were from Italy and Russia respectively. They both had strange accents mixed with some words of their own language and English. She said in her own language of Portuguese, "Bon Dia," good day or hello. Filomena found she was not alone in a strange country. She felt she had found some kindred spirits in these two women as they looked at her with kindness and compassion, even if they couldn't understand one another completely.

She had been working almost non-stop except for two bathroom breaks for over three hours. She suddenly realized that she had lost track of time and had forgotten that she had to pick up Alycea. She stopped sewing and went to look for the foreman, Mr. Stockman. He was in his office having his lunch and hunched over his desk knee deep in paperwork.

As she watched him eat his sandwich, Filomena realized that she had not had anything to eat all day. Her stomach started growling loudly.

She asked him if she could have a minute of his time. He stopped chewing, pushed his seat back, sat up to look at her and nodded his approval. She told him that she needed to go pick up her daughter at school since it was her first day and that she would be right back after she safely got her home.

Mr. Stockman told her in his limited Portuguese, "You can go pick up your daughter and get her supper. Come back to work afterwards to finish up until you are through with your quota."

Filomena promised, "I will do, obrigado, senyor." He went back to eating his sandwich and looked up at her with apology for his rudeness. He saw by her face that Filomena was eyeing his sandwich and must be hungry. He picked up the other half of his sandwich and offered it to her. Filomena just shook her head and turned and hurriedly left his office, through the mill and out the large double doors to the street.

She nearly ran all the way back to the school. Her poor Alycea would have been waiting over an hour and a half by this time. As she got closer, she could see the schoolyard was all deserted but for one little girl sitting on the front steps with her head in her hands. She called out to Alycea to announce she was finally here.

Alycea looked up with tears streaming down her face at her mother. She ran into her mother's arms and held tightly to her neck sobbing all the while.

Filomena held onto her and patted her gently saying in a calm voice. "I'm sorry, mia filha, for keeping you waiting so long. I promise it will not happen again,"she explained that she had waited for hours in lines at the mill and had finally gotten a job and had lost all track of time once she started working.

She took Alycea's little hand in hers and they walked home together. As they arrived at their building and headed down the hall to their rooms on the first floor, they saw Manuel sitting outside the apartment. He did not have a key to open the door since only one key was given to them.

Filomena reached inside the pocket of her dress and produced the key. She gave it to Manuel to open the door, and promised that she would try to get the locksmith to make another one for him. It would cost them more than they had right now. She would not get paid until the end of the week from her job as a stitcher at the mills.

Upon entering their rooms, Manuel turned excitedly towards his mother and sister and announced, "I found a job too!" He told them that as he was walking down the street from their building, he saw a sign in the grocer's store for a stocker and delivery boy. He had gone inside and spoken with the owner and had been hired on the spot. He started immediately to fix and stock the shelves and make deliveries to the neighborhood for Mr. Bohodoney. "He is a really nice man. He even gave me a tip of two cents on every delivery I made!" he exclaimed excitedly, shaking his pockets filled with coins at both of them. "I made a lot of deliveries! I will get a key made tomorrow, Mae, so you don't have to worry about it. Ok?" His face was bright and eager to please as he said this.

"That is wonderful, Manuel! We will eat well tonight. Go down to the butcher, grocer and baker for some meat, vegetables and bread for a stew. Don't forget to go to the dairyman for milk and cheese. See if he can give you a block of ice to keep the milk cold too. The other one we had is almost gone. Thank you, my dear son. You are most helpful."

Manuel beamed at them and rushed out the door to buy their celebratory supper. Mae was at the kitchen stove preparing the fire while Alycea spread out her homework. She also planned to write a letter to Antonio about their trip and her first day of school.

Mae asked Alycea how she liked her first day of school. Alycea answered with excitement showing on her beaming face, "It was good and I made two friends, Mary and Arnold. We did some arithmetic and spelling and geography and had lunch. Miss Hanley is really nice. I like her! I think I am going to like school here in America."

"I'm glad to hear, Alycea. Do homework quickly, then you set tabela, table and help with jantar, supper." Filomena was trying to speak in English as much as she could to increase her vocabulary.

Manuel rushed in almost an hour later with his hands full of food. Evidently his boss, Mr. Bohondoney, was feeling generous and had given him more than enough to feed them. He had sent Manuel over to the iceman for a block of ice to keep the milk cold and to the butcher for some meat. The baker also had provided them with a loaf of day old bread.

Manuel had his hand closed over something. He opened his hand to show his mother his new key for the house that the locksmith had made. He was feeling proud of himself, and smiled broadly at both his mother and sister.

Mae said she felt blessed and silently prayed and crossed herself, as she looked up to heaven and gave thanks to God for their good fortune. "Manuel and Alycea, you will have enough left for breakfast and lunch tomorrow too."

After supper was finished, Filomena announced somewhat reluctantly, "I have to return to work to finish my quota as a stitcher at the mills. Alycea, I expect you and your brother to behave yourselves and finish up your homework, wash and then go to bed. I will be home as soon as I can."

Manuel nodded, looked at Alycea with a smirk and said, "Don't worry Mae, I will babysit Alycea!"

"I don't need anyone to babysit me, Manuel - least of all you! You are only five years older than me!" She proclaimed sticking her chin up at him defiantly.

"Oh Alycea, it's okay, sweetheart. I know you are all grown up. I just want you to take care of each other for me, okay?" She smiled and bent over and gave them each a peck on the cheek before she opened the door and headed back to work.

Alycea walked over to Manuel who was sitting on the edge of his bed taking off his shoes and cuffed him on the ear. He jumped up and grabbed her and they wrestled onto the floor. He was much bigger than she but Alycea gave him a few good jabs in the ribs. He just rolled away from her holding his sides laughing.

She couldn't get angry with him and found herself laughing heartily too. Everyone always told Alycea that she had a big hearty laugh for a small person. It was infectious and always made everyone else laugh too. Her laughing only made Manuel laugh longer and harder.

Soon they both had tears from the laughter running down their faces. Sniffling and wiping their eyes and noses, they both settled down to do their chores. They washed and wiped dishes together and put them away and then Alycea sat down at the table to finish up her homework and the letter to Antonio that she had started earlier.

Manuel looked over her shoulder at what she was writing to Antonio. He said, "Alycea, please tell Antonio that I have a job of my own and am making money to send for him soon."

Alycea just looked at Manuel and said, "Why don't you write to Antonio yourself, Manuel, and tell him that? I am sure he would like to hear from his brother too, not just his sister. Don't you realize he is all alone without us?"

"Listen little sister, I don't write well and I don't know what to say. You just tell him that I am working to send money to cousin Grinalda so that she can buy him a ticket to America to be with us. Okay?"

"Oka, Manuel. Don't worry I will tell him. I still think you should practice your writing and just try. It would make him felix, happy. He loves you very much, you know. He won't notice if you make any mistakes. After all, he is a lot younger than you are. His Portuguese and English are not as good for writing as yours."

"Yeah, well maybe another time I will do just that. I will surprise him, how about that?" He grinned at her and then ruffled her long brunette curls as he passed by on his way to bed.

"Don't stay up too late, little sister. I am going to bed. I have a long day ahead of me tomorrow. Mr. Bohondoney has a lot of deliveries for me to make and I have to clean all the back room for him. I also promised to help out the butcher, baker and iceman for giving us all the food supplies. Good night, sweet little Alycea. You know, Alycea, you really are not at all sweet sometimes!" Manuel chuckled to himself as he hurriedly closed the door to the bedroom.

She looked up from her letter writing and replied, "Okay, big brother, I'm almost finished with my letter. I put in it that you miss and love Antonio too. I know that will make him happy."

"Hmmm, yeah, right," he mumbled as he drifted off into a sound sleep producing a loud snore.

# CHAPTER 8

## SEVERAL MONTHS LATER

The foreman looked at his watch and noticed that it was already 8:00 pm. He was never in a hurry to go home. No one was there anyway. He looked over at the bay of sewing machines and one wheel at the back of the room was still spinning. He walked down the long corridors and narrow spaces between the machines until he reached the whirling machine. He looked kindly at the petite and lovely young woman who was sitting busily working the fabric under the needle and pushing it along with practiced and skilled hands.

"Filomena, you have done an admirable job. You have more than met your quota. You have been working diligently staying way past your time for months now. I think you should pack up your area and go home earlier for a change. You have a child you said, right?"

"I have two children, mio filho, my son, Manuel, who is thirteen and mia filha, my daughter, Lubelia Alycea, who is eight."

"Well, go home to your son and daughter. They must need you. You can come in tomorrow at 7:30 instead of 7:00. Ok? Don't tell anyone that I am easy. I don't want that to get around. Everyone thinks I am a tough boss and I want them to continue to think that. All right, Filomena?"

"Of course, Mr. Stockman. Obrigado, thank you for your kindness. I will be here... 7:30, as you say."

As Filomena cleaned up her work area, Mr. Stockman watched her with sad eyes. He admired her for her strength and also for her beauty. She was doing all this on her own. She hadn't mentioned a husband. He didn't usually take note of this about his employees but had taken a more intense interest in Filomena.

He had lost his wife a few years ago at an early age from Influenza and she was pregnant at the time. He, unfortunately, never got to have any children. He envied those who had a life and someone to go home to. He led a lonely and sad existence for a man who was only thirty.

Looking at Filomena he figured she was under thirty. She must have had her children at a really young age. He thought back to his conversation with her yesterday and her musical Portuguese accented English.

As Filomena was walking out the door of the mill, she turned to wave at Mr. Stockman. He looked up from his thoughts to see Filomena waving at him and he raised his hand in acknowledgment.

She observed his sad eyes that displayed much of his personality which was of a man who had suffered a great loss, but was a survivor. He had a kind and sympathetic nature.

I don't think he has a mean bone in his body, Filomena said out loud to herself as she was walking home. I am fortunate to have such a man for a boss. St. Theresa is truly looking out for me and my family.

# CHAPTER 9

## BACK TO PRESENT TIME

"You two look lost in thought. What are you planning or conspiring to do? Mama, how are you? Are you getting tired yet? We can leave, if you are." Caterina interrupted the two conspirators and looked at her mother with concern.

"Caterina, I am fine. Stop hovering over me. I am having a nice conversation with my granddaughter, Jasmine. If I get tired you will be the first to know," she said curtly to her daughter so that she would leave them alone, then she could continue to share her thoughts with Jasmine.

"Auntie, it's okay. I will keep an eye on Avoa for you. She was just telling me about her life. It's fascinating. I will make sure she doesn't overtire herself." Jasmine smiled at Aunt Caterina to put her at ease.

Alycea then turned her attention to her granddaughter, once again oblivious to all the other guests at her 100th birthday party. She had become completely absorbed in the past.

# CHAPTER 10

The two men were wandering around the streets dressed in tattered and dirty clothes, in much need of a bath and a shave. They pulled their jackets tightly around their chests for the weather was getting chilly. Soon their meager clothes would not be enough to keep them warm.

They had been roaming up and down the streets looking for work or a place to get a meal. They were hungry and tired. Their families were home waiting for them to bring them something to eat. It looked as if they would have to go home empty handed once again.

As the men turned the corner to head home, they noticed a young woman walking towards them. She was petite and attractive. One man looked at the other with a barely perceptible nod to each other. They waited for her to get closer. They planned on robbing her of anything valuable that she had so that they could buy some food for themselves and their families and some booze to warm themselves up.

Filomena looked up and saw the two men standing at the side of the road watching her. She felt a tingle of apprehension at the back of her neck and slowed down looking behind and around her to see if she could find a way to avoid passing by them. She crossed the street and hurried on her way.

She didn't want to look behind her for fear that the two men were following her. She could hear their footsteps getting closer and louder as she also increased her steps.

Suddenly and painfully she was jumped from behind and knocked to the ground. As she landed, she skinned her right knee and putting out her hands to try to stop her fall, had possibly broken her right wrist. She tried to get up but someone was holding her down while the other person was checking her pockets for any money. She screamed out for help and the man jumped back off of her and they both ran away.

Fortunately enough, Filomena did not have any money on her. She did, however, have her wedding ring on and a St. Theresa medal around her neck hidden under her clothes. She looked at her left hand and saw the ring was still there and quickly felt around her neck for the medal. Thank God it was there, proving St. Theresa was watching over her once again.

She gingerly rolled onto her side and winced in pain. She tried to put her right hand down to push herself up but it would not support her and she felt a sharp jolt of pain running through her hand. She had to use her left hand, which was badly scraped, to push herself up. Filomena looked at her right knee which was skinned raw, blood running down her leg into her shoe.

She heard someone running towards her and was afraid that the men had returned. But then she heard a familiar voice calling her name. She turned to see Mr. Stockman standing over her. "Filomena, are you all right?" He reached out his hand to help her up. Putting his arm around the right side of her waist, he gently lifted her off the ground.

"I guess so," Filomena's voice shook with emotion and pain.

Mr. Stockman saw her bloody knee and the unnatural angle at which she was holding her right wrist. He feared that it was broken. He had noticed her walking a block ahead of him as he was on his way home. He had also noticed the two men standing at the corner and as they had jumped Filomena. He yelled at them to get them away before they could hurt her. He heard Filomena scream and ran as fast as he could to come to her aid.

She looked at Mr. Stockman with relief and gratitude and said, "Obrigado, thank you."

He just smiled at her and said, "Da nada, you are most welcome. Now please let me take you home and clean up your scrapes and set your wrist. It looks like it could be broken. I have had some medical training and wanted to be a doctor but never finished my training due to lack of money. Is your house far from here?"

"No…ugh…it is just a block away on the right. I don't know how to thank you, Mr. Stockman. I was afraid that they would kill me and my children would be left alone. I was fortunate that they left me with only a few cuts and scrapes and a broken wrist. You really can't fault them. They were just tired, hungry and desperate to take care of themselves and their families. These are difficult times for all of us just trying to survive," she said through the pain.

"Filomena, you really are a remarkable woman to not feel angry with these men. When I saw them attacking you I feared the worst. I am much relieved that you were not hurt in any other way. The scrapes and broken bones will heal but if they had….if…well, you know what I am talking about. You are an attractive young woman and I don't want to see anything like that ever happen to you."

"Mr. Stockman, I appreciate your concern. But I don't think they had anything like that in mind. They just wanted money or anything of value that they could sell to buy food to feed their families."

"Please call me Stan, short for Stanley. You are too kind and such a good woman not to think ill of anyone. I, on the other hand, think otherwise of these men. They should be taught a lesson and punished for what they did to you. If I had my way I would…"

She interrupted him before he could say anything that he would be sorry for later. "Mr. Stockman, er…I mean Stan. You mustn't get upset over this. It is all done and forgotten already. I would appreciate it if you could assist me home. I don't want to frighten my children when they see me in this state. If you are with me they may not notice my condition. I will tell them that you are a doctor who came to assist me when I had an accident at work. Ok?"

"Filomena, I would be honored to assist you and would love to meet your children. If they are anything like their mother, they must be angels."

"Well, angels sometimes, but not often enough! Ha ha!" She laughed but winced when the movement sent another jolt of pain to her wrist and down her hand.

"Stan, I am afraid I will not be able to work well with my hand. What will I do? Can I do another job until my wrist is healed? Maybe there is a job that I can do with only one hand." She looked at him with eyes, soft and luminous, that he couldn't look away. She had such a sweet nature that he couldn't refuse her anything.

"Of course, we will find you something to do so you can earn your pay. Don't worry about that now. Ok? Let's just get you home first. I will clean you up as best I can. Then I will go to the Apothecary to get the materials I will need to put your wrist into a cast. I will have to set it first and that may be a little painful. I apologize for any pain I may cause you, Filomena. I will also pick up some pain medicine to help you sleep better. I promise in a few days it will feel better and on its way to being healed. You will have to keep the cast on for a few weeks though."

"Stan, I don't know how to thank you for being there for me. I know St. Theresa was watching over me and sent you to assist me. I will include you in my prayers to her tonight that she will watch over you too. You are a kind and generous man."

"Please Filomena; there is no reason to thank me. I was there, as you say, sent by St. Theresa. I was only doing her bidding, right?" He smiled at her as he said this. The smile reached his soft brown eyes and illuminated his face. She looked at him and smiled back taking note of his light brown wavy hair and attractive face. She hadn't noticed how good looking he was when she had first met him several months ago.

They reached her building and entered, walking with his arm wrapped protectively around her waist. She leaned heavily against his strong shoulder. She pulled out her key and Stan unlocked her door quietly so she wouldn' disturb her children in case they were asleep.

Stan assisted her into the room and settled her down at the kitchen table. He put her wrist up on the table and hurried over to get a cloth to wet it with cold water and began gently cleaning up her scrapes and cuts on her hands, elbows and knee. He asked her if she had a pillow to elevate her wrist. She pointed to the bedroom and he entered the room tiptoeing as quietly as possible not to disturb the sleeping children and picked up her bed pillow. He returned and put the pillow under her wrist to elevate and take the pressure off of it and relieve the pain somewhat.

He whispered to her that he was going to the Apothecary down the block to buy the supplies he would need to set her wrist. He promised to be back as quickly as he could and that she should just sit and rest until he returned. He got her a glass of water to sip until he could return.

She looked up at him with a grateful but somewhat weary smile. She was feeling the pain much more now, he imagined. He knew that it would get worse and he must hurry. He turned and ran out the door and down the block quickening his pace like never before. He never knew he could have such an abundance of energy and spirit. This was the first time in many years he had felt alive and useful to anyone. He realized he now had a reason to live. It was Filomena.

# CHAPTER 11

Alycea turned over as she woke up and saw her mother with her arm in a sling. "Mae, what happened to you? Why do you have that white thing on your arm and hand?" Her voice was shaky and she was anxious and a little frightened to see her mother looking utterly vulnerable like that.

As they were talking, Manuel started grunting and moving around in his bed. He stretched his arms over his head and continued to stretch out his whole body like a cat. He opened his eyes and looked at this sister and mother.

His eyes popped open even wider when he saw his mother's arm in a sling. He sputtered out, "What…what happened to you, Mae? Are you okay? Did you hurt yourself at work?"

Filomena knew that she must think of something to tell her children. She certainly didn't want them to worry about her or her safety.

She smiled and said as calmly as she could muster, "I am fine, you two, don't worry. I had a little accident on the way home and slipped and fell on my right wrist and broke it and got a few bumps and bruises on my legs and elbows. I will be okay. My boss saw me fall and he helped me home and patched me up. It turned out that he was studying to be a doctor but had to drop out of school before he could finish. He did a good job making a cast to keep my wrist immobile while it heals. I will wear the cast and the sling for a few weeks until the bones are healed."

"Of course, in the meantime, I will need help from both of you to cook, clean up around here and also to do the shopping."

"Oh Mae, we will do everything for you. You will not have to do a thing. Does your boss expect you to go to work in this condition?" Manuel asked with concern etched in the crease between his brows. He was already seriously taking on the job as man of the house.

"No. He said I can take a few days to rest and as soon as I feel strong enough I can try to come in. He is going to give me a different job to do for a few weeks until I get the cast off. He really is a kind and generous man. I am truly fortunate to work for someone so thoughtful." Filomena's eyes got misty and took on a faraway look as she said this.

Her children looked at her then at each other in a questioning way. They had never seen their mother with that look on her face before. They were not sure what it meant but at the same time they were not sure they wanted to know.

Manuel got up from his bed with a start and gave Alycea orders to get dressed and come out into the kitchen to help prepare breakfast. He planned on giving his mother breakfast first before taking Alycea to school so his mother could rest in bed. He would be a little late for work but he knew that Mr. Bohondoney would understand once he explained the situation.

Alycea rushed around getting dressed and putting her books and homework in her backpack but not before bending over to kiss her mother's warm cheek. She told her, "I love you, Mae. Just rest and Manuel will take me to school. When we come home I will help make supper with him. Ok?"

"Obrigada, my sweet Lubelia Alycea. Do well in school today and study hard. You are a smart girl. I will rest now and pick you up from school this afternoon. The short walk will do me some good by then. Don't worry now. Go help your brother."

"Bon dia, Mae. Take care." She smiled at her mother and blew her a kiss which brought a smile to her mother's lips in between the pain.

As they were leaving, Manuel called out to his mother, "I will take care of the shopping for supper. You are not to do anything but rest." He was in control of everything. "Bon dia, Mae."

As he said this it gave him a warm feeling to be grown up and to have his family depend on him. He kind of liked the feeling. This was how it must be to have a family of your own, a wife and child. One day I will have both, he mused to himself.

*** 

Filomena lay in bed quietly for a little while longer but couldn't get comfortable. The pain in her wrist was starting to increase and she finally got up gingerly pushing herself up by leaning on her left side. She must take another one of the pain pills that Stan had left for her. She didn't like having her head feeling fuzzy but the pain was too intense to stand all day.

He really was wonderful last night fixing her arm, she remembered as she swallowed the pill with a glass of water. His calm and confident manner made her feel much better as he hovered over her. She couldn't remember the last time a man had catered to or pampered her. She always took care of her husband and their children. No one had taken care of her. She always had to be the strong one in the family.

Then she remembered what Manuel had said to her before he left with Lubelia. She liked the way he had taken over. He was a lot like his father with such a good heart, not always dependable but he meant well. She was sure he would be a comfort and help to her now that she needed to lean on him a little.

She knew Alycea would also be a help. She was headstrong and feisty, always full of life and passion. She would keep Manuel in line. Ha ha! Filomena laughed out loud just thinking of her little Alycea, mia filha, my daughter, with her long dark brown hair in curls and big amber colored eyes.

She was a lovely little girl who would grow up to be a beautiful woman and an intelligent one at that. She would be a tough one for any man to handle. She would always be the boss in any relationship. The poor young man who fell in love with her would certainly have to watch his step.

Manuel, mio filho, her son, was such a strong, handsome and loving young man who would be breaking a lot of hearts before he finally settled down with a lucky young woman. He would dazzle them all with his beautiful smile and thick, coarse brown hair that always fell into his deep brown eyes. His eyes always crinkled when he laughed. Filomena surely hoped that one day there would be a strong and decisive young woman who could handle Manuel and keep him in line. He definitely needed that kind of woman.

Filomena guessed she had to get used to their new names, Alycea and Manuel. They were in America now and their names were Americanized but they will always be her Manuel Antonio and Lubelia Alycea in her heart, even if she called them at times by their new names.

The morning was going quickly as Filomena sipped a cup of tea and nibbled on a slice of toast as she thought of her children. She was feeling a little better due to the effects of the pill. But she was getting sleepy and decided to go lie down again until she felt better. She would have to make sure she did not fall asleep too long for she promised to go pick up Alycea at school. She didn't want to see those tears of disappointment and look of fear of abandonment on her daughter's face like the first day ever again.

Her thoughts were not even finished before she had fallen soundly asleep on her bed from the relaxing effects of the pain pill.

# CHAPTER 12

She heard something in the distance, could it be knocking? What? Where was it coming from? She realized that she was not dreaming. It was coming from her door.

She struggled to get up but couldn't do it quickly or gracefully from her prone position. She staggered into the kitchen where the knocking was getting louder and more persistent. She heard a voice calling her name. "Filomena, are you all right? It's Stan. Will you let me in, please? I need to see you."

"Oh Stan, of course. I'm coming. I'm sorry if you had to wait. I laid down for just a minute and fell sound asleep. Please come in." She stepped back as she opened the door for him to enter.

"Filomena, how are you feeling today? Did you take another pain pill? Is the pain too bad for you to manage?" He questioned her with deep concern registering in his soft brown eyes and handsome face.

"I am feeling better, obrigado. I did take a pill. That's the reason I fell asleep, I guess. They do make me feel groggy and my head still feels a little fuzzy. But at least I don't feel the pain as much."

"That is a good thing. I know they are strong but you need to take them every four to six hours if the pain gets too bad for you. They will help your body heal faster too if you are more comfortable." He looked at her with such a serious face that she just smiled at him. He couldn't help but smile back at her.

She was lovely with all that thick brown hair piled up on top of her head and her big brown eyes. It must look beautiful down and cascading around her face. He found himself feeling warm and his cheeks were bright with just the thought. The pit of his stomach was filled with such a longing. He shook his head to clear his thoughts.

He looked at her and she was looking back at him with a puzzled expression on her lovely face. Unbeknownst to him she was giving him her own inspection. She found him intriguingly attractive and was as aware of him as he was of her.

"Filomena, your English is getting better all the time. Your accent is not as strong as before. But don't lose it completely; it's lovely and charming," he said with a wink.

"Oh, Stan, I try hard to speak correct English. My children help me. We have spoken English a lot since we arrived. It will get easier, I am sure. Obrigado, I mean thank you."

She lowered her eyes because she feared that her feelings may show on her face. She was definitely smitten with him. He had become more than a friend to her and it was a good feeling to think of a man again in her life.

"Oh, my goodness! I must go. I will be late again to pick up poor Lubelia Alycea. Please excuse me, Stan. You may stay here or come for a walk with me. I was going to invite you to have supper with us as a thank you for helping me."

"I would be happy to accompany you to pick up little Alycea. You shouldn't be out on your own just yet. You may be lightheaded from the pain medicine and lose your balance. I don't want you to hurt yourself anymore. Here, Filomena, let me lock up. Please take my arm. You can lean on me if you need to."

Filomena smiled her thanks and tucked her left hand into his arm and leaned into his side. She found herself a little woozy as she started walking out the door and was grateful for his company and his support.

***

Alycea was working conscientiously to finish up with her spelling test. She had gotten an E for excellent on the last one and wanted to get another E. Spelling was her favorite subject. She didn't like geography too much and had some difficulty with arithmetic. But she was managing to get G for Good on these subjects too. Mae would be proud when she got her report card and saw all E's and G's.

The school bell rang and all the children jumped up out of their seats. Miss Hanley stood at the doorway and collected the spelling sheets from each student before they went out. She smiled at Alycea after she had collected her sheet. She leaned over to whisper to Alycea, "You are doing a really good job, Alycea. You always work hard. I am proud of you and I am sure your family will be proud of you too when they see your report card."

"Thank you, Miss Hanley. I really like school and I have the best teacher in the whole school. That is why I like it so much!" Alycea's eyes were bright and sparkled as she looked at Miss Hanley.

"Thank you, Alycea. You are a sweet and thoughtful little girl. I like you a lot too! Now go along. Your mother must be waiting for you. See you tomorrow, Alycea."

"Bye, Miss Hanley." Alycea was moved along with the rest of the students in the corridor and saw her friends Mary and Arnold waiting for her at the end of the corridor. They talked about their plans to go to one another's houses to play or maybe do homework together. She waved goodbye to them and walked out of the building and looked up and down the street to see if she could see her mother walking toward the school. All the children were excited as they ran up to their waiting parents outside the school. Alycea looked dejected and was getting those butterflies in her stomach again like she did that first day when her mother was late. She was worried that her mother would not come and she would be left all by herself. Even though her mother had never been late like that again, she was still fearful of being forgotten.

Almost all the students were gone now so she decided to sit on the steps and look over her homework until her mother showed up. Just as she opened her book she heard her name being called and looked up to see a man and woman walking towards her. She realized that it was her mother with a man she did not recognize.

"Lubelia Alycea! Did you think I had forgotten you? Of course I am here. Did I not promise to pick you up every day?" She smiled at Alycea with crinkling eyes.

"Mae! I knew you would come. I was just doing my homework until you got here. Who is this man with you, Mae?" Alycea looked at Stan with a serious expression on her little face.

"Oh, mia filha, this is my boss and friend, Stan Stockman. He is the one who hired me to work at the mill. He is also the one who helped me when I injured myself on the way home from work yesterday. Remember I told you he put my wrist in a cast?"

Alycea noticed that Mae smiled at Stan with a different kind of expression on her face than the one she used to look at her.

"Alycea, be polite and say 'bon dia, hello' to Mr. Stockman," Filomena prodded her daughter gently.

"Hello Mr. Stockman. It is nice to meet you. Thank you for taking care of my mother."

Stan smiled and nodded to Alycea.

"Can we go home now, Mae? I have homework to do and I want to write another letter to Antonio about what happened at school today."

"Okay, sweetheart. What happened at school today?" She asked with a worried expression on her lovely face.

"Oh, nothing important. I just wanted to share it with Antonio," she said with a smug look as she turned to walk ahead of them on her way home.

Filomena and Stan just looked at each other and shrugged off Alycea's comment. They were too much into each other to realize what Alycea meant by it. They continued walking together with Stan supporting Filomena and Alycea skipping ahead of them without looking back.

# CHAPTER 13

"Manny, could you please come here and deliver these supplies to Mr. Dante for me. I appreciate all your diligence sweeping and cleaning out the storage room but this is more important right now."

Manny, as he now wanted to be called, turned towards Mr. Bohondoney to give him his attention. Seconds before his attentions were directed towards an attractive customer who had just come into the grocer's store. He hadn't taken his eyes off of her for the last ten minutes as he kept sweeping the same part of the floor back and forth.

"Umm, yes, Mr. Bohondoney, I will be right there." He strolled over to his boss while keeping one eye peeled on the lovely young lady. At this point she had her eyes on him too and gave him a coy smile before nervously looking down again at the floor."

"Now, Manny, do I have your full attention? I know it is hard to concentrate with such a lovely young lady present, but please do your best. This delivery is most important. Mr. Dante is one of my best customers. He expects his orders to be delivered promptly and with courtesy. Please remember to thank him and smile when he pays for his order."

"Of course, Mr. Bohondoney, I always thank our customers and smile. It comes naturally to me," Manny said with a wide beaming smile which was more for the benefit of the lovely young lady.

"Okay, Manny, be on your way. Hurry back because there is much to do. I have a few more deliveries and shelves have to be checked and stocked again."

"Yes sir, I will be back as soon as I can," he said as he grabbed the items and rushed out the door but not before he snuck another quick peek at the young lady.

He smiled to himself as he hurried on his way to Mr. Dante's house three blocks away. He wondered who this young woman was. She looked about his age, maybe a couple of years older. She was lovely with long blonde hair in curls that framed her fair face and big blue eyes. He had never seen anyone as beautiful. He felt his heart pounding a rhythm of love all its own.

He had seen many American women since they had been here but none that could compare to this one. He must find out her name and where she lived, he decided.

***

"May I help you find something young lady?" Mr. Bohondoney asked as he watched the young woman who appeared to be a little lost.

Looking at him shyly, she answered, "Yes, my mother sent me here to pick up her order. She called you this morning about an hour ago?"

"What is her name?"

"Oh, her name is Clara Da Silva."

"Let me see. Oh yes, I have her order right here. Let me put it in a sack for you to carry. Will you be able to manage on your own, Miss Da Silva?" He looked at her diminutive size as he said this.

"Oh yes, I will be fine. I am stronger than I look, sir." She gave him a dimpled smile as she walked out the door towing the sack behind her.

She was such a little thing, sweet and pretty too. I think she is interested in Manny and him in her. I am sure she will be back again to see him. He smiled as he watched her walk away a little unsteadily under the weight of the bag.

He remembered back to the days when he courted his wife, Louisa. They had been married for 30 years now. That was long ago but she was still as lovely and sweet as ever. This young girl reminded him of his Louisa. When he first met her she was around the same age, maybe 14 or 15 years old.

Louisa was his whole world. He wouldn't know what to do without her. She was a good wife and a wonderful mother. If only...our little Carolyn had lived. She would have grown up to look a lot like this young woman.

He picked up his phone and dialed a number. He identified himself to Mrs. Da Silva. "This is Mr. Bohondoney, the grocer. I need to ask you a favor... please let me explain."

# CHAPTER 14

"Be quiet now. He's coming. Lubelia Alycea, please turn off the lights in the kitchen. Everyone, hurry and hide in the bedroom so he doesn't see you. As soon as I say, 'Manuel you are home,' come out and yell, 'Happy Birthday!'"

The key was in the lock and Manny was turning the handle slowly. He was tired tonight for Mr. Bohondoney really worked him when he got back from doing all his deliveries. Manny was also disappointed that the girl was gone before he could find out her name. He just couldn't get her out of his mind.

As he opened the door, his mother was standing right there and saying loudly, "Manuel, you are home."

Right after that he didn't know what happened, a lot of yelling was going on and a rush of people were coming out of the bedroom. They were singing out to him all together, "Happy Birthday, Manuel!"

He was surprised. He had forgotten it was his birthday today! He was now 14 years old.

He looked around at all the people here and spied his boss, Mr. Bohondoney. No wonder he told him to lock up tonight, that he had something important to do and had to leave ahead of time. He was planning on coming to my birthday party, the thought bringing a smile to his lips.

Besides his mother and sister and Mr. Stockman, his mother's boss, he also noticed the iceman, Mr. Piantodosi, the baker, Mr. Spinatelli, Mr. Santos, the butcher, and all their delivery boys that Manny has gotten to know. Then he saw her…

She was standing at the back of the group looking a little lost and shy. She looked up just as he started to walk toward her in a fog. How…what…why? He couldn't think straight. How did she get here and how did she know it was my birthday? Many confusing thoughts and questions were spinning around in his head. He found himself at a loss for words which never happened to him.

She smiled that shy smile that brought light into her face and eyes and a dimple to each cheek. Her long blonde hair cascaded in curls along the side of her face and down her back. It shone in the light and he could almost imagine a halo forming around her head. She looked like an angel.

He reached out his hand to her and tried to make words come out of his open mouth. He only hoped that they made some sense if and when they somehow came out.

She, in turn, put her small hand into his larger one and lightly squeezed it. She didn't say anything either. All she could do was look at him with that ethereal, smiling face.

They were so absorbed in each other that they did not see everyone gawking at them and whispering. They were all witnesses to what it was to fall in love at first sight or maybe in this case, second sight.

Finally, Mae spoke up. "Hello everyone. I want to thank you all for coming to Manuel's birthday party. Let's all have some cake and I will make some coffee since Mr. Bohondoney was kind enough to bring the coffee and Mr. Spinatelli baked this beautiful chocolate birthday cake. Thank you both."

Mr. Bohondoney and Mr. Spinatell both bowed in thanks to Filomena.

"Manuel, come over with your friend and make a wish then blow out your candles so we can enjoy a piece of the wonderful chocolate cake."

Manny walked over with his friend's hand still in his and guided her over to his birthday cake. Without ever letting go of her small, cool hand he closed his eyes and then blew out the candles extinguishing every one. Everyone clapped and exclaimed congratulations to Manuel. I think they all knew what he wished for. She was certainly a lovely young lady.

Alycea watched Mae as she deftly pulled out the candles and cut the cake expertly as she passed the plates around to all the guests. The cake was delicious as was expected since Mr. Spinatelli was an excellent baker. Mae thanked him once again for his skill and workmanship. The cake was not only delicious but beautifully decorated too. Mr. Spinatelli bowed again to Mae and kissed her hand in thanks. He said he was happy to be part of this wonderful group of friends.

Manny was handed a piece of cake and he in turn gave it to the lovely young lady. He realized as he watched her eat it that he didn't even know her name.

He looked at her, expectantly, as he asked in a weak voice, "What is your name? You know mine now and you even know the date of my birth."

"I'm Gracinda Da Silva. You are probably wondering why I am here. I am as surprised as you are. My mother asked me to come here with Mr. Bohondoney. She said that he needed me to do him a favor and come with him to a party for his delivery boy. I knew it must be you. I didn't see any other worker in the store. He said that it would make you happy and provide an unexpected surprise."

"Hi Gracinda. That's a beautiful name for a beautiful girl. I am so happy that you came and it *is* a nice, unexpected surprise. I couldn't have asked for a better one. Thank you for coming."

"Do you live far from here? I can walk you home if you like," Manny said and looked at her eagerly as she pretended to think about it.

"Yes, Manuel, I would like that a lot. My house is only a few blocks away from here." She smiled again, causing him to feel weak in the knees.

"You can call me Manny or Manuel is okay too," he said as he looked at her like a lovesick puppy.

Manny then turned to the group and thanked everyone for the wonderful birthday surprise. He looked over at Mae and whispered that he would be walking Gracinda home and would be back right after that to help clean up.

"Manuel, you must open your presents from all your guests first. I am sure that Gracinda would like you to open hers too before she leaves."

"Of course, I'm sorry, I hadn't realized that I got gifts too! It was such a surprise."

He proceeded to open each gift and in turn thank that person for his kindness. All he could think about though was being alone with Gracinda.

Manny finished with the gifts except for the one from Gracinda. It was in a small tidily wrapped box with a blue ribbon tied tightly around it. He looked sheepishly at Gracinda as he carefully opened the little present. He couldn't imagine what it could be. His eyes grew wide with surprise and elation at the money clip shaped like a boat. He looked at Gracinda and smiled and grabbed her in a quick hug that surprised both of them. It was just what he needed to keep his money safe in his pocket. He would cherish this gift forever as a token of her love for him. At least, he hoped she loved him.

Manny smiled and holding tightly to Gracinda's hand looked over at his mother for her approval. Filomena nodded, stood at the door and watched as the two lovebirds walked away holding hands.

She never thought she would see the day that a woman would finally capture Manuel's heart. She seemed like a lovely and sweet young lady. She wasn't quite sure at first when Mr. Bohondoney told her that he was bringing a girl for Manuel. But, she thought to herself, things do work out with the help of St. Theresa. She has her work cut out for her watching over all of us though, Filomena sighed. I will say a special prayer to St. Theresa tonight to thank her for giving us so many blessings.

Alycea appeared at her mother's side, putting her little hand into her mother's and giving it a squeeze. She looked at her mother with her big amber eyes and said, "Mae, does this mean that Manny has a special girlfriend now? Will he still look at other girls too?"

"Yes, it certainly looks like he does have a special girlfriend. To answer your other question, time will tell whether Manuel will ever look at another girl. I think that he probably will not. I think he has found the one for him."

"Oh, I like Gracinda, Mae, don't you? She is pretty and has nice blonde hair too. Don't you like it too? I wish I had blonde hair like hers!"

"Yes, I like her a lot too and she does have beautiful blonde hair," she chuckled at her daughter's remark.

"Sweetheart, you have beautiful dark brown hair. I don't think you would be as beautiful if you had blonde hair. God gave you the perfect color just for you!"

"Do you really think so? Will I find a nice boy someday who will love me like Manny loves Gracinda?"

"I'm sure you will. You have plenty of time yet, my sweet little Alycea. Don't worry about such things yet. You must finish school first then we will find you a nice young man. Ok?"

It would be sooner than she thought and then she would no longer be a little girl.

# CHAPTER 15

Alycea had been writing to her twin brother since the day they arrived in America without any word back from him. She worried that something must have happened to him. She had asked her mother weekly if there had been any news about Antonio from Grinalda, her mother's cousin.

Evidently, Grinalda had taken sick and was not able to respond. One day Filomena received a letter from Grinalda's daughter saying that her mother had to send Antonio to a friend to care for him since she was unable to do that herself. She promised to send Antonio's new address as soon as she could.

Weeks, then months passed by and still no word about him. Filomena was distraught and tried to call someone back in Madeira for help in locating her son. She finally reached Grinalda's daughter who apologized profusely for neglecting to get back to her.

Filomena was patient and kind as usual. She explained, "Please, I need to know that my son is safe and well. Can you give me his address?"

"Of course." The young woman rattled off the address and apologized again. "Antonio is well and living with a kind family who took him in. They have two daughters of their own. He is happy and doing well. My mother told me to tell you that she will try to call you as soon as she is well enough to do that."

Filomena thanked her and put the phone down. She cried happy tears of relief. She had thought her son might have died. She looked at the address that she had received, sat down and wrote a long letter to her son and his new family.

She relayed the information about Antonio to a much relieved Alycea and Manuel. Alycea began a letter to him right away. There was much to tell Antonio about America. She wasn't sure that he had received her other letters with all the news.

Letters began to come from Antonio two weeks later. The family was thrilled to know that he was doing so well. Antonio never asked why he had been left behind. They were all afraid to enter into that conversation for fear of hurting his feelings.

Alycea wrote every chance she got to Antonio. It almost felt like they were together, in a way. She told him that she was saving up some money to send to him so he could come to America. She noticed that he never responded to that and always changed the subject in his letters. She never stopped trying to make him feel wanted and loved.

She wrote letters weekly to Antonio and shared all about school and her friends. He shared that he was good in art and arithmetic. She had sent him a photo of Mae, Manuel and her for his graduation gift. He had sent her a photo of him and his home in Brazil. She always ended her letters with, 'I love you, Antonio.'

*** 

It was eighth grade graduation day for Alycea and she was not happy about it. She really loved school, her teachers and having friends. She did well in all her subjects. Reading and spelling were still her favorites but she did manage to get good marks for Science, Arithmetic, and Geography.

Her two best friends since the third grade were there beside her in line, Arnold Santos and Mary Giuffrida. They were both going into their parents' businesses to work with the intention of taking over for them.

Her friends always asked her about her twin and when he was coming to America. She never knew what to say to them, for she did not know herself.

She, on the other hand, did not have any plans after graduation. She was working on the side with her mother at the mill doing menial work for Mr. Stockman. He and her mother were still close. But there was no talk of marriage for them as yet.

She knew her mother loved her father with all her heart. It was hard to replace someone like that. He was her first love, her mother had told Alycea. She had asked her many times if she loved Mr. Stockman and she said that she did in her own way. Alycea did not understand grownups at all. They don't always say what they mean, she thought to herself, trying to make sense of everything.

\*\*\*

Alycea had a party to celebrate her fourteenth birthday the week before. It wasn't a surprise like Manny's was because no one could keep anything from Alycea. She was too clever and would have known about it right away. One of her presents was a surprise from Mr. Stockman.

Time seemed to be passing quickly and Alycea was hurrying home from work from the mill where she had obtained a full-time position with the help of Mr. Stockman as a material handler even if she was only fourteen years old. He had told her the week before at her party.

He had a surprise gift for her – a position at the plant working for him.

Alycea now handed material off to her mother. Alycea had gotten a real kick out of that. Even though her mother wasn't too sure about it, she finally conceded when Stan convinced her that it was time for Alycea to find a job.

She was the youngest worker in the mill and she always told everyone she was sixteen and not fourteen. After all, she did look older than her age and she certainly acted older because of her bossy attitude.

With the help of her pay and Mae's they managed to rent an apartment a few blocks away from the former two-room complex building at which they had first stayed. This apartment had four rooms and felt like a luxury to them since they now had it all to themselves including a bathroom. They were not able to reach their sponsor since they arrived in America. Thus, they had to do what they could on their own.

As Alycea opened the door to their new place, Mae was standing there waiting for her. A man whom she had never seen before, with dark brown hair and handsome features, stood beside Mae. He was definitely much older than Alycea but she found him quite attractive.

When he saw Alycea, he smiled and a dimple showed prominently on each cheek and a cleft in his chin. His eyes mirrored his smile by sparkling with such delight that she couldn't help but smile back at him. She was absorbed in his face and did not hear Mae trying to get her attention.

"Alycea, I want you to meet Edouardo Carlos Rubelo, or Ed Rubelo. He works at the mill in the sheet metal room on the third floor. Stan just hired him this week and introduced me to him. He is Portuguese too and just came over from Madeira recently." She looked at her daughter eagerly waiting for her response.

"Oh…I…It's nice to meet you, Ed. Bon Dia," Alycea said with her stomach in knots and a funny feeling spreading throughout her body. This had never happened to her before. She hoped she was not getting sick, she thought to herself.

"It is a pleasure to meet you, Alycea. Your mother has told me all about you and what a good worker you are at the mill." He continued to appraise her with a twinkle in his green eyes.

Alycea didn't know where to look, his stare was quite intense and the feeling was getting stronger and she was feeling extremely warm all over.

She felt as if she could pass out. She tried to look elsewhere but his stare kept her focused on him. She wished she knew what was going on inside her. She almost expressed this feeling out loud. She was frightened and sick. Before she could register another thought, her vision darkened and she passed out right at his feet.

"Alycea, are you all right?" His voice was soothing and melodic.

She felt a cool cloth on her face being pressed by a hand that was not familiar to her touch. It felt fairly smooth but strong with a few callouses on the fingertips and palm. It was much larger than her hand as he placed it over hers protectively.

She opened her eyes to see his handsome face and green eyes staring at her in a concerned and troubled way. A smile touched his lips making his dimples appear in an appealing way which was again disturbing to her.

"I...I...don't know what happened. I...guess I'm all right. Did I faint?" She looked at him imploringly, not sure how or why this had happened to her. She was trying to make sense of it all.

He patted her on the arm and turned to Filomena who was standing behind him looking at Alycea with deep concern too.

Filomena smiled and nodded her head at her daughter and said, "Alycea, dear one, you did faint but Edouardo caught you before you could fall and injure yourself. He is quite strong and agile and easily lifted you up and carried you over to the couch. Are you feeling better now? Would you like something to drink or eat? You could be coming down with something or just hungry? It is time for supper anyway."

Mae moved over to the kitchen to warm up some watercress soup with little meatballs, and vegetables, Alycea's favorite. She felt herself getting stronger just from inhaling the fragrant aroma of the soup as it was heating through.

Ed was still looking down at her waiting to assist her if need be. Alycea just shook her head at him and got up gingerly, putting her feet down to test her balance. Once she realized that she could support her own weight, she went out to the kitchen and sat down at the table to eat her soup. Mae had put down three bowls of soup. Evidently, she wanted Ed Rubelo to stay for supper.

Ed followed closely behind Alycea to ensure her safety and sat across from her at the table. He inhaled the aroma of the watercress soup and then picked up his spoon and dug in.

"This is excellent, Mrs. Ataide. You certainly are an excellent cook. Can Alycea cook like you?"

Mae walked over to the table with a basket of crusty bread that she had just cut into slices and placed it on the table. She looked at Ed and chuckled, saying, "Ed, please call me Filomena. I have taught Alycea everything I know about cooking. She does help me in the kitchen to prepare meals each day. I think she is quite adept at cooking on her own. She is reasonably capable of taking care of her own kitchen."

Alycea almost choked on the spoonful of soup she had in her mouth when she heard the tone in her mother's voice as she spoke to Ed. There was something in that tone that Alycea did not like. It almost sounded like she was trying to sell Alycea to him! Her mother was definitely up to something and Alycea thought that he may be in on it too. It would be nice if they would clue her in too.

Alycea finished her soup, got up and announced that she was tired and needed to go to bed early tonight. "I am taking an earlier shift tomorrow at the mill," she announced flatly.

Mae eyed Alycea curiously and nodded her reluctant approval but stated at the same time, "Alycea, please say good night to Ed before you go."

Alycea looked at mother with the same curious expression but did as she was told. "Ed, it was a pleasure to meet you. I hope you have a good night."

"Alycea, it was definitely a pleasure to meet you too. I hope we will see each other again real soon and spend more time together. Please get some rest. You seem to be tired and stressed. You are working much too hard for a young woman."

"I am not a young woman; I am only a girl of 14! I am not ready to spend time with you. You are too old for me!" Alycea's face was crimson and her temper was rising as she stormed out of the kitchen, headed into her bedroom and slammed the door loudly.

Alycea could hear her mother's excited voice rising in apology. Alycea could imagine what her mother would say to her later when Ed left. She soon heard the murmur of voices fading as they moved away from the kitchen and then the apartment door closed softly.

Alycea hurriedly took her clothes off and pulled her nightgown over her head. She then simultaneously pulled the covers down and jumped into bed pulling them over her head. All she wanted to do was hide from her mother's wrath. She was going to be really angry and disappointed with Alycea. Her mother was a loving and patient person but sometimes Alycea pushed her too far.

She heard her mother's soft footsteps as they got closer to the bedroom door. Her mother hesitated, then opened the door and entered.

Filomena touched Alycea softly on the shoulder as she said, "Lubelia Alycea, I can understand that you are frightened about your feelings about Ed. I know he is an older man but you are now a young woman. You have had your monthly time for about a year now. I think it is time for you to find a husband. Ed is a wonderful man, handsome and strong. He can support you and a family exceptionally well." She patiently waited for any response or reaction to her proposition.

Alycea couldn't believe this was happening. She couldn't be serious! Alycea sat up abruptly and turned to face her mother and through tear-filled eyes she proclaimed, "I am not ready to get married. I am still a child! I don't want to have babies yet! I am not in love with him. I do think he is attractive but I don't want to marry him! Please, God, help me!" She prayed silently for his intervention, "I will do whatever He wants. I will pray to St. Theresa too for help. I don't want to do this, Mae. Please don't make me! I don't want to leave you." Copious tears were falling from her eyes. She let them fall, wetting the covers and her nightgown as she looked pleadingly at her mother.

"Oh Alycea! Mia filha, please don't cry. I hate to see you cry. It will be okay, I promise you. You can live here with Ed and use the other bedroom. In time, you will learn to love him and be happy as I did with your father. We were matched by my parents but he was such a good man that I fell in love with his goodness and kindness. He loved me so much too."

"Mae, it is not the same thing! You told me that you always loved Pai and that he was the love of your life," Alycea stressed through tears and a stuffy nose.

"Oh, mia filha, yes, I did tell you that. But you know we were destined to marry and I guess I did love him from the first time I met him. I did not know it at that time but we were pushed together to meet and my parents hoped that we would fall in love on our own. They were patient and we did and then we decided on our own to get married. They did not have to force us. I had hoped it would be the same for you and Ed."

"We can wait awhile and see how you feel. You may need a little more time to get to know him. He is coming by tomorrow again for dinner. He needs a place to stay. I told him he could use our extra bedroom. He is going to help us with the rent, food and expenses also. I had planned to rent the extra room out if we needed the money. I told you that when we found this place. Now, please be kind to him. He is a nice young man. Okay, Alycea?"

Alycea reached for her handkerchief at her bedside table and wiped her tears and blew her nose. Mae reached out to her and took Alycea into her arms. Alycea laid her head against her mother's soft bosom inhaling her sweet lilac perfume. Filomena rubbed Alycea's back and whispered into her ear that she loved her. Alycea instinctively hugged her mother tighter, not wanting to let go. She was fearful of what she must face and was not yet ready to grow up.

Alycea remembered the day she had her first monthly over a year ago. She was tremendously frightened back then. She was feeling just as frightened now. Mae had explained it to her in a way that left her wondering what she was talking about. She had said that she was now a woman and this would happen once a month. She told her how to take care of it. That was all she had told her. Alycea didn't understand anymore now a year later.

She had even asked her friends at work about this. They were all older than she and had just laughed when she asked them. They said that she would find out soon enough what it meant. Alycea felt angry and hurt that they wouldn't tell her more.

She didn't want to grow up yet. She was afraid of what she didn't understand and of Ed. She was strongly attracted to him but didn't know what to do. She was still a child inside.

"Alycea, try to get some sleep now, dormir, dos mia filha, we will talk some more tomorrow. I have to clean up the kitchen and do a little sewing before I go to bed." She tucked Alycea into bed and kissed her softly on the cheek, leaving her to muse over what she had just told her.

Alycea's head was spinning and she couldn't believe what was happening. She knew she was not ready for this but didn't see any way to escape. She found herself slowly drifting off to sleep with dreams of Ed coming to live with them.

# CHAPTER 16

Manuel had moved out of his mother's and sister's apartment to live with Gracinda's family after they had gotten married. They had a large house five miles away. Her family was well to do for the time. Her father was in the coal business.

Manuel had courted and dated his girlfriend, Gracinda, and they had finally gotten married when he was sixteen and she was eighteen.

Gracinda had gotten pregnant within the first year but had suffered three miscarriages in a row, much to their disappointment. Manny wanted to have a child of his own. That was all he had dreamed of for a long time – to be a father.

They finally had a daughter, Cristina Maria Ataide, just short of his nineteenth birthday. She was a sickly baby at first but soon developed into a lively and healthy little girl.

Mae was ecstatic about being a grandmother and Alycea was thrilled to be an auntie. Cristina Marie was a beautiful little girl with her mother's blonde hair and dimples and her father's hazel eyes. Manny brought her over to see them often so they could spoil her as only a grandparent and aunt could do.

She was the apple of Manny's eye and wanted to go everywhere with him. It was hard for him to sneak out to go to work. She would put up such a fuss over him leaving without her.

Life throws unexpected events our way. Some we can accept and overcome, while others can destroy us. Manny would have a long, hard road ahead of him. The question was – would he survive it?

# CHAPTER 17

"Oh Avoa, I am sorry you had such a hard time back then. You were forced to marry Grandpa too early. Did you really love him? Did you even know what love was being that young?" Jasmine looked anxiously at her grandmother. She couldn't imagine what it would have been like to be only fourteen and have to marry someone much older.

"It was a shock at the time. But I did what I had to do, to please my mother. She was a forceful woman but she was thinking of my best interests and wanted me to be secure in a marriage. I guess she thought that maybe I wouldn't be able to take care of myself. Well, she would have been surprised how well I have taken care of myself," she chuckled softly at the thoughts running through her head.

They continued to go back to a time and place that seemed long ago.

# CHAPTER 18

Alycea woke up with a start, thinking that everything had all been just a dream. She rushed through her daily routine, washing, dressing and then eating before she realized the dreaded truth.

"How are you this morning, Lubelia Alycea? Are you feeling better, dos Alycea? Don't forget that Ed is coming over today. He will be bringing some of his things with him during the day. I have given him a key so he can get in to drop them off."

Alycea looked at her and her face showed the shocked recognition. All the words were coming back to her now; the realization that it was not a dream.

"Mae, I am not…I don't…I have to go to work. I will see you later. Mr. Stockman wants me there earlier than you. Don't worry about me. I am fine." She grabbed her sweater and lunch and rushed out the door. She really didn't want to go to work today, she was too depressed, but she had nowhere else to go.

Alycea arrived more quickly than she expected since she was in such a daze and walked faster than she usually did. She guessed she was trying to escape her problems but couldn't. They just kept following her.

She got right to work and stopped in to see Mr. Stockman to get her workload orders straight. She dropped off her things at her locker first. She needed to have her hands free to carry her work back to her desk.

Mr. Stockman was a pleasant man and she could see how her mother had fallen for him. He told Alycea to call him Stan but she just couldn't do that. He was attractive in a different way than Ed but his personality was even tempered and kind. He was sensitive to his employees' needs but tried to hide that fact under his brusque way. He didn't want to be thought of as a pushover. He especially liked Alycea since she was an extension of her mother who he loved dearly. He looked at her mother with such a dopey expression. It could be sickening at times! But Alycea was glad that she was one of his favorite employees, thanks to Mae.

Mr. Stockman handed Alycea the workload with some extra instructions. She was on her way back to her desk when she saw Ed coming towards her. He smiled at her with his eyes and she found herself smiling back. She was caught now and couldn't get away.

"Bon dia, Alycea," He said as he assessed her arms full of material and papers. He rushed to her side to assist her. Alycea told him that she did not need any help. But he didn't listen and began to take some of the material off the top of the pile lightening the load considerably. She couldn't help but say, "Obrigado, Ed."

As she hurried on her way, he followed closely behind and deposited the material on her desk. He smiled at her intently and said, "I will see you later on, Alycea. Don't work too hard now."

She felt at a loss for words. He was too sure of himself. He was going to move right into her life without asking her permission. What a nerve! Why was it that he irritated her one minute and the other she couldn't help but smile at him? He was driving her crazy!

How was she going to live with him in the same house, only a room away!

\*\*\*

Alycea heard the closing bell but couldn't believe that it was that time already. She didn't want the day to be over because she knew what was waiting for her at home. He… would be there again.

She looked around to see if some of her friends were still at their desks but of course not, they were already running for the exits. They were always the first ones out the door a second after the bell sounded.

Mr. Stockman was heading her way as she sat down at her desk. He had a funny look on his face. She wondered if he wanted her to do some more work to prepare the lot of material for tomorrow.

As he got closer to her, she could see his face was showing some strain and his eyes were sad. He stopped at her desk and just looked at her, opened his mouth but nothing came out.

Boy, this didn't look good. Alycea got up and reached out to him to touch his arm. He seemed like he was not aware of her touch until Alycea pressed on his arm. He jumped like he had gotten a shock.

"Mr. Stockman, is everything all right? What's wrong? You look like you received a shock or something?"

"Oh, Alycea, I just got a call from your mother. She told me to escort you home right away and that she had something to tell you," he said in a soft but shaky voice.

"What did she have to tell me? Did she tell you? You're making me nervous, what is it?" She emphasized her anxiety as she looked into his troubled eyes.

"I don't know, Alycea. But, I feel that it's not good. Your mother sounded unnervingly upset. We must hurry now. Get your things and I'll lock up. I'll walk you home. I may be needed by your mother and you," he said with resignation and sadness.

They walked out in silence, after locking up, and continued that way until they got to the apartment. He turned toward Alycea and put out his hand. She put her hand into his and he held it reassuringly and smiled wanly at her. They headed toward the door. They walked in together to face whatever they had to face. Just having his hand in hers made her feel a little stronger as if her father was with her.

Her mother was standing in the kitchen with her hands covering her face, a limp lace handkerchief, which she had embroidered, was sticking out of her right hand. She turned at the sound of the door opening to look up. Her face was white. Tears were running down her cheeks making a shiny path before dripping off the edge of her chin. Her eyes were puffy and red and she had a look of sheer devastation on her face.

Alycea let go of Mr. Stockman's hand and ran into her mother's arms, hugging her tightly and saying, "Mae, what's the matter? Why are you crying? What happened? Are you sick or something?"

She led Alycea over to the kitchen table and sat her down in one of the chairs and then sat down next to her. She put her hands over her daughter's and pressed tightly. Alycea watched her mother's face as she tried to compose herself. Behind her Alycea heard a noise from the bedroom and turning around saw her brother, Manny walking toward them. His face had the same look of devastation as Mae's. Alycea couldn't stand this a moment longer and yelled, "Manny, what's wrong? Please tell me!"

Manny sat down next to them and wiped his face as tears started overflowing and sliding out of the corners of his eyes. He looked at Alycea and spoke so softly that she had to strain to hear him.

"They are gone, Alycea, my wife and daughter, they are gone! My beautiful Gracinda and Cristina! I can't believe it!"

"What…what do you mean, Manny, where did they go?"

"They are dead. They drowned." He broke down now and couldn't explain anymore. Mae wrapped her arms around his shaking shoulders as he let out deep wracking sobs. In between the sobs he would exclaim, "No, No, No, Mae, please help me! What will I do without them?"

Alycea looked back at Mr. Stockman who was crying openly and watched as he walked over to her mother and brother and wrapped them both in his arms. He held them there until they both stopped shaking and the sobs got softer. He pulled out his handkerchief and offered it to Manny who took it and wiped his eyes and loudly blew his nose.

He patted Manny on the back and whispered something into his ear. Alycea could not hear what he said but evidently it made Manny look relieved.

Alycea asked Manny what Mr. Stockman had said to him. He looked at her as if he hadn't known she was in the room. He took her aside and hugged his sister fiercely. She had to push against him to get her breath back.

Alycea stepped back and looked up at Manny and waited for him to explain something, anything to her. She was still in the dark. She didn't like being treated like a child even though she was only fourteen.

"Alycea, I'm sorry. Did I hurt you?" His voice was soft and tender.

"No, Manuel," Alycea said using his given name when she was upset, "I'm okay. Please tell me what Mr. Stockman said and if you are ready, can you tell me what happened to Gracinda and Cristina Maria?" She asked tentatively.

"Well...I...they wanted to go out on Mr. Dante's boat which he had used to go fishing with me. He is a business man who wanted me to work for him. I met him a few years ago when I was working for Mr. Bohondoney. Well, Mr. Dante said I could borrow his boat any time I wanted, so I took Gracinda and Cristina for a short boat ride." He stopped when he couldn't talk suddenly due to his voice getting thick with emotion and the tears welling up in his eyes.

Alycea patted him on the back and he looked up at her with gratitude and love. He took a deep breath and continued his tragic story. "The weather was bright and sunny, not too many clouds overhead, just in the far distance. We were only going to be out for a short time and not far from shore but...the storm came out of nowhere. I had tried to get to the cove and moor the boat so we could get onto the little beach there but we didn't make it... Cristina...was happy and loved riding in the boat. She had such a look of joy on her little face. Gracinda...was holding Cristina a second before the sky darkened and the wind picked up and tossed the boat around like a cork. But Cristina moved out of her mother's arms and was looking over the side and...I reached for Cristina at the same time that Gracinda did but neither one of us could get to her in time...she fell overboard and Gracinda jumped in after her before I could stop her. I jumped in to save both of them but couldn't find either one of them. It was dense and dark under the water and I kept going down and coming back up, again and again and again."

"I finally had to stop and go back to shore and get help. Divers went down and looked in vain for hours. There was no sign of either of them." He raked his fingers through his hair that was still damp. "I...couldn't...I couldn't save them, Alycea, I couldn't save my family! I don't know what I will do without them! There is no reason to go on living now!"

96

"No, Manuel, you will not say that! Do you hear me? You have every reason to live. What would Mae and I do without you! It would kill Mae to lose you! Can't you see that! She lost Pai and had to leave Antonio behind. You can't do this to her! How can you be so selfish?"

He lifted up his head, his face shiny with the streaks of tears and his nose was cherry red. He wore an expression of shock and then anger on his face. "What do you mean, selfish?! What do you know about anything? You only think of yourself and you can't imagine what it is to have a family. You are just a child." He turned his face away, too ashamed to look at his sister. He got up and stormed out of the apartment.

Filomena called after him and tried to follow him but was stopped by Stan's strong grip. "Don't, Filomena. Leave him alone. He has to deal with this. He will come back after he has cooled down. It has been quite a shock for everyone. It will not be an easy road for him. He really didn't mean what he said. Remember that. Ok?"

Alycea looked to her mother for guidance and comfort. "Mae, what did I do to hurt him? Will he forgive me? I am sorry for whatever I did or said." She ran to the second bedroom and threw herself onto the bed.

Her mother came in to see her. "You need to rest and not worry. Manuel will forgive you. He was just angry and grief stricken over losing his wife and child. He will heal in time but we must be here for him and to help him. Ok, child. Now get ready for bed. We will talk more tomorrow. Say your prayers and get to sleep, mia filha." Filomena kissed her daughter's wet cheek, tucked her into bed and shut off the light.

Filomena came back to the kitchen where Stan was sitting at the table, his eyes with a glazed and faraway look.

"Oh, Stan, you...I know you understand. You lost your wife and child too. It is not something that you can get over quickly. I don't know how to thank you for being here to help and support us. We all need you! I love you, Stan!" She stopped to think about what she had just said to him.I do love him; I know that now without a doubt, Filomena said to herself.

"Filomena, I love you too! I know that this is not the time or place but I will ask you a question soon and I hope you have the answer that I have prayed for."

He took her into his arms and held her and she cried out of sheer grief for the great loss of her daughter-in-law, Gracinda, and her precious little granddaughter, Cristina.

Suddenly there was a knock at the door and they were startled out of their embrace. Filomena went to the door slowly and opened it to see Ed standing there with his arms full of his belongings. She had forgotten that he was coming over to move into the extra bedroom.

Stan, seeing how distraught Filomena was, took matters into his own hands. He asked the man standing at the door, "What can I do for you, sir? I know you. I just hired you a couple of weeks ago."

"Yes, you did, and I thank you for the job. It is a pleasure to see you again, Mr. Stockman. I will be back in a second to shake your hand after I drop off my things in the bedroom," Ed said, feeling good about having a job and now a place to stay.

Filomena said, "It's okay, Stan. This is Edouardo Carlos Rubelo. I was expecting him."

Turning toward Ed, Filomena responded, "Please come in Ed, and get settled. The room is down the hall." Filomena directed Ed to the second bedroom without a thought of Alycea sleeping in the bed.

Mentally and emotionally spent, Filomena plopped herself down on the coach and put her face into her hands.

Stan directed a questioning look at Filomena over Ed's head as he was going into the bedroom. Filomena just shrugged her shoulders and placed her index finger up to show one minute. She would explain to him later.

Ed returned in less than a minute and went right over to Stan and gave his hand a firm handshake.

"Are you staying here long, Ed?" He was trying to find out what this was all about without Filomena's help. His curiosity got the better of him. Also, he did not like a good looking young man living in the same house as his future wife. Ed was younger than he by several years. Stan figured he was about twenty-three or four.

"Well, Filomena was kind enough to let me stay here until I can find a place of my own."

Filomena was busying herself around the kitchen cleaning up the dinner dishes and putting away the food that they had not eaten. No one had an appetite tonight. She kept wiping her eyes with her handkerchief, the tears just kept creeping up on her each time her mind returned to her son.

Turning toward Filomena, Ed again thanked her for her hospitality and generosity. She waved her hand at him but did not turn from the sink to look at him.

He walked toward her when he realized that she was upset. "Filomena, are you all right? Did I say something to upset you? Do you want me to leave?" His face registered confusion and concern.

"No, Ed, it is not necessary for you to leave. I am upset, but not at you. We had a tragedy in the family…my son, Manuel's wife and daughter drowned at sea." Just saying this brought on more tears and painful sobs from Filomena.

"Oh no, Filomena. I'm sorry. Where is Manuel now? Can I do anything to help? I met Manuel only once with his wife when they came by the mill to see you last week. She was a lovely girl."

Filomena at this point was too distraught to answer any questions. Stan just took her to her bedroom and put her down on the bed to rest. He came back to talk to Ed.

"Ed, I don't think Filomena is in any mood to talk to anyone right now. She has had a severe shock and I fear that she may get herself sick if she does not rest. Please excuse her. Why don't you get yourself unpacked and settled in? I am going to stay here on the couch to watch over things in case I am needed. Goodnight, Ed."

Ed was left standing there looking somewhat confused. He turned and went into the bedroom to start unpacking and getting ready to go to bed.

He turned on the light in the bedroom and suddenly his eyes went to the form in the bed. He didn't realize that he was going to have to sleep in the same room as Alycea. He quickly shut the light so as not to disturb her. He hadn't noticed her sleeping form in the bed when he had hastily dropped off his things a short time ago.

He leaned over to look down at her sleeping peacefully. The covers were pushed aside and he gently pulled them up and tucked them under her chin. She moaned and settled in comfortably grabbing hold of the covers and tightly pulling them toward her and at the same time brushing against his hand. He jumped back with the shock of her skin touching his. It was like an electric current.

He moved around in the dark, now trying to organize his stuff and finally gave up and grabbed the extra pillow off the bed and the

100

afghan that was on the back of a chair by the window and curled up on the braided rug on the floor to try to fall asleep. He closed his eyes but could hear Alycea breathing softly with a little nasally sound. He couldn't think of anything else but Alycea's soft skin that had brushed against his hand and how much he would like to touch her. This was going to be a long night, he thought to himself.

Later that night Filomena would kneel and pray in the privacy of her bedroom to seek the guidance of St. Theresa to help her son heal. St. Theresa was always there for her. Filomena was sure that with St. Theresa's help they would all survive and go on with their lives in spite of the tragedies they had to bear.

As Filomena was falling asleep, she was unaware of the uncomfortable situation in the other bedroom down the hall.

# CHAPTER 19

"Oh my God! What are we going to do, Paul? We have lost our Gracinda and little Cristina! How could something like this happen? Where is Manuel? He came to tell us and then left to go see his mother. Will he come back? I must speak with him and find out what and how it happened?" Clara covered her face with her hands as she cried softly.

Paul went to his wife, sat down beside her on the couch and gently took her into his arms to comfort her. She threw her arms around his neck and held on tightly, leaning her face into his neck and breathing in his manly scent which helped to calm her.

He could feel his wife's tears running down his neck and onto his chest, wetting the front of his shirt. He reached into his back pocket and pulled out his handkerchief and handed it to Clara before she soaked him thoroughly.

She accepted his handkerchief and wiped her copious tears and gave her nose a loud blow, sniffling a little, before giving it back to him. He just shook his head and tucked it back into her hand to keep.

"Clara, bad things happen sometimes. We don't always understand the reasons behind them. We can't blame anyone for this. It was an accident. They are with God now and we must go on. It won't be easy, my love, but we will do it for their memory. I loved them both more than my life, you know that. I wish I could make it all go away and have them back with us, but I can't do that. I wish I could, just to see you happy. We need each other more than ever now, Clara. Please be strong. I am here for you to lean on and I may lean on you a little some days too. It is still sinking in. I feel like it was all a dream but I know it is reality."

"Oh Paul, I love you so much. I need you too, darling. I know we'll make it, but right now I am completely lost without them. I hope they did not suffer. I take solace in the fact that they are together in Heaven. I hope they are looking down on us and help us get through this terrible time." She reached for her husband. They held each other in a comforting embrace, leaning into one another for support as their tears mingled on their connected cheeks.

The doorbell sounded and they both looked up and then linking hands walked toward the door.

Standing on the doorstep was their son-in-law, Manuel. He looked like he had been in a tempest. His hair was tousled and standing up on end and his clothes were still damp and rumpled from his ordeal. He had not taken the time to change. He just stood there looking miserable.

Clara pulled him into the house and hugged him tightly trying to comfort him too. He leaned on her and held on, wracking sobs coming from his chest as his whole body shook.

Paul wrapped his arms around them both to hold them steady. After a short while, Manuel become still, and stepped back to look at his in-laws. He had such a tortured look on his face that it hurt Clara to look at him.

Manuel cleared his throat and spoke, "I don't know how to say I am sorry for what happened. If I could turn back the clock and make different choices I would. If I never took them out in the boat, they would be here right now. Please forgive me.

I tried so hard to find them. I kept diving down…but it was too dark and I couldn't see them. The divers who came later on couldn't find them either. I don't know if we will ever find them…"

"Manuel, it was not your fault. They made a choice and you wanted to make them happy. You did the right thing. It was an accident. That is all. Please do not torture yourself anymore. We must support each other and we will survive this together. I loved them dearly as you did and will miss them more than I can say. But we must take care of one another now. They would want us to continue on in their memory."

"Paul, you are an honorable and forgiving man. Gracinda always told me that you were a wonderful father and then grandfather. I must add, you are a wonderful father-in-law too."

"Thank you, Manuel. You are a good man. My daughter was fortunate to have found you. I know you made her happy."

"Thank you, Paul. I know in time we will heal the wounds of this loss but for now I must grieve. I wanted to come see you before I went away. I am going to sail out on the first ship that comes into dock. I need to be away from here and the memories. It is just too painful to look at everything and everyone that will remind me of my loss. I hope you will understand. I just need to pick up some of my things, ok? I will come back one day to see you, I promise. Until then, take care of yourselves and know that I love you both." He gave them one last hug and went upstairs to the bedroom he had shared with his wife and packed his things. He passed by his daughter's room but did not look in. It hurt too much to see her room without her in it. He came back downstairs with a large duffle bag over his shoulder and turned to look at his mother-in-law and father-in-law once more before closing the door behind him, leaving a void for his in-laws that would never be filled.

Paul and Clara Da Silva stood there looking at the door for what seemed like an eternity and then turned away to go on with their empty lives.

Alycea had kept in touch with the Da Silva's in the beginning but it became trying. They did not know what to say to one another after a while and just looking at one another only reminded them of the tragedy they each had to bear.

The Da Silva's struggled for ten years over the loss of their daughter and granddaughter. They never saw their son-in-law or his family again. They died within a few days of one another, most likely from broken hearts.

# CHAPTER 20

"I am so sorry, Avoa, about Uncle Manny's family. I never realized what happened. I had heard that he had a child but didn't know what had happened to her. You and Granny Filomena must have had a terrible time keeping the family together. That was such a tragedy." Tears welled in Jasmine's eyes as she expressed her sympathy to her grandmother. A deeper respect was growing inside her as her grandmother's life had begun to unfold. Jasmine was beginning to realize how strong and resilient her grandmother really was.

"I always loved Uncle Manny. He was a wonderful man, funny, always smiling and cheerful. How did he do it after all he had gone through in his life? He never let on about any of this to me. He didn't come to visit often but when he did I always had fun with him," Jasmine sighed as she felt the deep loss of her beloved great uncle.

Jasmine thought back to one of Uncle Manny's visits when he played hide and seek with her and they ran around the yard together. He had to sit down afterwards because he was exhausted. He kept telling me that he was old. He would laugh much like Avoa did, heartily, and tears would form in his eyes afterward. He would always call me his little amendoim, peanut, or macaco, monkey, because I was small but active and mischievous.

Alycea added, "Well that was Manuel. He was a fun-loving person. It took him many years to get over the loss of his family and of course he never forgot them. But he did go on with his life and married Ernestina. She kept him sane. He did miss not having another child, though."

"So sad for him. It was a horrible tragedy," Jasmine said and sighed deeply.

"Manuel doted on your mother and aunt when they were growing up as much as he could every time he came home. Over the years he did come to visit you and your brother and cousins too. He loved you all deeply. We only wished that he would come home more often. But I don't want to get too far ahead of the story," Avoa said with deep sadness and regret in her voice.

# CHAPTER 21

Filomena woke up and went out to the kitchen to prepare breakfast like she always did. She saw Stan on the couch; his long body was draped uncomfortably hanging over the side.

She went over and kissed him softly on the cheek. He opened his eyes and smiled at her. Her heart skipped a beat and she felt a warm feeling inside.

He reached out to her and she went into his embrace willingly. They kissed at first softly then more ardently and then remembered that they were not alone in the house. Alycea was in the other bedroom. Oh my God...and, so was Ed!

"Oh no, Stan, I forgot Alycea was in the other bedroom last night and we sent Ed in there, too. What was I thinking? Alycea was supposed to stay in my room with me from now on! I was out of my mind with grief last night and forgot." Filomena wrung her hands and paced back and forth in front of Stan.

"Now Filomena, don't worry. Ed is a good man and he would not take advantage of a young woman. After all, he is several years older than she. You are not at fault. I was the one that sent him in there. In fact, I ordered him to go to bed last night. I was upset too. It will be okay. I'll go see him and straighten this out right now."

Stan went over to the other bedroom at the back of the apartment and knocked softly on the door. He waited a minute and then opened it.

The room was dark. He had to step in and wait for his eyes to get acclimated to the lack of light. What he saw sent a wave of relief through him. There on the bed lay Alycea sleeping soundly and on the floor a few feet from the bed lay Ed all tangled up in an afghan.

Stan tiptoed out of the room so as not to disturb them and went out to the kitchen to report his findings to Filomena. He wanted to relieve her of any guilt over this mishap.

After telling her what he saw, she let out a great sigh and just smiled the sweet, angelic smile that he loved. She hugged him in thanks and went back to preparing their breakfast.

They were soon joined by Ed who still looked quite rumpled in his shirt and pants that he had slept in. He rubbed his eyes and stretched his arms over his head and greeted them with, "Good morning. I could smell the bacon, eggs and coffee and it woke me up. My stomach was growling this morning. I didn't eat anything last night," he said between yawns.

"Oh, I'm sorry, Ed. With everything that had happened yesterday, I forgot to offer you some supper. I had prepared it but we did not eat...couldn't eat, more like it. I did put it away but you can take some of the meatloaf for lunch today. We will finish it all tonight though so it won't go to waste."

"Oh, what is wrong with me?! I apologize. I didn't mean to sound like I was complaining. I know what you went through yesterday. I am half asleep and don't know what I'm saying. Please forgive me!" He looked embarrassed as well as angry with himself for being inconsiderate.

"No Ed, that's okay. I will feed you plenty today to make up for neglecting you yesterday," she replied trying to sound normal, though her voice sounded sad and tired.

She hadn't slept well herself with all the dreams of her granddaughter calling to her and going under water. She tried to save her innumerable times but was unsuccessful. She couldn't imagine what her son was going through. It felt like someone was stabbing her in the heart and it would break in two.

As her thoughts of her son were going around in her head, she suddenly heard his voice. She thought she was imagining it when she felt his arms around her shoulders. She turned and was embraced by him as she stood at the stove.

His eyes were red rimmed and puffy but he smiled wanly at her through the new tears pooling in his eyes. They were both crying now but happy to see one another. She had thought he would not come back to them.

"Mae, I had to come see you before I went away. I'm leaving on the schooner that is docked today. They are leaving port in a couple of hours. I went to pick up some things that I would need and said goodbye to Gracinda's parents, Paul and Clara. I will be off for six months at a time. I promise I will be back to see you and Alycea and you too, Stan."

He turned to see Stan sitting on the couch. He went over to shake his hand and pat him on the arm but Stan pulled him into his arms and gave him a bear hug instead. Manuel returned the hug and thanked him for being a friend to his mother and said, "Stan, please take care of Mae and Alycea for me. I will be back again but it may not be for a long time. Ok?"

"Of course, Manuel, I will be here to take care of your family. They are my family now too," Stan said as his voice broke with emotion.

"Thank you, Stan. You're a good man," Manuel said with as much emotion.

As Manuel was heading toward the door, he noticed Ed standing in the corner of the room in the dark. He raised his hand to Ed and said, "I am sorry I did not see you there. You are Edouardo Carlos Rubelo from the plant. Are you having breakfast here this morning?" He asked in a puzzled voice.

"Yes, I am also staying here at your mother's invitation until I can find other quarters," he replied in a hesitant way. Ed did not want to interfere in any way with this family scene.

"Oh, okay, well I am off. Mae, please take care of yourself. I love you. I will send home some of my wages to a post office box and let you know what it is as I find work in different ports. If you need anything please contact me through the post office."

"Bye Manuel, take care of yourself, mio filho. I love you too! I will miss you. Please write to me to let me know how you are doing. Ok? I promise to write back." She walked him to the door, her arm around him trying to prolong the contact. Her heart was too full with grief to comprehend this new loss.

"Manny, where are you going?" Alycea heard his voice as she came out of the bedroom. She ran over to him and hugged him to keep him from leaving.

Manny turned and looked at his sister, grief deeply showing in his face and tear-filled eyes.

"You can't leave me; take me with you, Manny, please!" She begged him in a tear choked voice.

He put his finger under her chin and lifted up her face to meet his. "My little sister, Alycea, I love you dearly but I can't take you with me. This is a journey that I must make on my own. You have to stay with Mae and Stan. You can help take care of them for me too. I promise I will be back to see you soon. I will write to you and make sure you write back to me," he said to her with his usual smirk. He kissed her on the cheek, and gave her one more hug and his trademark wink before going out the door.

"Mae, why does Manny have to go away? We need him. I need him! I will miss him so much!" She said with tears coming quickly now.

"Alycea, be strong, mia filha. He will return one day. We will write to him and keep in touch that way. He will tell you all about his adventures at sea. You know how you loved the stories your father used to tell you. Manuel needs to do this right now to keep his sanity. This journey will help heal him. The sea may have taken away his loved ones but it will also heal him now." She looked at her daughter's sad face and felt the same pain deep inside herself.

"Okay, Mae, I will write to him, but he better write back to me. You know how awful he is about writing!" She said in an exasperated tone. This tone caused everyone to lighten up a little and they all let out a much needed laugh.

Alycea looked around the room hearing a different laugh, spotted Ed standing in the corner looking seriously rumpled. She remembered getting up from her bed and stepping on a pillow and afghan that were on the floor. Now she knew why they were there. He had slept in her room last night while she slept in her warm bed. The thought made her shiver even though she wasn't cold. In fact, she suddenly felt her face turning pink and warm with her thoughts of him, cold one minute, warm the next. What was going on with her?

Ed looked back at her with his eyebrows raised and his eyes crinkling into a smile. He realized what she was thinking. He was feeling similarly warm just looking at her face as it continued to blush to an attractive, bright pink tone.

Mae, watched the exchange of facial emotions on their faces and broke up the silence with, "Breakfast is ready everyone. Please sit down and enjoy it while it is still warm."

They all sat down to eat and try to get back to life as grief and loss were pushed into the back of their minds while their bodies were nourished.

# CHAPTER 22

Life did go on, but not in the same way. There was a void that could not be filled with Manuel gone. He had a spark that was needed and which couldn't be replaced. Also, they missed Gracinda and little Cristina, who had been much like her father, full of life.

Alycea wrote long letters to Antonio to relate everything that had happened to their sister-in-law and niece. Antonio wrote back how distraught he was for Manny. He promised to write his brother as soon as Alycea sent him an address. Alycea also wrote about the new border, Ed. She left out her feelings for him but did say that Ed was being pushed on her by their mother. Antonio didn't have much to say but that he wished her well whatever she did in these new state of affairs.

Alycea went to work and came home each day to sit at supper with Ed. They got to know one another better and spent every night telling each other all about themselves, talking long into the night. They still slept separately - Ed on the floor and Alycea in the bed. It became familiar and comfortable. Well, at least it was comfortable for Alycea because she had the bed.

One day Mae came home with an announcement. She and Stan were getting married. She showed off her engagement ring to them as she bustled about the kitchen preparing supper. She looked happy and more like herself again. It had been almost six months since the death of Gracinda and Cristina, and Manuel had sailed away on the schooner.

Manuel had been good about writing at first. They had received a letter every couple of weeks for the first three months then once a month for the next three. Alycea still wrote a letter every other day and mailed them out once a week to him. She wanted him to have letters coming all the time so he wouldn't forget her. She missed him constantly even if he had teased her all the time. Of course, she continued to keep Antonio in the loop of things and he responded with his news back in Brazil.

She was lonely without Manuel but now had Ed who was always kind and attentive to her. She found him looking at her in a different way which made her more nervous. She did find him intriguingly attractive, and one day when he kissed her, she found herself kissing him back.

One evening when Mae and Alycea were alone in the kitchen, the men had not arrived home yet; Alycea asked her mother what it was like to love a man. Filomena turned to look at her with a smile on her lined but lovely face.

"Why do you ask, Alycea? Do you love Ed?" She asked her with a hint of a smile on her face.

"Oh, I like him a lot, but I don't know if I love him. I think he likes me a lot too. He kissed me the other day, Mae, and I kissed him back. I liked it. His lips were soft and gentle. He had a funny look on his face after he kissed me and left the room. He didn't come back for a long time. I don't know what I did or why he had to leave. Did I do something wrong, Mae?" she asked innocently.

"Oh no, I don't think you did anything wrong, mia filha. I think Ed just had to think about his feelings for you. He may be getting serious and didn't know what to say to you. I think you will know soon, though, what his intentions are," she said matter of factly.

Just as their conversation was finished, Stan and Ed walked in laughing, both in a jovial mood. They had become close over the past six months and were like father and son. They loved Filomena and Alycea. Ed loved Alycea while Stan loved Filomena romantically.

They had many discussions over the past six months about their feelings for the two women. Stan had already proposed to Filomena and they were planning their wedding which would take place at the local church in a few weeks.

Ed had talked to Stan about his intention to marry Alycea and planned on asking Filomena for her blessing before proposing to Alycea. Alycea was, after all, not yet fifteen and needed permission from a parent before they could get a license. He never loved anyone as he loved Alycea. He would promise to love and protect her with his whole being and make her happy.

Filomena went into Stan's waiting arms as he came into the room. They were so much in love. Alycea could see it and feel it in the air. She didn't know if she felt as strongly for Ed. Maybe she would one day. She was in no hurry. She was not yet fifteen years old. Her birthday was six months away.

Stan took Filomena over to the couch to sit next to Ed as he guided Alycea into the kitchen to help her continue with preparations of their supper. He wanted to ensure that Ed had some privacy so he could ask Filomena for her blessing of his proposal to Alycea. He planned to ask Alycea that evening after supper when he would take her for a walk so that they could be alone.

Alycea was surprised by Stan's offer of help with the supper because he knew nothing about cooking and always said so. She also wondered why her mother and Ed were whispering on the couch together. They were up to something and most likely it had something to do with her.

After their meal Stan and Filomena went over to the couch to discuss their plans for their wedding and reception which would be simple. They planned to have just Alycea and Ed and a few friends, the grocer, baker, iceman and their wives back to the apartment where they would serve coffee and cake before they went to New York City for the weekend.

Once they were married they planned to move to New Bondford or River Falls in Massachusetts. Stan had lived there when he was a young child and wanted to go back to his roots. Stan had already procured a position in the local clothing factory there. He also thought that Filomena would like the area since it now had a large population of Portuguese immigrants.

After dinner, Ed helped Alycea with the dishes and then suggested, "Alycea, let's go for a walk since it is such a warm evening. It would also give your mother and Stan some privacy so they could make their wedding plans," he added.

"But Ed, I was going to help Mae with her plans," she almost whined in protest at his suggestion.

"Alycea, I would like to have some time alone with you tonight. Is that okay with you? I would like to talk to you about something important," he propelled her towards the door as he spoke.

He waved to Filomena and Stan as he pulled Alycea out the door. She had on a big pout that only Alycea could produce. Stan and Filomena both laughed out loud when they saw Alycea's face as she turned to look at them, pleading for help.

Once they were away from the apartment and down the street Ed took Alycea's left hand in his right and stopped to face her. He put his hand into his left pocket and pulled out a small black box.

She looked at him with a puzzled expression. She had no idea what he was doing or what was in the box. It was a lovely little box and she was curious about what was in it.

He looked into her amber eyes and said, "Alycea, I love you and want you to be my wife. Will you marry me?" He looked at her with pleading eyes.

Alycea felt the wind go out of her lungs and could not speak. She was shocked. Did she hear him correctly? Did he just ask her to marry him? How could he? She was too young, wasn't she? What could she say to him?

These and a million other questions were going around in her head. She didn't know what to do. Did she love him? Was she ready to get married, not only that; was she old enough to get married?

She came back to the present and saw him looking at her, anxiously waiting for her answer.

"Well Alycea, what do you say? Did you hear me? I want you to marry me." His face was white and he was looking fearful at this point since she had not said a word or even blinked for a long time.

"Alycea, are you all right?" He asked her as he squeezed her hand and shook her arm to try to get a response.

"Ed, I don't know what to say. I like you a lot, maybe even love you. But I am too young to get married. I need more time to grow up. Do you understand?" She pleaded with him in her little girl voice.

He dropped her hand and averted her eyes putting the little black box back into his pocket. He looked like a man who had received a terrible shock. He was quite stricken and disappointed with her answer or lack of one, that is.

"We might as well go back to the apartment now, Alycea. I will escort you back and take a long walk by myself. I need to think this all over. I guess it was a bad idea for me to ask you this. Maybe you are right; you are too young," he said resignedly.

"Ed, I didn't want to hurt you. I'm sorry. But I do care for you more than I can say. I have never cared for anyone like I care for you. Give me some time and then ask me again in a few years," she said trying to make him feel better.

"I don't know, Alycea. I just need to give this some thought. I will see you later. Go into the apartment now. We have arrived. I will talk to you later." He turned and walked away leaving her gawking at his back.

Alycea opened the door to the apartment and her mother and Stan rushed over to greet her hugging and kissing her and expressing their congratulations. They looked around behind her for Ed and then saw her face.

"What's wrong, Alycea? Where's Ed? Didn't he ask you to marry him? Didn't you tell him, yes?" her mother asked her all these questions without taking a breath. She approved of Ed as her future son-in-law but not unless her daughter loved him and would be happy to be his wife. She saw how they had looked at one another. They were in love. What could have happened?

"Mae, I told him I was too young and not ready and that he should ask me in a few years," she said sadly, avoiding looking at her mother who was clearly upset.

"Alycea, he loves you so much. He must have been heartbroken. You are young, mia filha, but I was your age when I married your father. We had a good marriage and I grew up with him. Ed will take care of you and will be good to you. Don't be afraid, Alycea," she put her arm around Alycea's shoulder as she said this guiding her to the couch.

Stan got up and walked over to sit down on the soft chair opposite so mother and daughter could sit together. He wished he could help in some way or had something wise to say to Alycea to make her realize that she was a woman now and not a child anymore.

He watched with love as Filomena explained things to Alycea about marriage and love. She was such a wonderful woman. He was happy to have found her and that she had agreed to be his wife. Their life together was just beginning. He wished the same happiness for Alycea and Ed.

# CHAPTER 23

"What a lovely story about Granny Filomena. I didn't know that she had found a second love. That's so romantic, Avoa. She must have been lonely being without a husband for a long time and then coming to a new country to bring up her family on her own. She was quite a woman. You definitely took after her for your stubbornness and strength. I guess she had to be tough to bring up you and Uncle Manny on her own." Jasmine smiled lovingly at her grandmother.

"Thank you dear, for being so sweet. You are your own mother's daughter. You are a lot like your mother, Belinha. She was always saying sweet things about people and never thought ill of them. Well, she didn't at first but then that all changed." She looked a million miles away as her mind wandered over the years.

"Avoa, what do you mean?" Jasmine looked puzzled and disturbed at the insinuation that something was wrong with her mother.

"Oh nothing really, Jasmine. Please let me continue and then you will eventually understand what I mean. Don't look so upset. It is not anything serious for you to worry yourself about." She patted her granddaughter's hand to reassure her.

# CHAPTER 24

Alycea knew it was inevitable that she would have to talk to Ed and give him an answer about his proposal. She felt so uncertain about it. She did love him in her own way, but was she ready for what she would have to do to be a wife? Her mother never really explained what to expect. She just said that she would have to be subservient to her husband. Now, what was that supposed to mean?

Alycea opened the door to her room or what was now their bedroom. Ed was sitting in the chair beside the window in the dark. He looked like he was sleeping; his head was lowered and he was leaning on his right fist.

She tiptoed into the room trying not to disturb him and get ready for bed. As she opened one of the drawers in her bureau, she heard Ed clear his throat and say, "Alycea, we need to talk. Are you ready to tell me what you want to do?" His voice was scratchy and sounded tired.

She jumped back with the sound of his voice and closed the drawer after taking out her nightgown. She turned without looking back at him and went out of the room and down the hall to the bathroom to wash up and change for bed.

Ed did not move from the chair but waited for her to return. He knew that she did not have anywhere else to go. He had planned to leave tonight if she refused him again.

Upon returning from the bathroom Alycea stood outside the bedroom door with her hand on the knob not wanting to go back inside to face Ed. She had to think about everything but couldn't think straight if he was there. What was she going to do? Would she say 'yes' to him? If she didn't, would he leave forever? How could she live without seeing him again? She knew she was strong even if she was young. This was a big decision and she must make the right choice. It would be something that would haunt her forever if she made the wrong one. Alycea opened the bedroom door and went inside.

***

Alycea and Ed had begun sleeping in the same bed that night but not doing anything else. Ed knew that he had to take it slowly with Alycea. She was young and unsure of what she wanted. She did not know anything about being with a man or making love.

He started off by cuddling with her each night, spooning and then rubbing her back until she relaxed. She seemed to like this. Feeling satisfied he was doing the right thing, he took it to the next level and started rubbing himself against her but he couldn't help himself and leaked all over her nightgown, much to her dismay. She had been confused and had asked him why she was all wet. Did he urinate on her? He had chuckled and gotten up to clean himself and had brought her a fresh nightgown.

They made love finally several nights later. It was her first time and she did not know what to do. Alycea was frightened about being with a man. She did not know what to expect being immature and inexperienced.

Ed, on the other hand, was an experienced older man and he guided her hands and mouth and taught her gently what to touch and taste. The first time he entered her she let out a soft cry and whimper, then she relaxed. He brought her to her first orgasm, then her second and a third when he reached a climax. By the fourth time they made love she was doing it all on instinct. It was their first of many nights of passion.

She will grow to be a passionate and able partner that would keep me happy hopefully for many, many years, Ed thought to himself as he smiled holding her in his arms. He felt sated, happy and content with his new life and partner.

He didn't think about the fact there would be some pain that would come because of this pleasure.

# CHAPTER 25

"You look beautiful, Mae. That dress is so pretty on you. Ivory is the color for you. It shows off your complexion and hair. I like the way you put up your hair too. Stan will be happy when he sees you. He will say you are beautiful too. He loves you so much. I can see it in his eyes." Alycea stepped back to admire her mother. Filomena was still lovely. Alycea noticed, even as her mother was getting older, her beauty had not diminished. I hope I look as good when I am her age, Alycea thought.

"Thank you, mia filha. I am happy. I love Stan with my whole being. Of course it is different than the love I had for your father. I think each time you love, it is different. It shouldn't be the same, for each person is different. I just hope your brother will be here in time." She gazed out the window searching for any sign of him coming.

"Mae, I wrote and told Antonio of your wedding day. He said he was happy for you and sends his love."

"Oh, how sweet of him. I miss him so much. I am saving more money and hope that he will come soon. I sent him some already but he did not write back to me about it."

"I'm sure he will soon, Mae. I also wrote to Manny and he said he is coming home to attend your wedding. He promised me he would be here. Don't worry about him, Mae. He will keep his promise to you. I know he will. He loves you and wouldn't want you to be unhappy." Alycea took her mother's hand and kissed it and rubbed it against her own cheek to reassure her.

"Manny sounded good in his last letter. He said that he met a woman in his travels and he may be bringing her back here to meet the family. It would be nice to see Manuel have a family again. I know he can't bring back Gracinda and Cristina but at least he wouldn't be so sad all the time." She looked up at her mother for her reaction to this.

"I agree with you, Alycea. I only want to see Manuel happy again. He deserves to be happy and to have a wife and children. He lost too much. I have been praying to St. Theresa for just that. She must have heard me," Filomena made the sign of the cross as she said this.

"Well, Alycea, are you ready to go to church? You are my maid of honor, bridesmaid and witness all in one. Do you think you can handle all that responsibility?" She hugged Alycea as she kissed her cheek. Filomena pulled a stray hair away from Alycea's face and tucked it behind her ear along with a pink rose which matched Alycea's pink taffeta dress.

Filomena reached for her bouquet of ivory lilies and roses and they headed out the door arm in arm to go to church. There was a car waiting outside to take them. Mr. Bohondoney was kind enough to send his delivery man to escort them to church. He had been their close friend since Manuel worked for him. He was always doing them little favors by sending over fresh fruits and vegetables or other sundry items that he thought they might need. He knew that life had not been easy for Filomena since she had lost her daughter-in-law and granddaughter and then her son had gone away.

Ralph Bohondoney and his wife, Felicia, had become good friends with Filomena and Stan. They had been to each others' homes for dinner many times over the years. Ralph and Felicia always loved going to Filomena's because she was an exceptional cook, making all kinds of Portuguese fish dishes and her fabulous pot roast with Portuguese Port wine.

Ralph was pleased to see Filomena happy now that she was going to marry Stan. Stan was a good man and perfect for her. He wished them well and his wedding gift to them was a reception at the church hall catered by himself with the help of his friends, the butcher, the baker and the pastor.

The butcher, Mark Santos, would provide all the meats cooked along with Ralph's salads and potatoes and the baker, Salvatore Spinatelli, would provide the breads and wedding cake. The priest, Father Silverio, was in charge of decorating the hall and church with ivory ribbons. The local winery would provide the wine. In fact, they had found a special Port wine from Madeira to surprise Filomena.

This was all going to be a surprise to the couple. Alycea and Ed knew all about this and would be responsible to get the newly married couple over to the hall next to the church so that the festivities could begin. The couple was planning a short honeymoon to New York City for a night at a hotel.

Alycea had packed her mother's things for her including an extra day of clothes. She and Ed had paid for their two-night honeymoon stay at the hotel unbeknownst to her mother and Stan. It was to be their wedding gift to them. Alycea had been carefully saving up as much as she could from her weekly pay check and Ed had made up the difference.

Filomena and Alycea arrived at the church. The driver got out of the car and opened the door for them. They walked quickly up the stairs and into the cool, dark interior of the church waiting for their eyes to adjust to the darkness. A few friends were seated in the front pews along with a tanned, handsome man who Alycea soon realized was Manuel.

Father Silverio spied them coming in and waved his hand toward the organist and the music began. Alycea reached over, whispered that Manuel was there, and then squeezed her mother's hand. She stepped forward to walk down the aisle ahead of her mother on the arm of Ed who was waiting at the back of the church.

Manuel rushed to the back of the church, took his mother's arm, much to her surprise, and escorted her down the aisle to her future husband. Manuel whispered to his mother, "Did you think I would let you walk down the aisle alone. I would be honored if you let me give you away, Mae."

Filomena's eyes filled with tears of joy and all she could do was nod to her son in assent. She couldn't believe how fortunate she was to have such a wonderful and thoughtful son.

Walking arm and arm with her handsome son, Filomena looked around her in the church. She felt truly blessed to have not only her children and a wonderful man like Stan but also many good friends in her life she loved and who also loved her.

At the altar, next to the pastor, stood Stan looking handsome and smiling nervously. His eyes looked pleased and filled with love at the sight of Filomena in her ivory embroidered dress, her hair in a bun with ivory roses in a ring resting on top of her head and a bouquet of ivory lilies and roses. Filomena's eyes were sparkling and she wore a lovely smile just for him.

Manuel kissed his mother's cheek and shook Stan's hand. After placing his mother's hand into Stan's, Manuel walked back to his seat in the front pew to sit next to a tall, elegantly attractive woman.

The ceremony went smoothly, and afterward everyone came over to greet the newlywed couple and wished them well. Manuel stood in line patiently waiting to give his mother a hug and kiss. As Filomena saw him she put out her arms. He came rushing forward to pick her up and swing her around giving her a tight squeeze and a kiss on both cheeks before putting her down again.

Filomena said, "Manuel, thank you for giving me away on my wedding day. It was such a pleasant surprise. It meant so much to me. It made this day extra special to have you be a part of it." Filomena's voice choked up when she continued, "The only thing that would make this day even more perfect is if Antonio was here too."

"I know, Mae. I wish he was here too. I had to be here for you. I wouldn't have had it any other way, Mae. I love you and I am happy for both of you."

Standing behind Manuel and waiting patiently, was a tall, attractive woman with light brown hair. She came forward and offered her hand to Filomena and Stan saying, "Congratulations on your marriage. It is such a pleasure to finally meet you both. Manny talks about you all the time and asked me to come along to meet you. I hope you don't mind that I am here," she said with sincerity and kindness in her eyes.

Filomena appraised this new woman in her son's life. She was nothing at all like Gracinda but she was attractive and had kind eyes. She only hoped that this woman could make her Manuel happy and fill the emptiness from his loss that she knew he still held deep inside his heart.

Filomena reached forward and took the woman's hand and turning to Manuel said, "Mio filho, aren't you going to introduce us to your new friend?"

"Oh, I am sorry, Mae. I was excited to see you again I forgot to tell you who this is. Mae and Stan, this is Ernestina Sousa. We met in Lisbon, one of the ports that I stop at every couple of months. I stayed in Lisbon for a couple of months recently and we got to know one another. I invited her to come to your wedding so she could meet you. Ernestina and I are going to be married when we get back to Lisbon." He smiled and took Ernestina's hand in his as he said this.

"That is wonderful for you. I wish we could be there at your wedding but I don't think it is possible. We are going to New York overnight for a short honeymoon. Then we are back to work the next day. I hope you will be happy. Please keep in touch and come to visit us again. Stan and I are going to be moving in a couple of weeks to New Bondford and the River Falls area as soon as we can find an apartment there. I will send you our new address after we are settled. In the meantime, you can write us here. Alycea will be moving with us along with Ed."

Alycea had gone next door to the hall to check on things and had just returned to see Manuel talking to her mother and Stan. She also noticed a tall woman standing next to Manuel holding onto his hand. She wondered who she was and if this was Manuel's new girlfriend.

She ran down the aisle of the church and called his name out. Manuel turned just in time to catch his sister in his arms. She was crying and hugging him and berating him all at the same time.

"Manuel, you haven't written to me in over a month. I sent you more than a dozen letters during that time. I told Mae you were coming but I didn't know if you were. You never answered me when I told you about the wedding." She wiped her eyes and gave him one more hug before looking over his shoulder at the woman standing behind him.

"Alycea, this is Ernestina Sousa, my fiancée. We are going to be married when we get back to her home in Lisbon." He pulled Ernestina forward as he introduced her to his sister.

Alycea looked her over and then leaned in to hug Ernestina. Open affection was not something that Ernestina was used to receiving.

She was reserved and leaned into Alycea to take the hug but did not return it with any fervor. She smiled at Alycea and shook her hand before moving away.

Alycea wasn't sure what to make of that but she smiled back at Ernestina and said, "I will write to you as soon as you send me your address in Lisbon."

Ernestina nodded and smiled.

Alycea was happy for her brother that he had found someone to share his life. Ernestina just wasn't someone she would have picked for her brother. She was completely different from Gracinda. She only hoped that Ernestina could make her brother happy and maybe give him the children that he dearly wanted.

Alycea leaned closely to her brother and whispered in his ear that they were all going over to the hall next door for a reception that was a surprise for their mother and Stan. She needed his help to bring them over there.

She walked out leading the way for the newlyweds and the guests to follow her. Stan and Filomena walked behind Alycea and out to go to the car that was still waiting there for them compliments of Ralph Bohondoney. But instead, Alycea grabbed her mother and Stan and guided them toward the hall. The couple just looked confused at each other and let themselves be led away.

As they opened the door to the hall everyone yelled out, "Surprise! This is your wedding reception!" As they opened their mouths in shock, they were guided in. Everyone took turns slapping Stan on the back and hugging Filomena as they led them to the head table all decorated by the pastor, Father Silverio, with an ivory tablecloth and ribbons.

There was one table laden with all kinds of meats and salads and another table with the wedding cake decorated with ivory roses by Salvatore Spinatelli, the baker.

Filomena and Stan had a wonderful time at their reception and were thankful to all who came and organized this special day for them. Glasses of Port were lifted as a toast to the bride and groom. After the wonderful buffet and opening presents, the happy couple was ready to leave for New York to begin their honeymoon. Filomena stepped forward and threw her bouquet and turned around to see who caught it. To her surprise Alycea held the bouquet in her hands. Her face was flushed with pure joy.

Filomena hugged and kissed both of her children and waved to all the guests throwing kisses to them all. Alycea hugged Stan and whispered to him that she and Ed had booked an extra night for them at the hotel. He hugged her in thanks and smiled at his new step-daughter who he had come to love like a daughter and said, "Alycea you are a treasure. Your mother will be quite surprised and happy. You have made this day extra special for us. Thank you and Ed for all that you and our friends have done to make our wedding so wonderful. We will never forget this perfect day."

Alycea said through tears, "Stan, I love you. You are now my pai, my father, and I am so happy that Mae has you in her life. Have a wonderful honeymoon. We will see you when you get back."

She gave her mother another tight hug and told her, "I will miss you, Mae, but will see you soon. Have a nice honeymoon and enjoy the sights of New York."

"Thank you, Alycea, for all that you and Ed have done. You made this day extra special. We will never forget your generosity." She hugged and kissed her daughter again and smiled at Ed who was standing nearby. Ed came over and gave Filomena a kiss on her cheek and wished her and Stan well. He leaned in a little longer and whispered, "Don't worry about Alycea. I will take care of her."

Filomena nodded and responded, "Thank you, Ed. I know you will."

The newlyweds called out their thanks and appreciation again to their friends and the pastor for all the blessings that they had received. After waving one more time at her daughter holding the bouquet, they went out to the car that would take them to New York City to begin their life together.

Alycea stood there with the bouquet still in her hand. Did this mean that she would be the next bride?

# CHAPTER 26

Filomena lay in Stan's arms and nestled closer to his chest breathing in his scent. She hadn't felt as content for many years. It had been many years since her husband had died. She had forgotten what it was like to be with a man. It was pleasant she thought to herself with a smile spreading across her face and a warm tingling feeling coming back into her loins.

She turned in Stan's arms, looked into his eyes and kissed his lips softly while her hands ran up and down his chest and his leg until she found the core of his heat. Their kissing got more intense and soon she was drifting along a strong current of desire and intensity as she reached her peak.

They had not left the room the first day and now it was noon and they had been drifting in and out of sleep between their lovemaking. It was time to get up and have something to eat and maybe go see some sights. The fresh air would do them both good.

She pushed back the covers and swung her feet off the bed. She sat up putting her feet into her slippers before getting up. Stan watched her walk away into the bathroom and felt desire return. He was completely blissful and thanked God for Filomena. She had saved him. He would surely have died of loneliness without her. She was full of love and life.

He found himself whistling as he got up from bed. He went to his suitcase and pulled out his razor and shaving soap and got busy cleaning his day old beard. There was a sink in the room which he used while he was waiting to use the bathroom.

The newlyweds dressed, ordered room service and ate. Soon after they headed out for some sightseeing. They strolled Central Park and stopped for a hot toddy in between the sights. They were in awe over all the tall buildings. Lunch was enjoyed in a little café that was known to have claims of famous people eating there. Other diners looked around to see if there were any there today. Filomena and Stan looked at each other and giggled when they realized they were doing that also.

It was a wonderful day spent as Mr. and Mrs. Stanley Stockman.

A few months later they enjoyed a second honeymoon in New York that was even better than the first. When they arrived home, this time, things were brewing.

***

"Should we tell them today when they return, Alycea?" Ed turned to look at her face for some positive reaction. He was hoping Alycea would finally say 'yes' to his proposal.

"I don't know, I suppose we will have to tell them soon. Mae will know what is wrong as soon as she looks at me. I'm not feeling well right now, Ed. I need to go lie down for a little while. Call me when they arrive." Her face was pale and sickly as she turned toward their bedroom to lie down.

Ed was worried about Alycea. She had not been feeling well for the past two days. She had not given him an answer yet to his proposal. How long would she make him wait? What would she say? She said, we should tell them? What did she mean that her mother would know when she saw her? What did she want to tell them? Did she mean that her answer was 'yes?' Was she seriously sick?

He shook his head and could not believe what was happening to him. He was a mess since he had fallen for Alycea. She controlled him like a puppet. He couldn't think for himself anymore. She made all the decisions. He was supposed to be the older one and more mature. He had to act like a man and take charge of her and make her marry him.

He put his head into his hands and laid his head on the table when he suddenly heard the door opening and laughter and happy voices coming into the room. He looked up and Stan and Filomena were standing there looking at him with concern.

"Are you all right, Ed? What happened? Where is Alycea? Is she okay?" Filomena asked without hesitation.

"No um, I…we're all right, Filomena. I was just thinking about Alycea and wondering when she would give me an answer to my proposal. I love her. I know she loves me too. What can I do to convince her I can make her happy?" he asked with desperation in his voice.

"Where is Alycea, Ed?"

"Alycea is resting. She hasn't been feeling well since you left a few days ago. She may have the flu or something. I'm sorry, I almost forgot, did you have a nice second honeymoon?"

"Yes Ed, we had a lovely time. Now Stan, talk to Ed while I go see how Alycea is doing? Ok, my love?" She kissed him lightly on the lips before moving away. He felt a tingle as their lips met and wanted to kiss her back more fervently but not with Ed looking on. They had been married now for three months and had enjoyed their three-day second honeymoon at the same hotel in New York. They were more in love than ever.

Filomena knocked on the Alycea's bedroom door before opening it, then walked in to check on her. Alycea was lying across the bed with her head over a metal pot. She had filled the bottom of it already with her breakfast.

Filomena put her hand on Alycea's forehead to determine if she had a fever but her head was cool. Alycea looked up from the edge of the bed at her mother. Filomena could see her Alycea's face was pale and strained.

She sat on the bed next to Alycea and rubbed her daughter's back to calm her down as she began to question her about her sickness.

"Alycea, how are you feeling, mia filha? Do you have a stomach ache or just feeling nauseated? What did you eat today?"

Alycea rolled over to look at her mother as she answered, "I haven't been able to keep anything down today. I started to feel uncomfortable a couple of days ago but it's worse today. My stomach feels upset and even the slightest thing I try to eat makes me throw up. Could I have some water please, Mae? My mouth tastes terrible and I feel so dry."

"Yes, of course, my dear, I will get some for you right away." She left the room and returned quickly with a large glass of water. She put it to Alycea's lips for her to take a sip.

After a few sips Alycea announced that she felt a lot better and could sit up. Her face was still pale and her lips stood out like blue-red roses against her white skin.

"Alycea, when did you last have your monthly time? I know you are a woman now and that could be what is wrong," she announced matter of factly.

"Oh, I haven't had it for quite a while, probably three months ago. What is wrong with me, Mae?" She looked at her mother with the frightened eyes of a child who is now a woman.

"I think my, dear Alycea, you are with child, probably a few months along. You have been sleeping with Ed, is that correct?" she asked, watching her daughter's reaction closely.

"Well, we...um...we sleep in the same bed now. I felt badly for him sleeping on the floor. I told him one night he could sleep next to me with his clothes on.

I woke up one night in the middle of the night with his hands touching me all over my body and he was rubbing his penis against my back. It had some sticky stuff coming out and going down my legs. I asked him what it was and he just laughed at me.

Another night he made me kiss him and rub his thing and kiss it. He rubbed me down there too. It felt nice, Mae. I let him do it every night after that. Then he pushed it into me and it hurt a lot but then it felt good. Did I do something wrong, Mae? Is it okay to kiss him and let him put his thing into me?"

"Oh, my sweetheart, it is okay as long as you love Ed and he loves you. You are now a woman and you are going to have a baby. You have made love to a man. That is what happens when you do this. We must tell Ed if he doesn't already know. You will have to marry immediately so that this baby will have a name. Come, get up, my child. We need to tell the men the good news. I am going to be a grandmother." She helped Alycea out of the bed and walked with a little skip in her step out to the kitchen to celebrate with her husband and soon to be son-in-law.

"What! She's pregnant? That can't be!" Ed announced excitedly after hearing the startling news. "She is too young. I did not expect her to get pregnant this soon." He looked at Filomena guiltily.

"Ed, I know that you have been sleeping together. Don't you think I can hear what is going on in my own house? I know you were careful and did not hurt Alycea in any way and you did not expect her to get pregnant this quickly. But you know, God must have wanted her to have a child to replace the one we lost. We must write to Manuel and Antonio to tell them the news of your marriage and pregnancy."

Filomena felt so happy that she could burst just thinking of a baby in the house again. She had missed Cristina so much it hurt. She would hold her grandchild in her arms in six months. She just couldn't contain her exuberance. She wanted to announce her news to the rooftops. That night she wrote a long letter to Manuel telling him of the good news and asking him to come visit his new niece or nephew when it was born. She told him she would write again after Alycea gave birth. She also wrote to Antonio hoping that he would come too.

"Mae, I don't want to get married and I don't want to have a baby yet," Alycea announced petulantly like a child.

"Oh yes, you will do both. I will make sure of it, Alycea," she said sternly to the surprise and dismay of all in the room.

"Filomena, don't be too hard on Alycea," Stan said kindly as he looked at the sad face of his stepdaughter. "She is, after all, just a child. There is still six months left. Give her some time to think this over before rushing her into a marriage. This is a lot to take in all at once. She is a child having a child."

Filomena responded, "Stan, Alycea is growing up and is now a young lady. She will accept responsibility for her pregnancy and agree to marry Ed. It is the best thing for both of them and for the baby."

Stan couldn't believe it. Alycea was going to have a baby. He would be a step grandfather, I guess, he thought to himself. He could understand how much this must mean to Filomena to have another grandchild to replace the one she had lost. He looked tenderly at his wife with more understanding now.

"Yes, of course, Filomena. You are right. They must marry for the sake of the baby."

Ed stood up and reached into his pocket where he had kept the ring for the past few months and kneeling down at the Alycea's feet, proposed marriage to her once again. He did love her and hoped, now that she was pregnant with his child, she would have to say 'yes.'

Alycea just looked at him with disbelief. She couldn't believe he still wanted to marry her. She did love him in her own childish way and did like the things that he did to her every night. If he left she wouldn't be able to do that anymore and would really miss how he made her feel. It felt really good.

She thought about it for a minute or two and then said, "Yes Ed, I will marry you." Then she whispered in his ear that she wanted to do the thing again and would marry him only if he promised to do it every night. He smiled at her and agreed that was the deal that he would do it to her every night in all different ways to make her feel good. She smiled back at him and kissed him quickly on the lips.

Ed was so ecstatic that he picked her up and hugged her closely kissing her passionately with Filomena and Stan watching. He finally stopped when Alycea started breathing heavily. He knew how she was when she started breathing heavily and he didn't want anything to happen in front of her mother and stepfather.

After he thought about it, Ed was happy that he was going to be a father too. He decided to get their marriage license right away and make plans with the priest to marry them as soon as possible. He put Alycea carefully back on the couch and announced that he had a lot of things to take care of if they were going to get married.

Filomena told him that she would be more than happy to help them with their wedding plans. Stan stepped in to offer his assistance too.

Alycea said that she could do her share since she had planned and helped coordinate her mother and stepfather's reception along with the priest and their friends.

It seemed that everyone had a job to do and soon there would be two newlywed couples living under the same roof.

Alycea's life as a child ended on this day. Within six months she would have many more responsibilities to carry on her small shoulders that would force her to grow up much too quickly.

# CHAPTER 27

"Mae, I need you! It hurts so much; please help me! When will the baby come?" Alycea gasped out each word between the pains which were coming quicker now.

Filomena was by her daughter's side and tried to calm her and applied cool cloths to her forehead between contractions. The baby would be here soon. She could see the head now. If only she could make Alycea push a little harder to help the baby out.

"Alycea, the baby is almost here. You must listen to me and do what I tell you. When you feel the pain coming take a deep breath and start to push as hard as you can. This will help the baby come easier. Your baby is doing all the work, Alycea. You must help him or her come into this world." She took Alycea's hand in hers and squeezed it as the pain started again. Then Filomena moved to get into position to guide the baby as it came out of the birth canal. She had towels and warm water to clean the baby. The doctor was on his way but the baby was born before he arrived. Filomena would have to take care of everything on her own as she did with her own births.

Ed was pacing back and forth in the kitchen as Stan tried to distract him with conversation about the weather, sports and the economy and impending recession and possible depression. Ed couldn't think of anything but Alycea and he jumped each time he heard her scream out, "Ed, I hate you! What did you do to me?"

They had moved to New Bondford a few months after Ed and Alycea's wedding and had settled into a nice tenement with three bedrooms. There would now be plenty of room for them and the new baby.

Suddenly it got eerily quiet except for a tiny cry. Ed ran to their bedroom door and gently knocked. He heard Filomena talking to Alycea and then another tiny cry. He opened the door and walked in to meet his new son or daughter.

Filomena wrapped the baby in a towel, cut the cord, and placed her into her mother's arms. She cleaned Alycea and assured that the afterbirth was completely out. It was a messy scene and Ed felt a little queasy at all the blood but also was curious as to what sex the baby was. He moved closer until Alycea saw him.

She held out the baby to him so he could see his little daughter. "I named her Caterina after my grandmother, Mae's mother. Is that okay with you, Edouardo?" She had taken to calling him his birth name especially when she was pleased with him or happy about something. He would always relax when he heard it and dreaded when she called him Ed for he knew he must be in trouble.

He held out his arms to accept his new little daughter, Caterina. He liked the name and it seemed to fit her. She was lovely, pretty and pink and larger than he expected for a newborn. That was probably why Alycea had such a hard time delivering her.

The doctor poked his head in as Filomena was finishing up washing her new granddaughter. The doctor went over to look at the baby examining her eyes, nose, mouth and chest. All seemed normal and he was satisfied. He told Filomena she had done a great job and apologized for not arriving sooner to help. He also examined Alycea and gave her an anesthetic so he could stitch her up where she had torn and stop the bleeding to help her heal.

Dr. Bradley expressed his congratulations and said, "If you need me, please call, but the baby looks healthy. I do not expect any problems to arise. Good job, Filomena. You may put me out of business if you keep this up," he chuckled to himself as he left the room.

Filomena watched her daughter and son-in-law getting to know their daughter and left the room. She went out to the kitchen and sat down with Stan on the couch. She hadn't realized how tired she was until then.

"Stan, we have a granddaughter. Her name is Caterina and she is beautiful!" She exclaimed with pure joy on her face evident, even though she was showing severe signs of exhaustion.

Stan looked at her with concern. "That's wonderful! Filomena, dear, you look fatigued. Are you okay? Lie down here, my love, and rest. I will get you a cup of tea and some Portuguese biscoitos. You haven't eaten anything all day." Stan put a kettle of water on the stove and went into the cupboard to find the biscoitos. When the water was ready, he strained the tea into the cup and brought it and biscoitos over to the coffee table in front of Filomena. She was fast asleep. He smoothed her hair back from her face and pulled an afghan off the back of the couch and placed it gently over her.

He sat across from her on the side chair to keep watch over his precious wife. He would be there if she needed him when she woke up. He sipped the tea and nibbled on the biscoitos suddenly feeling hungry himself. He hadn't eaten anything all day either. They had been engrossed in taking care of Alycea and the birth of her baby girl.

He could hear the soft cries of Caterina and then the shushing sounds of Alycea and Ed speaking and singing Portuguese to their daughter.

# CHAPTER 28

"I can't believe how much she has grown in the past two years, our little Caterina. She is certainly becoming a real beauty with her dark curls and big brown eyes like her mother," Filomena said to Stan as she watched over her granddaughter run around the apartment.

Stan reached over and picked Caterina up to give her a hug and kiss. Caterina reached up and grabbed a handful of Stan's now graying hair and gave it a tug. He promptly put her down after releasing her grip on his hair and laughed his deep resonating laugh.

"She does love you, Stan, but she has this thing about your hair. Maybe you need to get it trimmed, huh?" Filomena said with amusement as she saw the stunned look on Stan's face. He liked to keep his hair fairly full and did not cut it more than once every couple of months. He joked that it was the source of his masculinity and strength.

Alycea waddled into the room after her afternoon nap. She was again with child, due any day now. Filomena had spoken to Dr. Bradley and he was on alert this time. She was not sure if Alycea would have a larger baby than previously and could have a more difficult time if that was possible. She would feel better if the doctor was there in case Alycea started bleeding excessively. Luckily she had curtailed the bleeding somewhat last time and then Dr. Bradley had arrived to stitch her up.

"Alycea, how are you feeling, my dear?" Filomena asked tentatively. She did not want to rile her daughter since she had not been in the best of moods lately.

"Ugh, I feel fat and ugly! This baby must be ready to come. I can't wait! I can barely walk and I can't see my feet anymore." She sighed heavily as she plopped down on the couch and put her feet up on the coffee table.

"Yes, mia filha, any day now the baby will let you know when he or she is ready. Dr. Bradley will be available at a moment's notice, he promised me. I know I can handle the delivery but I will need him to take care of you and the baby afterward in case of any emergency situation that may arise," she responded in a calm voice and manner, careful not to excite Alycea in any way.

"Did Ed come home from work yet or did he call saying he was going to be late again?" Alycea said with some bitterness clearly visible in her tone.

"Um, no, we haven't heard from Ed as yet. I know they had a lot of work to do because there were some workers out with the flu. He was covering for them and doing extra work," Stan reported in a soft, tentative voice.

Ed was staying late at work to avoid dealing with Alycea and her vile moods. He also was playing the mandolin with a group of musicians. They practiced at night and on the weekends they played at local clubs. He didn't make much money but he did enjoy it and also being a musician attracted a lot of attention from the women. He was a sensual man and needed his stimulation. He certainly wasn't getting any from his wife right now.

Before Ed and Alycea were first married they did go out to the clubs, danced and listened to the music until their first child was born. They continued to go once a week leaving Caterina with her grandmother.

Ed had been taught to play the mandolin by his father when he was just a young boy. He had wanted to play it again and this was his chance. It gave him an outlet away from Alycea who was getting more and more demanding of him. He hoped after she had their second child that she would return to the sweet young girl he had fallen in love with before they got married. He missed her and didn't want other women but they flocked to his handsome face and debonair attitude.

Ed looked at the clock on the wall at the mill and noticed it was after quitting time. He decided to call home to check in with Alycea and see if she was doing all right before he went to the club to meet the guys.

Filomena answered on the first ring and whispered to him that Alycea was sleeping on the couch and had been in her usual grumpy mood. He told her he would be at the club and would be home after 8:00. If she needed him sooner she could call him there. He gave her the number before thanking her and hanging up.

Thank goodness for Filomena, he thought. She was definitely a saint taking care of Alycea and Caterina for him. She had stopped working at the mill at the request of Stan. He was making enough money as a supervisor and wanted her to stay at home so she could be a housewife and take care of Alycea and her granddaughter.

He thought back to the time when Stan and Filomena had planned to move to New Bondford. Alycea did not want to go at first with them and begged her mother not to leave. Filomena wouldn't have left her daughter to deal with a baby on her own. She had convinced Alycea and Ed to move with them. Now a second baby was on the way. Ed was certainly glad that they had made the move too. He and Stan both found jobs in the local plant and were doing okay. By combining their wages they were surviving even with the economy faltering.

Stan had noticed that Filomena wasn't feeling well lately and seemed to be exhausted all the time. She was drinking an excessive amount of water and craving sweets. She couldn't get enough to eat at times, but she was still losing weight.

He insisted that she see Dr. Fusco instead of Dr. Bradley, who he did not like or trust for a physical. Stan had this funny feeling about Dr. Bradley that he couldn't shake. He knew that the doctor had taken care of Filomena and her daughter and son since they were young, but something just wasn't right about him.

Stan made the appointment and took Filomena to his office instead of having him come to their home. After the physical, Dr. Fusco told them that Filomena had diabetes and there wasn't much they could do for it. He suggested that they watch her diet and make sure she rested.

Stan, being the consummate husband, did all he could to make sure Filomena did everything she was supposed to do. He watched over her like a mother hen. Now with the added burden of taking care of one grandchild and another one on the way, he feared she would neglect herself and get sick.

Stan had come home early that day to help out. He knew that Alycea could be unreasonably demanding and did not want her to overtax Filomena. He felt better being there to help out if he was needed and also to watch over his precious wife.

Filomena bent over Stan and kissed him lightly on the cheek saying that she was going to lie down for a little while to rest while Alycea and Caterina were both napping. "When either one of them wake up, call me. Ok, darling?" Stan nodded in agreement planning to do no such thing. She looked exhausted and he planned to take care of Alycea and Caterina and let Filomena get some much needed rest. After a half hour of peace and quiet Alycea woke up followed shortly thereafter by Caterina. He went to pick up Caterina from her crib and brought her out to her mother who was sitting in the chair with her feet up on the coffee table.

He went to the kitchen to prepare something for Caterina to eat. Filomena had made enough the previous day so he could easily heat the leftovers.

Alycea put Caterina on her knee since she did not have a lap any more and held her there until Stan could take her over to the table to feed her. Alycea did not feel like doing anything. She was miserable. She wished she had not gotten pregnant again. Having one child was work enough for her. She was thankful for her mother and Stan's help though, otherwise she wouldn't have known what to do. She missed going out with Ed to the club and dancing at night. She had this to look forward to as soon as she was feeling better again though, she thought.

Alycea heard music in the background. The radio was on like it always was from the time Stan got up in the morning and again once he got home from work until he went to bed at night. She listened at times to The Voice of Firestone or The Bell Telephone Hour. They all listened to the Waldorf Astoria Orchestra on Sunday evenings. The house was always filled with music.

She liked it at times, but at other times, it was maddening. She did like to listen to the presidential speeches about the economy. She was somewhat fearful, though of what lay ahead for her family. She looked at the clock and noticed it was past 6:00 pm and Ed still hadn't come home. She scooted herself to the edge of the couch and holding Caterina in one arm, pushed herself up to a standing position with the other and headed toward the kitchen to call Ed at work.

When Stan saw her wobbling into the kitchen he went right over to take Caterina from her arms. Alycea didn't look too stable to be holding the little one. He placed Caterina in her high chair and brought over her dinner and some dinner for Alycea too. He would eat later on with Filomena when she woke up.

"Stan, did Ed call yet?" She asked without looking at him.

"Yes he did, Alycea. Your mother talked to him. He was working late and then going to the club to play with the group. He said he would be back after 8:00 pm."

"Oh sure, he is at the club. That is all he ever does. He comes home late smelling of other women! He doesn't love me any more in this condition. I hate him! I hate myself! I hate being pregnant!" She threw her hands up in the air crying and screaming.

Caterina took one look at her mother and started crying too. All this commotion woke up Filomena who staggered out of the bedroom half asleep. She took one look at the scene and in her inimitable way, took over the situation, and calmed everyone down.

Stan apologized for not being able to control Alycea and the baby. He said, "Filomena, I hope you got some rest. I am terribly sorry about this outburst but Alycea was upset after I told her that Ed had worked late and then had gone to the club. I didn't realize it would upset her like that, otherwise I wouldn't have said anything." He looked overwhelmed by it all and couldn't imagine another baby coming into this turmoil.

"Stan, it's okay. I will handle everything. Why don't you go sit down and read the paper. I will finish up feeding the baby and talk to Alycea. We will have our dinner once all is settled, okay, my dear?" she said with such a calm and determined voice that he did as he was told.

"Now, Alycea what's wrong? You upset poor little Caterina with your antics. You must try to stay calm for her and for the baby you are carrying. It is not good for anyone if you act this way." She looked at Alycea with her stern and serious expression when she meant business.

Alycea knew that she was in trouble when she saw that expression on her mother's face. She pouted and looked ashamed of herself. "Mae, I'm sorry but I am angry with Ed. He stays out quite late and I think he is having other women. I don't think he loves me anymore."

"Of course, he loves you, Alycea. Don't be silly now. Ed loves you and Caterina and the baby deeply. Don't you remember what a lovely wedding and reception you had? Ed was sweet to you, dancing you around the floor tenderly so as not to hurt the baby. He loves you more than life itself," she said as she reminded her daughter of happier times.

"Now, eat up while I feed Caterina. You can go to bed early tonight and rest up. That baby may come in the middle of the night or by tomorrow the latest. You have already dropped quite a bit since this morning and the baby is getting into place. That is why you are not feeling well. It will soon be over, mia filha, and then you will feel much better, I promise you. I prayed to St. Theresa to make this an easier delivery for you. I am sure she will be watching over you."

She put her hand on her daughter's back to support her as Alycea got up from the chair.

Filomena was silently praying for the delivery to be soon to relieve her daughter's suffering.

That time would come two hours later and go into the next morning before the second grandchild was born. Dr. Bradley came in as the child was delivered ably by Filomena again. He had stitched Alycea this time needing more stitches to close the tear and checked over the new baby who was named Belinha. Once Dr. Bradley was sure that both mother and baby were healthy, he left to make his other rounds and then go home to sleep. Just before leaving, however, he had bent over Alycea, kissed her cheek, patted her on the hand wishing her well, and congratulating her on another beautiful daughter. He smiled sadly at her and left the room.

***

"Alycea, are you awake? Belinha is beautiful just like her sister but she has blond hair like I had when I was a child. She also has dimples like mine. I think she looks like me, don't you?" Ed excitedly told Alycea as he touched her face tenderly, his eyes showing all the love she thought she had lost.

"Edouardo, you are here. I missed you. I must have fallen asleep. Belinha is beautiful, isn't she? Did you get to hold her? Is she sleeping now? Where is Mae?" She was feeling more like herself again except for the intermittent pains between her legs where the doctor had stitched her up. She was happy to see Ed again and sat up gingerly for him to hug and kiss her.

"Edouardo, I was angry last night that you weren't here when your daughter was born. You need to be home with us more. We miss you and need you. I…I love you, Edouardo." She looked at him with tears forming in her eyes.

"I love you too, Alycea. I promise I will be home earlier and when I go to the club you can come to hear me play. Ok? I would like you to be there, my darling." With his handkerchief he wiped her tears that were now running down her flushed cheeks.

They held each other closely for several minutes, kissing and touching one another. When Alycea moaned deeply as he caressed her breasts and pinched her nipples, he had to leave because he was getting an erection from all this stimulation. It had been a long time since they had made love and by the sounds of Alycea's pain in that area, it would be a long time before he could even think about going there. He could be creative though. He would have to think this one through a little and make some adjustments and suggestions to Alycea. He was sure she would be eager to resume their lovemaking in any way they could. This pleasant thought brought a smile to his handsome face.

Life returned fully after a few months and Alycea and Ed grew closer and more in love. He was fearful of Alycea getting pregnant again but he need not have feared because she never had any other children after Belinha.

***

Jasmine had to take a deep breath over all that her grandmother had told her – especially about her love life. It was a little shocking to say the least. She never expected her to describe everything in such detail.

"I'm sorry if I shocked you, Jasmine. But you did say you wanted to know everything about my life. Loving Ed was a major part of my life."

"Yes, Avoa. I understand. But…I was still surprised to hear about it."

"Sorry, my dear. That is what I do. I shock people with my boldness. I always have," Alycea laughed out loud and covered her mouth when she began to cough.

"Are you okay, Avoa?"

"Of course, I am. I am just an old woman who laughs too loud, too long, and too deeply. It sometimes hurts me in my chest when I do that. But, look at me. I am 100 years old. I guess I won't die from laughing. Nothing else has killed me thus far." This brought on another laughing spell that infected Jasmine who joined in.

# CHAPTER 29

When the United States had entered WWI the year before Alycea came to America she had been a child. Alycea was frightened about what would happen to her mother, brother and her. They had to hunker down and try to make ends meet as best they could in their new homeland.

In the 1920's times were still hard nearing the end of WWI. They had started out in a recession which soon grew to be known for all time as The Great Depression. Everywhere you looked people were waiting in long lines to find jobs or food. Both at this time were scarce.

Alycea was one of hundreds standing in line this early foggy and damp morning. She had been in line for over two hours already. She had been listening to the radio last night when President Hoover mentioned the food subsidies that would be available at this warehouse. She was hoping to obtain some cheese and bread to bring back to her family.

Alycea had lost her job at the plant as a material handler. Clothes were not being made now. People still needed clothes to wear but most couldn't afford new outfits and only mended their clothes with patches to keep them from falling apart.

She and her mother did their best to keep the house and family together. They did help the war effort also by giving all they could of needed metals and donating their time where needed.

Most men had gone to war and many did not return. Stan did all he could to prevent his plant from closing. He and Ed did their share for the war effort by collecting and donating hundreds of garments when needed. They were not called up because Ed's hearing did not pass the physical due to having pneumonia at a young age and losing part of his hearing in his left ear. Stan had back problems after a fall down a flight of stairs when he was young.

At the plant they let all the women go first and were only keeping a few men, who did not go to war, to keep the place barely running. They didn't have the heart to let these men go because they were the only supporters of their families who were struggling too.

Stan had been taking in clothes to be mended in the plant charging menial amounts to help people out. He also used some of the scrap material he had to do this mending. He and Ed were single handedly keeping busy doing this. It brought in a minimal amount, but enough to pay their rent.

Mae was also embroidering and patching their clothes to keep them together. She had taught Belinha and Caterina how to embroider and do needlepoint as soon as they were old enough to hand a needle. She told them that these talents would be useful in their lives one day. Filomena's family in Madeira owned a needlepoint factory. She had learned how to needlepoint at a young age and had even worked in their factory for a short time.

Belinha didn't mind having her clothes patched but Caterina was outraged at the idea she couldn't have new clothes even though she was still a young child. Alycea sometimes didn't know what to do with her older daughter. She was always so challenging. Mae told Alycea one day that Caterina was a lot like her when she was that age. After all, Alycea was still somewhat like a child in a woman's body.

Alycea shrugged her shoulders, pulled them back and made up her mind that she would take control of her daughter's stubborn nature. She would not allow this petty bickering over unimportant things.

She would keep the family together and work hard to get back to prosperity again. Things would get better; she was sure of it. If they didn't, she would think of something to do.

# CHAPTER 30

"Well, it's about time you came again to visit your nieces," Alycea scolded her brother. Manny had only visited his nieces a couple of times when they were toddlers. "They are nearly grown up now. Caterina is ten and Belinha is eight. You just missed their birthdays in February and May." Alycea always had a sharp tongue and an attitude but she dearly loved her brother. Her eyes softened when she looked at him. She ran into his open arms pressing her cool cheek tightly against his warm one.

"Alycea, mia amendoim, my peanut, you are filling out to be a beautiful woman. Look at those daughters of yours too! Wow, they are beauties. Caterina looks just like you and Belinha favors her father," he said as his nieces looked at him with bright eyes and smiling faces. They had heard a lot about their uncle and looked forward to seeing him.

Caterina stepped forward first and leaned toward Uncle Manny to give him a kiss on his cheek. He picked her up and spun her around like he used to do to Alycea when she was little. Caterina giggled and held on tightly as he gave her a hug and kiss and then placed her back on her feet. She walked away feeling a little woozy from the spinning.

Manny next set his eyes on Belinha who was running in circles to try to get away from him, knowing what her fate was. He picked her up and spun her around as he had done to Caterina. Belinha's eyes opened wider and she felt sick to her stomach but held on tightly. Seeing her frightened little face, Manuel abruptly stopped and hugged and kissed her on both cheeks before he put her down.

"Well, it seems that Caterina is the tough one like you, Lubelia Alycea, while Belinha is the sweet, frail one like Ed," he said this as he turned to face Belinha and asked her, "Are you all right now, little Belinha, my sweet niece?"

Belinha was especially sensitive and had tears in her eyes when she answered her uncle in a soft, shaky voice, "I'm okay now. I get dizzy when I spin and sometimes I get sick. I kind of like it though, the spin...not the sick part," she told him with her green eyes sparkling with unspent tears.

"That is good, little one. Sometimes we like things even if they are not good for us. I know I like a lot of things that are not good for me. Right, Alycea?" He smiled and winked at his sister.

Alycea just thumbed her nose up at him and laughed. "You were always into trouble, big brother. I knew it wouldn't be any different now that you are a man!"

"Didn't Ernestina come with you? You did marry her, did you not?" Alycea couldn't help but be curious about her sister-in-law. They hadn't seen Ernestina since Mae and Stan's wedding. Manuel never talked about her either. It was strange.

Manny waved his hand in dismissal.

"You never answer my letters, Manny. So I don't know what you are doing," Alycea stated, exasperated.

"Yes, Lubelia Alycea, we did get married shortly after we went back to Lisbon. She and I...well...I was out at sea a lot. I went home to see her as often as I could. She was pregnant and lost the baby a few months ago. I should have been there for her but…it was hard on both of us. I didn't think she was up to coming here to see your two girls. I thought it would have been too hard on her. I will bring her back another time to visit with you all."

"I am so sorry for you both, Manny. Are you doing okay now? Are you still out fishing at sea a lot? Maybe you need to be home more now that…" She couldn't finish her thought when she saw her brother's face turn pale and a visible shudder go through him.

She abruptly changed the subject by saying, "Well, it would be nice to have a visit from you and Ernestina next time. I look forward to it."

Manny nodded and tried to smile.

"Manny, can you please watch the girls while I go out to the grocer and butcher to get something for dinner. We will celebrate my - long lost brother is back. I want to cook up something extra special for you. Ed and Stan will be coming home from work shortly. Mae went out for a walk with a neighbor and will be back soon too. They will all be ecstatic that you are here." She pecked his check and rushed out the door, feeling light headed and happy.

Manny sat down and patted the seats next to him on the couch and beckoned his nieces to come and sit down and talk to him. He wanted to know all about them and what they had been doing for the past ten and eight years respectively that he had missed. Since Manny had only seen his nieces a couple of times when they were babies, they did not remember him.

Caterina was the first to run over and sit down right next to her uncle. Belinha was a little shy and took her time strolling over to sit next to her sister. She was always in her sister's shadow.

Manny noticed the different personalities and temperaments of his two nieces as he listened first to Caterina talk about herself. He tended to want to protect Belinha from Caterina but knew she had to find her own way. He would though, always keep an eye on her and guide her in any way that he could.

Caterina at once began by telling her uncle about her life from as early as she could remember up to the current time. She never once seemed to take a breath between all the exclamations of what she could do, how many friends she had and how all the boys liked her. She was about to tell him about her singing and dancing lessons when Manny stopped her.

"Caterina, you are hogging the floor. It's your sister's turn now to tell me about what she has been doing. You will have another turn to tell me all about your dancing and singing." He looked at Belinha who was sitting with her eyes downcast.

He called her name. She looked up with her big green eyes and the saddest expression on her face. "What's wrong Belinha? Don't you want to tell me all about what you have been doing in school and the friends you have? What kind of ice cream do you like? What is your favorite color?" He smiled, waiting for a response.

"I don't really like school and I don't have any friends. I like pistachio and coffee ice cream and my favorite color is blue," she said almost too quickly to get it over with.

"Belinha, why don't you like school? I am sure you have friends. Don't you sit with someone at lunch or play during recess?" He didn't know what to make of this. Something was definitely wrong. She was clearly shy but surely she had found others who were just as shy to befriend.

"Oh, Uncle Manny, she doesn't have any friends. She always sits by herself at lunch and the kids make fun of her. Grandma brings her lunch every day because she always forgets to bring it herself. Grandma sits with her to make sure she eats all her food too. Everybody calls her a baby!" Caterina exclaimed, eager to tell all to her uncle.

"Caterina, I don't think that's a nice thing to say in front of your sister. It will make her feel sad. Why don't you sit with her if she is all alone? Maybe if you did, no one would make fun of her. It would probably make her happy too." He watched Belinha's expression to see if she showed any relief at all about his suggestion.

"No, I sit with my friends and they wouldn't want to sit with my baby sister." Disdain showed in her face at just the thought of doing what he requested.

"What do you say about all this, Belinha? I would really like you to talk to me." He patiently waited for her to acknowledge that he was speaking to her.

With her eyes focused on the floor, Belinha began by saying, "I...I forget my lunch sometimes and Grandma brings it to me. I get really hungry every day and almost passed out one time. Grandma said she would bring me a snack too to have later on in the afternoon. I don't care if anyone wants to sit with me. I don't mind sitting alone or with Grandma. I don't like your friends either, Caterina. They are mean to me. They are the ones who make fun of me all the time." Tears started to form in her eyes and she sniffled and wiped them away with the back of her hand at the corners as they fell.

Manny reached into his pocket and brought out a handkerchief which he handed to Belinha. She said, "Thank you" and used it to wipe her eyes and blow her nose loudly.

"It's okay, Belinha. No one is going to make fun of you anymore. I will make sure of it. I will come to your school and have lunch with you tomorrow and fix the problem. Then you will not be alone anymore. I will bring your lunch instead of Grandma. Ok?"

"Oh, Uncle Manny, would you do that for me? I would be pleased to have lunch with you tomorrow. I can't wait to tell Mae and Pai and Papa and Grandma." Her sweet little face became at once animated and happy as her eyes sparkled.

The only one who wasn't looking pleased was Caterina. She pouted and sulked when she heard what her uncle said.

Manny glanced at Caterina and winked at her expression of displeasure. "Well, I'm glad that I made you happy, little one. Now what would you like for lunch?" He was feeling a lot happier himself at the thought of having lunch with his little niece. She made him think of his sweet Cristina. He missed her terribly.

He felt happy being around his nieces and would enjoy staying for a week or so. He would send word to Ernestina that he would be staying longer than he had expected. He would tell her that his sister needed help with the children.

He knew that it only prolonged the inevitable that he would have to go home to face his wife. He couldn't stand to see her face when she looked at him with such hatred. She blamed him for the death of their baby. He wasn't there when she needed him. If he had been there he might have been able to protect them both and prevent her from falling.

\*\*\*

He had been gone for a month and had enjoyed every minute being with his mother, Stan, Alycea, Ed and the girls. They had hugged him tightly not wanting to let him go. The girls cried as they waved goodbye and told him to come back again soon. They threw kisses and said, 'We love you, Uncle Manny."

He had watched them standing on the dock waving until he couldn't see them clearly anymore. They were probably still standing too there watching his boat disappear into the horizon.

He was glad that he had helped his shy niece, Belinha, to finally find some friends at lunch time to sit with her. The kids had all flocked to him and her when they saw him come into the school with some of his sailing paraphernalia. He had talked to the principal and Belinha's teacher ahead of time about coming into the classroom to talk to the kids about his sailing adventures.

They were all animated when he had told them that if they had any questions to ask Belinha and she would write him with their questions. He said he would answer them back as soon as possible. This would ensure that Belinha would have plenty of people to talk to for a long time.

He had turned his attention toward the sails to help his fellow fishermen and crew with the rigs to unfurl them to speed their way home. He always loved the feel of the sea-salt spray on his face and the smell of the sea air even when it was cold. The air was beginning to get a bite to it and the winter would be here before he knew it. He then would have to store his boat until the warmer weather returned. He never liked this part of the year when he would not be able to sail and feel free.

Mr. Dante, the man he had met when he worked for Mr. Bohondoney, had generously given him this boat to use whenever he wanted. He had said to Manny one day after he was working for him, 'Consider it yours, Manny. You have done a lot for me over the years. I appreciate your help in getting my business going by delivering my supplies and introducing my products to the other ports.'

Manny had enjoyed working for Mr. Dante until his wife and daughter had lost their lives when they had drowned falling off the boat. After this tragedy Manny had told Mr. Dante that he could not accept the boat but Mr. Dante had insisted that Manuel take a different boat so as not to remind him of their deaths.

Manny had needed to sail away and try to heal after the loss of his wife and child. He had finally come back and picked up the boat from Mr. Dante. He was glad to have it now. He could get back and forth without having to use other means to visit his family. He looked up from his reverie and realized he was at the dock. He headed home and saw Ernestina standing at the front door looking sadly at him. She raised her hand in welcome and peace.

She ran to him and he opened his arms to catch her in a warm embrace. They kissed and held each other for a long time before either could say a word.

Peace had finally come to their home. Love was always there. Anger, hurt and disappointment were now gone.

# CHAPTER 31

Nearly every day since Manny had a few years ago, Belinha asked Alycea the same question. "Mae, when do you think Uncle Manny will visit again?" Belinha's face looked radiant as she asked her mother.

"Oh, dear one, he won't be back for a few more years if I know my brother. He has written to you almost every week since he left. He never wrote that much to me when I was your age." She winked at her younger daughter and threw her a kiss as she continued preparing their dinner.

She was relieved to see how content her daughter, Belinha, now was at home and at school. She had received excellent reports from her teachers. They all said that Belinha was doing well and becoming more outgoing.

She knew it was all due to her brother's intervention. He always seemed to make people laugh and everyone was relaxed around him. He was a special person. She only wished that he lived closer so they could see him more. She felt like Belinha did. She missed him terribly but at the same time hoped that he was happy with Ernestina and all was forgiven over the loss of their unborn child.

Her prayer now was for her two daughters to get along. They always seemed to be quarreling. They never agreed on anything and got upset with one another over everything from clothes to boys.

Caterina was a dark beauty with her long dark brown hair and big brown eyes. The boys all flocked to her like bees to honey. It was difficult for Belinha to bring home any boys now because they would always ignore her once they saw her sister.

Belinha was a beauty in her own way. She was paler and blonde with green eyes and dimples in her cheeks like her father. She had a sweet innocent way about her while her sister was more worldly and sure of herself.

Caterina had already met many boys but had not been serious with any of them until she met Dean. He was different from the rest. He was a young man while the other suitors were just boys. He was strong, tough and wore an air of confidence. He was also quite handsome and athletic. He played football and boxed in the local gym.

The thing that really intrigued Caterina about him was that he did not fall all over her like the others. He had asked her straight out to go with him to the school dance in his no nonsense way. She was afraid if she didn't answer him right away he would find someone else to go with him. Her answer was 'yes' before he had turned away from her to walk back to class. She ran after him and walked beside him, proud to be seen with the captain of the football team.

***

Alycea was proud of her daughters and felt content with her life. She and Ed went out at night to the clubs and she watched him play his mandolin with the other musicians. They manage to dance when he had a break from playing.

Her mother still watched over her daughters and doted on them. The girls were growing up swiftly, however, and soon wouldn't need all the doting by their grandmother.

Filomena and Stan didn't go out as often now and were busy with their lives just caring for all the family. Filomena cooked, cleaned, shopped and was there for all of them. Because of her mother's unselfish nature, Alycea did not give her a second thought most of the time. She was just there to do everything, giving Alycea and Ed lots of free time to do what they enjoyed doing, going out with friends, dining and dancing.

This carefree lifestyle for Alycea would soon change.

# CHAPTER 32

"Filomena, would you like to go for a walk? It's awfully hot in here, and you are looking a little pale, my dear." Stan rubbed Filomena's frail shoulders as she stood over the sink washing the dishes.

"No dear, I need to finish up here. We can go after I wash the clothes though. Ok?" Filomena looked at her husband's face, the face she had come to cherish all these years. He was always worried about her and wore a frown between his brows when he asked her how she was feeling.

He had noticed that she wasn't well lately and looking tired and thin. She was still doing everything in the apartment with little assistance from Alycea and their granddaughters. The girls were teenagers now and both in high school and well able to help around the house. He would have to insist that they help their grandmother more. She was getting older and couldn't keep up this pace.

He had to admit that Belinha was a kind soul, much like her grandmother. She kept offering to do things around the kitchen for her grandmother. Filomena had always shushed her out of the way and said she didn't need any help.

He went to see Belinha who was in her room doing her homework as usual. She studied hard since most things did not come easy to her. She was a good student but had to work at it. Her sister, on the other hand, found help from her boyfriends and all her girlfriends when it came to doing her projects for school. She didn't do her own homework either. She somehow always managed to get good grades though.

Stan knocked on Belinha's door. "Belinha, can I come in? I just need to talk to you. I promise it won't take too much time so that you can get back to your homework. Ok?" He hesitated at the door waiting for her to acknowledge him. She seemed to be deep in thought.

"Oh of course, Grandpa Stan. Please come in. I am studying for a science test. I always have such a hard time with it. I can never remember everything. What can I do for you? Are you all right? Is it Grandma? Is she sick again?" Belinha's voice registered deep concern as she looked Stan in the eye. He had become precious to her. He was her grandfather since she never knew her mother's father. Stan was always kind and thoughtful to both her and her sister and he loved Grandma more than his own life.

"Oh dear one, she is looking extra weary lately, that is all. I just wanted to request, if I may, that you and your sister might do a few more chores each day so that she won't have to work as hard around the house. Do you think you could help her out a little, sweetheart?" He said with such tenderness as he looked at her sweet face and sad eyes.

He knew that she adored her grandmother and thought of her more like a mother than a grandmother. It was due to the fact that Alycea seemed to favor her older daughter over Belinha since Caterina was more like herself. Also, Filomena always doted on Belinha being the baby in the family and took care of her when Alycea went to work in the local plant.

"Of course, I will do whatever needs to be done. I already make my bed, clean my room, set the table, help wash the clothes, empty trash and wash the front steps. Caterina is supposed to take turns with some of the chores but she has been busy with her dancing and singing lessons and other stuff. I cover for her and do the chores when she can't," she said in all one breath as she smiled up at Stan.

He just looked at her in amazement. He didn't realize she was doing that much already. He would have to have a talk with Alycea about Caterina slacking off on her duties. She should be helping out more. He kissed Belinha on the cheek. Before turning and leaving the room, he thanked her for doing all she did. She was such a sweet young lady and more and more like Filomena all the time. They would all need to help out and he knew he could count on Belinha.

The country was not yet out of The Great Depression and they still had to scrimp and save to make ends meet. At least he and Ed were working and Alycea was starting back to work soon. He did what he could to find her a spot in his department.

He did not want Filomena to have to worry about anything. He would be the provider for the family with the aid of Ed. They would survive.

Now all he had to do was make sure Filomena's health improved. He would do all he could to make her well.

***

Alycea was getting ready to leave the plant and looking out for Ed when she saw Stan walking toward her. He didn't look happy. He was now a manager and in charge of all the stitchers and material handlers and the processing of cotton on the first and second floors.

She was adept as a material handler at two plants doing this position since she was fourteen years old before she got pregnant. She thought back about the day and what had transpired and didn't remember making any mistakes to cause him any concern. Well, she guessed she would find out soon what was bothering him. He was heading her way and quickly.

"Alycea, I need to see you right away. Please come to my office." Stan abruptly turned and headed back to his office with Alycea in tow.

She followed him. Looking at the back of his head she noticed that his hair was thinning and graying. He did worry a lot about everything. It was aging him evidently, Alycea thought to herself.

Stan opened the door to his office and stepped aside to let Alycea come in. He went around his desk and sat down and gestured to her to take a seat too.

Alycea didn't like the looks of this. He looked awfully stern and serious. Maybe he was going to fire her, she thought. She wouldn't be able to pay for all the things she liked to buy and do if he did fire her.

He noticed the frightened look in her eyes. "Alycea, I didn't mean for you to be afraid. It has nothing to do with your position here. This is something personal. It is about your mother. I am worried about her health. I can't talk at home in front of her. It would only upset her more." He waited for this much to sink in for Alycea.

"What's wrong, Pai? She didn't call him father at work only at home. But she used this term of endearment since they were alone and he was visibly upset. "Is she sick again? Did she go to the doctor? Is it her diabetes?" she asked with a modicum of concern. She knew he worried sometimes unnecessarily about her mother.

Alycea was still a child inside and never really grew up. Her mother always took care of her and Alycea's children not leaving much for Alycea to do but enjoy life and think of herself.

Filomena had made a tragic mistake bringing her up to be selfish. Stan knew that Filomena was only doing what she thought was right by helping her daughter with everything. It was time for Alycea to take responsibility for her life to enable Filomena to live hers.

"Your mother is exhausted. She does everything in the house. You and the girls need to help her out more. I know Belinha does her share but Caterina doesn't. I have been part of this family for a long time now and I feel I can talk to you on this level. I know I am not your father. I don't want to replace him but I have been a father to you and your brother. I am here for you always. All I am asking from you in return is to help your mother. I fear for her health. She is not well."

Stan dropped his head into his hands and sighed deeply. He didn't realize saying all this would disturb him this profoundly. He was deeply fearful of losing his Filomena. He couldn't comprehend how he would live without her.

"Pai, Stan, you are a father to me. I love you and I can understand how you feel about Mae. I love her so much too. I want to help her in any way I can. I know I have been selfish but she has always taken over and done everything for me. There was never anything left for me to do. She took care of my girls from the time they were born until now. I didn't worry because she was always there to make things work. I guess you are right. I need to grow up and stand on my own two feet. I promise I will do just that from now on." Alycea leaned over the desk and touched Stan on his head. He looked up at her with tears in his eyes, surprise showing in his distraught face over her words of wisdom and sudden maturity.

"Thank you, Alycea. I knew you would do whatever you could to help your mother. Let this conversation stay between us two. Ok? I don't want your mother upset or to worry about anything. Is that okay with you, dear?" He looked so forlorn and tired. All Alycea could do was nod at him and smile to try to relieve some of his apprehension.

That night Alycea prepared dinner and washed and dried the dishes, cleaned the floor and finished up washing the clothes. She even got Caterina to wash the front steps which was something she hated to do. She always finagled her way out of doing them by asking her sister to take her turn at this dreaded chore with the promise that she would do some chores for her too.

Alycea enlisted Belinha to take charge of changing the sheets and washing them and hanging them out on the clothesline. She was also responsible to make sure her grandmother was sitting on the couch with her feet up and resting. Belinha had checked on Grandma before she started the beds and noticed Grandpa Stan sitting next to her on the couch keeping a watchful eye on her. He waved at Belinha to reassure her that he would take care of her Grandma.

Alycea felt for the first time in charge of her family and her life. It was a good feeling. She hadn't realized how much she had been missing by letting her mother do everything. She looked over at her mother and the man who was a father to her all these years and felt a swelling of love for both of them. She would be in charge of this family from now on. It was not like her to kowtow to anyone. She had always been the strong, resilient one in the family.

She was deeply engrossed in her thoughts and washing the dishes when Ed came up behind her and kissed her on her neck. He was surprised to see her doing this mundane thing. He arched his eyebrow at her when she turned to face him.

She gave him a quick peck on the lips and said she was now in charge of the kitchen and everything else in this household for that matter. He smiled and snapped to attention and saluted her.

She playfully slapped at his hand and he grabbed her in a bear hug that made her catch her breath. He released her. She laughed and looked at him with a yearning in her eyes.

He took her hand in his and led her to their bedroom with his own plans in mind. He looked quickly around him and saw the rest of the family were busy with their own projects. It seemed safe for them to spend some much needed time privately together. He could never get enough of her. Besides he had some new ideas in mind how to please his sweet Alycea that he wanted to test out.

***

Alycea stretched and rolled over to look at her sleeping husband. They had been amorous, more than normal lately with all his new ideas added to their lovemaking. They were definitely doing her complexion justice. She woke up each morning feeling rested and sated and her cheeks kept their rosy glow all day.

She dearly loved her Edouardo. He was a good man and father. He worked long hours at the mill with Pai and provided well for his family even in the tough times since the Depression. They never were left hungry and with Mae's patching of their clothes they were never naked. Thank goodness for that!! She chuckled to herself. She spent a lot of time naked in bed with Edouardo as it was!

Ed always spent some time with their daughters too. He took them out to the club to listen to him play or to their friends' houses or just out for a walk. He talked to them about what they were doing in school and if they had boyfriends.

He was several years older than Alycea and he always felt that he would not live as long as Alycea. He had been known to state this fact for years as the girls were growing up. They would laugh at him and hop onto his lap and give him a big hug and say, "Pai, you are going to live forever and see us grow up and get married and have children."

Ed would just smile and hug his daughters and tell them he hoped to be around long enough to see his grandchildren. He didn't want to frighten them too much but he had this funny feeling that Alycea would outlive him by many years.

# CHAPTER 33

"Mae, are you awake?" Alycea looked down at her mother who had been sleeping all day. She was looking extremely pale and losing weight which made her look even frailer. She wasn't a big woman to begin with standing less than five feet.

Alycea smoothed her mother's brow, kissed it and noticed all the new gray hairs around the crown of her head. There were a few more wrinkles around her eyes too. She did smile a lot though. I guess they could be called happy lines, thought Alycea.

Her mother had not been feeling well lately and Pai was usually at her bedside. She had made him go out for a little fresh air so that she could sit with her mother for a while and give him a break. The doctor had been over to see her two days ago and had given her something for her pain. She had been getting sores on her legs that would not heal and she had pain in her feet and couldn't walk or stand for too long.

Alycea hated to see her mother incapacitated like this. She had always been active doing something around the house.

She pulled up a chair to sit next to her mother, picked up her hand and gave it a squeeze. "Mae, how are you feeling today? Can I get you something to drink or eat? I made some watercress soup for you with the little meatballs that you like."

Her mother moaned and tried to push herself up in bed. Alycea jumped up to aid her, putting pillows behind her back and head and propping her up.

"Lubelia Alycea, don't you worry about this old woman. I am just fine. I would love to have some of your watercress soup. You make it better than I do now. You have become a good cook, mia filha." She opened her eyes and smiled at her lovely daughter who was now a beautiful woman and no longer a child. She could see the maturity and confidence in her mannerisms and felt relieved that she had done a good job with her. She knew that Alycea would be able to take care of the family when she was gone.

Filomena knew that she may not get to see her grandchildren married and with children of their own. Her health had been declining and the doctor told her that she may lose her foot or even her leg to diabetes. He told her that if he took her leg she may be free of pain. She had told him to schedule the surgery and that she would get around somehow with only one leg if she did not have the debilitating pain anymore. She had not told Stan or Alycea yet about her decision. That would be the hardest part, convincing them that this must be done.

That night Filomena prayed especially long and fervently to St. Theresa for guidance. She had already made up her mind what she was going to do but she needed to have the strength to go on and face her life which would be more difficult on one leg. She felt that with St. Theresa's help she could do whatever she had to do.

\*\*\*

Back to the future

"Oh my God, Avoa, Granny Filomena lost her leg when she was only in her forties. I remember my mother talking about her all the time. She really loved Granny and said she was a saint. She was

178

good to everyone but especially those who were needy. She was unselfish, always putting the needs of others before her own. I wish I could be more like her," Jasmine sighed as she shook her head over such a tragedy.

"Don't get all upset. Your great grandmother was a feisty one, you know. She didn't let anything get by her. She was a good person and all but a tough one sometimes too. I guess she had to be to keep me and my brother in line." Alycea smiled then let out a chuckle as if she had just shared a joke with her granddaughter.

"We all did what we could to make her comfortable even if she was obstinate about wanting to do everything herself. Your mother did take care of her for me when I couldn't. For that, I was thankful, because, at times, I did not have the patience to deal with her as your mother did."

***

Back to the past

Filomena had the surgery against her family's wishes. The surgeon had to remove her right leg from the knee down. Gangrene has eaten it away to that point. If they hadn't removed it then she would have lost the whole leg and maybe – her life.

"Alycea, you don't have to dote on me. Stan does that enough for both of us. I have been home a week from the hospital and I need to get up. Dr. Carter, the surgeon, and Dr. Fusco and Dr. Bradley, our family doctors, all said it is time for me to try getting around. Dr. Carter left me with a crutch and I will need to practice. Now, move aside, dear filha. I need to try it out." Alycea stepped aside as she observed her mother. She was extremely anxious about her mother falling and hurting herself but she knew her mother was a determined woman. Alycea knew she would be the one to get hurt if she did not move away.

"Okay Mae, but I will be close by in case you need me to catch you. Stan is outside the door and he wants to come in. Can I let him in now?" Alycea wanted Stan there in case she needed him to lift her mother back into bed.

"No, I am fine, dear one. He will just get in my way. Let me get myself up and walk a little and then you can let him in. Once he sees me up and about, he will relax and so will you. Now stop worrying." Her voice was a little shaky but her eyes were clear and strong with her message.

***

Six months later

"Mae, Grandma's left leg does not look good. She is getting around amazingly well but she is in pain again. She may lose her left leg too, it if doesn't heal. What can we do for her? The doctor gave her some salve but it is not working."

"Belinha, you do worry a lot, dear child. Go to the kitchen and separate two eggs and bring me the white of the eggs in a dish with a spoon. Go quickly child." Belinha looked at her mother with a frown and puzzled expression.

"Don't question me, mia filha, just do what I say." Alycea's voice was strong and commanding as she waved her daughter away to do her bidding.

Belinha brought back the white of the two eggs with a spoon in a bowl and handed this clear, slimy mixture to her mother. She stepped aside as her mother spooned a little of the mixture over her mother's sores on her leg and waited until the mixture started to dry and seal in each sore. She instructed her daughter to do the same every few hours.

Three days later Belinha continued as she was instructed by her mother to bath the sores with egg whites and noticed that the sores were now beginning to heal and close up. She ran to tell her mother what she saw.

"Mae, surely St. Theresa is blessing Grandma and healing her sores." She looked at her mother for some sign that this was true.

"You can believe whatever you want, mia filha. I feel sometimes it is just luck when something like this happens. I prayed many times for some guidance and I found that I had to make my own luck. There will be many trials that we will have to bear in life. We need to try to make the best of what we have. For what we have, may be all we will ever receive," Alycea looked solemn when she said this. She smiled wanly at her daughter's sweet, innocent face and wide, surprised look in her eyes.

Grandpa Stan was sitting in a chair next to Filomena's bed as Belinha entered her grandmother's room. He patted Belinha on her hand and excused himself to let Belinha spend some time alone with her grandmother.

Belinha looked at her Grandpa Stan and smiled sweetly at him. Thinking to herself, what a wonderful husband her grandmother had. He was devoted to her. She hoped one day to find someone as wonderful.

She sat down next to her grandmother's bedside to hold her hand and talk to her. She felt confused about what her mother had said to her. She needed to believe in something like her grandmother Filomena did.

"Grandma, do you believe in God? Do you think what happens to us is what God wants to happen? Did He want you to lose your leg?" Belinha's questions were coming out so rapidly that Filomena looked sadly at her granddaughter before she opened her eyes and struggled to prop herself up to respond to her questions.

"Dear child, God is always with us. He guides us in our travels here on earth. He doesn't want us to suffer but we must make our own decisions and deal with whatever happens to us. We must not ever lose sight of Him. We must believe and pray to Him so we can be with Him in His Heavenly home one day. Whatever good we do on earth will be rewarded in Heaven. Listen to your heart, dear one, pray if you need guidance and He will help you. Don't ever give up your faith." Filomena closed her eyes and fell back to sleep exhausted by own words. It was getting more difficult for her to stay awake for long and moving or talking exhausted her.

Belinha kissed her grandmother on her cheek, thanked her for the much needed words of guidance and left her room. She felt better after talking to her grandmother and would continue in her beliefs and pray every day for her grandmother's good health to return.

Alycea was standing outside her mother's room and heard their conversation. She smiled to herself content to know that Belinha would listen to her own heart and do what was right for her. She was always such a sweet child and now was a kind and tender young woman. She did not want to see her hurt and tried to toughen her up like herself. Alycea knew how tough life could be if you were too soft.

She thought about her life and how many years it had been since she had seen her twin brother, Antonio. He had stopped writing to her several months ago.

She had tried to send him money to have him visit her but he refused it. He had been living in Sao Paulo, Brazil for many years now and had recently moved to a new home there but had not sent her his new address yet. Alycea knew that he was angry about being left behind and forgotten for many years.

He had made a life for himself, had gotten married and had two children of his own. She had sent him pictures of her children and he, in turn, did the same. She made a vow to visit him one day and would write to her cousin, Grinalda's family, in Madeira to try to obtain Antonio's new address. Her cousin, Grinalda, had died many years earlier but her children were still living in the same house.

She also had not heard from her older brother, Manuel, for over a year. She knew that he was like that. From time to time he would not write for several months then he would surprise them with a visit and stay for a month and then be on his way again. He was a gypsy and couldn't stay in one spot for a lengthy time.

Manuel and Ernestina were still together but did not have any children. When she lost their child she had to have an operation later on after which she was rendered sterile. Manuel was heartbroken but went on with his life and never talked about it with Alycea. She knew he was devastated but she couldn't do anything to help him. When he visited, Alycea had kept him busy. They had taken trips to see the Statue of Liberty and relived their travels to America from Madeira each time they looked out over the harbor from the Lady's torch.

Alycea talked to Manuel about their brother Antonio. Manuel had never written to Antonio regularly or kept in touch as she had. He said he would visit him one day. He never seemed to want to talk about Antonio though.

Alycea's bond with her twin was stronger than Manuel's was with their brother. She vowed to do what she could to make up for all the time they had been apart. She would save up her money and travel to Brazil to see her twin one day since he refused to accept any money from her to come to America.

# CHAPTER 34

Jaco had seen Belinha walking by the platform at the train station as he was waiting to get on a train. He had thought she was the loveliest thing he had ever seen. He got up the courage, caught her eye and went up to her to introduce himself. She was a little shy and had such beautiful green eyes that when she looked at him his heart skipped a beat.

Belinha thought Jaco was handsome. He told her that he had just enlisted at sixteen but had told the enlistment officer that he was eighteen. Jaco was only two years older than Belinha but she was delighted that he even noticed her since she was so young. They met several times after that for coffee at the train station until it was time for him to go to the Marine base to begin training. They talked about their lives and their dreams and in a short time grew closer. Jaco had asked Belinha to write to him when he went overseas and she promised she would.

War was coming closer to them and Jaco knew that he was going to have to leave soon. He did not want to lose contact with Belinha and gave her his PO address so that her letters would get to him wherever he was stationed.

On the day that Jaco was being shipped overseas, Belinha met him at the train station once again to say goodbye. They held each other tightly and promised to keep in touch with one another. Jaco said,

"Belinha, I want to see you when I come back and I promise to come back to you. Will you wait for me? I want to marry you one day." Tears were sparkling in his eyes as he held Belinha's hands gently in his.

Belinha couldn't believe her ears. "Jaco, I will wait for you. Please be safe and come back to me. I promise to write to you every day until then." She gave his hands a squeeze as the tears covered her face when she looked at him. She felt as if she was losing her best friend. She sensed a warm feeling growing inside her just being this close to him. "Was this how it felt to be in love?" she asked herself.

She hugged Jaco tightly and then they parted. She waved continuously and didn't leave the station until she couldn't see Jaco's train anymore. She was lost and lonely without him. They had become close and good friends in a short time. She never had felt comfortable with boys at school until Jaco. He was special and different from other boys; after all he was a young man. She couldn't wait until she could tell her mother about Jaco. She never invited him to her home for fear her mother would not let her see him. With the war imminent, there would be time to prepare her mother before Jaco returned.

"Mae, I have some good news! Where are you? I need to see you." Belinha came bursting through the front door of their apartment looking in every room for her mother. She had just left the train station and couldn't contain her excitement over having a boyfriend.

She had never had a boyfriend before. Her sister, Caterina, on the other hand, had many, many boyfriends, that is, until Caterina had starting dating her latest, Dean. He did not like Caterina dating anyone else now that they were going steady.

Her sister would be really surprised to hear her news. She gave up trying to find her mother when she spied her sister, in the room that they had shared, standing in front of the mirror admiring the new dress she had just bought.

Belinha ran into the room and called her sister to get her attention. "Caterina, I have good news. Do you want to hear my news?" Belinha's eyes were bright and sparkling as she waited patiently for her sister to pay attention to her.

"Okay, Belinha. If I listen to you, will you please leave me alone? I need to get dressed. Dean is on his way here to pick me up. We are going to the movies and then out for ice cream," Caterina said with some exasperation in her impatient voice. She didn't pay too much attention to her little sister. She was such a shy little mouse and always seemed to be gawking at her and watching her every move. She was only two years older than Belinha but felt a lot more grownup and more worldly than she.

"I said goodbye to my friend, Jaco, at the train station. He went overseas to fight the war. He gave me his address so that I can write to him every day. He wants me to wait for him. He wants me to marry him one day when he returns," Belinha spoke as quickly as she could to prevent her sister from interrupting her or asking her to shut up. Belinha watched her sister's expression as her face showed her shock at these astounding revelations from her baby sister. Caterina was, for the first time, speechless.

Belinha couldn't help the smile that spread over her face as her sister opened her mouth but nothing came out. She was pleased with herself that for once Caterina didn't have anything to say or was not being mean to her.

Caterina shook her head and finally blurted out the first words that came into her head. "Are you crazy Belinha? How can you marry someone you just met? What makes you think that this man will not find someone else in the meantime? Do you really think that he will save himself just for you? You are only a child!" Her words came out to sting her sister like a snake stings its prey with venom leaving it stunned and ready for the kill.

Belinha wanted to run away from her sister's words. They hurt her too much to even respond. She tried to keep the tears from falling by covering her face as she turned and hurried out the door. She ran into her mother who was standing outside their bedroom and had heard every hurtful word her elder daughter had uttered.

Alycea's face was a white mask of anger. Belinha had never seen her mother look that way and hopefully she would never see it again. She was relieved to realize that this anger was directed away from her.

Alycea caught Belinha in her arms and held her as she cried. Belinha's small shoulders shook as the tears cascaded down her face.

"Belinha, my dear, are you finished crying? Don't waste your tears on your sister. She doesn't mean what she says. She is just jealous that you have found someone who loves you and wants to marry you. Her boyfriend, Dean, has not asked her to marry him yet. She wants to be the first to get married. That is all. Don't worry, mia filha. Caterina and I will be having a little talk and she will not say another unkind word to you. Now go to the bathroom. All this crying is taking a toll on you. Go wash your face and fix yourself up. Your eyes and nose are all red. I will be back to see you after I speak to Caterina." Alycea gently pushed her daughter in the direction of the bathroom as she opened the door to her daughters' shared room.

Caterina was still standing in front of the mirror and saw the stern expression on her mother's face. One look and she knew she was in trouble. Her mother must have heard what had transpired between her and Belinha.

Caterina turned toward her mother and steeled herself with a determined resolve to face whatever her mother would throw at her. She kept her facial expression serious, for a smile, would only get her mother's dander up.

"Caterina, have a seat on the bed. We need to have a serious talk right now." Alycea's eyes were no longer amber but gray and unyielding as she stared her daughter down.

"I heard what you said to your sister. Those words were unkind and uncalled for. How can you say such mean things to your sister? She is the only sibling you will ever have. You should be kind to her and love her. She always looks up to you. She came in here to pour her heart out and share her good news with you. All you could do was break her heart. What is wrong with you, Caterina? Is it sheer jealousy that she is happy and you are not? You have everything, beauty, brains, talent and boyfriends. What else do you want?"

Alycea sighed deeply and looked visibly shaken on the edge of the bed next to her daughter. She didn't know what else to say or do to get through to her. Alycea knew Caterina was a good person and did not mean to hurt her sister. She was just too quick with her tongue and didn't think before she spoke.

Caterina looked at her mother and knew that she was right but didn't want to admit it. She knew right after the vindictive words left her mouth that she was wrong to say such terrible things to her sister. She loved her sister but didn't know how to get rid of this jealousy she was feeling towards her. She knew that her father and her grandmother favored Belinha but she also knew that she was her mother's favorite.

She had to do something to make her mother forgive her. She wanted to see her mother look at her with her usual radiant smile. Caterina couldn't stand for her mother to be angry with her.

Caterina leaned toward her mother and put her arm around her shoulders as she said, "Mae, I apologize for my awful behavior. I shouldn't have said those terrible things to Belinha. I am truly sorry. Will you forgive me?" Caterina looked at her mother with a measure of contrition spreading across her face.

It was true that Alycea could not stay angry with Caterina for long. All Caterina had to do was look at her with a sorrowful expression and her mother's anger dissipated quickly. They were soon crying in each other's arms.

"Caterina, you need to say you are sorry to your sister, not to me. Okay? I am not the one who is hurt. I am the one who is extremely disappointed in you though. I know you will make this right between you and your sister. Please go see her right away. She is distraught." Alycea gave Caterina one last hug and coaxed her out of the room.

Caterina went looking for her sister and found her sitting on the front steps leaning against the front of the building. Her eyes were red and puffy and her nose was still bright pink from blowing it.

She settled down next to Belinha on the steps and pushed her shoulder into her sister's arm playfully saying, "Hey, Belinha, what are you doing out here?"

When Belinha didn't look up or answer her, Caterina continued, "I wanted to tell you that I...I am...I'm sorry about what I said before. I didn't mean it really. I was just surprised that you had a boyfriend and that he was serious so soon. It didn't seem right that you got a proposal of marriage before I did. I am, after all, the older one. I thought I would be the first one to get a proposal. Dean hasn't asked me yet but I think he will after we graduate from high school."

Belinha was quiet but she sighed heavily and nodded to her sister. "You know, Belinha, Mae won't let us get married until we are at least eighteen. She said she was married too young and she didn't want us to make the same mistake. She wanted us to enjoy our childhood as long as we can. I plan to get married when I am nineteen or twenty."

Behina nodded again at her sister and sniffled.

"Do you think your boyfriend will wait that long for you to be that age? You are only fourteen now. That will be at least five years away from now." Caterina was looking intently at her sister who had not looked up from the ground yet.

Belinha finally focused her blood-shot eyes on Caterina and said in a tiny voice which was still quite hoarse from crying, "I forgive you Caterina. I know you really didn't mean it but it hurt to hear those words just the same. And, yes, I believe Jaco will wait for me that long. He has four years to do in the Marines first; and in the meantime I plan to finish high school and go to school to be a Beautician before we get married. That will take four years to do that. I will be eighteen by then," she said with a hint of a smile returning to her pale face. "I also want to save my money for a year before I get married."

She looked at Caterina and opened her arms to her sister to embrace her in between more tears and sniffles. Belinha felt relieved to be on speaking terms with her sister once again even if Caterina could be trying at times. Caterina was also relieved for now her mother would be nicer to her again, just in time, because Caterina was planning on asking her mother for a few favors soon.

# CHAPTER 35

"Alycea, what do you say about going out for a bite to eat tonight? You work too hard, cooking and taking care of everyone. Let me take care of you tonight, sweetheart?" Ed looked at Alycea with his devilish grin.

She knew he had more than plans just for dinner. He was friskier lately. He should be slowing down a little, but not her Edouardo. He was always ready even if she wasn't.

"That sounds nice, Edouardo. Let me fix dinner for the girls and Mama and Stan first. I need to change my dress and comb my hair then we can go. Okay?"

She had been more tired lately having to do all the cleaning and cooking since her mother had taken to bed more often than not. Filomena did hop around on one leg holding onto the furniture as she did this but it was difficult for her to stand for long stretches to do any kind of cleaning or cooking.

Of course, Stan was always one step behind Filomena to make sure she didn't fall. He doted on her constantly and was a big help to Alycea since she couldn't watch her mother all the time. They both feared that Filomena would injure herself the way she insisted on getting up on her own to go the bathroom without her crutches or their assistance.

Her mother, even with her disability, never lost her smile and pleasant disposition. She was always willing to listen when Alycea had a problem with the girls or if she just wanted to vent about Ed's bad habits, drinking and going out to the club with the guys.

Alycea sometimes wished she was more like her mother but then Ed would have walked all over her and probably cheated on her too if he hadn't already. He had a roving eye as it was and she did what she could to keep him in line.

Alycea finished up serving the pot roast, potatoes, carrots and salad to her girls and her mother and stepfather. As they sat down to enjoy this delicious meal she excused herself to get ready to go out with Ed.

Ed had cleaned himself up too and was looking dashing with his hair growing grey at the temples and on top. He just seemed to get handsomer as he got older. She looked at him and her heart gave a little start. He could still stir the fires in her, of that she was sure. She was afraid that other women were affected the same way.

He had a way of looking at her with his eyes crinkling and his dimples deep on each side of his cheeks. He even had a sexy cleft in his chin that she loved to touch when they were making love. She would rub her thumb across the indentation as she reached her peak.

She had to snap out of it quickly or she would be taking him to bed and then they would never get out to dinner. She smiled back at him and took his arm as he led her out of the apartment and for a stroll to the diner two blocks away.

She enjoyed being out with him but the food was never as good as her own cooking. He admitted that many times but he wanted her to be waited on for a change as he told her again this evening.

Ed was doing his own appraising of his lovely wife. She was fuller than she was when they were first married but she was only a child then and she had birthed two children since then. She looked really delectable tonight with her full breasts and round hips and he visualized doing some naughty things to her later in the privacy of their room. He leaned over and pecked her cheek with a light kiss and sniffed the cologne she had dabbed earlier at her neck and behind each ear. It had a sweet smell like honeysuckle and roses. Alycea purred when she felt his whiskers brush against her neck sending shivers down her spine. She loved this man more than life itself and knew that she was tough at times on him. She didn't want him to take her for granted. She acted tougher than she should. This way she could hide her true feelings.

She didn't know why she needed to have the upper hand in their relationship but she just did. She always needed more than she had whether it was food, love or people around her. She was afraid to be alone and unloved. She probably felt that way because of the separation from her twin brother when they were only eight years old. She had never gotten over that.

Alycea tried to get her mind back to her food. She had ordered a roast chicken dinner. She found it too salty and the white meat of the chicken was dry. They didn't put enough milk in the mashed potatoes and the green beans were rubbery.

She looked over at Ed who seemed oblivious; he was eating all his food without taking a breath. He acted like he was starving. He had ordered a boiled dinner with slices of pork shoulder. It looked like the cabbage was overcooked and mushy but this didn't stop Ed from eating it all.

He burped as he wiped his face with his napkin. He looked at Alycea who was picking at her food, seeming to have no appetite at all, while he had finished all of his food and was eyeing her plate now.

"Alycea, aren't you hungry, dear?" He showed his dimpled smile to get her attention.

"I…guess I'm not that hungry. Do you want some of my chicken or vegetables, Ed? You look like you are still hungry."

"Well, if you aren't going to eat it; I guess I could eat a little more. It would be a shame to waste it," he said as she slid her plate over in place of his empty one.

Alycea couldn't believe what this man could put away. He usually ate twice as much as she did and sometimes even finished everyone else's plates at home if there was any food left over. He never gained any weight either. This fact could be frustrating for her. She had to watch everything she ate or she would gain weight.

She always took a walk after dinner each night with or without Ed just to keep the weight down. Ed usually unbuttoned his pants and sat in his overstuffed chair and put his feet up on the stool and fell fast asleep with the radio on.

As Ed was finishing up her plate of food, she was thinking back to earlier in the day when Caterina had asked her for two new outfits. She said she was going to the school dance and also a football banquet with Dean both within a week of each other.

Caterina had picked out the dresses she wanted and told her mother the cost of both, much to her chagrin. The prices were too high for Alycea's budget and she told Caterina this.

Of course, they had a disagreement and Caterina had stormed out of the house to go pout outside on the front porch. Alycea let her go out so she could cool off and come to her senses.

Alycea had told Caterina that she had more than enough dresses to wear that would be perfectly fine for either occasion. She had only worn some of the dresses once or twice. Alycea also had told Caterina that if she wanted any new dresses, she would have to find a job and pay for them herself.

Caterina had not spoken to Alycea when they had left to go out to dinner and refused to even look at her mother. Alycea could live with this, at least there would be peace and quiet for a little while until Caterina blew up again with her usual tantrums when she did not get her way.

Alycea did not plan on giving her daughter her way this time. She just wouldn't do it. Caterina always got her way and sometimes it cost them more than their budget could take. It was time that Caterina learned the value of money and maybe getting a job would help her learn.

Ed had finished up all the leftovers in Alycea's plate and was looking at her with a frown. "Alycea, what is wrong, dear? You look deep in thought. Did I do something wrong? Are you angry because I finished up all your food?"

"No, don't be silly, Ed. I am fine with you eating the rest of the food. I didn't want it anyway. I was thinking about Caterina. I didn't tell you what her latest request was." Alycea relayed what had transpired between Caterina and herself.

Ed folded his hands across his full abdomen and took on a look of deep contemplation as he tried to come up with a solution to the ongoing trials of having a daughter like Caterina.

"I think you are right, Alycea. It is time for Caterina to find herself a job to pay for all the extravagances that she is always demanding. Belinha doesn't demand anything but the bare necessities. Why can't Caterina be more like our Belinha?" Ed always did favor Belinha because she was like him in temperament and never demanding in any way.

"No two children are ever alike, Ed. Don't you know that? You can't compare one with the other ever. When are you going to realize that? I know you favor Belinha over Caterina. You cannot be fair in any exchange."

"Well, dear Alycea. You certainly favor our Caterina more than Belinha. Am I not correct? That means you cannot be fair in judgment either. What will we do about this situation?"

"I will talk to Caterina one more time to try to put some sense into her head. If she does not agree to our suggestion of her finding a job and paying for her own dresses, then I will punish her and forbid her from going to the dance and the banquet." Alycea looked smug as she glanced at her husband for his approval. She desperately wanted to have Ed's approval at the same time she wanted to be fair to both of her children and not show any favoritism to one over the other.

Time would tell soon if this would work.

***

"Caterina, what's the matter?" Belinha had just come into the room to see her sister lying on the bed looking upset. Caterina was a tough one. She seldom cried, and, if she did everyone would know something terrible must have happened.

Caterina turned over to look at her sister. Her tears were clearly visible from the tracks they had left on her cheeks. "I can't believe Mae! She said I can't go to the dance or banquet unless I get a job. Then I can buy my own dresses. I don't want to get a job. Why can't she buy me the dresses? I know she can afford it. She keeps extra cash in the jar in the kitchen hidden behind the sugar and coffee canisters."

"She doesn't know that I found the hiding place. I was supposed to be in my room doing my homework one day but I happened to walk out to the kitchen and saw her put some money in there. I should just take the money and go buy my dresses. She won't notice the money is gone until next week when she gets paid and puts more money in there."

"Oh Caterina, you shouldn't touch that money! Mae will be angry with you. She will never forgive you. She told me that she has been saving money to pay Grandma's doctor bills but I didn't know where it was. Maybe it would be good for you to get a job. I would like to get a job too." Belinha smiled innocently at her sister.

"Belinha, you are annoying! Why would you need to get a job? You don't need to buy any dresses! You are too young anyway. You never understand anything! Just leave me alone!" Caterina turned away from Belinha and pushed her head into her pillow and let out a wail of frustration.

Belinha just shook her head and agreed that she never would understand her sister. She went out to the kitchen to find her mother. She would ask her if she could get a job and help out; maybe even buy Caterina her dresses so she wouldn't steal Mae's hidden stash of money. She didn't want her mother to be upset. She always did what she could to keep peace in the family.

Alycea was in the kitchen where she seemed to spend a lot of time lately cooking and cleaning. She was preparing their dinner, a roast chicken with all the fixings. Alycea had had a hankering for a good roast chicken dinner since she had such a miserable one at the diner two nights ago. She heard her younger daughter calling her name as she was stirring the rice and looked up to see the sweet face of Belinha.

"What is it, dear one? You look a little upset. Did Caterina give you some trouble again? I don't know what to do with that girl! She drives me to distraction!" Alycea started sputtering under her breath at the thought of another confrontation with Caterina.

"No Mae, she is the one that is upset. Can I get a job too like Caterina? I want to help you take care of Grandma's doctor bills and maybe help pay for Caterina's dresses. I don't like to see her this unhappy," she said with her little chin thrust upward without any hesitation.

"Oh my goodness, Belinha, you are always sweet, mia filha. You never cease to amaze me with your kind and unselfish nature. You are definitely more like your grandmother who is closer to sainthood than anyone I know. I only wish your sister was more like you. Life would be a lot easier for all of us and we would have more peace in this house."

Alycea closed her eyes and took a deep breath. She didn't want to cry in front of her daughter. Belinha was definitely a joy to behold and such a Godsend. She said a silent prayer that St. Theresa would watch over them all and help them through the tough times ahead.

Alycea found herself getting more emotional all the time about her mother. She worried about her health and whether she would lose her other leg. She could use all the help she could get if both her girls got jobs. She wouldn't have to work extra hours to afford the medicine and treatments for Filomena. She could also relieve Stan so he could get out once in a while. He was getting older and was not feeling well himself lately. She would have the doctor check him out next time he came to visit her mother. She realized that Belinha was talking to her and turned her attention back to her daughter.

"I am sorry, Belinha dear, I did not hear you. I guess I was daydreaming a little. What did you say, sweetheart?"

"Nothing really, Mae. I was wondering if I could go to the drugstore and see if Mr. Polito needs any help. I could sweep the floor and stock shelves for him." Her face was eager with anticipation as she watched her mother's reaction.

"Of course, Belinha, you can go see him. He may not let you do that since you are only fourteen. But I guess it wouldn't hurt to ask. Run along now. Don't be too long. Dinner will be ready in an hour." Alycea resumed her stirring of the rice and checked on the vegetables cooking on the back burner as the front door closed behind her.

Belinha ran all the way to the drugstore to inquire about a job. She was excited about the prospects of having a little spending money after she gave some of it to her mother. She could buy herself a book or the embroidery set that she had liked. She never would have imposed upon her mother to buy her anything that was not necessary.

*\*\**

Alycea felt blessed to have such a daughter as Belinha. She more than made up for having Caterina. She loved both of her daughters fiercely but had to admit that she always did favor Caterina since she was like herself. But because of the similarities between them they did tend to lock horns more.

Caterina was a spit fire. That's what Ed always called her. He had said she was just like his Alycea was when she was that age. These thoughts brought a smile to Alycea's face. She remembered the early days when Ed had moved into her mother's three-room first floor tenement. She found herself feeling a little thrill and was looking forward to seeing him come through the front door shortly.

The phone rang bringing her out of her reverie. It was Ed who seemed to be out of breath. "Alycea, honey, I have to work an extra hour to help the supervisor with the inventory. I should be home by 6:30. Okay dear? Don't wait for me to eat. I will warm up the leftovers when I get home."

"Ed, do you have to do this? I need to see you and talk to you. I had plans for us tonight after dinner. Do you want to know what I plan to do to you?" Her voice was husky with desire.

"Oh, Alycea, I will hurry through the inventory and be home as soon as possible, my love. Hold those thoughts. I want to hear all about your plans. I love you, darling." He clicked off before Alycea could say anything else.

Alycea sighed heavily and went back to checking the food and setting the table. This mundane job was supposed to be done by Caterina who was nowhere to be seen. Of course, she was probably still sulking in her room.

Belinha arrived at the drugstore and spoke to Mr. Polito and surprisingly, he hired her to sweep and clean up around the store. He knew she was only fourteen but told her not to tell anyone that he had hired her. She was to say she was just volunteering her time there to help him out. He would pay her under the table until she was sixteen then she could work there legally.

Mr. Polito liked Belinha and thought she was a lovely young lady, someone he could trust to do a good job. She was sweet, kind and thoughtful to others and people took to her easily. She was also quiet and not talkative like her obnoxious older sister. He didn't think he could stand having Caterina around the store. She would be too busy checking out all the male customers. He had seen her in his store doing just that recently.

His thoughts were interrupted by Belinha. "Mr. Polito, do you think you could use another helper? My sister, Caterina, needs to find a job too. She would be a good worker. She is smart besides being beautiful." Belinha's eyes widened and sparkled at him as she anticipated his positive response.

"Well, I don't think…I need another helper just yet. You will be enough for the time being." He saw the look of disappointment register in her big green eyes and hastily added, "Maybe a little later I will have a job for her too. Tell her to come see me and I will see what I can do. Okay, Belinha?" He hated to see her unhappy but at the same time didn't look forward to the prospect of having Caterina around causing distractions with his customers, especially the male ones.

"Oh thank you, Mr. Polito. I will tell Caterina to come see you as soon as possible. What time do you need me tomorrow? I get out of school at 3:00. I can come right over afterward. Is that okay?" Excitement was evident in her reaction to his favorable response. He felt some relief for the time being. Time would tell how this would all work out.

Mr. Polito sighed heavily, "Yes, Belinha, that is fine."

Belinha opened the door to their apartment loudly exclaiming, "Mae, I got a job, I got a job! Mr. Polito hired me to sweep up and clean the store. He told me not to tell anyone but I know I could tell you." Belinha was jumping up and down with excitement and running around in circles as her mother stood rooted to the spot, a surprised expression on her face as Belinha told her mother the good news.

"Mr. Polito said he would hire Caterina too. All she has to do is go to see him tomorrow. I am starting right after school tomorrow. I will be able to give you some money every week now, Mae, to help you out. Can I keep a little to buy a book or embroidery kit?"

"Of course, dear. You can keep some to buy whatever you like. I am really surprised though that Mr. Polito hired you this young. Did you force him into hiring your sister too?" Her brows were furrowed as she questioned her daughter.

"Oh no, Mae. He said he could use her too. He is such a nice man. I think I will like working there. I can also save up some money to pay for beauty school. I know you can't afford that with the doctors' bills for Grandma. I want to help you, Mae." Her innocent face was radiant as she looked at her mother.

"Belinha, I appreciate that you want to help, but I can manage. You should save all your money for school and anything extra that you might need. That would certainly help me not have to worry about these extra things. Okay, sweetheart? Now make sure that your school work does not suffer if you work every day after school. Promise me, Belinha. You are doing well in school now and I don't want to see that change. Okay?"

"Oh yes, Mae. I will work extra hard at school to keep up my grades. School is hard for me but if I work harder I will be able to keep up with my B's and C's. I have to go tell Caterina. She will be surprised that we will be working together." She happily ran off to tell her unsuspecting sister the news.

Alycea stood there looking aghast. She knew that Caterina would be horrified that her little sister had finagled a job for her in a drugstore, no less. She would soon hear the yelling and screaming coming from the bedroom as Belinha announced her 'good' news to Caterina.

"I will not work in a drugstore with you or anyone else! I don't need my baby sister taking care of me either. If I wanted to work I could find my own job and a better one than in a drugstore!" was the retort that was uttered by her stubborn sister. Belinha stood still and shocked as she looked at Caterina who was ranting and raving at her.

Alycea knew she would have to intervene sooner or later or Caterina may try to kill her sister. Well, not really kill her but she could never tell with Caterina what she would do.

Alycea went into the dark bedroom and all was now quiet except for the sobbing she could hear coming from both girls. She turned on the light and sat in the chair by the windows and waited for one of her daughters to acknowledge her presence.

Belinha was the first to go to her mother. Her green eyes were red and tear filled and her lower lip was quivering. Her eyes looked at Alycea with a sorrowful expression. She pressed her body into her mother's lap and hung on tightly to her legs.

Alycea just patted Belinha's head and smoothed her hair away from her tear-soaked face saying, "It will be all right. Don't worry, Belinha. I will talk to Caterina. Go out to the kitchen now and go get Grandma and Grandpa Stan and get them seated for dinner. We will be right out." She released herself from Belinha's grip. She got up from the chair and went over to the bed to sit beside Caterina who was visibly trembling from anger.

"Caterina, dear. You do not have to take this job if you do not want it. I think it would be a better idea if you found your own job. What do you think?" Alycea was trying to find a way to help Caterina keep face and do the right thing. She knew Caterina was upset that her younger sister took the initiative before she could go about finding a job.

"Mae, how dare she get me a job? I can find one myself. I don't need her help. She is a nuisance. She is always trying to help me but gets in my way. I am the older one and I can take care of myself," she said in a trembling voice as she looked up at her mother. Caterina's dark brown eyes were red and puffy from a lot of crying. She was embarrassed more about this whole thing than angry; Alycea could see it in her eyes. Caterina was angry and Alycea knew that Caterina was feeling out of control with her feelings and her position in the family as the older child. She wanted and needed to be in control at all times as her mother did.

Alycea knew that what Belinha had done was the catalyst for getting Caterina out to look for her own job. Belinha was unaware of what she had done and only wanted to help her sister. All would work out in the end, thought Alycea. She felt a rush of love for her daughters and wrapped her arms around her sobbing daughter while whispering in her ear, "Everything will be all right."

"Come on, Caterina. Get up and stop crying. You look quite a sight. You wouldn't want your father to see you like this. He will be home a little later. We are going to start dinner without him. Go wash your face and blow your nose and make yourself more presentable. You don't want to frighten your grandmother. She will think I beat you or something." Alycea patted Caterina on her behind as she got up from the squeaky bed.

As she left the room she could hear Caterina blowing her nose and sniffling as she stood in front of her mirror assessing her face. Alycea felt all would work out and that life could be good at times when everyone got along.

Alycea didn't know what was ahead when her daughters were a little older. Things were going to get more complicated than she ever imagined.

# CHAPTER 36

"Are you sure you heard correctly, Ed? Did he say that she had a gun? You can't be serious! Why would she want to bring a gun to church?" Alycea was getting herself ready for the wedding of her youngest daughter. She had gotten a call from her future son-in-law's family telling her the groom's mother was extremely upset about her son's impending wedding and had threatened to harm Belinha.

Belinha was unaware of what was happening or could happen on her wedding day. Alycea did not want to upset the bride or cause any chaos with the guests. She vowed to handle this situation by talking to the groom, Jaco Gomes.

Alycea couldn't believe that her younger daughter was getting married. Belinha had met Jaco before he had gone overseas to serve in the Marines. They had kept in touch by writing to one another faithfully for four years. She had asked them to wait another year after Belinha had finished beauty school before they got married. By that time Belinha was nineteen and Jaco was twenty-one. Alycea had wanted to make sure they still felt the same way about one another after a year. This time they spent together would help them get to know one another better too. Alycea did not want her daughter to make a mistake and marry the wrong man. The year has also given them time to save some money to get an apartment after they got married.

Alycea went to see how Belinha was doing and if she needed any help from her. When she opened the door to her daughters' room she saw a vision standing in front of the mirror all in white. Next to Belinha were her sister, Caterina, who was her maid of honor and Mary Castina, Belinha's best friend from grade school, hovering around the bride. They were helping Belinha put on her veil and pinning flowers in her hair.

Alycea had never seen her daughter looking more beautiful and radiant with happiness. She was deeply in love with Jaco who was not only handsome but kind and loving toward Belinha. He truly loved her too. This made Alycea pleased to know that her daughter had made such a good choice. Alycea had never felt she had made a choice on her own but was forced into her marriage. She did love Ed now but at the time she wasn't sure. She was too young to know what was right for her. She felt as if she was raped when she was fourteen years old, a mere child. She really did not know about being with a man. Ed had to teach her how to make love. She was fortunate that he had married her after he knew she was pregnant. He did love her, but looking back, it had all been quite traumatic for her. She had lost her childhood.

She was lost in her thoughts when she suddenly was aware that Belinha was talking to her. She smiled as she walked into the room and went directly to her daughter to kiss her on each cheek and hold her lightly as not to wrinkle her gown.

Belinha looked beautiful and Alycea told her daughter, "Belinha you are a vision and you look radiantly happy. I hope you and Jaco have a wonderful life together. I am sure you will be content. I came in to see if you needed any help but it looks like your attendants have taken good care of you. I will be downstairs waiting for you. Your father wants to stop in to see you. He is waiting outside the door. I told him to let me check first to see if you were decent."

"Oh Mae, I am blissful! I thought this day would never come and I would never find such a wonderful man as Jaco. Thank you for this beautiful gown. I know it cost you a lot of money. I wish you would let me help you. I have saved up some money from my hairdressing that I could give you."

"Of course not, dear. You will need that money to help you and Jaco get settled. You will need to find a place of your own. You will have to set up housekeeping and there are a hundred things that you will need to do that. Now, don't worry your pretty head over anything. Enjoy your special day and let me take care of everything. Okay, sweetheart? Your job today is to look beautiful for Jaco. Now I will let your father in or he will be breaking down the door. He is anxious to see his daughter to wish her well."

Alycea took one more look at her daughter, feeling such emotion welling up inside her as she opened the door for her husband. She stepped aside to allow him to spend some time with Belinha.

"Pai, you look dashing in your suit! The dark brown suit definitely brings out the green in your eyes." She smiled brilliantly at her father as he took her hands in his. She could feel the tremble in his touch.

"My sweetheart, you look lovely, so lovely that you bring tears to my eyes," he said with a choking feeling. He felt as if he would break down with tears of joy just looking at her. He was losing his daughter to another man. He had a hard time with that. He loved her more than he could express. She had always been a joy in his life. He prayed that Jaco would love her and appreciate her special qualities, her kindness and unselfish nature. She was definitely one of a kind. He worried that she could be hurt easily too.

Ed kissed her on both cheeks and hugged her, being careful not to knock her veil off her head. She kissed her father and chuckled at his ineptness as he was trying to avoid messing up her makeup or hair as he held her closely.

"Well Pai, are you ready to take this walk down the aisle with me? I need your strong arm to hold onto. I am a little nervous and don't want to stumble or trip on my train. Will you help me?" She smiled at her father sensing that he was anxious. She was fine and not nervous at all and just wanted him to be relaxed too.

While the bride was preparing to go in the limousine with her father and her attendants, strange events were unfolding unbeknownst to her. These events were keeping her mother busy at the church.

# CHAPTER 37

"Avoa, I'm sorry to interrupt your thought, but you look tired. We can continue with this on another day. Why don't I come over to see you in a few days and you can tell me more about my mother and father's wedding. I would love to hear all about it." Jasmine patted her grandmother's hand as she got up from her seat. She looked over to see her aunt heading their way.

"Auntie is coming over to check up on you again, Avoa. She doesn't look too happy either. I will go talk to her and calm her down before she gives you heck again. Ok?" Jasmine winked at her grandmother and walked over to meet Aunt Caterina.

Aunt Caterina announced, "Jasmine, I think my mother needs to rest now. You have been keeping her busy talking up a storm. She is 100 years old, you know, and can't extend herself too much. She gets tired." Caterina seemed to be disturbed about something more than just her mother's health. There was something else bugging her, Jasmine thought to herself. It was not like her aunt to be impatient with her. She had always been kind and attentive. Oh well, she would just give her some space.

Jasmine hugged her aunt and kissed her on her cheek and said, "I will see you again soon, I'm sure." She excused herself and went back to her grandmother to kiss her and thank her for sharing her life thus far. She told her, "I look forward to meeting in a few days, Avoa." She set up the time before she went back to her husband,

Giovanni. He and the rest of the family looked like they were just about ready to leave the celebration.

"Well, you must have gotten a lot of information from Avoa by now. You two had your heads together for quite a long time. No one else could go over and talk to Avoa. You really hogged her through the whole party. Just what were you two talking about so avidly?" Giovanni asked, curiosity getting the better of him.

"Oh, honey, she was just giving me some background on her life. I hope one day to tell her life's story in a way. Maybe I'll put it into a novel based loosely on her interesting life." Jasmine gave her husband a playful peck on the lips which brought a smile to his handsome face.

"Well, I think your Aunt Caterina was a little upset with you too for hogging Avoa. Maybe it was a little jealousy on the part of the other grandchildren who did not get a chance to spend some time with Avoa also. Aunt Caterina's kids were angry that you had all Avoa's attention, I guess. Families can be such a pain sometimes, huh, honey?" Jasmine's husband said. Giovanni was funny at times. He wasn't always this observant, so his recent revelation surprised her.

Jasmine took his arm and they walked out of the hall. All this talk about love and things with her grandmother had put her in a mood that she knew Giovanni would certainly enjoy.

*** 

Jasmine couldn't stop thinking about everything that her grandmother had told her. It was too much to absorb. She was a little surprised at all the sexual things that her grandmother had shared with her too. But nothing about Avoa would surprise her after this. She certainly was an unforgettable character.

A few days later Jasmine looked forward to meeting with Avoa as she headed over to her apartment in the west end of Dracut not far from the local farms and open land which was down the street from her house.

Jasmine and Giovanni had spent a lovely night after Avoa's party. They both had Avoa to thank for that. Avoa had made Jasmine appreciate everything that she had, especially her loving and wonderful husband, Giovanni.

As she pulled into the driveway she saw her grandmother at the door waiting for her with a big smile and an even bigger wave.

Jasmine couldn't help but laugh at the sight of her grandmother's exuberant expression on her still not too lined 100-year old face. Avoa always brought a smile to Jasmine's face too.

"Come in, dear child. Come in. We have plenty to talk about. I am not getting any younger and I have much more to tell you. Hurry up, dear one," Avoa said this as she shuffled along as quickly as she could into her sitting room and settled down in her favorite rocking chair. Jasmine pulled a straight backed kitchen chair next to her and sat down.

"Avoa, can I make you a cup of coffee or tea before you begin? I think I could go for a tea myself. I brought you some Portuguese biscoitos."

"Yes, I would love a cup of coffee and one of your delicious cookies. It's nice to see that you continue with the recipes I gave you. Your cousin, Katrina, just left a thermos of coffee which should still be fairly hot. Get yourself a cup of tea then please sit down and relax with me," she said with a sweet conspiratorial smile showing that she couldn't wait to continue sharing her life's experiences. She also was enjoying the surprised and shocked expressions on her granddaughter's face from some of the things she shared about her life.

Jasmine got up and put the kettle on to make the tea for herself and then poured a cup of coffee from the thermos that had been brought over to her grandmother by one of her cousins just before she arrived for a visit.

The kettle whistled and Jasmine prepared her tea and brought it back with her as she sat down next to her grandmother who was noisily sipping her coffee. Jasmine placed a small plate of biscoitos in front of her grandmother.

Avoa's eyes sparkled as she began again to travel back in time reliving the memories that gave her more joy and that seemed more real than present time to her now.

\*\*\*

"Father Silverio, can we get some help here?" Rosa Freitas was scurrying around the church placing the white ribbons at the end of each pew.

Father Silverio bent over to pick up some of the silky white ribbons and attached them on the opposite side of the aisle as Rosa had instructed. She was a big help to Father Silverio since she was his housekeeper and cleaned not only his apartment but the church as well. She washed and ironed all the embroidered pieces that were used on the altar. Father Silverio wouldn't know what to do without her. But she was a bossy woman much like his mother had been. He let out a big sigh as he attached another ribbon to the next pew.

Rosa Freitas had become a good friend to Filomena when she met her on the boat as she came to America from Madeira. Her husband had fallen off the boat and had drowned. She had found this position in the church working with the previous priest and had stayed on with Father Silverio. She was getting older now but still had a lot of energy and never lost her dictatorial skills, much to all the priests' dismay. This had become her life and kept her busy and feeling productive and needed.

"Rosa, the church looks perfect! Thank you for all your hard work," Father Silverio said.

"You too, Father. You know I love doing this."

"Of course, Rosa. I know and I'm glad to help." Father Silverio nodded to Rosa and gave Alycea a big smile of gratitude when she walked up to him. He quickly slipped away before Rosa had him doing another chore. He needed to prepare for the wedding mass anyway.

Rosa, looked up to see Alycea walking toward her. "Alycea, how are you, dear? Is your mother here yet? How is she doing? I worry all the time about her. Do you like the ribbons? I pressed each one after making the bows. I wanted everything to be perfect for your lovely daughter." Rosa was exhausting to listen or talk to; she never took a breath between her questions.

"Yes, my mother is here already. Stan is helping her out of the car and will be bringing her in to sit in the front pew. She cannot make the long walk down the aisle by herself. I wanted him to get her situated first. Then I can take care of all the other details before Belinha gets here. Have you seen the groom yet?"

"Yes, he is downstairs getting ready with his best man and another attendant. He looks handsome. He is quite the dashing fellow, if you ask me. Where did she meet him? She is a one lucky young lady. I wish her well in her life. I am sure she will be happy. Oh, here is your mother now. Excuse me, dear. I want to go see her. It has been too long since we have seen each other. I am sure we will have lots to talk about."

Rosa rushed down the aisle to meet Filomena who was nearly being carried in by Stan. She was fighting him all the way for fear that he would injure his back trying to carry her.

Upon looking up Filomena saw Rosa Freitas hurrying toward them. She raised her hand in greeting and leaned against Stan for support before she put out her arms to hug Rosa. Filomena was happy to see that Rosa was looking well and keeping busy with the church. She knew this was the best place for Rosa to utilize all her energy and talents. She was a great housekeeper and organizer. Rosa, though, had never remarried after she came to America.

Alycea watched as Rosa hugged her mother, nearly knocking her off balance in her exuberance. Her mother was smiling her sweet smile as she listened to Rosa go on and on about herself. She didn't know how her mother could stand to just listen so patiently to people like that. Alycea knew she was not the patient type and could only put up with so much chattering from Rosa. She was glad that her mother was now the recipient of Rosa's attention.

There was suddenly a ruckus outside the church. Alycea ran past her mother, Stan and Rosa to find out what it was. She yelled out to Stan to get her mother situated and out of the way. She feared that something was happening out there and it had to do with a disgruntled mother of the groom.

Rosa ran after Alycea to see what was going on. She was right behind Alycea when the first gunshot went off which hit Alycea in her left shoulder. Rosa was hit with the second shot right between the eyes. She never knew what hit her. She was dead before her body fell to the floor.

It was soon all chaos as people who were entering the church were rushing back and forth. Father Silverio came running out of the sacristy to help the wounded. He took one look at Rosa and realized that he was too late to administer last rites. She looked peaceful since she never knew what had hit her. He closed Rosa's eyes and went to the phone to call for a hearse for her and an ambulance for the more fortunate who were just wounded.

Outside the church, Maria Gomes had been standing with her three other sons and two daughters waiting for her husband to help her up the stairs into the church. She had worn a strange look on her face, a mixture of sadness and depression. This was a dark day for her. She did not want her youngest son to marry this woman who she had just met a couple of months ago.

Maria Gomes was a disturbed woman and had been depressed for a long time. Her husband, Bento Gomes, tried his best to care for her. The children, as they grew older, did what they could to assist him. Bento had taken to drinking to try to forget and deal with his wife's depression. The drink though, only made him more depressed and dependent on another drink to keep him going.

It had all happened quickly. One minute Bento was closing the door of the car and walking toward his wife when he noticed she had a gun in her hand. She was aiming it at the doorway to the church where the bride was standing with her father. They had just arrived and had walked up the stairs to stand at the back of the church in the shadows to keep anyone from seeing them until the music began.

Belinha had noticed some of Jaco's family coming up the stairs behind her and moved aside so that they could get by her to find seats in the pews.

Belinha had met Jaco's three brothers and two sisters and liked them all. She also had met his parents and loved his father but was not too sure about his mother. She had felt uncomfortable with Mrs. Gomes because she had just stared at Belinha not saying anything for the longest time when they first met. Mrs. Gomes only took Belinha's hand and shook it when Belinha offered it to her and said, "Hello."

Belinha had replied, "It is lovely to meet you, Mrs. Gomes."

Belinha had looked over her shoulder and saw Jaco's mother staring at her with a blank expression in her eyes. It was a little disturbing and Belinha felt the hair on her arms and the back of her neck quiver and rise up. It was not a good feeling and she sensed that she should get out of the way and not say anything to her future mother-in-law in case she was in a bad mood. By the look on her face, Mrs. Gomes did not look like she was in the mood to make small talk.

As it turned out, Belinha's premonition saved her life because she got out of the way just in time. Maria Gomes was aiming at her future daughter-in-law, and had pulled the trigger barely missing Belinha. She pulled it multiple times when she realized she had missed her target but then had hit Alycea in the shoulder and Rosa point blank and a few other guests had suffered flesh wounds from the stray bullets.

Ed and Stan grabbed embroidered doilies off of the altar to staunch the flow of blood on Alycea's shoulder until the ambulance could arrive. Alycea was not going to let this stop her daughter's wedding. She called out to Father Silverio to get the show on the road. He signaled to the organist to start the wedding march. All the guests, some limping and holding their minor wounds, got seated for the wedding to begin.

Belinha was horrified that her mother had been shot and didn't want to continue with the ceremony. Belinha was crying softly now and her father was holding her and trying to calm her down. Ed took his daughter's arm and slipped it through his own and started walking down the aisle.

Jaco was standing at the front of the church next to his best man, his eldest brother, Erico, and Father Silverio. Jaco looked visibly shaken and his face was white but he looked handsome just the same. He looked at his bride and was grateful that she was not injured but was worried about Alycea's injury.

Jaco couldn't believe what his mother had done. The police were on their way over to pick up his mother. She would surely go to an asylum or possibly prison he imagined. His father and brothers had taken the gun out of his mother's hand before she could shoot anyone else and wrestled her to the ground to hold her there to calm her down.

Jaco's two brothers and father were outside church as they heard the music start. Their mother was trying to get up when she heard the music. She was still intent on stopping this wedding at whatever cost to herself and her family.

Bento stayed with his wife until the police arrived and then went to the station with her for support. Bento had instructed his sons to stay with the wedding party and that he would call them if he needed them at the police station. He knew it would be a long day and night for his wife and him. Once his sons gave their statements to the police, it was not necessary for them to go with their father. Bento would call his lawyer when he arrived at the police station and his sons would meet their father at the station after the wedding ceremony was over. Bento wanted them to stay to support their brother, Jaco, and also to get their families home safely after the wedding.

Bento was horrified at what Maria had just done. Bento couldn't believe that she would resort to something like this at their son's wedding. This was supposed to be a happy occasion for the family. How could Maria do this? How will their son ever forgive her? Bento was beyond distraught. He now knew how sick Maria really was.

As the door was closing to the police car, Bento could hear the organ music ending and felt relieved that his son would get married this day after all. It would always be a sad day for his family but at least Jaco would be married to the woman he loved.

Maria Gomes was not in a sane frame of mind, and never would be. She would spend the rest of her life in an asylum and her husband would eventually drink himself to death.

Jaco would be scarred for life from this tragedy along with his siblings. He would try to make it up to his bride for all the hardship his mother had caused them on their special day. He only hoped that his mother-in-law would not blame him for his mother's tragic mistake.

***

Alycea survived the gunshot wound to her left shoulder which narrowly missed her heart as it had passed through her body. The doctors told her she was extremely lucky. If the bullet had been a few inches lower she would not be here today. The doctors said she would recover full use of her shoulder and arm but would be plagued with pain off and on for years afterward as a reminder of that fateful day.

Alycea was relieved that the wedding went on in spite of all the chaos and she had refused to go in the ambulance until the ceremony was over and she saw her daughter married. Fearing she would die, Father Silverio moved the ceremony along speedily skipping the mass.

Alycea had missed the reception at the hall but it seemed that a few other people who had gone to the hospital to treat their injuries had missed it also.

She would have to make this up to them in some way and have another reception for them later on after things settled down. The couple had gone to Niagara Falls, New York for their brief honeymoon. Alycea had insisted that they take a full week but they returned in a few days still too shaken about everything that had happened. Belinha was concerned about her mother's injury and wanted to be close by in case her mother had needed her.

Alycea was angry with Maria Gomes but at the same time felt sorry for her. Maria had killed Rosa Freitas and nearly killed her. She had wounded a few other guests who would recover but this woman had taken away her daughter's happiness on her wedding day. It was supposed to be a special day for a bride and groom and now it was forever tainted by this tragic shooting by the mother-in-law.

Maria Gomes had also destroyed her own family. Maria was evaluated and it was determined that she was insane. Bento Gomes continued to drink to forget his troubles. He had died within a few months after seeing his wife go into the insane asylum. He was not an old man but he looked older than his fifty-seven years when Alycea saw him in the casket the day of his wake.

Alycea expressed her deep sympathy to the Gomes' family and told them to keep in touch with her. She wanted to help them in any way she could. She had watched the distraught faces of Jaco and his siblings as they prayed by their father's casket at the gravesite. She held Jaco as he cried that day holding onto his wife, Belinha's, hand for both support and courage. He was profoundly affected by this tragedy and would always be extra careful with his own family, treating them like they were precious objects that would break.

It was tragic for them to lose both parents this close together; their mother to the asylum and their father in death. The Gomes' siblings had ostracized themselves from their mother blaming her for killing their father. They could not forgive her and never went to see her in the asylum. She would die alone many years later an old woman; oblivious to any of the suffering she had caused her family. They would see her only after she died and was laid out in her casket.

# CHAPTER 38

Life went on for Alycea and Ed calmly and uneventfully considering what had transpired in the past few months. The wedding was more than memorable for everyone but in a tragic way. They needed some peace and quiet in their lives for a while.

Just when they were getting back on their feet financially and physically, Caterina delivered a whammy. She had come home from her job at the plant where she had obtained a job due to Stan's and Ed's influence as a material handler as her mother had done. Alycea was now the manager of her department and Caterina worked under her, which was a challenge in itself to keep her daughter in line not only at home but now at work.

Caterina had announced in her usual inimitable way that she and Dean were getting married within a month's time. Alycea and Ed just looked at each other and couldn't say a word. They were shocked and speechless. How could she even think that her parents could afford another wedding so soon or even have the strength to endure another one?

They had met Dean's parents, Rose and Rolando Cortelino. They were both wonderful, warm people but was Caterina ready to start a family and think of others and not just herself? They surely hoped so.

They had watched her grow up to be a bright, beautiful, and talented young woman. She sang with her father's band at the club on Fridays and traveled to other cities and towns to sing at other clubs. She was beginning to make a name for herself.

Well, they had given their blessing and started making plans for the wedding and reception at the church and hall. Father Silverio was there and looked at them with a wary eye. He welcomed Alycea and Ed and inquired about Alycea's shoulder and how her mother was doing.

Alycea told him, "We are both doing as well as can be expected. Father. We came here today to hopefully book the church for a month away on the last Saturday of July for the wedding of my older daughter, Caterina."

"Ah, I see."

"How are you doing, Father?"

He smiled and nodded. "Fine as can be expected without…" he choked up and couldn't finish.

"Yes, I understand, Father. Rosa was a wonderful woman," Alycea said in response.

Father Silverio hadn't gotten over losing Rosa. He had missed her formidable manner and preciseness and had still not found a suitable replacement for her to clean his house or the church. Mrs. McCarty was the most recent woman to take over booking the hall. She couldn't handle much else though.

Rosa had become like a mother to Father Silverio and he mourned her in the way a son would mourn his mother. She had been a kind woman who had tragically been in the wrong place at the wrong time. He prayed for her soul and was sure she was in Heaven with the Lord.

It was hard to think about Belinha's day back in April when Alycea thought of what she had to do next for the preparations for Caterina's day. She and Ed had discussed everything beforehand and she had tried to allay his fears. "Somehow, we will get through this, Ed. Don't worry. I will take care of all the plans. Caterina will do her share too," she said to her husband who did not look too happy about the whole marriage thing. He felt jinxed and was worried about something else happening to them. Alycea assured him that he was just being silly and superstitious and that everything would go smoothly as planned.

Father Silverio smiled and nodded to them both. "Yes, let me look in my book and see what we have for July that is open. Ahh yes, the last Saturday of July is open. Let me put it down right away. What is the name of the groom?"

Alycea told him, "Dean Cortelino. You may know of his family or of him. He plays football and has been in the newspaper for making records as a quarterback, Caterina has told us. We don't follow football or any other sport for that matter. Do you, Father?"

"Ahh yes, I do remember seeing an article about him in the paper. Yes, he is quite the player and a strong, strapping, good-looking young man. Your Caterina has chosen well. The family is a good, Catholic family. They don't attend church here but go to a church in the next town. I met a priest at a conference from that church recently and he did mention he had a football star who attended his parish. It is a small world, isn't it?"

"Yes, Father. I guess it is."

"Well, I think we are all set for the day. I am sure you have a lot more plans to attend to. Do you want to book the church hall again,

Alycea? If you do, then go over to the hall and see Mrs. McCarty. She will take care of you. It was good to see you both in good health. May God bless both of you and Caterina and her fiancé on their wedding day. Good day."

"Good day to you too, Father. Thank you. We will see you on Sunday for services." They left the church and walked next door to the church function hall to book the date in July with Mrs. McCarty, Rosa's latest not quite replacement.

*** 

Everything was in order on the day of Caterina's wedding. Alycea knew she had taken special care to make sure that Caterina's day would be perfect. It made Alycea feel guilty about Belinha's wedding day. She had done everything right that day too, and look what happened! It turned out to be a disaster and utter chaos!

Well, Alycea knew that she couldn't control everything but she would certainly try to ensure this day was uneventful and a happy memory for all.

Alycea had checked in with Caterina to see how she was doing getting into her wedding gown. She was in good hands with her sister, who was her matron of honor by her side. She looked beautiful and elegant in her white gown with the lace and beads at the bottom of the hem and covering the bodice. She had a white crown of flowers pinned to her dark hair with an extra-long veil reaching below her waist. She looked like a fairy princess.

Alycea waved and threw a kiss to her daughter as she left the room to find Ed. She wanted him to see their daughter and wish her well as he had done with Belinha. She knew that Caterina would notice if he didn't take the time to see her before their walk down the aisle.

"Ed, Caterina is almost ready. Please go see her and wish her well, my dear. I know you had planned to do just that and I don't mean to rush you but it is almost time for us all to go to the church. Are you all right? You look a little pale and sweaty." Alycea reached over to feel her husband's forehead.

"I'm fine, Alycea."

"You don't feel like you have a temperature. Are you feeling sick?" Her voice showed her concern if her face did not.

Alycea knew that he was nervous about the wedding. There had been no indication that anything would go wrong but there was none at the time of Belinha's either. Only Alycea had a premonition that something was going to happen. She had never told Ed that she had woken up that morning with a strange tingling at the base of her neck and a funny feeling in her stomach. This morning she was feeling fine, no odd sensations or feelings of any kind. She felt that it would be a good day.

"I'm fine Alycea, don't fuss over me. I was just on my way up to see Caterina. Just make sure you have the checks with you for the priest, the hall and the caterer. I will take care to get Caterina to the limousine and to the church on time. He turned abruptly and walked upstairs to his daughter's room.

They had moved to a second floor tenement apartment in Lowell, Massachusetts, while Belinha had moved to the downstairs apartment. Caterina and Dean were going to live with Dean's parents for the time being until they could find a place of their own.

It was a big change for Ed and Alycea after living in New Bondford for many years as the girls were growing up. They moved because there had been many layoffs at the plant where Ed and Stan had worked. They had heard that there were positions available in Massachusetts at the Lowell Mills.

Ed and Stan had spent some time downstairs in Belinha's apartment visiting and playing cards with Ed's new son-in-law, Jaco, and sometimes Dean would join them. At times they would go out for a beer at the club just to have some sanity while Ed's wife and daughters were planning the wedding. The women had more fights over what should be done or not done and how. There was just so much a man could take living with three women. Ed was amazed that he had survived this long. He really liked Belinha's husband. Jaco was an easy going, really good guy. Ed hoped that he would get along as well with Caterina's husband.

Dean was a lot different. He was a rough and tumble kind of guy who was into sports having played football in high school and boxing in local arenas. Ed was not into sports unless you call bowling a sport. He loved to bowl or watch others bowl at the local bowling alley. Ed would do his best to get along with Dean and even invited him to the club for a beer or to the bowling alley to bowl a few a couple of nights.

Ed reached Caterina's room and opened the door to see his daughter standing in front of the mirror much like the day he saw Belinha on her wedding day. Caterina was as lovely as her sister had been but in a darker more exotic way. Her dark hair framed her face and set off the stark white of her crown of white roses and long veil. He felt himself taking a deep breath and holding it just to look at her in all her glory.

Caterina ran over to her father hugging him tightly, excitement radiating all over her face as she exclaimed, "Pai, I am incredibly happy today. Do I look beautiful? You look handsome in your suit. Did you see Dean yet?" She stepped back to the mirror for one last check of her hair and dress to make sure they were perfect. Belinha was watching from the sidelines as her sister hugged and gushed all over their father.

Belinha knew that she was her father's favorite but wanted him to show Caterina some attention on her special day. Well, he was doing a good job, she thought. He hadn't even looked at me yet, she fretted. Just as this thought came into her head she squashed it feeling guilty. After all, this was Caterina's day, not hers. Hers had been a disaster but it was not her family's fault. If only Mrs. Gomes hadn't....She shook her head to clear those memories away and looked back at her sister doing her last minute check of herself in the mirror. Caterina definitely was stunning and Dean would be thrilled when he saw her.

Belinha reached out to her sister to give her a tentative, careful hug so as not to mess up her hair or dress. She said in a loving tone, "Caterina, you look beautiful! You make a stunning bride. Your day will be absolutely perfect in every way. Look at the weather – it couldn't be better – sunshine and in the 80's. I am happy for you. Are you ready? We should be going down to the limo now. Pai, are you ready too?"

Caterina took her father's arm and walked out the door to begin her new life with her sister in tow holding up Caterina's long train. As they reached the limo, Ed helped Caterina in first and then turned to Belinha and gave her a kiss on each cheek and hugged her fiercely to show her that he hadn't forgotten her. He had noticed her sad little face as he had told Caterina how beautiful she had looked. He had whispered in her ear that she was looking quite lovely herself for a matron of honor and that Jaco was a lucky man to have her.

Belinha just beamed at her father and returned his hugs and kisses before bending her head and getting into the limo with his assistance.

The wedding went well as did the reception and the rest of the day. The couple went on their honeymoon to New York City to see the sights, that is, if they ever got out of their hotel room over the next five days and nights.

# CHAPTER 39

"Would you please soften that radio, Ed? I can't stand that program one minute more! I have a splitting migraine and I feel sick to my stomach. Can you get me a cloth with some ice to put on my head and some aspirin? I'm going to lie down in the bedroom."

Alycea felt awful. She had been having these migraines for the past several months and they only seemed to increase in frequency, duration and intensity. She felt as if her head would explode. Her vision had been fuzzy and she had intermittent blind spots. She knew Ed was getting tired of her complaints but she didn't know what to do. She just lay in bed and moaned her way through each headache.

Ed finally came in to give her the cloth with ice and asked her, "Alycea, I'm sorry you're not feeling well. Can I get you something to eat or drink? Maybe a cup of tea would make you feel better." He was feeling guilty that he had been avoiding her. He couldn't take her temperaments. She would fly off the handle at any little thing that he did. He thought it best to stay as far away from her as possible. It was safer.

"No, I feel too sick to eat, Ed. You will have to make your own dinner again tonight. Thank you for the ice. Can you put it on my head please? I'm sorry that I'm grumpy and irrational about everything. I just can't think straight with all this pain. Did you bring me some aspirin?" She looked at his empty hands.

"Oh, my love, I'm sorry, I forgot. I'll get some for you right away."
He came back in a flash with a glass of water and two aspirin and
handed them to her and waited as she drank all the water and handed
the glass back to him. He took it and excused himself as quickly as
possible saying, "I will leave you alone. That way you can get some
rest and feel better. I will take care of my own dinner and then go
downstairs to visit with Belinha and Jaco. Ok? If you need me you
know where to find me, Alycea." He closed the door softly, not to
disturb her.

The whole apartment had become deathly quiet after Ed had closed
the door and gone down to their daughter's apartment. The radio had
been turned off and all she could hear was the steady drip of the
kitchen faucet. Alycea turned over and moaned as another pain shot
through her head starting at the front and going down the back of
her head to the base of her neck. She shifted the ice pack to her neck
and moaned once more.

Her mother and Stan had gone out for a stroll or more like a hobble
and then stop-to-rest kind of walk. Filomena had insisted that she
needed some air. She was feeling cooped up and wanted to get up
and move around. Stan helped her with her crutch on one side and
his shoulder for her to lean on for the other side. They took the walk
leisurely. The hardest part was going down the stairs to get to the
sidewalk.

Alycea knew her mother was an amazing person in many ways. She
accepted her disability without questioning the Lord. She prayed
constantly to St. Theresa for everyone else but never prayed to curb
her own suffering. Alycea couldn't stand any pain and would not
have had any patience to deal with losing a limb as her mother had.

She had a tough time dealing with a headache. She had been having
more and more migraines and was getting a little worried that
something may be seriously wrong with her.

***

"Hi Pai, what's up? You look fatigued. Are you okay?" Belinha greeted her father with her usual bright smile just for him. She noticed that he was not looking well, very tired and strained around the eyes.

She wondered what her mother was up to now. She knew her mother was tough on him at times and always demanding. Poor Pai, he seemed to be coming down to visit a lot since they had moved there evidently just to get some peace and quiet away from his wife, she thought to herself.

There was going to be a lot of moving around which Pai did not know about yet. I guess Mae decided not to tell him because he seemed to get too nervous about change.

Belinha didn't look forward to telling her dad that they were going to be moving out to let Caterina and her husband, Dean, move in. Caterina had been living with Dean's family and wanted to have a place of their own.She was pregnant also and had convinced her mother to move downstairs to the first floor apartment so it wouldn't be as difficult for Grandma to get outside. She and Dean would move upstairs, in other words, just swap apartments.

The second floor apartment was a little bigger with three bedrooms, while the first floor had two bedrooms. Caterina wanted to have the extra room because they had planned to have a big family.

Jaco had found another first floor apartment around the corner with three bedrooms and wanted to have a little more privacy from the rest of the family. At times he felt like they were smothering him. Anyway, he and Belinha would soon need more room with a baby on the way too. Things would work out well for everyone this way without any hard feelings. He planned to move soon.

"Hi my lovely daughter, how are you today?" Ed said in his usual sweet way. He dearly loved his daughter, Belinha, and treasured spending time with her. He enjoyed playing cards with his son-in-law but found him quiet at times. Maybe he was spending too much time in their apartment. Jaco may not enjoy his company quite as much as he did.

"Pai, it's always good to see you. Would you like a cup of coffee and Danish or something else? I don't want to spoil your dinner. Mae might get upset with me." Belinha was always afraid to get her mother's ire up. Sometimes she still felt like a child around her mother, afraid of doing something wrong that would displease her.

"I would love a cup of coffee and Danish. Your mother has a migraine again and is lying down. She said I have to make my own supper anyway." He rolled his eyes and snorted his discontent about having to cook for himself. He was not adept at it and usually burned the pan just boiling water.

"Oh Pai, you are going to stay for dinner here. I am making Italian tonight, spaghetti and meatballs. How's that sound?" she said with a chuckle knowing that he would be happy to eat whatever she cooked.

"Are you kidding? Of course, I would love to eat dinner with you. You know I can't cook at all. I would probably have had to make toast and tea tonight for dinner and probably burn the toast. I love your tomato sauce. It's delicious! You are a good cook like your mother." He smiled his satisfaction and relief that he didn't have to fend for himself another night. Alycea usually had a migraine for two or three nights in a row. He was starting to lose some weight from not eating enough.

Jaco looked over at his wife with an exasperated expression on his face. Belinha could tell that he wasn't exactly thrilled to have her father for the evening. He could take him in small doses. Living downstairs from him made them too accessible to Ed. He had been coming down to visit them almost every night this week. They never seemed to have any time to themselves. The move to the new apartment couldn't come soon enough.

Belinha just smiled at her husband and shrugged her shoulders as if to say, 'Please understand, sweetheart, just this once.'

Jaco smiled back at her and couldn't refuse whatever she wanted. He would grin and bear it. After all Ed was really a nice man and he never won at cards. He always left all his money on the table and went upstairs a little lighter in the change department. Luckily for Ed they only played for pennies.

***

Alycea lay as still as she could because every movement was sheer agony for her. She listened for the door to open but Ed had not come back yet. It had been a few hours. He must be having dinner with them. She thought impatiently.

He could be exasperating and helpless. He couldn't even boil water. She would have to teach him a few things in the kitchen so he could survive especially since Belinha and Jaco would be moving around the corner to get away from them and have some time to themselves. She knew this fact even though they did not admit it to her.

Having Caterina downstairs instead of Belinha would be fine for Alycea. She could visit with her daughter and chat over coffee and pastries but Ed would be upset. He wouldn't visit with Belinha and Jaco if they were not in the same house unless they invited him. He would sense what the real reason was they moved away. He would probably be hurt by it too. Well, she wouldn't worry about that right now. She just wanted this pain to go away.

She tried to swing her legs out over the edge of the bed but nearly passed out from the pain and nauseated feeling she got. What was she going to do? She had to call Belinha and ask her to send Ed up to help. She needed to get the doctor to come. Maybe there was something stronger than aspirin to lessen the pain in her head.

Alycea struggled between the sharp daggers of pain and managed to sit up but couldn't get her equilibrium. She felt unsteady as she reached for the phone on the end table by her bed. Thank God Ed had put one there. She had fought him about it, saying that she didn't need it. Now she definitely did.

She put her finger into each hole, dialed the numbers painstakingly slow, held the handle to her ear and waited for the ringing.

Alycea heard Belinha's voice on the other end as she said, "Hello, who is this? Is there anyone there?" Belinha was about to hang up when she heard a groan.

"Mae, is that you? Oh my God, you sound terrible. I will be right up to help you. Do you want me to send Pai too?" She turned to her father and told him to go upstairs to help her mother and she would be right behind him.

"Yes...send him...I have so much...pain. Hurry!" The phone went dead as Belinha cried out to her father. "Pai, it's Mae. She needs you. Hurry!" Belinha said as she dropped the phone and ran out the door taking the stairs two at a time on the heels of her father who had never moved that fast in his life.

Ed opened the door quickly and ran into the bedroom and found his wife on the floor with the phone beside her. She was unconscious and her mouth was slack and her face was covered in vomit. He went to get a wet cloth to wash off her face as Belinha came running into the room. She let out a soft cry as she saw her mother on the floor.

Belinha went over to her mother and felt her head which was clammy and warm. She took the wet cloth from her father when he returned to the room and cleaned up her mother's face.

Ed picked Alycea up and put her back into bed smoothing her damp hair out of her face. She could drive him crazy at times but he did love her with all his heart. He felt his hands shaking as he pulled the covers over her and tucked them under her arms. As he did this Alycea moaned and opened her eyes to see both of them standing over her with worried expressions.

"Oh, what happened? I must have fallen out of bed when I was on the phone. I felt extremely dizzy and nauseated." She stuck her tongue out and her mouth felt dry and tasted terrible. She realized she must have thrown up.

Her head started pounding again and she felt as if she was going to throw up again. She put her hands over her mouth and looked wide eyed at her husband and daughter.

Belinha knew right away what her mother wanted and reached for the basin under the bed and put it in front of her. Alycea grabbed it just in the nick of time. Afterward, she wiped her face with the cloth that Belinha had given her and asked for some water.

Ed, not having much resistance to such displays, gladly went out to fetch it for her. He was afraid that he would lose his supper right then and there if he didn't get out of the room quickly. He had really enjoyed his daughter's spaghetti and meatballs too. It would have been a shame to lose them. His stomach was now quite content and full for a change.

"Are you feeling any better now, Mae? Would you like me to get you some tea and crackers? I know you shouldn't eat anything heavy for a while. Do you still have the headache?"

Belinha looked extremely concerned about her mother after looking at her face which was pasty white and she was still clammy. She decided to call Dr. Bradley, whom her mother had been seeing for years. He must have been ancient by now. She made a note to herself to try and find her mother a new younger doctor to take care of her.

"Mae, I am going to call Dr. Bradley or another doctor if you want. You don't look well and you're still in a lot of pain. Just relax and I will take care of things. Now don't worry. Okay, Mae? I will be right back after I talk to the doctor."

Alycea was feeling a little better, she thought, but she always hated throwing up. It was such a disgusting thing to do and her mouth tasted terrible. Some tea and crackers might do her good. The pain had subsided a little but had not gone away completely; at least she could sit up a little without feeling nauseated and dizzy. Belinha was born to be a nurse; she was kind and gentle. Alycea was thankful that she was there to help. Ed was useless. He always got panicky when she was sick. He was afraid she was dying. Though a little while ago, Alycea felt like she was too.

Ed came back into the room with a tray of crackers and a cup of tea for Alycea. He gingerly placed it on the night table and propped up her pillows so she could sit up straighter to drink and eat comfortably. Alycea patted Ed on the hand and said, "Thank you, dear. How nice of you. It will make me feel a lot better, I am sure."

"Are you feeling any better, Alycea? You aren't going to throw up again, are you?" Ed looked nervous as he said this and started to back away from her bed just in case. His face was almost as white as Alycea's which made Alycea smile a little. He was such a baby sometimes but she did love him. He was her husband and he was a kind man and good to her even if he was a sissy and weak at times about sickness.

Belinha came back in to report that she had called Dr. Bradley, "The doctor is on his way over, Mae. He has another doctor working with him now and is bringing him over, Dr. Silva." This made Belinha feel better knowing that there would be two doctors conferring over her mother's health.

\*\*\*

"Belinha, how is your mother doing?" Jaco asked as his wife entered their apartment. She looked a little frazzled and worn out. She had stayed while the doctors had examined her mother to make sure everything was all right.

Jaco had cleaned up the kitchen and put away the leftovers after his wife had run out of the apartment to check on her mother. He was doing his share around the house now since she was pregnant and didn't want her to get overtired.

Belinha was relieved to be back in her own little apartment with her husband where it is quiet and peaceful. She was feeling tired and worried about her mother's condition. The doctors had examined her mother and said she needed to be hospitalized so that they could do some tests. They did not want to say much in front of her mother but took Belinha and Ed aside to tell them what they thought the diagnosis was.

Ed had been fearful and held onto his daughter's hand as the doctors explained what they thought was wrong with Alycea. They suspected a brain tumor causing the pain and pressure in her head. They needed to do some x-rays to verify this and also some blood tests. She seemed a little pale and she could be anemic.

Alycea refused to go into the hospital when she was told that she needed to have some tests to determine the cause of her headaches. "I don't want to go to the hospital. That is a place that old people go to die. I will be fine. Just give me something to take away the pain once and for all." Alycea waved her hand at the doctors impatiently.

Ed had been firm with her, for once in his life, and insisted that she listen to the doctors and do what they said. "Alycea, you will go to the hospital and do what Dr. Bradley says. He only wants to help you feel better. I will be there with you. Now let me pack your overnight bag for you."

Alycea was shocked which showed in her face at Ed's bossy attitude and take-charge manner. She did what he told her to do though and she just smiled at him. She felt proud of him for taking care of her and relieving her of the decision making for once.

Alycea arrived at the hospital, driven there by her son-in-law, Jaco. Alycea liked the new doctor, Dr. Silva, a nice young Portuguese man and clever too, who had come to her house along with Dr. Bradley to examine her.

She told Dr. Bradley, "You can send Dr. Silva to check up on me daily instead of coming yourself. I think it would be good for the new doctor to get more practice dealing with patients. I could be his guinea pig." Alycea smiled and appeared to be happy to have a handsome and younger doctor to take care of her.

Dr. Bradley was getting a lot of this from his other patients. Dr. Silva was young and handsome and had a great bedside manner with the patients. He guessed it was time for him to retire and hand over his practice to Dr. Silva. He would talk to Jose, Dr. Silva, after his rounds to get him indoctrinated with the rest of his patients before he announced to them that he would be retiring.

But the last thing he would do before he retired officially was make sure that Alycea Ataide Rubelo was well cared for. He always had a thing for her. She was an attractive woman and a fascinating one too. She was a tough woman but there was softness underneath that tough exterior that he had seen on many occasions. Ed Rubelo was a fortunate man to have her. He sighed to himself and he thought of what could have been.

He headed off to the lab to check her blood tests and then to x-ray to check the results of her films. He had a funny feeling about these headaches which he didn't like.

***

The CAT scan showed a shadow resting against her optic nerve. He didn't think it was anything malignant on the vein but needed to treat it carefully and couldn't take a biopsy because of where it was positioned.

He didn't want to jeopardize her vision in any way. He would find some way with medication to reduce the swelling of the tumor on the vein to keep it from infringing on her vision.

He thought of sweet Alycea with her rich brown hair that was now salt and pepper colored. She was still an extremely attractive woman. He would do all he could to stop her migraines and insure that she had her vision back so she could live a long healthy life.

He remembered back to the first time they had met and she had told him that he was a nice man and quite good looking. She seemed to be as taken with him as he was with her. She was only ten years old and he was twenty years her senior.

He had been examining her when she complained of cramps and headaches after starting her monthly. He had to give her an internal exam to make sure she didn't have any fibroids or any other woman problems.

Alycea had jumped at his touch and he had to reassure her that he would not hurt her. He knew he shouldn't have done what he did to her but he couldn't help himself. He had just wanted to calm her down and then it had become an obsession just to have her come each time in his hands. He felt empowered by it. Alycea didn't know what he was doing but all she knew was that it felt good and she wanted him to do it again and again. She went back to see him each time she complained of a headache and started making up the headaches just to see him.

He never told her what he had been doing to her for over three years and then she had gotten married the following year to Ed. She would belong to another man and he would not see her or examine her in that way ever again.

He had made sure that he was late each time to deliver her children. He had felt he would have wanted to touch her again. He had arrived after the delivery of both her children. He really was not needed due to the expert care of the delivery by her mother, Filomena.

He did have to stitch her up though afterward and did that as tenderly as he could. He left soon after examining her and the babies to make sure they were healthy.

He remembered drowning his sorrows in a bottle of Port, a bottle that was given to him by Alycea for Christmas the previous year. He knew that one day soon he would have to make amends to Alycea for what he had done to her. He hoped the Lord would forgive him for loving her in that way when she had been just a child, too young to understand such things.

# CHAPTER 40

After Alycea had told Jasmine about her secret, she sat back with her face flushed and looked away. She avoided making eye contact with her granddaughter.

"Avoa, I understand if you don't want to tell me some things. I know we all have secrets in our lives. Some things should be kept that way. Please do not feel you need to tell me everything if you are uncomfortable." Jasmine could see the consternation in her grandmother's face as she had abruptly stopped talking.

"Thank you, dear. There are many secrets in my life but most of them I have told you. This one is something that would make you ashamed of me, even if I was only a girl when it happened. I really didn't know that it was wrong at the time but I did figure it was strange." Alycea looked sadly at her dark haired, attractive granddaughter who sat there with her pen and paper in hand taking copious notes.

Alycea wasn't sure she wanted to see this item in print. She requested, "Jasmine I told you about this tawdry secret but please promise not to publish your book until after your aunt and I are both gone from this world. I wouldn't want her to see this. Ok?" she said this with a wink as she threw a kiss to her granddaughter.

"Oh Avoa, I am so sorry that happened to you. You were just a young girl. It must have been a shock to find out later on what he had been doing to you. Shame on him! He was a grown man, many years older than you at that time. He should have known better. If that were today he would have lost his license to practice medicine and gone to prison. After all, you were a minor." Jasmine just shook her head in disbelief. At the same time she wanted to laugh out loud at her grandmother's reaction to being manipulated like that and enjoying it!

She was definitely a sexual person. Even at 100 she still got flushed at the thought of sex. She was definitely one of a kind! Jasmine thought, as she felt her own cheeks flush with embarrassment and shock.

Jasmine promised not to have her book published until after both her grandmother and her aunt had died. She was sure that whatever she did, there would be some relatives that would disapprove of what she wrote. She hoped they would understand that basically the story she was going to tell was dedicated to the memory of her grandmother and would be loosely based on her grandmother's life. Jasmine would change many things in the story and protect the innocent parties any way she could.

Avoa was a fascinating person who had become the matriarch of their huge family and would provide a lasting legacy for them all. Jasmine only hoped she would do justice to Avoa's story in her novel, she mused as she looked with love and wonder at her grandmother.

# CHAPTER 41

Dr. Bradley turned when Dr. Silva came into the office to stand next to him as he looked over the x-rays and CAT scan.

"Hello, Dr. Silva. I just looked over Alycea Rubelo's films. There is definitely something there pressing on her optic nerve. We have to treat it carefully with medication to get the swelling down and take the pressure off the optic nerve." Dr. Bradley snapped off the light he was using to look at the films and picked up his pen and prescription slip to write down the medication he thought would be the best course to use.

"Did you want me to go see her at the hospital or do you want to go?" Dr. Silva looked expectantly at his superior and the man he would be replacing over the next few months. He was already familiar with the office procedures and staff and had reviewed all the thousands of files of patients that Dr. Bradley had been treating over the past forty years.

"Thank you, Dr. Silva, but I will go see her. I would like to explain things to her. I do not want her to worry about her condition or anything else for that matter." Dr. Bradley seemed far away in his thoughts, looking at Dr. Silva but not really seeing him. All he could see was Alycea in his mind.

Dr. Silva knew that Nicholas Bradley was dying from liver disease. He had always been a heavy drinker and had done great damage to his body. He also knew Nick didn't have much time left and was anxious to see his patient, Alycea Rubelo, well before he was too ill to help her. Nick seemed to have a special attachment to this woman, Dr. Silva had noticed. It was probably due to being her physician since she was a little girl.

Dr. Bradley was aware that Dr. Silva knew he was dying and had requested that no one else be told about this fact. He wanted his patients to think that he was retiring to do some traveling. He didn't want them to worry about him.

Nick Bradley was going to go see Alycea for the last time to talk to her about her migraines and the solution he had to make them go away. He wanted to reassure her that she would be taken care of by Dr. Silva who would be following the regimen he had set up for her.

When he got to Alycea's hospital room he took one look at her and wanted to cry. She looked tired and still in pain. He placed a cool cloth on her forehead and sat next to her bedside.

He took her hand in his and stroked it lightly saying, "Dear Alycea, you are still not feeling any better. I was hoping you would be by now with rest. I have prescribed some medication for you that should help relieve your headache so that you can sleep. Here, please take this pill and then we will discuss your problem some more." He handed her the pill and took the glass of water off her night stand and brought it to her lips. She swallowed it and laid her head back on her pillow.

He started by saying, "Alycea, you and I have known each other for many years. We have had a friendship…a strange relationship…and I promised myself I would never say this but…I feel it is time." Alycea looked at him through the haze of pain and saw tears glistening in his eyes.

She squeezed the hand that was holding hers and tried to sit up to look at him more closely. "What's wrong, Dr. Bradley? Are you worried about me? Is it serious? Am I going to die?" She looked at him with a deep frown forming creases on her forehead.

"Oh no, my dear, you are not going to die. You are going to live a long life. You will get through this time now. I am sure of it. Dr. Silva will take care of you and make sure that the swelling in your head goes down. That way you will not have any more headaches.

Dr. Silva will keep a watch on you and do regular x-rays or scans to ensure the vein does not swell any larger. Having migraine headaches like you have are caused by a swelling of the veins in the head. One particular vein seems to be swollen a little larger than the rest causing you great discomfort. We are treating the headaches and the swelling at the same time. We want to take away the pain and decrease the swelling and then you will feel much better." Dr. Bradley watched Alycea's face for any sign that she did not understand what he was trying to tell her.

He waited for her to respond. She just looked at him and said, "I understand, Dr. Bradley. I am not going to die, am I? I know you will...or Dr. Silva will take good care of me. Is this why you look sad? Are you worried about me?"

"No, I am sure you will be just fine in a short time." He took a deep breath before going on. "It is...I am going to die. It's my liver. I have been imbibing too much over the years. I guess it was all that Port that I came to love almost as much as I love...," he stopped as his voice choked up and tears ran down his cheeks.

"I don't understand. You are sick. You are dying, not me? How can that be? You don't look like you are dying. You do look a little tired but I thought you were retiring to rest, travel and enjoy what was left of your life. I don't want you to die. You are right; we have had a strange relationship. I know we never talked about what happened back then. I am still a little embarrassed over the whole thing but that was so long ago. It is all forgiven and we are friends and have been ever since then." Alycea squeezed his hand again and smiled at him.

"Alycea, I never told you this but I tormented myself over what I did to you when you really didn't know what was happening. You were innocent and sweet. I am deeply sorry, but at the same time I wanted to love you then as I want to love you now. I have always loved you. There has never been another woman in my life but you. But you belong to Ed and I respect that. Can I kiss you goodbye as a man kisses a woman?" He hesitated, then leaned forward and kissed Alycea on her lips, first lightly then with more fervor before releasing her. He had such a sweet smile of satisfaction on his face as he got up and moved away from her bedside.

He walked toward the door and turned one last time to look at her with tear-filled eyes, then walked out closing the door softly behind him.

Alycea touched her lips and could still taste his lips on hers. It was a shock to her that he confessed that he loved her. She hadn't expected that. She knew he liked her but never thought it was more than a passing thing with him. She didn't love him but cared for him in a way. He was the first man to touch her.

She remembered feeling good the first time he examined her after her complaints of severe cramps with her first monthly. For the next several months after that she went back because he made her feel better. She knew something wasn't right but didn't understand what he was doing to her. All she knew was that he relaxed her and took away the pains by massaging her down there. She never told anyone about it. Inside, she must have felt it wasn't right to let him do that to her.

Alycea never asked him about what he did during his exams and it was left unspoken until now when he had come to see her to say goodbye. It would always be a bittersweet memory for Alycea. She had secretly cared for Dr. Bradley as a childhood crush but he felt much more deeply involved.

She knew after she had married Ed what Dr. Bradley had been doing to her was something of an extremely personal and sexual nature. She wasn't angry with him for taking advantage of a child because she liked it and could have stopped him or told her mother about it. She never did.

When she first slept with Ed he did something like that to her too. She almost told him then but seeing his face looking happy that he had pleased her, she just couldn't tell him.

It was a secret that she vowed she would take to her grave. She feared that her husband would have felt betrayed and her mother and family would be disappointed in her if they knew. She knew she could not share this secret with anyone.

Alycea started to feel sleepy. The pill that Dr. Bradley had given her was beginning to work to relax her. She closed her eyes and the last thought she had before she nodded off was how sweet the kiss was from Dr. Bradley. She felt a tear run down her cheek as she started to dream of Dr. Bradley and how she would never see him again.

*** 

"Alycea, how are you feeling today?" the nurse asked as she was taking Alycea's pulse and listening to her heart and chest.

"I am feeling a little groggy but the pain is a dull ache now. Is Dr. Bradley here today?" She asked anxiously. She had not seen him for two nights and she was scheduled to go home today.

Her latest x-rays and blood tests, she was told, showed marked improvement in the shadow. The swelling had gone down and was no longer pressing on the optic nerve; therefore, the headaches were almost gone now. Ed was coming to pick her up within the hour if Dr. Silva signed her release papers in time.

Nurse Coral looked up from checking over Alycea's chart to say, "No, Dr. Bradley is away and Dr. Silva is taking over for him permanently. Unfortunately, Dr. Bradley admitted himself to a hospital in Boston. He hasn't been feeling well. We are all saying prayers for his quick recovery. He is such a wonderful, caring doctor," Nurse Coral said with a sigh as her eyes glistened with unspent tears.

She really cared for him more than just a doctor/nurse relationship. It was plainly seen on her face, Alycea surmised, as she watched Coral go about helping her get ready to be released.

Before she could ask Coral about her feelings, Ed walked in looking handsome in his suit and tie and his hair all slicked back, still wet from his shower. He could still take her breath away at just the sight of him. Coral's smile showed how much she appreciated the way he looked. Ed could always turn heads of the female gender wherever he went.

"Hi Ed, I am almost ready. Coral here has been a great help to me. I am feeling much better thanks to Dr. Bradley and Dr. Silva."

"I saw Dr. Silva at the front desk. He was signing your release papers. He said he would be in shortly to see you and make sure you are all right to go home." Ed smiled at his wife, relief flooding through him as he noticed her pink color had returned and the creases between her eyes had almost disappeared along with the headaches.

Ed had missed her but had gotten by eating at both of his daughters' houses. Belinha and Jaco had moved around the corner to their five-room apartment, while Caterina and Dean had moved into Alycea and Ed's former second floor apartment. He and Alycea in turn had moved downstairs where Belinha and Jaco had formerly lived. It was smaller with two bedrooms but that was all they needed. Filomena and Stan were still with them. They were getting older and Filomena couldn't get around without some assistance. She did surprisingly well though for a one-legged person. Filomena still refused to use crutches opting for hopping around holding onto furniture as she negotiated herself around the house.

Filomena insisted on doing most of the cooking and cleaning, too, with Stan's assistance while Alycea had been in the hospital. Ed did eat occasionally at home but most of the time he had eaten with his daughters. He was lonely too. Filomena and Stan went to bed early each night leaving him alone with his thoughts. Ed tended to stay late at his daughters' houses so he wouldn't have to be alone too long and could just return home and go directly to bed.

Ed looked forward to having his wife back home. He longed to get their life back together. He missed Alycea's cooking even though his daughters were great cooks. Alycea just knew what he wanted without asking and always made his favorites.

He was sure that now that she was feeling much better she would be cooking up a storm for him once again. She did enjoy being in her kitchen. The kitchen looked empty when she wasn't there. Ed smiled to himself at the image of Alycea in her apron in their little kitchen.

Alycea looked at Ed with a silly grin on his face. Now what was he thinking? He was such a mischievous man. She had to admit she missed him and their lovemaking and his sweet kisses. The kiss she got from Dr. Bradley had stirred something in her and she wanted to satisfy that urge with Ed soon, real soon.

Well, she was definitely feeling a whole lot better now. It was good to be going home again. She smiled and sighed, thinking of what she planned to do.

***

"Is she home yet, Caterina?" Belinha was rushing around as fast as she could move now as her belly was growing bigger day by day. She rested the phone on her shoulder as she rubbed her aching back.

"Yes, she is home and back to her feisty self, bossing everyone around. Poor Grandma Filomena, she went to hide in her bedroom to get away from Mae. Stan just went out for a quick walk around the block. He was upset with Mae because of the way she treated everyone around here. He didn't want to say anything that he would regret later on." Caterina loved gossiping and couldn't get all the details out fast enough.

"Caterina, she isn't all that bad you know. Aren't you at least happy that she is going to be okay now? Weren't you at all worried about Mae?" Belinha couldn't help but be surprised at her sister's attitude. Caterina never changed and never worried about anyone or anything except herself.

"She will live forever, who are you kidding, Belinha? She will outlast both of us! She can be ornery at times! You were smart to move out of here. At least you have some peace and quiet now. Mae is always coming upstairs and barging in on us. She walked in on us the other day making whoopee or at least trying to considering my large condition! Would you believe she didn't even bat an eye! I had to yell at her to get out and come back in an hour to give us some privacy. I am going to start locking my door!" Caterina said with exasperation noted in her voice.

"Oh, goodness sakes. I'm glad she didn't do that to us when we lived there. She didn't come down frequently but Pai was down all the time much to Jaco's chagrin. Pai just needed to get away at times from Mae too, I guess. I know she can be trying." Belinha had to move the phone away from her face to keep her sister from hearing her chuckling over the mishap of her mother walking in on them. Caterina was funny but took things too seriously at times.

"I have to go, Caterina. This baby is kicking up a storm and I need to lie down and try to take a nap if he or she would only keep still long enough for me to fall asleep. How are you feeling? Are you getting tired lately? Is your back killing you?" They were both pregnant and shared their aches and pains on a daily basis. Belinha was due two months after her sister.

"Yes, I feel as if I am going to explode. This baby just keeps growing and is always kicking the daylights out of me. My due date is in two weeks. I have a feeling I may go before that though. The baby has been quieter yesterday and today. Who knows, maybe he or she is getting ready to come into this world?" Caterina said goodbye and thought her sister had a good idea. She planned to take a nap too before her husband came home from work. If only her mother would stay away long enough for her to get some rest, she would be thrilled.

Belinha put the phone down and would postpone her nap. Instead she decided to walk over to visit and check up on her mother. She would bring over some coffee cake she had made earlier that day and they could sit and have some cake and coffee.

Alycea went to the door quickly as she heard a soft knock and her daughter's voice calling out to her. "Mae, can I come in to visit with you. I brought some coffee cake."

"Belinha, how nice of you, sweetheart. Please, come in. You don't have to knock, just come in any time. Hmmm, that cake smells and looks delicious. I will get Ed. He would love a piece of it too, I'm

249

sure." Alycea went into the living room to rouse her husband from his afternoon nap.

"What...wha...I'm up, I'm up, Alycea. What do you want, dear?" He sat up and buttoned his pants and pulled up the zipper, which he had a habit of opening when he was full and comfortable and ready for a nap.

"Belinha is here and she brought a delicious coffee cake she baked just for me. Come out and have a slice with us. I will make some coffee too." She turned and left Ed sitting there, still loopy from sleep. He did love Belinha's coffee cake but really needed to catch a few more winks. But no one could sleep if Alycea requested your presence for whatever reason.

He begrudgingly dragged himself out to the kitchen to see his daughter. She looked sweet and pregnant as he bent to kiss her on both cheeks. It was always a pleasure to see his Belinha.

"Hi Pai, you look a little sleepy. Were you taking a nap? I'm sorry Mae woke you up. I'm planning to take a nap myself once I go back home. But I did want to see Mae first to make sure she is feeling well. Would you like a piece of coffee cake and a cup of coffee? Mae is making the coffee now. It will wake you up a little." Belinha tried to make her father feel better. He didn't seem to be in a good mood after being awakened abruptly by his wife.

"Ahhh, you may be right. I could go for a cup of coffee and your delicious coffee cake. It smells heavenly, Belinha. Thank you, dear."

Ed watched as Belinha sliced him a generous piece of the cake and placed it in front of him. She also poured him a cup of coffee that her mother had just brewed and brought over to the table.

When they were all settled down, sipping coffee and eating the cake, Belinha asked her mother how she was feeling.

Just as her mother was going to answer, the phone rang. Ed jumped up to answer it. He listened for a minute or two and then exclaimed loud and clear, "Caterina is going to the hospital to have the baby! This is Dean. He is going out the door with her now and will call us once he gets to the hospital to let us know how far along she is. He is hoping for a boy! Me too! We have enough girls in the family as it is!" He looked embarrassed after he said it when he saw his wife and daughter's shocked faces staring at him.

"What did you say, Ed?"

"Oh, dear, I didn't really mean that. I was just trying to make Dean feel better. He really does want a boy. He says that he wants to have enough boys to make up a football team. I don't know if Caterina feels the same way, however," he said as he chuckled to himself at the thought of his bold daughter talking to her husband about this preposterous idea of his.

"Oh my goodness, she is a little early. I thought she looked a little peaked yesterday and I told her that she was dropping like a lead balloon. I think it's going to be a girl. She is carrying all around. I carried all around for both of my girls and was tired all the time. She has been complaining of being exhausted from the beginning. I hoped she picked out girls' names and not just boys' names like Dean wanted her to do. Men, they know nothing at all about having babies!! Ha!"

"Mae, you may be right. I am going to go home now to prepare dinner for Jaco. Let me know if Dean calls you back with the news. Ok? I love you both. Take it easy, Mae, and you too, Pai."

She put her cup and empty plate in the sink and left their apartment. She didn't tell them that she was feeling exhausted too because then her mother would say that she was having a girl also. Jaco wanted a boy. Oh well, they would try again whatever it was as long as it was healthy. Belinha sighed as she began her short walk home and rubbed her lower back to ease the ache. She looked forward to getting home and putting her feet up for a little while before starting dinner. She might even grab a quick nap too. That concept really sounded good.

# CHAPTER 42

"It's a girl, Mae. She looks just like Caterina. I'm glad she has her nose too. I wouldn't wish my nose on any daughter of mine," Dean laughed happily after announcing the news of his daughter's birth.

"Oh, how wonderful, Dean. I'm pleased to have another girl in the family. I never wished to have a boy and was always happy with my two girls. Now I have a beautiful granddaughter. Thank you, Dean, for calling. I will stop by and see Caterina as soon as I can. I'll call Belinha to let her know too. Give Caterina a kiss for me."

She picked up the phone to dial Belinha at the same time announcing to Ed that he now had a granddaughter.

"Belinha, it's a girl! Isn't that wonderful? Dean does seem to be happy though. I know how he wanted to have a boy, you know, for his football team. Poor Caterina, she doesn't know what she is in for. He plans to have at least six or seven children. He hopes to have more boys than girls with the odds in his favor. I hope for Caterina's sake that he gets a boy the next time."

"I'm happy for Caterina. How is the baby doing? Did she name her yet? She had talked about boys' names mostly but I think she said she had a girl's name in mind." Belinha didn't tell her mother that Caterina had prayed for a girl for the first child she had, then afterward she wouldn't mind if all the rest were boys.

"You know, Dean didn't tell me what they named her. I didn't even think to ask either. Don't worry, we will know when we go visit her tonight. We are going to have supper first and then we can all go together. Ok? Did Jaco get home yet?" Neither Alycea nor her husband had their driver's licenses and depended upon Jaco to take them everywhere."

"He just came in the door now, Mae. I have to go get his supper ready then we will call you when we are coming to pick you both up. All right, Mae?" Belinha hurried off the phone to greet her husband with a kiss at the door. He had looked at her as she had walked away from putting the phone down. He saw by her facial expressions that she had been talking to her mother.

Belinha had a hard time with her mother. Always knowing how her mother favored her sister really hurt Belinha. No matter how old she got she still felt like a child in her mother's presence and always did what her mother told her to do. This was one thing that irked Jaco deeply. He wanted to separate their lives from his in-laws but the attachment was too strong and thick as a steel cord. He just couldn't cut them loose.

"How are you feeling, sweetheart? Is everything all right with your mother?" He felt some apprehension just saying those words to her about her mother's health. He knew how worried she had been about her mother's condition. Thank God she was home. Now Belinha wouldn't have to run back and forth to see her every day. It had been tiring Belinha out and he was concerned about the health of his wife and unborn child. They were precious to him.

"I'm fine, Jaco. Please don't worry about me. Mae is doing well. She is definitely back to her feisty self again. Just ask Pai. He will tell you how feisty she is! She just called to tell us that Caterina and Dean had a little girl." She smiled one of her sweet smiles for her husband who felt his heart skip a beat. She could still do that to him. He loved her deeply.

At times he still thought about their wedding day and thanked God she was not injured or killed by his insane mother.

Jaco put his arms around Belinha feeling the baby kicking as he hugged her. In a couple of months they would have a child of their own. He had hoped secretly for a son but would be happy with a daughter. He wanted to have a few children, not quite as many as his parents did though. They had had nine children. He had three sisters and three brothers. Two siblings died when they were just infants, two boys, one from illness and the other from crib death.

He would definitely treat his children with respect and make sure that they had enough food to eat, nice clothes on their backs and receive more education than he had. He had to leave school in the sixth grade to help out at home. He must have had a serious expression on his face as he was thinking about the future because Belinha roused him out of his thoughts.

"Jaco, is everything all right, dear? You look awfully pensive and worried. I hope you are not worrying yourself over me. The baby and I are just fine. Before we know it, we will be able to hold this child in our arms. I am really looking forward to that and also having no more backaches and feeling fat. I am quite a sight, I know, since my breasts have gotten much bigger. I haven't gained a lot because I just can't eat much but what I eat the baby takes. But all the weight is up top. I know you are happy about that!" Belinha laughed out loud at her own observations.

Jaco raised his eyebrows at her remark and laughed too.

"Let's go eat, supper is about ready. I will put it out for us. We have to go to the hospital to see Caterina and the baby. We are taking Mae and Pai with us. I hope you don't mind, Jaco, but I made favas and linguica. It was a quick and easy dish to make and I didn't have much energy to make anything more. Slice yourself some of the crusty bread and dip it into the juice." She placed the steaming plate in front of her hungry husband who dug right in. She was always amazed at his appetite; and he never seemed to gain weight.

***

A couple months later...

"Caterina, she is just beautiful! I just can't wait until I can hold my own. You are breastfeeding her, right? I decided I don't want to do that. It creeps me out a little." Belinha shrugged off a convulsive shiver that made her hair stand on end just thinking about it.

"Oh, Belinha, you are excessively dramatic about it. It really isn't any big deal. I plan to breastfeed all of ours. The number that Dean keeps mentioning though, may run me dry. Would you believe he wants to have nine children? He thinks he is going to have eight boys. I told him I need at least a few years in between each one." The baby, named Katrina, started to cry and Caterina picked her up from her crib. She was already two months old and pretty as a picture.

"Ooh, that was a bigger one than the last one." Belinha gasped as she held onto her distended belly. "Caterina, I think I may be in labor. I better go home and call Jaco so he can bring me to the hospital. I just may make his birthday after all. Jaco's birthday is tomorrow and he is hoping that I will have the baby. They can share their day together. Jaco will call you if I go into the hospital tonight. Ok? Bye little Katrina, soon you will have a cousin."

Belinha gingerly got up from the chair she was resting in and left her sister's apartment to go home around the corner. Thank God she didn't live far away or she may not have made it.

It was getting increasingly harder to walk with the pains coming closer together. She had to stop every minute to wait out the pain.

She could see her house up ahead but it still seemed really far away and she had to climb a flight of stairs to get to the porch and then into the house even though they lived on the first floor.

Caterina watched her sister as she moved slowly out of the apartment and down the short flight of stairs and then around the corner to her house. She wasn't sure if she should follow behind her in case she couldn't make it up the porch stairs to her house. She watched sufficiently until she was sure that she was finally in the house before turning away to breastfeed Katrina who was still fussing.

She sat in the rocking chair with her daughter in her arms and they were both soon quite content and getting sleepy. Caterina had just about forgotten about her sister when the phone rang. She jumped up feeling quite startled by the sound and went over to pick up the phone.

Her brother-in-law was frantic on the other end. "Caterina, Belinha has to go to the hospital. Her water broke and she is in pain. I am driving her over to the Dover Hill Hospital. I will call you if and when she has the baby. She told me that she has been in labor all day. Did you know that? Why didn't she call me?" He dropped the phone back on the cradle without saying goodbye and rushed out the door with Belinha puffing and waddling as she leaned into him.

Jaco tried to move Belinha along faster but she was in too much pain to move quickly. She kept stopping to hold onto her stomach and back and was sweating and groaning with each contraction.

The houses were close enough together to give Caterina a view of Jaco and Belinha leaving the house, getting into their car and driving away. Jaco hit the gas and took off with a squeal, leaving a little rubber behind.

Caterina had to laugh at him. He was a nervous wreck, nothing like her Dean. Dean took everything in stride and nothing seemed to bother him. She was much the same way. Her sister was a worrywart just like her husband. How could two sisters be so different? She wondered.

Well, she figured she had better call her parents to let them know they could be grandparents once again before the end of the day. But before Caterina could call her mother the baby had arrived.

"Mae, it's Jaco. Belinha had a girl! She is a little hairy but beautiful! If Caterina and Dean can't give you a ride over to the hospital, I can come and get you. I will be here in Belinha's room if you need me." Jaco hung up the phone and looked over at his wife who was beaming as she fed their new daughter.

They had named her Jasmine. When he first looked at her she was covered in a soft, black hair all over her body. Both he and Belinha were first shocked at their daughter's appearance. The nurses reassured the parents that this hair would all fall out in a short time.

Alycea and Ed had visited their new granddaughter and were also alarmed at her appearance. They weren't sure what to make of all the hair. But they loved her from the moment she opened her dark eyes and looked at them and smiled. They swore that she smiled at them no matter what everyone else said of newborns not being able to focus, see color or smile right away.

By the time they got her home in less than a week, Jasmine had lost most of the black hair except for the full head of hair she still sported. Belinha soon coiffed and styled it with pink ribbons and bows. After all, she was a hairdresser and no daughter of hers would go out without her hair being done just so.

Anxiously waiting at home were Filomena and Stan who greeted them as soon as they got into the house. Alycea had dropped her mother and Stan off at Belinha's and Jaco's so that she could straighten out the baby's room and bring over some new items as a surprise. They had done the same thing for Caterina after she had Katrina.

Filomena had embroidered a christening dress and cap and a doily for the top of the baby's bureau. She had also crocheted an afghan and pillow to place in the bassinet.

Alycea had bought the sheets and coverlet and had decorated the baby's first bed, the bassinet, with pink ribbons and bows which Jasmine would use for the first month before going into a crib.

When Belinha and Jaco arrived home they were pleased and grateful for the lovely things and generosity of their family in putting things in order for their new daughter. Maybe it wasn't too bad to be in close proximity to the in-laws, Jaco thought.

Jaco felt terrible about his thoughts about his in-laws a few months earlier. His in-laws were good to him and replaced the parents that he had lost so tragically. He was grateful to have such warm, loving and generous in-laws.

A few months after Jasmine's birth the family would all be mourning the death of sweet Filomena. Belinha was grateful that her grandmother had done all the embroidering for Jasmine's room. For it was the last time Filomena would do any embroidering, sewing or crocheting for her great grandchildren.

They had Filomena's funeral mass at the Portuguese Church, St. Peter's in Lowell. Besides all of the family, many other people were there to pay their respects to Filomena. She had touched many lives in her fifty-eight years on earth. She gave food to those who were starving and money to those who were struggling during The Great Depression. Even though she didn't have much for herself and her family she gave what she could. She was truly a saint of her time and would be greatly missed by everyone whose lives she had touched.

Alycea was distraught over her mother's death and the fact that Antonio wasn't there to say 'goodbye' to her. She had written to Antonio and had told him that their mother was failing. He had apologized but could not come out for the funeral. Manny had made it to the funeral but had not seen his mother for several months before her death.

Alycea was angry at her twin but did not know what to do to convince him that she would pay his passage. He had said that he couldn't leave his family there. What was he thinking? They were his family too! Alycea cried in disbelief.

The St. Theresa statue, Filomenta had lovingly kept in her room each time she moved, was given a prominent place in Alycea's bedroom as a memorial to her mother. Alycea knew how much her mother had loved and prayed to St. Theresa over the fifty-eight years she had lived. Filomena had a good life but had been sick the last twenty years of her life with severe diabetes. She had lost her right leg and was wrought with constant infections on her left leg. Alycea had feared she would lose that leg too. God showered her with mercy by taking her before that could happen.

Her husband, Stan, was at her bedside holding her hand when she died. He never left her side until the undertaker came and took her body away for preparation and burial. He was inconsolable and walked around the house as if in a zombie state. He refused to eat and only took a cup of tea or coffee when forced by Alycea or Ed.

After the funeral and burial of his much beloved wife, Stan felt his life was now over and that night he cried as he tried to sleep in their now empty bed. He could still feel Filomena's presence all around the room. He prayed to her and to her patron St. Theresa to take his life so that he could join his wife in Heaven. He promised that he would confess all his sins to the priest the next day. He hoped that he could ensure a place in Heaven.

When Stan woke up from his fitful night, his covers in a bunch, he told Alycea and Ed that he was going to church and would be back shortly. They both looked at the pallor of his skin and his hunched over appearance and just nodded to him. They were deeply concerned that he was not going to fight to go on. He was extremely depressed.

They, too, missed Filomena immensely. She was a strong, resilient and resolute woman who made her mark on all their lives. She was the one responsible for forging a new life for them all by coming to America. Who knows what would have happened if they had stayed in Madeira, Portugal?
Stan arrived shortly thereafter at St. Peter's Church and met with a new priest, who he did not know, to receive his confession. He kneeled at the bench and said his penance, crossed himself and left the church to return home. He was now ready to go whenever God wanted to take him. Stan prayed it would be soon.

Stan's prayers were answered during the night. He passed away in his sleep peacefully with a smile on his lips.

# CHAPTER 43

"I am sorry that I didn't get to know my great grandmother and her husband Great Grandpa Stan. She sounded like she was a wonderful person and so saintly. Stan was devoted and loving toward her. She has to be in Heaven, don't you think, Avoa?" Jasmine interjected as she interrupted her grandmother's thoughts.

"Well, you are seeing only the good in her just as your mother always did. I loved my mother but at times she could drive me crazy. She was always telling me what to do and how to do it. I guess I never did anything right for her."

"Pai Stan was a wonderful, loving husband and stepfather. I loved him with all my heart. I didn't know my father for long since he died when I was only eight years old. Pai Stan was there for both of us and was our father in the true sense of the word."

"Yes, he certainly sounds like he was."

"You know, now that I am much older, I can understand how my mother felt. She had to leave my twin brother behind and she was always angry with herself for having done that. She made a choice between my brother Antonio and me. Sometimes I think she was sorry she didn't leave me behind instead. I gave her plenty of trouble and heartache," Alycea stated with sadness in her voice.

"Oh Avoa, she loved you, I am sure of it. You were her daughter. You took care of her and lived with her all her life. I am sure she regretted leaving Uncle Antonio behind but it could not be helped. Please don't blame yourself for what she had to do. It was her choice and a difficult choice to make," Jasmine said as she laid her hand on her grandmother's and patted it to try to make her feel better.

Alycea raised her eyes to her granddaughter and smiled. Her eyes took on a glassy faraway look as she went back in time once again…

# CHAPTER 44

Both girls were growing quickly. They were close, being born only two months apart. They were more like sisters than cousins.

They were as different as different can be. Jasmine was petite and dark haired while Katrina was taller and fairer. They were always together crawling around either at one house or the other and learned how to walk almost at the same time.

Caterina soon realized that she was again pregnant. This greatly pleased her husband who was still hoping for a boy.

He got his wish nine months later with his first boy, Nolando. He was a robust little boy and every two years afterward was followed by Matthew, Bartholomew, Noel, Bertrand, Edward, and Stanley. The last two boys were named after their grandfather and great grandfather. Two babies were lost in between Bartholomew and Noel which were also boys. Dean now had part of his football team.

Meanwhile Belinha and Jaco had a miscarriage a couple of years after Jasmine, then finally had a healthy boy two years after that. They were happy with their daughter and son and thought that their lives were now complete. They didn't feel a need to keep up with her sister and husband's large tribe.

Alycea and Ed were kept busy babysitting all their grandchildren, when they could. The granddaughters, being the oldest, helped out taking care of the younger siblings. Their houses were always filled with love, laughter and sometimes tears.

Holidays were chaotic and joyful and the noise reached great levels, enough to pierce eardrums. Santa was kept busy in these households trying to fulfill the long lists of all the children. Life seemed hectic but wonderful for everyone. It seemed as if nothing could go wrong. But life has a tendency to take each of us by surprise and shake things up a little from time to time.

***

One day Alycea was not feeling well. She noticed her vision fading in and out with some black spots in front of her eyes.

She thought she was just tired after having taken care of her eight grandsons while Caterina and Belinha had gone out shopping with the girls for some new clothes for school. It was too crazy to bring the boys. They could buy the boys' clothes without them but not the girls who liked to pick out everything themselves.

Belinha and Caterina had come to pick up their children and noticed that their mother was looking at them strangely. The boys were all playing around the living room with their little cars and trucks, making their usual busy sounds.

Alycea was in the kitchen with her hands thrust out in front of her as she walked towards them. She called out to them to come to her since she said she couldn't see them well, the reason for her unusual squinting stare and wobbly gait.

They both rushed to her side, each taking one of their mother's hands and leading her over to the couch to sit. They both talked at once asking her what was wrong.

Alycea just sighed and said, "I really don't know. I was fine one minute cooking supper and the next I couldn't see the pot I was stirring. There were all these spidery things and black spots in front of my eyes. I tried to wipe them away but I couldn't no matter how much I rubbed my eyes with my apron."

"Mae, we're going to call Dr. Silva to come over and check you out. You could just be tired but we would both feel better if he told us that it is nothing to worry about. Ok?" Belinha said as she looked over her mother's head at her sister with a worried frown creasing her brow.

Caterina picked up the phone in the kitchen and made the call to Dr. Silva as Belinha put on the kettle to boil some water for a cup of tea for her mother to keep her preoccupied until the doctor arrived.

Belinha also went to check on the kids to make sure they were not getting into any trouble. She looked in on them quickly and noticed that they were getting along fine. But when they saw her, they asked for something to eat. They all joined in at the same time saying, "We are hungry; can we have some cookies before supper?"

"Yes, I will get you all some biscoitos. Now go sit down at the table and I will bring you some milk to go with the cookies."

Belinha patted each of them on the head, Caterina's brood, as they passed her to go out to the kitchen. She marveled at how good-looking they all were and how many hearts they would break as they grew up to be handsome young men and beautiful young women one day.

She brought over the tea and biscoitos to her mother after getting the children settled at the kitchen table with their milk and cookies.

Alycea was sitting on the couch where she had left her. Caterina was sitting next to her holding her mother's hand. Belinha asked her mother, "Would you like to sip your tea before it gets cold?"

"Belinha, don't hover over me now. I am just fine. I will sip the tea and eat the biscoitos just to keep you happy, dear. I am not sick. I know Dr. Silva will find me in good health and that my eyes are just tired and getting older, that is all." The look on Alycea's face said otherwise. She looked frightened and kept putting her hand up to her face to look at her fingers turning them this way and that. She was definitely having a difficult time focusing on anything.

Caterina kept patting her mother's hand and trying to reassure her that she was probably right. She was just fine and there was nothing to worry about. She exchanged a quick, anxious look at her sister after she said this, though.

Dr. Silva arrived shortly after Alycea had finished her tea and biscoitos. He was still a handsome man with a kind face and sensitive eyes. He asked Caterina and Belinha to give him some room on the couch next to Alycea so he could examine her eyes.

He took out his stethoscope and listened to her heart and palpated her back. He put on a small flashlight and looked into her eyes flashing the light back and forth across her vision to check her pupils for dilation and sensitivity to light.

He asked her some questions about what she was seeing in front of her vision and how long she had been experiencing this phenomenon. After some more questions he told her that he wanted to have her admitted to the hospital for further tests on her eyes. These tests had to be done in the hospital.

Dr. Silva knew how cantankerous Alycea could be about going to the hospital. He promised her that it would only take a day or two to do everything he wanted to insure that her vision was not endangered in any way.

He gave her a gentle pat on her hand before turning to Caterina and Belinha and with a nod of his head indicating he wanted to talk to them further in another room. They walked out to the kitchen where the boys were finishing up their milk and cookies. They hurried them up and out of the room so they could have some privacy.

Caterina spoke first. "Dr. Silva, what do you think is wrong with our mother?"

Before he could answer, Belinha asked, "Do you think it's serious, Dr. Silva?" They both wore such serious expressions of concern on their faces that he just smiled wanly at them before answering.

"First of all, I need to do some more tests but I think it may be a detached retina. Yes, it can be serious. Your mother could lose her vision if we don't do something right away. I am going to call the hospital to get her admitted today. Can you drive her over now or I can call an ambulance? I will meet you there. I will be bringing in an ophthalmologist to confirm the diagnosis and treat her." He went back to see Alycea and whispered to her that she would be fine and that he would see her at the hospital shortly.

Caterina went to pack her mother's small brown suitcase which she always kept in the hall closet. She put a couple of nightgowns, a bathrobe, a pair of her favorite slippers and a change of clothes in the suitcase while Belinha packed a few cosmetic essentials for Alycea. They both knew their mother always wanted to look good no matter where she was going, due to her vanity.

Since neither Caterina nor Belinha had driver's licenses they had to decide which husband to call to drive them and their mother to the hospital. The final decision was to call Jaco. He could be reached more easily at the rubber plant where he worked than Dean who worked in construction and would need to get cleaned up.

Alycea was patiently waiting on the couch as they rushed around getting things ready for her journey to the hospital. The boys were all of a sudden too quiet as they had noticed their mothers moving back and forth between the bedroom and the kitchen carrying a suitcase and cosmetic case.

They were curious and wanted to know what was going on? "Where are you going with the suitcase? Are we going on a trip?" Their eyes lit up at the prospect of going somewhere. It wasn't often that they went anywhere but to each other's houses and to school and back again.

"No, we are not going anywhere," Caterina announced to her children. "Avoa Alycea is going to the hospital. She isn't feeling well. You will have to be good and try to be quiet. She needs to rest until Uncle Jaco comes to pick her up. Okay?" She smiled at the children to show them it was not something for them to worry about. She also promised to buy them some ice cream from the ice cream man that always came by each day at noon.

There were cheers heard all around from the children who loved ice cream. They each had their favorite kind from the ice cream truck. They were talking excitedly back and forth about what kind of ice cream bar they would get. She heard them say 'creamsicle, drumstick, fudgicle and ice cream sandwich' and argue back and forth which one was the best.

Jaco arrived shortly thereafter and taking the suitcase in one hand and his mother-in-law in the other, guided her out to his car to take her to the hospital. Caterina said she would stay behind with the children and Belinha and Ed could go to the hospital to make sure Alycea was settled.

Once Dean came home, Caterina would feed the children their supper and then get a sitter, one of the neighbors, to watch them so she and Dean could go to the hospital and see her mother and relieve Belinha and Ed. Ed was failing at this time. The sisters did not want to leave him there and wanted to have him home with them to make sure he ate and rested.

Tests done on Alycea did indeed reveal a detached retina. A laser was developed at that time in its early stages to repair the detachment and was successful in restoring vision to Alycea. She would have to wear a patch and rest with little movement for the first two days until it healed. It was best to keep the patient in the hospital during that time to ensure that she did indeed keep still.

Alycea was bored after two days of doing absolutely nothing in her hospital bed. Dr. Silva had come in to check her vision and all was well. The black spots and spider webs were gone and she was seeing well once again. She told the doctor that she had had enough of sitting around in bed and was determined to go home to cook and do whatever she needed to do for her husband and family. Dr. Silva agreed that she could now go home. But she should still take it easy, no lifting or bending over for a few days.

Alycea called Ed and told him to come and get her. Since he didn't drive, Ed had to call Jaco once again. He didn't care to call Dean because he always seemed upset about having to leave work in the middle of things. There was no one to cover for him.

Jaco, on the other hand, was an assistant to the supervisor at the rubber plant and could luckily come and go without too much harassment from management. He was in constant demand by his in-laws who always called him to be their chauffeur. He did whatever was asked of him just to keep peace between his wife and her family. He knew that if he kept Belinha happy, he would be happy too. That was the secret to a happy marriage. The wife must always be happy. Sometimes though, Belinha could be excessively demanding.

If he didn't love her so much, he would not put up with all this. But, he did and she was his whole life. Belinha and their two children were the true joys in life. One day though he would take them and move away from Belinha's family. In the meantime he would work hard and save all he could until they could afford a home of their own, he thought as he drove with Ed to the hospital to pick up Alycea and bring her home.

Alycea was relieved to be home again. She had missed Ed and he assured her that he had missed her too. He did look well fed though. Her guess was he had been eating well at both of their daughters' houses. They always took care of him when she had been in the hospital or too sick to cook for him. For this, she was thankful.

She found it was getting a little tiresome to keep asking for a ride here and there and decided that as soon as she felt up to it, she was going to go to the Registry of Motor Vehicles and apply for her driver's license. She knew that Ed would not do it and neither would her daughters. They both had husbands who drove them around.

It would give her and Ed a lot more freedom to go out at night and on weekends without having to bother their son-in-law, Jaco. He was a good sport about it and never complained to their faces, anyway. But she knew that he was getting fed up with the whole thing. It wasn't fair to him either.

She told Ed about her plans. He was surprised but happy about the prospect of more freedom for them. He did admit that he didn't want to drive himself but was glad that she had the ambition to do it.

Two weeks later Alycea had applied, passed and received her driver's license at the age of forty-seven. She had celebrated by taking her husband, her daughters and their husbands to dinner at a restaurant that had just opened locally. They had to get two babysitters quickly for all the kids.

Her daughters couldn't believe that their mother had managed to get a license. They both were deathly afraid of driving and didn't see the need as long as their husbands could drive them anywhere they needed to go.

Jaco was the happiest of all since he now would be free from having to drive everyone around. Now he would have more time for his immediate needs and those of his family.

Alycea observed Jaco smiling broadly and having a grand old time at dinner that night. She knew secretly that he was celebrating not only for her but for himself as well. She couldn't help but smile back at him and wink when she caught his eye. He winked back and smiled shrugging his shoulders at the same time apologizing for his celebratory manner.

She looked at him and said, "Now Jaco, you will have more time to do what you need to do without worrying about your in-laws. We appreciated all you did for us over the years. If you ever need a ride and can't drive, you know who to call." She chuckled at the thought of having to drive Jaco somewhere.

He smiled at her and hoped secretly the day would never come that he would have to rely on Alycea to drive him around or anyone else for that matter. He was an independent guy and did not like to lean on anyone. That day would unfortunately come for him many years later when he would have to lean on others. It would be a sad day for him indeed.

# CHAPTER 45

"Ed, look what came in the mail today? It's a letter from my brother, Antonio. He wants us to come visit him in Brazil. He has two children and four grandchildren now." Alycea was excited and couldn't contain herself as she skipped around the room waving her brother's letter. By this time she had reconciled to the fact that Antonio hadn't come to their mother's funeral. She had forgiven him and wanted to get closer to him now.

"Oh, Alycea, I don't know about going all that way. Why don't you go yourself? He is, after all, your brother, your twin, and you will need time together catching up on many years and experiences." Ed looked distraught over the idea of flying. He had never flown and had no desire to start now at his age. He was fifty-four, seven years older than his wife, and did not have the energy that she always seemed to exhibit.

Alycea was not surprised in the least at Ed's reaction to flying. She knew her husband and how frightened he was about everything and anything new or different. She, on the other hand, liked change and enjoyed new experiences. In fact, she craved excitement and wanted to get out into the world as much as she could.

Ed then said, "The only place I would ever fly to would be my native home of Madeira, Portugal." He had always wanted to go back but never had enough money to do that until now. He promised Alycea, "Once you come back from Brazil, we will save up enough to travel to Madeira and see our relatives, if any of them are still alive." It had been nearly forty years since Alycea had been back there. It had been less time for Ed because he had come to America when he was in his teens.

"Ok Ed. I will go on my own and will hold you to your promise that you will fly with me to Madeira, Portugal at a later time. I'll make plans to go to visit my brother in Brazil and see when I can leave. I'll make sure you are taken care of, my dear, don't worry. I am sure that either Caterina or Belinha will let you stay with them or they can come here and check up on you and bring you dinner each night."

"You can surely make your own breakfast and lunch, can't you? Just boil an egg and make a toast for breakfast and for lunch you can have a sandwich. I will ask Caterina or Belinha to buy you groceries each week I am gone. I expect to be gone about three weeks since it is a long trip. The travel will be the hardest part of the trip. I'm sure I will be exhausted by the time I get there and also when I get back from the flight."

Alycea was getting more excited at the idea of not only seeing her brother but also seeing another continent. It would do Ed good for him to be on his own for a while and not to have to depend upon her. Distance is supposed to make the heart grow fonder too. It would also be good for their sex life possibly. It was getting a little boring and old. She couldn't help but smile at the thought of something new and interesting to do in bed. The thoughts going through her head gave her a little longing deep inside her, making her feel warm all over. She looked over coyly at Ed and smiled her most intoxicating smile and batted her eyelashes at him.

Ed, who had been thinking of something in an entirely different vein, looked up at her questioningly. He was thinking about having to do everything around the house himself for three whole weeks. It would be lonely, too, sleeping without Alycea. He saw the look in her eye and knew exactly what she wanted. He realized suddenly he wanted the same thing.

He reached out his hand to her and led her back to their room. He would worry about those other things later but for now he had something more important to do.

***

Alycea had wanted to drive herself to the airport but Jaco had insisted that he drive her to the airport to take her flight to Brazil. Ed, Caterina and Belinha had come along to say goodbye and wish her a safe trip.

Alycea kissed and hugged everyone and gave an extra hug to Ed who had tears in his eyes as he held on tightly to her. She waved goodbye to him and hurried along with her suitcase to the line forming for her flight to Sao Paulo, Brazil. She looked back one last time to see her daughters with their arms around their father as he cried. She felt badly leaving him in that state but knew he was in good hands and would survive until she returned. They had a lovely time the week prior making love every night as if it were their last week together.

As she was standing in line, a uniformed airport policeman came over and asked her to step out of line and follow him to an office nearby. Dragging her suitcase along and a large pocketbook over her shoulder, she followed him into a small office where there was another airport policeman sitting at a desk. He looked up as they entered the room.

They asked her, "What is your name? Where are you going? How long will you be there? Is this business or pleasure?"

She answered each question without a thought. "Alycea Rubelo is my name. I'm traveling to Sao Paulo, Brazil and will be there for three weeks to visit my brother." She figured that is what they do when you travel far away. She smiled sweetly at them and waited for them to stamp her ticket so she could get on board her plane.

They did not ask to see her ticket but continued to ask her other questions about her destination. "Where are you staying? Who is meeting you at the airport in Sao Paulo?"

The next thing she knew, they had handed her a small package tightly wrapped in brown paper with a white cord wrapped around it twice in a knot.

She obediently took the package. But before she could leave the office, they gave her more instructions. "Alycea Rubelo, you must take this package with you all the way to Sao Paulo. When you arrive at the airport there will be two men in uniform who will ask you for the package. You will give it to them. You must not show or mention this package to anyone during the flight or afterward. You must not tell anyone of our conversation. Do you understand all this?" They looked at her with stern expressions waiting for her response.

"Yes, I understand. I will give it to two men in Sao Paulo. Will you stamp my ticket so I can get on the plane now?" She asked matter of factly as she slipped the package into her oversized pocketbook as if she hadn't cared about it and was more interested in getting to her destination.

The two men looked at each other and shrugged their shoulders and seemed confident that she would do as they had requested but were surprised that she had not asked any questions of them. They nodded at her and then one of them escorted Alycea back to the line so she could be processed for her flight. The other man continued to watch from a distance as Alycea got into line and was processed through security and walked up the ramp to her plane.

The flight was long and tedious, sitting for over fourteen hours. She had to get up and walk around several times and use the bathroom. She felt as if she would go crazy if they didn't land soon. She had only brought a magazine to read and was tired of looking at it now. She had watched a movie, eaten snacks, dinner and more snacks and drinks and was relieved to finally feel the descent of the plane into Sao Paulo.

Just as the men at Logan Airport had told her, there were two men waiting for her as she was being processed at the Sao Paulo Airport. As had been done previously, these two men took her aside out of the line and brought her to a small office. There they asked for the package which she gave them without question. They looked it over to ensure it had not been opened and then one of the men escorted her back to the line where she had been standing previously. Before leaving Alycea, her escort thanked her for her assistance and wished her a good visit and safe travel back home.

After Alycea picked up her luggage and went outside the terminal, she looked up and down the street for any sign of her brother. She thought about the package for the first time. But her thoughts soon were interrupted by a voice excitedly calling her name. She looked around and spotted a small man not much taller than herself smiling broadly at her.

She dropped her things and reached out to hug him tightly saying his name over and over again, "Antonio, Antonio, Antonio! I've missed you so much! You look wonderful. I would know you anywhere. You really haven't changed that much in forty years. You do have a lot of gray but you are getting older as I am too!"

"It's good to see you too, Lubelia Alycea!"

"Well, since I went to America I am now called Alycea."

"Okay, Alycea, it will be. You haven't changed much either, sister!" Antonio gave her another tight hug.

Antonio or Tony as he was being called now, couldn't stop smiling at his long lost twin sister. To Alycea he would always be Antonio. His eyes crinkled as he looked at her. Tears were rolling down his cheeks as he hugged Alycea and then held her at arm's length again to look at her. He couldn't believe they were together after forty years apart.

Alycea was crying softly now as she felt the same emotion as her brother and didn't want to let go of him for fear he would disappear. They had much to celebrate and make up for all the lost years.

Behind Antonio stood his wife, Sonada, and their two children and four grandchildren. The names Alycea couldn't remember because all she could think about was she had her brother back.

Antonio picked up her luggage and Alycea grabbed her pocketbook. They got into his car and drove to his house overlooking the harbor of Sao Paulo. It was a beautiful place and bustling with activity much like their native Madeira.

Sonada showed Alycea to her room and told her to freshen up and take a nap if she was tired. If not, they would be having dinner in a few hours and she could go out to the veranda and have a glass of wine and sit with Antonio. She said they had some Port just for her to celebrate her coming.

Alycea freshened up and lay down on the comfortable bed, and before she knew it she had fallen asleep for an hour and a half. She woke up with her brother sitting by her bedside holding her hand.

It was wonderful to wake up and see the sweet face she thought she would never see again. She sat up abruptly apologizing for falling asleep and took his hand as he guided her out to the veranda to have some refreshments before they dined in a little over an hour. Antonio handed her a glass of Port wine, her favorite, Sandaman's.

As Alycea took a sip she felt the warm burn down her throat as it settled into her stomach, warming her all over. Life could be good, she thought. She wished that Ed had come to see Antonio, his beautiful family and the lovely home he had.

Antonio brought Alycea into his studio where he had numerous paintings bursting with color and vibrancy of his native home of Madeira and his present home of Brazil. He pointed out to her his favorite place to paint. From the window of the studio room she could see a prominent hill smaller than the mountains around it but situated close enough to the shore and high enough to give a spectacular view. She could just picture Antonio with his painter's smock and brush and pallet of paints in hand creating yet another masterpiece.

She spotted one painting that caught her eye. It was a painting of the field across the street from their home back in Madeira, the one in which they had hid from the men who had taken their father away forty years ago.

The grass was tall and seemed to be moving. The sun was shining down on two small figures lying in the grass peering across the road at a house, their parent's house. Another small figure was seen in the distance as if walking toward them. She gasped when she realized who the figures were and looked at her brother with eyes full of tears and a heart full of love.

She threw herself into Antonio's arms and held on tightly as the tears began to flow. She said, "Oh Antonio, I'm sorry! I didn't want to leave you. I begged Mae to take you. Please forgive her and me. I love you, Antonio!"

Antonio cleared his throat that was thick with emotion and tears before he could speak. "I know, dear Lubelia Alycea, I know. But I just had to paint this to never forget you and the short time we had as brother and sister. One day I will have it sent to you when I die. I already told Sonada that she is to send it to you in America. I want you to keep it always. Please forgive me if I cannot part with it now. It is my only connection to that time and you. I love you too, sweet Lubelia Alycea. Now let's dry our tears. It is time to celebrate that you are here. Sonada has made a wonderful meal for you. Let's go enjoy it."

They ate a delicious fish stew and a wonderful creamy flan with coffee. They sat for hours afterward talking about their separate lives and the experiences they each had since they had been separated.

They moved to the living room and Alycea held tightly to her brother's hand as he relived that fateful day. She could feel tears forming in her eyes and watched Antonio's expression get gloomy and his usually crinkling eyes took on a slack and glassy look with unshed tears. She could see there were a lot of unspent feelings bottled up inside him. She felt her heart breaking over how he must have been devastated being left behind by his mother and siblings. He must have been angry and disappointed when no one came back for him…ever.

Antonio told Alycea that he had left Madeira shortly after she and their family had sailed to America. He had moved with a cousin of Grinalda's husband and his wife who had visited them, and did not have a son. They asked if he would like to go with them to Brazil. Even though they did not adopt Antonio they did take him under their wing and brought him up as a son in Brazil along with their own two daughters.

Grinalda had allowed him to go in order to keep him safe once Filomena had left with Alycea and Manuel. She feared that the police would come after him and take him away because of the possibility he may have Influenza that had killed his father. Fortunately for Antonio and his new family, he was not infected.

Alycea apologized for what their mother had done and wished that Antonio would have let her send money for him to come to America. Antonio had told her, "Manuel did send me money years ago but I sent it back to him saying that I had found a new home. I did not wish to go to America, for Brazil was now my home."

Alycea was shocked. She had not known that Manuel had sent Antonio money. She had not heard from Manuel for many years now since their mother's funeral. He was in Portugal with his wife Ernestina and the last time he had written back to her, he said they were moving to America down south possibly to Florida.

Manuel had promised to get in touch with her once they were settled. She hoped to talk to him about her visit with Antonio and tell him all the stories Antonio had been sharing with her. Maybe one day Manuel would visit Antonio too. She wished she could have her brothers back together again.

Alycea promised that she would make up for all the lost years they did not spend together. Before she left to go back home she made definite plans with Antonio for him and his family to come visit her in America. They set a date and hugged and kissed on the promise. Alycea felt a great heaviness leaving her heart when she saw that Antonio was smiling at her with his crinkling eyes bright with happiness.

The day of her flight back to America, she looked out her bedroom window at the harbor of Sao Paulo and breathed in the Brazilian air smelling of the sea for the last time. She knew she would probably not get back there but, hopefully, the next time she saw her brother would be in America. She looked forward to that day with great anticipation and joy. She would make sure that her two brothers were together at that time and would do whatever she could to convince Manuel to come home again to see Antonio.

***

At the airport she saw the same two men watching her as she got in line to check in for her flight to return home to America. They made Alycea nervous as they kept their eyes on her. She didn't know where to look and found herself looking down at her feet to avoid their stares. What could they possibly want with me, she wondered? I don't have a package for them and I didn't even look at it or tell anyone about it.

Once she was on the plane her anxiety dissipated somewhat and she found herself relaxing enough to fall asleep. In her dreams there were two men chasing her, in their hands were guns and murder in their eyes. She jumped up with fright and refused to go back to sleep for the remainder of the long flight.

Should she tell someone about this package? Would these men come after her if she did? What was in the package that she had carried from America to Brazil? Maybe she should have refused to take it. What would they have done to her if she had?

What was she to do? Who could she trust with this information? There had to be someone – her brother – Manuel.

# CHAPTER 46

"Aleeeeesea! I'm thrilled to see you! I missed you, my darling! You look wonderul - healthy and tanned! Did you miss me too? How were Antonio and his family? Did you like Brazil? It must have been scorching there?" Ed couldn't contain his excitement; he was much relieved to have his wife finally back home after three long weeks.

Even though he was taken care of by his two daughters and never lacked for anything, he knew he needed Alycea. He loved her more than life itself. He had been worried about her and had a strange dream the night that she was flying out to Brazil. He had seen two men following her and he sensed that she might be in danger.

He woke up the next day and only felt better after she had called long distance from her brother's house telling him that she had arrived safely. He didn't like these feelings he had from time to time of impending doom. He always felt like that about himself. He knew that he would not outlive Alycea, but of course being seven years older only increased those odds. He shook his head at himself for being so inane and ridiculous.

Alycea was hugged and kissed innumerable times by Ed and he nearly took the breath out of her holding her so tightly. He seemed to be afraid to let her go.

She looked at his still handsome, slightly lined face and smiled. It was good to be home with him. She did miss him too. He finally released her and she could now answer all his questions.

"Yes, I missed you too, Edouardo. Antonio looked great, healthy and happy with his family. His wife was lovely and his two children, Antonio and Carina, I think, were sweet and polite. They are in their twenties now and have families of their own. Antonio has four grandchildren now. I got to meet all of them but don't ask me their names and ages. I couldn't keep up with all the information he kept giving me. He promised to visit us next year and bring his wife with him. He is not sure if his children and grandchildren will be able to make it though. It's too expensive to travel here. He planned on saving as much as he could over the next year just for his wife and him to come." Alycea sighed and laid her head back on the back of the couch and put her feet up. It was good to be home, she thought.

"Edouardo, would you make me some tea and bring over some of those biscoitos. We can have a little tea party, just the two of us. How does that sound dear?" Alycea fluttered her eyes at Ed and he did her bidding as always. He couldn't resist her. He knew that she had desires and he had plans to quench her needs and those of his own. It has been a long dry three weeks. It was certainly good to have her home again, he thought, as he put the kettle on for tea and rummaged in the cabinet for the cookie jar. Luckily his daughters had baked plenty of Portuguese biscoitos for him during the past three weeks.

\*\*\*

Life was soon back to normal and Alycea had almost forgotten about the package. But she was watching TV one afternoon with her feet up and a cup of coffee in one hand and the newspaper in the other, when she saw a news flash. The airport authorities had caught an older woman with a package trying to slip through security.

It seems that the woman was carrying a package containing drugs worth over one million stateside. She was taking it to Brazil, South America. They had arrested her on the spot and taken her away along with the package.

Alycea almost dropped her coffee as she watched the woman being led away in handcuffs by the police. She knew that could have been her, and decided then and there to call her brother Manuel to tell him about what she had done or had been requested to do. He would know what to do and if she should go to the police with her story. She would also relate to him the story she had just seen on TV.

Alycea called information to get his new listing for his phone in Florida. She did not know his new address since he had not written to give it to her; Manuel was not good about writing. She finally reached him and they spoke for more than half an hour after the usual pleasantries. She related all the details to him and waited for his response.

He had started off by saying, "Alycea, I love you and miss you and everybody. How are the girls doing? Say hello to the girls and Ed." Manuel was shocked when Alycea told him about her experience and asked about the package that Alycea had carried to Brazil. "Do you realize what could have happened to you?" Manuel mentioned all the possibilities of what it could have been such as drugs, stolen articles, and other contraband. "You were really fortunate not to get caught as that unfortunate woman had been. You would have gone to prison and never gotten out, especially in another country."

"I'm sorry. I know that now, Manuel." Alycea felt her heart beating wildly with fear of what might have been. She was thankful that she did not get stopped or checked at the airports that closely. Her life might have ended in a prison somewhere and she would never have seen her family again.

Manuel went on to tell her to forget about the package and not to worry about it anymore. It was over and it could not hurt her now. No one saw her with the package other than the men who had given it to her.

These men would not be telling the authorities about it any time soon or they would get themselves in trouble too. But he also recommended that she never tell anyone else about this. These men were dangerous and they could come back to find her and harm her or her family. It was best to forget that it ever happened and to go on with her life. Manuel promised that he would take this secret to his grave.

Alycea knew that someone up there was watching over her. That night she said an extra special prayer to her mother and St. Theresa to express her gratitude for their help.

She never told her family about this package until Jasmine for fear of retribution of some kind to her and her family. She was sure now they were all safe after many years. It had taken a long time for her to feel this way. She had looked over her shoulder for a long time.

# CHAPTER 47

"Ed, hurry up! We have to get to the airport to pick up Antonio. I don't want to be late and have him waiting around for us. This is a strange country to him. He doesn't know his way around and his English is not too good either." Alycea was getting exasperated at Ed for being so poky in the bathroom, shaving and combing his hair. Where did he think he was going, to see the Queen?

"I'm all set, Alycea. Relax. We will get there in plenty of time. You already called the airlines and they said the plane had not yet landed. We will be there in less than an hour and that is when he should be arriving. He has to go pick up his luggage too. That will take a little time." Ed escorted his wife out the door before she could say anything else to berate him. He knew she was just excited about the prospect of her brother and his wife coming to see her. She wanted everything to be perfect.

She had worked day and night, when she knew they were coming, to clean the house top to bottom. She had baked a cake, Portuguese biscoitos, and had marinated some baucolau and a roast beef for their dinner that night. Ed had promised to help her set the table and get Antonio and his wife, Sonada, settled with refreshments so she could attend to the cooking.

Alycea and Ed got to the airport in plenty of time and Antonio and Sonada arrived half an hour after their scheduled time. Alycea was always impatient with Ed when she was nervous or worried about something. At this point in his life, Ed expected and accepted her behavior in stride.

He was kind, sweet and patient with her at all times and never raised his voice. She was the opposite of him normally anyway.

She always took all her frustrations out on poor Ed. Alycea knew she did this but couldn't help herself. She always felt that Ed was her rock even though he was quiet and just listened most of the time to her ranting and ravings. He was strong for her when he needed to be but was otherwise a real softy.

He knew how to handle her and always put things into perspective when she was out of her mind with worry. All he really wanted was to have peace in his life. He would say anything and everything to her just to obtain this peace and quiet.

She had a tendency to exaggerate and blow everything up, yelling and screaming if anything did not go her way. She really hadn't changed from the strong, stubborn little girl from long ago.

Ed knew that Alycea would behave herself with her brother and his wife visiting for a few weeks. He just may get his wish for some peace and quiet during that time anyway.

The two couples sat around feeling full to bursting from the delicious roast beef dinner. They sipped their coffee and ate cake and biscoitos while they talked about their lives and countries and all the similarities and differences.

Antonio and Sonada had taken Alycea to see all the sights while she was in Brazil and now they wanted to see the sights in America. Alycea had promised to take them to see the Statue of Liberty and Ellis Island. She had written over the years about the great Lady and wanted Antonio to see it firsthand to feel the incredible power of her presence as she had.

She also hoped to take him to Niagara Falls to stay there overnight before coming back home. But before they would take these two trips she wanted to have a big cookout at her daughter Belinha's new house in Dracut. They had moved there when Jasmine was eleven years old and Raymond was only six. Five years after they had moved Belinha had another child, a little girl named Shannon. She was a sweet little girl with platinum blonde hair and the apple of Jaco's eye. He doted on his little daughter and like never before he came out of his shell. He loved his children deeply but was always afraid of losing them due to his upbringing by his crazy mother who wouldn't let him out of her sight when he was just a child.

With Shannon, he began to relax more and enjoy her as she was growing up. They became closer and did everything together in the yard, even painting the house as she got old enough to climb a ladder and help him.

Belinha and Jaco's house had a large backyard where the whole family gathered every weekend over the years to have a cookout. Caterina and Dean had also moved just prior to Jaco and Belinha to the same town of Dracut a couple of streets over from each other. They had both always stayed close to their parents who still lived in Lowell moving from tenement to tenement over the years.

The split had been good for both daughters and the moves gave them some much needed privacy and more space for their families to grow. Alycea and Ed visited each of their daughters often and were there every Sunday for the cookouts in the summer and the cook-ins in the winter months.

The whole family was there at the cookout to celebrate the visit of their Uncle Antonio and Aunt Sonada. Alycea was ecstatically happy to be with her twin brother and to introduce him to all his extended family after too many lost years. Life was full and rich and complete for her. It couldn't be any more perfect except...maybe if Manuel were there.

Ed watched Alycea as she hovered over her brother not letting him out of her sight. She was just happy to have him there to share him with her family. She just couldn't stop smiling from ear to ear. It brought tears to Ed's eyes just to see her this happy. He was a softy, that's for sure. He found his eyes tearing up at the slightest thing lately. It must be because he was getting older.

He knew that she was missing her brother Manuel though and had wanted him to be there when Antonio came to visit. He had asked Belinha and Caterina to write a letter to the last address they had for their Uncle Manuel to tell him that his brother was coming for a visit from Brazil and would only be there for three weeks.

Belinha had received a letter back finally from Manuel who was sailing in the Caribbean the week before the cookout. He said he would try to come up this way within a week or so by plane with Ernestina. Belinha had told him about the cookout planned at her house and hoped he could be there to surprise Alycea and Antonio. He had promised he would do his best to get there on time.

\*\*\*

The food was plentiful and delicious as usual. The meal was prepared by Belinha and Caterina who were both excellent cooks with their own distinctive styles. Belinha prepared her special potato salad, fried chicken, stuffed cabbage leaves and tossed salad while Caterina made her crown roast pork with raisin sauce and favas and linguica and Portuguese rice. There was plenty for all and would be leftovers for anyone who wanted to take some home.

They were just starting to clean up the table outside when they saw a man and woman coming up the walk to the backyard. The man looked familiar to Belinha and she suddenly realized who it was.

She put down the dishes she was holding and ran out to meet them calling over her shoulder to her mother.

"Mae, look who is here? Come quick! Oh my God, Uncle Manuel and Aunt Ernestina, you made it!" Belinha hugged and kissed them both then stepped aside for fear of getting run over by her mother who was barreling down the sidewalk at the three of them.

Manuel put his arms out to catch his sister who was screaming out, "Manuel, you made it! I can't believe you came. How did you know we were here? I didn't tell you about this cookout and Belinha's new house. Who told you?"

Manuel didn't answer but just whirled his sister around until she was dizzy, hugged her fiercely to him and kissed her on both cheeks before putting her down again. He gave her his signature smile and wink and said, "Alycea, are you going to feed us or are you going to talk all day?" He patted her on her tush and pushed her along to the backyard so he and Ernestina could meet the rest of the family.

Everyone was rushing forward when they saw what the excitement was all about. There were many more hugs and kisses to go around and pats on the back and introductions to his wife Ernestina who had not met most of the family yet. Then, last but not least, Antonio and his wife stepped forward to greet Manuel. Antonio had tears in his eyes as he put his arms around his big brother and sobbed against his brother's strong sailor's shoulders.

They stayed like that for enumerable minutes before separating to let Manuel meet Sonada, his sister-in-law. Manuel said, with his usual quick wit, "Brother, you did a good job picking out this beautiful wife. Too bad I didn't see her first. Ha ha!" He said with a chuckle after giving Sonada a hug and peck on the cheek and in turn introducing her to Ernestina who just rolled her eyes at her husband's remarks.

Antonio quipped back at his brother for the first time in their lives, "She would be too much woman for you, big brother." He then laughed even louder than his brother when he saw the surprised expression on Manuel's face.

Manuel grabbed his brother and playfully hugged and ruffled his coarse and wavy hair. They both had a good laugh together as if they had never been apart. The only difference was Antonio stood up to his brother and was a lot more assertive than he had been as a child.

Antonio had missed both his sister and his brother. He had been closer to Alycea but had always looked up to his big brother with adoration and respect. He had always wanted to be just like Manuel when he grew up.

Antonio had grown up to be a mild tempered and stable person always in control of his life. Manuel had always been cavalier about life in general and carefree and sometimes emotional but not as openly as was Alycea.

Manuel had some tragedies in his life to deal with that had hardened him a little and he was no longer as cavalier as he once had been. He was now a much quieter and complacent person, Antonio had observed, as he talked to Manuel about his life without his siblings.

He told Manuel, "I'm sorry I sent back the money you sent me to go to America. But it was because I had made a new life in Brazil and didn't want to leave. Also, I was afraid of going to America to see my family there. I was certain that you all did not love me and wanted nothing to do with me. That was the feeling I got when I was abandoned at eight years old."

"I'm sorry, Antonio. I was upset, too, when Mae told us you wouldn't be coming with us."

Antonio nodded solemnly and said, "It has taken me many years to come to terms with what Mae had done to me. I understood later on when I had children of my own. I knew that it must have been a heartwrenching decision for Mae to make. I felt sorry for her and also for not going to America to see her before she died. I always loved Mae but felt somewhat disconnected from her."

"I understand, Antonio. I think I would have felt the same." Manuel patted Antonio on his back to reassure him that he was loved.

Antonio had lived with his adopted Brazilian family for most of his life and they became his parents and siblings. He still loved his sister and brother but time did strange things to families; it split them apart. He was happy to be here with all his American relatives but longed to return to his now native home of Brazil. He already missed his children and grandchildren who could not afford to come for the trip.

Antonio looked over at his lovely sister, Alycea and his handsome, rugged and tanned brother, Manuel. He tried to capture their faces and the faces of all the family in his memory for eternity. He knew that he would not return to America. He was under the care of his doctor for a heart condition and knew that another long trip like this one could kill him. He would make the best of the time he had here to spend with Alycea and Manuel.

Alycea watched her brothers talking together animatedly. This sight filled her with much happiness that she thought she would burst. She had thought she would never see this day come to fruition.

She knew that Antonio was not well. Sonada had told her in private during the first days they were in America that she was worried about Antonio's health and that he was under the care of his doctor back home.

Alycea had noticed him wincing at times going up or down stairs. He had put his hand over his chest and stopped to take a breath each time he had to walk a long distance or climb. Sonada asked Alycea not to tell Antonio that she had mentioned his health to her. Alycea promised not to tell him that she knew but she found herself watching over him more closely during the three weeks he was with her.

The day before Antonio and Sonada were scheduled to return to Brazil, Alycea found him in her mother's old room kneeling down beside St. Theresa's statue that belonged to their mother.

Alycea stopped at the door of the room Antonio and his wife were using while they were with her. She overheard Antonio praying to their mother in front of the statue asking for her to forgive him for not coming to see her while she was alive.

He suddenly turned, hearing Alycea at the door. She noticed the tears that were flooding his eyes. He got up from his knees and went to his sister, arms outstretched for a hug. He rested his head on her shoulder since they were approximately the same height of 5' 2" and he let Alycea hold him until he stopped crying. Alycea's tears were mingling with his and she was soon quite soaked down the front of her blouse.

Alycea spoke softly as she told Antonio that their mother had heard his prayers and that he should not worry about this anymore. She told him, "Antonio, Mae loved you more and because of her deep love for you she feared that you were not well enough to travel with us. She feared that she might lose you to sickness or death if she brought you to America. You must believe this. She knew in her heart that you would be safer with Gracinda and that she would take care of you." Alycea patted Antonio on the arm as she smiled reassuringly at him.

"Thank you, Lubelia Alycea. I love you! I've missed you with all my heart. Some days I felt like I was missing part of myself. But I always felt that we would be together one day before I died. Now here we are."

"Yes, here we are, Antonio. I love you too, brother. You know what? I think Mae was right," Alycea said. "You certainly turned out perfect! Look at you, Antonio! You are handsome and you have a wonderful life and a family who love you in Brazil. And now you have family in America who love you a lot too! Don't forget us!"

"We have to keep in touch by writing and visiting one another over the years we have left. Let's shake on it – make me a promise that you will write to me and visit again. Please Antonio, do this for me. I have missed you deeply and feel whole now that we are together even if it is only for a short time." Alycea put out her small hand to receive her brother's hand which was a little bigger than her own. It felt warm and soft in hers and she squeezed it back and then brought it up to her lips and kissed it lightly.

Antonio's voice was a little choked with emotion as he replied, "Yes, dear sister, I will write to you and if I can travel I will certainly try to come visit you again. If I cannot come this way please travel to see me again instead. Ok?" He, in turn, kissed his sister on the cheek, as he shook her hand then held her close sealing the deal. He knew well that this could be the last time he would hold his sister in his arms. He felt the prickling of more tears start and fought to hold them back.

Alycea heard her brother sniffle trying to hold back the tears which she was sure had filled his eyes, for she was having a hard time herself keeping the tears in her own eyes from flowing. She whispered to him, "Antonio, I love you, dear brother, with all my heart. These three weeks have been wonderful getting to know you again. Take care of yourself and your family. We will keep in touch and see one another again."

Antonio smiled the same sweet smile she had always remembered on the day they left him behind. That smile had haunted her thoughts and dreams for over forty years as they would continue to haunt her until the last day of her life.

The day came too quickly for Antonio and Sonada to travel home. At the airport Antonio reassured his sister that all was forgiven about the past and that he would write to her often and think of her every day.

He said, "May God bless you, dear sister, and all your family. I hope we can see each other again if not in this life but in the next. Stay well and be happy." Antonio kissed Alycea on both cheeks and shook Ed's hand before he turned and picked up their luggage, took Sonada by the arm and walked into the lobby to check in for their flight.

That would be the last time Alycea would see her brother. He died six months later from a massive heart attack while he was doing what he loved most in life, painting the seacoast from the top of one of the surroundings hills of his home.

The painting arrived one week after his death with a note that had been written by Antonio.

> "Alycea, sweet sister, please accept this as a remembrance of our close bond, even though we were separated, we remained close in heart.
> Never forget that I love you and will be with you in spirit always."

> Love, Antonio

Along with the painting and Antonio's note, was a short note from Sonada.

'My heart is broken. The love of my life, Tony, is no longer with me. He passed from a massive heart attack. I miss him so much, Alycea. I know you understand my sorrow better than anyone else. You know the pain of losing someone dear to you. Tony asked me to send you this painting after his death. I know you will treasure it always.

I also found some letters that you had written to Tony over the years when I was cleaning out his studio. I included them in the package with the painting.

Stay well and keep in touch.

With much love, Sonada'

They kept in touch until Sonada's death five years later.

\*\*\*

"Avoa, please don't cry. I know how much you miss him. I remember the day that Uncle Antonio and Aunt Sonada came to my parent's house. It was such a joyous time for us all."

"I was fascinated by Uncle Antonio because he was the complete opposite of you. He was quiet and soft spoken and sweet. Oh, I don't mean anything by that. I love you, Avoa. But you are more robust, demonstrative, emotional and outspoken and you have a laugh that would crack up anyone, even Oscar the Grouch." Jasmine noticed her grandmother had abruptly stopped crying and had a surprised look on her face at Jasmine's remarks.

Jasmine couldn't help herself and started to laugh. Her grandmother then suddenly threw back her head and let out her signature booming laugh to join in.

Jasmine was at once relieved that she had not hurt her grandmother's feelings, heaven forbid. Her grandmother could be a formidable woman and quick to anger. She did not want to upset her at her advanced age. The laughter quickly diffused the situation and all was forgiven as they continued on with the past most of which was known by Jasmine but it was nice to hear Avoa tell her version of it.

# CHAPTER 48

"Timothy Matthew, how's my little great grandson doing today? Do you want Avoa to put you in your swing or do you want to play in your playpen?" Alycea was now taking care of Jasmine's first child who was three months old. Of course, he was too young to answer her but she spoke to him as if he were an older child and sometimes in her native Portuguese.

Alycea had started taking care of Timothy while Jasmine was working at a lawyer's office. Jasmine had started working when Timothy was just seven weeks old. It was a tough transition to leave her son but she knew that he would be well cared for by her grandmother. The extra money was needed since they had just bought their first house.

Timothy Matthew was a handsome baby with his soft, dark blonde hair and green eyes. He was going to be a heartbreaker for sure. He was bright from an early age and loved to sing and dance as soon as he could walk and talk.

Alycea enjoyed taking care of Timothy and they became quite close. She would drive over to Jasmine's house from her Lowell tenement leaving her husband Ed behind each day. He did not want to leave the house and preferred to be in his own house. He wanted to watch his favorite shows and just relax.

Alycea didn't fight with Ed about that but actually enjoyed getting out of the house and away from him each day. She would return to make their supper each night at six or seven o'clock when Jasmine came home. Ed was now seventy and slowing down quite a bit, while Alycea was still active and vibrant at sixty-three.

She stayed active taking care of Timothy and loved every minute of it. She took him for walks in the warm weather and in the winter they played on the floor with his toys and she read him stories from an endless supply of children's books.

When it was nap time she would sing in Portuguese to him as her mother had once done to her and her brother when they were little. Timothy would fall fast asleep before she finished the tune. He would learn the song as the years went on and learned a little Portuguese through immersion which he would pass on to his own children one day.

When he was two years old Alycea decided that she was no longer able to take care of him. She was getting a little tired running after him. He was extremely active. Jasmine asked her mother, Belinha, to take over the care of Timothy to give Avoa Alycea a rest.

Belinha had left work due to a problem with her knees and the diabetes that she had inherited from her grandmother, Filomena. But she was well enough still to take care of Timothy. Some days he did wear her out though too. She did this for two more years and was assisted at times by Alycea who came to visit because she had missed Timothy.

Jasmine had been home after being laid off from work for a month when she realized she was pregnant again. Just seven months later Jasmine would call upon her grandmother once again for assistance when she fell down the stairs and sprained her ankle. She somehow managed to drive to her mother's house where her brother and grandmother were at the time. Her brother, Raymond, picked her up, all 150 pounds of her and took her to the hospital to have her ankle x-rayed.

Alycea and Belinha took charge of Timothy until Jasmine could get back home. Once she was home she could not walk or use crutches due to fear of possibly harming the baby and had to crawl around or be aided by her mother or grandmother to get to the bathroom. Alycea came every day with Belinha in tow during the last two months of Jasmine's pregnancy to help her with Timothy and prepare the meals for her family.

The day Jasmine's water broke Alycea rushed over to the hospital to see the new baby, this time a little girl, Brittany Marie. With her blond curly hair and blue eyes, she was a real beauty. She had a dimple in each cheek and a cleft in her chin both of which she had inherited from her Grandpa Ed. Alycea was the first one to notice that right away.

Another event happened that would affect everyone profoundly that day. While Brittany was coming into this world, another life was leaving, Ed, known as Grandpa Ed to all his grandchildren, had a fatal heart attack.

Earlier Alycea had called home to announce the good news to Ed and he was just thrilled that Jasmine had a little girl. Alycea had told him about the dimples and cleft in the baby's chin just like his and said she would be home soon.

When Alycea got home Ed was waiting as usual in his favorite lounge chair in their small den with the TV on. Ed looked relaxed as always with his hands in his lap and his head back against the chair probably fast asleep. But something wasn't right, Alycea noticed as she walked towards him.

She called out his name and realized as she stood over him that he was not sleeping. All she could do was scream and cry and throw herself at his feet calling out his name over and over,"Edouardo, Edouardo, no Edouardo, noooo!"

The neighbors heard her screams and called an ambulance and ran over to assist her. There was nothing they or even the EMTs, when they arrived, could do for Ed. He was gone. He had died from a heart attack most likely during his nap. He had died peacefully in his sleep.

The kindly neighbor, Mrs. Pareter, helped Alycea up after the ambulance had taken away Ed's body to be brought to the morgue until arrangements could be made. She asked Alycea what her daughter's phone numbers were. Belinha and Caterina were soon there to console their mother who had finally stopped crying but now was in shock and deathly quiet. They thanked Mrs. Pareter for staying with her until they arrived.

Caterina called the funeral parlor and arranged to have them pick up her father's body from the morgue and prepare him for burial. Alycea heard her on the phone and told her daughters that she was ready to pick out his casket and help them with the burial plans.

They looked surprised to see their mother suddenly sitting straight backed in the chair and with a determination in her eyes they had not seen for a long time. She had gotten herself together and was now in charge. She would grieve more later when she was alone but now, she had more important things to take care of to ensure that her precious Edouardo was put to rest.

***

To keep busy now that she was alone, Alycea went often to visit Jasmine, Brittany and Timothy. She would offer to take care of them along with Belinha for assistance. She enjoyed seeing her great grandchildren growing up to be such handsome and beautiful children.

Jasmine enjoyed being home with her children, teaching and nurturing them and also appreciated the extra help from her mother and grandmother when they came to visit or babysit. The children got along well and Brittany loved her brother, Timothy, and would mimic him every chance she got.

When Timothy had to go to school, Brittany was crushed but Alycea was there to lend a hand as always to ease the transition for all. She came over and played with Brittany as Jasmine took Timothy to the Kindergarten class for the first day.

Life has a habit of sending obstacles one's way. Alycea would once again have to deal with another loss.

*** 

"Oh, no, please tell me that isn't true? I don't think Mae can handle another loss in her life right now." Belinha reacted to the latest news from her sister, Caterina.

"Was he sick? How and when did it happen?" Belinha asked, feeling her heart pound and her hands begin to shake.

Belinha couldn't believe that her Uncle Manny was dead. She had loved her Uncle Manuel. He had been instrumental in bringing her out of her shell when she was just a little girl. She had never been short of friends after he had visited her school that day with his Merchant Marine paraphernalia and tales of his sea travels. These sweet memories managed to bring on more tears for Belinha.

Caterina talked over her sister's sobs and continued her tale of his death. "Evidently he had been on his way to visit Mae after hearing about Pai's death. He had been living in Florida and was planning on sailing up the coast to Massachusetts to dock and then rent a car to drive up to see the family. He never made it though and was lost at sea. His body was just found by some sailors when it washed up at a port close to the Carolinas. It was badly decomposed and not much of it was left after being out at sea so long. It took a while to do an ID on the body due to difficulty finding his dental records. He had traveled far and wide and had seen many dentists at different ports he had passed through."

"I don't understand why Aunt Ernestina did not contact us that he was missing. That must have been about three years ago when Pai died. What, he has been missing all this time? No wonder he did not answer our letters. The last letter I received from him must have been just before he set sail. I had told him about Pai's death and he had promised to come right up to spend some time with Mae."

Caterina hesitated before responding to her sister. "Belinha, I talked to Aunt Ernestina. She is the one who called to tell us that his body had been found. They had been separated for the past five years. She was living in their home in Florida and he had found himself an apartment along the coast of Florida where he could be close to his boat. It was not unusual for them not to talk or see each other for months or years at a time. She had gotten used to him being away at sea most of their married life."

"Aunt Ernestina said that she would be going through Uncle Manny's things. It seems that he had left most of his stuff at their house and only took what he needed at the time he had moved out. He never went back to pick up the rest of his stuff. She will be sending out some of it to Mae - letters and other things that she thought Mae might like to have as keepsakes."

"Oh, Caterina, we have to tell Mae about his death. We better go over there to tell her now before she finds out by watching TV. It will probably be on the news. You know how Mae likes to watch CNN. I will get Jaco to bring us over to her house. Be ready and we will just beep the horn for you out front." Belinha hung up the phone and ran outside to find Jaco who had been cutting the lawn and cleaning up the yard.

After dragging Jaco in to take a shower and hurrying him up, they were finally sitting in their car outside Caterina's house waiting for her to appear. Caterina came out and ran to the car and hopped in and they took off quickly. No one wanted to complete this task but they knew it must be done and better to get it over with as painlessly as possible. They would have to take Mae back to one of their houses to stay until she could handle this new loss. They didn't want to leave her alone, not knowing what she would do to herself.

They arrived quickly and went in to face their mother. Alycea was sitting in her rocking chair watching CNN when they opened the door. They sat down next to her.

She hadn't turned her face until they called her name, and when she looked up at them there were tears in her eyes. Their eyes went to the TV screen where the announcer was saying, 'A sailboat was recovered from the waters outside of the Bermuda Triangle. A man's body was pulled from the waters that may be connected to the boat. He may have fallen overboard during the rough surf due to the hurricane strength winds that he must have traveled through.'

There was a picture of the sailboat and on it was the name 'Cristina Maria.'

***

Alycea had received the package of Manuel's belongings from Ernestina shortly after his death. As Alycea had sorted through it, she had found her letters to him neatly tied up with a string in a sailor's knot, so like her brother, and a sweater that Alycea had given him one Christmas.

What was surprising was the stuffed animal tucked at the bottom of the box. Alycea left out a cry of anguish; it was her twin brother, Antonio's, stuffed lion, Simmy. Antonio must have put it in his will to have it sent to Manuel as she had inherited Antonio's painting.

She picked up the lion, tattered and worn from many years, and carefully pressed it to her heart. She felt transported back to the day Antonio had stuffed it into his backpack.

Tears were running down her cheeks but all she could do was hold onto Simmy, the only thing left of her brothers. Now she was really all alone.

# CHAPTER 49

Alycea was slowing down a little at seventy after her husband's death and three years later the death of her older brother, Manuel. She missed them both desperately.

She never thought about ever getting married again. She didn't yet consider herself old but knew her chances of finding another good man like her Edouardo was slim at her age.

She visited with her daughters, babysat all the great grandchildren, taking turns at her daughters' houses and saw a few friends occasionally. The strange thing was that a lot of her friends were getting older too and they were sick and dying off one after the other. She feared that soon she would be the only one left from her generation.

She found her vision starting to blur again and black spots appearing and knew from her past history that she may have another detached retina. She called Dr. Silva right away and made an appointment to see him. He referred her to an ophthalmologist in the area who saw her immediately because of her symptoms and history.

Her son-in-law, Jaco, offered to take her as always. Belinha came along to talk to the doctor while Jaco stayed in the waiting room as the chauffeur, a job he had mastered over the years.

The doctor told her, "Yes, Alycea, you do have a detached retina. I want to admit you directly to the hospital. I will follow close behind to correct this problem before you lose your vision completely." He didn't know how she had managed to see anything at this point. There was a chance that she may not regain her vision completely even after laser surgery which he omitted telling Alycea. The doctor promised, "I will do all I can to save your vision in your right eye, Alycea."

Belinha held her mother's hand as this news was delivered to them. Her mother was stoic about it and just nodded her head and said, "Thank you, doctor. I'm sure you will do all you can." She got up and walked out, tightly holding onto Belinha's hand.

Surgery was scheduled shortly after Alycea was admitted and it went as well as could be expected. The tear was repaired but some vision was lost and she would never see well in that eye again. She would always have to use a magnifier to read anything.

Alycea continued to devour several love stories from romance novels. She used her trusty magnifier and kept requesting larger print books in order to see better. Her vision over the next several years continued to dim in that eye forcing her to give up driving and some of her freedom and independence.

One day Caterina and Belinha were talking about their mother and discussing what could be done to perk up her spirits. She seemed more depressed lately and it was becoming too difficult to read. They decided to buy her a radio and cassette player along with cassettes of all her favorite singers, Frank Sinatra, Dean Martin and Perry Como. They planned to give it to her at her big birthday celebration that weekend. She was going to be seventy-five years old.

All the family was there and also, Francisco Tavares, a cousin of Ed's who had come as a surprise. Francisco and his wife Lynn, who had died a year before, used to go out dancing and to dinner with Alycea and Ed when they were much younger. They had since lost touch with each other. Caterina and Belinha knew this old friend might be just the medicine to cheer their mother up.

They had not told Alycea about the party but had said they wanted to take her out to dinner to celebrate her 75th birthday. She was thoroughly surprised when they walked into the restaurant function hall that was all done up with colorful balloons and a large banner proclaiming, 'Happy 75th Birthday, Alycea!'

The biggest surprise was when Caterina and Belinha brought over Francisco to wish their mother a happy birthday. Alycea looked up at the pleasant but shy looking man who stood in front of her. He smiled at her when she realized who he was. Alycea put out her arms to Francisco and hugged him and kissed him twice over. She was happy to see him. It was like having a piece of Edouardo back again, being her husband's cousin.

Francisco hugged Alycea back and told her, "Thank you for inviting me to your party. It's good to see you again. I'm sorry I haven't kept in touch."

Alycea looked around for Francisco's wife. "Where's Lynn?"

"She died a year ago from cancer. It has been difficult losing her just as you lost Edouardo. It's lonely without her."

"I know what you mean, Francisco. I feel lonely without Ed, too."

Francisco had been living alone in Rhode Island at the same house ever since. He hastily told Alycea, "You are welcome to come and visit me any time. I have plenty of room with three bedrooms and a large back yard where I grow all my own vegetables and a lovely flower garden."

Alycea's eyes sparkled for the first time since Ed had died. She felt a new stirring inside her just looking at Francisco. She had always thought that he was a good looking young man back then and now she could still see a good looking but older man in front of her.

"That sounds nice, Francisco. I may take you up on that invitation sometime." Alycea smiled coyly and batted her eyes. Even at her age she still knew how to flirt.

Francisco never left Alycea's side for the rest of the evening and there was a buzzing going around the hall as the family talked about Avoa Alycea's new boyfriend. It was good to see her as happy and animated as she once was. She had become solemn and depressed since she lost Ed. They all knew that Ed would have definitely approved of Alycea and Francisco getting together. Francisco was, after all, part of his family and a good man who was well off and could take care of Alycea in her golden years. He was a few years younger than Alycea. Her family all felt that he would probably be around to take care of her and may even outlive her.

\*\*\*

Within that year of their courtship, Alycea and Francisco were married. They had lived together for most of the year anyway at Francisco's Rhode Island home and finally decided to get married to make it all legal.

They set up housekeeping in their home and Alycea put in her own touches to make it her home now. She cooked and cleaned and loved her new life and her new husband. He was kind and good to her and provided for her in every way. But it was inevitable that one of them would get sick and possibly die leaving the other alone. They had been fortunate to have had a wonderful life together for nearly fifteen years before things changed drastically.

Francisco was the first to get sick, suffering from dementia. Alycea was beside herself when he was put into a nursing home because she was unable to take care of him anymore on her own. She visited him every day, hand feeding him each meal. He didn't remember who she was at this stage but that did not deter her from talking to him for hours and telling him about their life.

The fateful day came when Alycea received a call from the nursing home about Francisco. He wasn't responding and they asked her to come right away. She called one of her neighbors to drive her since she had stopped driving years before.

When she got there he had passed away peacefully. She looked at the serene expression on his face and kissed his still warm lips before the tears started to fall.

She backed away and sat down next to his bed and reached out to take his hand for the last time. She told him that she had loved two men in her life each differently. Both men were special to her and she cherished the time she had with them.

She told Francisco she would miss him greatly but knew that one day she would see him again. She looked forward to that day. She stayed with him until they came and took his body away.

Her neighbor came to get her and brought her back to her now empty home. She called her daughters to tell them of her husband's death. Caterina said she would call the funeral home and make all the arrangements for his burial and she and Dean would be driving over there in a few hours to be with her.

They, in turn, called all their children. One of Caterina's boys offered to drive to Rhode Island and pick up his grandmother to bring her back to live with him after the funeral. He said he would make an apartment for her in his home to give Avoa her own space.

Alycea was nearly ninety now and was still able to take care of herself and clean her own house but could not take care of the entire garden and flowers as Francisco had done.

She would have Caterina and Dean and her grandchildren take care of the garden when they got there and pick all the vegetables, she thought. Francisco would be dismayed if the vegetables spoiled before they picked them. This thought disturbed her and only brought on more tears. Her beloved Francisco; how would she go on without him? She felt empty inside and her heart was broken once again. Would she be able to heal this time or would she die of a broken spirit?

\*\*\*

Alycea sat at her small kitchen table and sipped a cup of tea as she thought over everything that she would have to do now that Francisco was gone. She would have to look for his will, clean out his clothes and pack up his things to give away. She would also have to put the house up for sale and move. She was too old to have to do all this by herself but she knew that her daughters would help.

She drained the last sip of tea and got up and went into the bedroom she had shared with Francisco for nearly fifteen years. She looked around at the flowered lavender and blue print drapes and matching bedspread, the ginger jar lamps in lavender and white to match and felt a great loss. She missed him desperately, especially his laughter and joking manner. He had made her happy and content. She found herself almost laughing out loud at some of his silly jokes and antics from him she remembered over the years.

She opened the top drawer of his chest and noticed how neat he had been with his socks and underwear. She got out a box from the closet and started removing all his socks and underwear and placing them into the box. She did the same to each drawer, carefully removing all the neatly folded tee shirts and shorts and sweatshirts and sweaters. Next she went to the closet and lovingly stroked and inhaled the fragrance of his woodsy cologne before folding each article of clothing.

He kept all his clothes in good shape and she was sure that someone could use his things at the local shelter or Salvation Army Store. She chose a sweater and sweatshirt that were always his favorites to keep for her. She placed them in a drawer in her own bureau before picking up the box and putting it on the bed. The box was heavier than she expected and she felt winded afterward. She would have Dean carry it out to the car to take to the shelter or wherever he wanted to go with it.

The phone rang as she was walking into the kitchen. She picked it up hesitantly. She really did not feel like talking to anyone right now. She was still upset and would start to cry at the slightest thing if anyone gave their condolences to her.

She picked up the receiver and said, "Hello. Yes, this is Alycea Tavares. No, I did not know that. Ok, I guess you can come over but can you come when my daughter is here? I think I would feel better if she were here to listen to what information you have. Ok, I will call you later when she gets here. What is your number? Ok, I got it. Thank you, Atty. Stevens."

Alycea looked at the clock; it seemed to be moving in slow motion. She was anxious for Caterina and Dean to get there. She did all she could in her room for the time being. There was a whole house to go through yet and a cellar chock full of all kinds of planting stuff and tools. She never went down there; it was Francisco's domain. She would have Dean go down and take what he wanted and then she would give away the rest to her neighbors or anyone else who may want something. She couldn't imagine any of it being worth much.

It was about time for dinner. She had not had much to eat, she realized, when she heard her stomach grumble. She went to the refrigerator to view what was remaining from yesterday's meal and found a chicken leg and thigh and some rice. She put the plate in the microwave and sat down at the table to wait for her food to warm.

She was dozing off at the table and jumped suddenly when the timer to the microwave went off. She got up unsteadily and removed the plate and sat down to try to eat something. She felt exhausted and knew that it was due not only to not eating and also to the shock of losing Francisco.

She was determined to clean her plate. She needed to feel stronger and less tired to tackle all the things she would have to do in the next few days, weeks, months or year, however long it took to get her house sold and for her to move back closer to her daughters.

She was finishing up her dinner when the doorbell rang. She put her plate in the sink and went to the front door. She looked through the peephole and saw the familiar faces of Caterina and Dean. Their faces looked strained and anxious.

She feared she looked a sight. She fixed her hair by running her fingers through it quickly and straightened out her dress before opening the door. She tried to put a smile on her face but failed. When Caterina ran to put her arms around her, she just collapsed into her and with Dean's help they guided her over to the couch.

"Oh Mae, I'm deeply sorry about Francisco. I thought he was doing better last week. It was too sudden for him to….Please don't cry. I know how hard it is for you, but we are here for you now and we will make plans to take care of you." Caterina got a few tissues from her purse and gave them to her mother.

"Mae, I have to ask you some questions and I know they will be hard for you to answer. What is the name of the funeral home that took Francisco? Do you know if Francisco had any other living relatives that we have to call?"

"It's Doherty's Funeral Home and yes, he had a few cousins but they don't live around here. He also has a grandniece who lives about five miles away from here. I didn't call her. I forgot all about her until you just asked. I should call her now. She had been here occasionally to sit with me to have tea after Francisco went into the nursing home. She was comforting and sweet. Her name is Carolyn. Now where did I put her number?" Alycea fumbled in the drawer where she had put the address book with telephone numbers the last time she had used it. She was getting a little forgetful, she thought, and then was relieved when she came across the book buried underneath other household bits of this and that.

"Mae, do you want me to call Carolyn? I can talk to her if you are not up to it. Did you eat dinner yet? Dean can take us out or I can see what I can make for us here. We didn't get to eat on the way over figuring that we would take you out somewhere," Caterina said as she looked up Carolyn's number in the address book.

"Yes Caterina, I ate some leftover chicken and rice that I had made yesterday. I hate cooking for one person and I always make too much. I always have leftovers for the next day. I have some leftover meatloaf in there if you and Dean want some. I could make a tossed salad for Dean. I know how much he likes his salad." Alycea opened the fridge to look for the meatloaf and some salad fixings as she heard Caterina in the background talking to Carolyn.

The coolness of the inside of the refrigerator felt good against her face which suddenly felt flushed. She heard Caterina softening her voice and whispering something that she couldn't quite hear. She knew that they were talking about her and if she was all right. Alycea wondered that herself. She had now lost two husbands and was again alone. What was she going to do? She suddenly felt depleted and grief-stricken.

She heard Caterina saying goodbye and hanging up the phone. She felt daughter's hand on her back as Caterina stood next to her at the opened refrigerator door. "Mae, please go sit down. I will fix something for me and Dean. How about a cup of tea or coffee for you in the meantime? Dean will have a glass of wine, I am sure, if you have some Chianti around or any red wine will do." She looked over at Dean who just raised his eyebrows at her. She knew what he was thinking, nothing but Italian wine for him.

Alycea looked at Dean and saw the disgust on his face and knew how fussy he was as she poured him a glass of red wine of unknown origin she had found in the liquor cabinet. She and Francisco were not wine drinkers. They only had some Bailey's Irish Cream liquor or apricot brandy at night after dinner occasionally. The wine that was there had been brought by visitors over an inestimable amount of time.

The doorbell rang giving Alycea something to do. She felt useless and depressed. When Alycea opened the door, there stood her younger daughter, Belinha and her husband, Jaco.

"Oh, Belinha, it's good to see you and Jaco. I didn't realize you were coming so soon after your sister. Please come in."

Alycea was happy to see them and welcomed them into her house and into her arms.

Belinha held onto her mother and whispered words of comfort and love. "Mae, I am so sorry about Francisco. I can't imagine how you feel. We are here now. We will help you get through this, I promise. We want you back home with us where we can watch over you."

Jaco kissed Alycea and said, "Mae, I'm sorry about Francisco. I will do whatever you need me to do. I am here for you."

Alycea smiled but her eyes were deep pools of sadness as she said, "Thank you both for being here for me. I will need some help getting this house in order to put it on the market and pack up all of my stuff.

I want to give away most of the furniture or sell what I can. Will you help me with that?"

"Of course we will, Mae." Belinha and Jaco said in unison.

Caterina came out of the kitchen to greet her sister and her brother-in-law. "Belinha, I didn't know you were coming this soon. I expected you in a few days. Dean and I can handle most of the packing. You really didn't have to come. "Caterina pecked her sister on the cheek as she hugged her and then Jaco.

"Caterina, I wanted to come. Mae is my mother too, you know." The same antagonism was evident between the sisters Alycea noticed with a sigh and a shrug. She couldn't do anything about it, not now. She had enough on her mind.

The sisters turned to look at their mother and saw her walk away from them with her shoulders sagging and her feet shuffling along. They stopped thinking of themselves for just a second and realized that their mother needed them and they had better get along together for her sake.

Caterina rushed forward to help her mother to the chair at the table. Dean was sitting at the table where she had left him sipping his second glass of wine as he looked up surprised to see his sister-in-law and her husband there. He was deep in thought and hadn't heard them at the door.

"Hi Dean," Jaco said. "What are you drinking?"

"I think it's some kind of wine, if you can call it that. I guess it's better than nothing. Do you want some?" Dean grabbed a wine glass out of the cabinet and poured some wine for Jaco. He wanted a drinking buddy since this stay would be a long one, longer than he wanted.

"Thanks, Dean. I think I could use a glass or two myself. It will be a long night, I think. The girls are at it again. You know what I mean?"

"Oh yeah, I certainly do," Dean said as he took a large sip of the poor excuse of a wine.

The next day the men would be sorry they had too much wine, for they would be knee deep in moving boxes and lifting furniture with miserable hangovers.

# CHAPTER 50

Alycea's daughters and their spouses stayed a few days with her until the house was packed up. She left the selling of the house and most of the furniture to her lawyer who would contact her when all was finalized.

Alycea and her daughters had met with the lawyer, James Stevens, at his office the day before they left to go back to their own homes. Atty. Stevens had told Alycea about some legal ramifications and then had reviewed with them some stipulations that Francisco had left regarding his death. Francisco had wanted to be buried in the gravesite he had bought with Alycea back in her hometown and she would subsequently be buried next to him, her first husband, Ed, her mother, Filomena and her second husband Stan.

Atty. Stevens had said he wanted to come back another day with more papers for Alycea to look over and there was another item he needed to discuss with her. Caterina and Dean and Belinha and Jaco said they would stay another day if he needed for them to be there. Atty. Stevens said it was just mundane stuff and they would not be needed.

Atty. Stevens came back the next day after Caterina and Dean and Belinha and Jaco had gone back home. Nolando, one of Caterina and Dean's sons was coming down the following morning to pick up Alycea to bring her back to his home.

Atty. James Stevens pulled out a sheet of paper for Alycea to sign. It was about the matter of the gold coins that Francisco had hidden in the basement amongst the tools and other paraphernalia he had stored there.

Alycea had gone down to the cellar after Caterina and Dean and Belinha and Jaco had gone back home. Her sons-in-law had done a great job of clearing out all the junk but had left Francisco's tool box untouched. Alycea had told them that she was going to leave the tools to her next door neighbor. Alycea opened her husband's tool box to see what she wanted to throw away, that is when she found the small metal box under all Francisco's tools.

Alycea had called Atty. Stevens right away to find someone who could appraise the gold coins for her. He had hurried over to pick up the box and Alycea insisted that she go with him to the appraiser who announced to them that they were worth upwards of $50,000.00.

Atty. Stevens suggested that she put them into a safety deposit box and she could trade them in when the time was right. He had said that gold had continually gone up over the years and never seemed to dip like the stocks, bonds and real estate markets did. He offered to put them in a safety deposit box of her choice near where she would be staying with her family. He returned the next day with a key and a box number.

He had told her to keep quiet about these coins until later on when she could trade them in and then decide how to disburse the money. She and Atty. Stevens were, therefore, the only ones aware of these coins and their worth.

Alycea had put the coins out of her mind for the time being and was relieved somewhat of the responsibility of the house and its care. She knew she would always miss having her own house for that was the first and only time she would have a house of her own. She had always previously lived in tenements and apartments.

Alycea did not know why she hesitated to tell her family about the coins but she thought if something happened to the rest of her money at least she had the coins to fall back on. She also feared that she would be put into a nursing home if she became incontinent or too feeble minded and unable to take care of herself. She still had all her faculties but was slowing down, that is all.

It would take three months after Francisco's death to complete the selling of their house and the transfer of all the property to Alycea's name, along with her two daughters as beneficiaries in case of her death.

\*\*\*

Nolando picked Alycea up the next day. She was all packed and ready to go. She slept part of the way to his house back in Massachusetts and was relieved when she was finally deposited in her new apartment.

Nolando had transformed his cellar into a small apartment for her. It had a little kitchen, dining/sitting area with a TV, a small bedroom and bathroom. She had a separate entrance next to the garage and another door going out to the large backyard that had several fruit trees and a garden. It also had a nice patio with an umbrella and table set and comfy chairs that she could use to get some sun and fresh air. It was lovely and well cared for.

She always prided herself in her clean house. She was aware of her surroundings and just couldn't get down on her hands and knees to wash the floor as she used to do only ten years ago. She now did not cook much either. She managed to survive on little help for fear that they would think she was incapable of taking care of herself and put her away in a home for the elderly and infirm.

She would make herself a boiled egg, a toast and coffee for breakfast and a grilled cheese or ham sandwich for lunch. Nolando's wife, Cyndi, would send down dinner each night, for which she was grateful. She never was too hungry now though. She just couldn't digest a lot of foods. She felt better eating as little as possible, just enough to keep up her strength.

Alycea was happy in her new apartment but still felt lonely. She would call her daughters to talk to them every so often and find out how all the children and grandchildren and great grandchildren were doing.

There were many more of them now. She couldn't keep track anymore of their names or who belonged to which family. Some of the grandchildren would call from time to time to check up on her when they were reminded by their mothers. They came seldom now, always busy with their own lives, but she understood.

Cindy and Nolando were away a lot visiting their daughter at college or just traveling on vacation. They insisted that she have some help. They didn't want to worry about her while they were away. Alycea had a nurse coming in daily now to make sure she took her prescription medication and a housekeeper who cleaned her house and washed her clothes two to three times a week. She had three meals delivered from the Senior Center daily. Also, a kind neighbor would deliver any groceries she would need weekly.

She looked forward to seeing the nurse and housekeeper just to have someone to talk to. She would make tea and offer them some cookies or whatever she had. They sometimes made Alycea a cup of tea but never took any food or drink from her. They were working and were not allowed to do that. Alycea didn't understand this. What harm would a cup of coffee or tea do?

Alycea was happy as long as they sat with her a few minutes after their duties were completed just to talk or listen to her. She would tell them about her long life and her loves but was careful to keep her deepest secrets to herself.

These caretakers always got a kick out of Alycea. She was known to all the nurses and housekeepers as the sweet little old lady who loved to talk.

Her family was planning her ninety-fifth birthday party which was a week away. At that time she would see all of them together. She looked forward to getting out of her little but cozy apartment to see everyone.

***

It certainly was good to see the whole family gathered together in front of her. But Alycea thought, for how many of these parties was she going to be around. She was already ninety-five and there seemed to be no end in sight for her. She was tired and had lost all of her friends. There was no one left her age with which to socialize.

What else did life have to offer her? What else could she do? What else did she want to do? She missed her second husband, Francisco. She thought of him often and wished she had died instead of him. She was too old for everything and mostly she was lonely. She was too old to get married again and sex was out of the question…or was it? She still got urges but couldn't do anything about them. Who would want her at ninety-five years old? She no longer had her face or figure to attract anyone. What did she have to offer anyone?

She watched her large family gathered in front of her as she mulled over what she wanted to do with what was left of her life. They were bringing over her presents. Now, what could they possibly have in those large boxes? I don't need anything she thought. What do you buy an old lady? I don't need any clothes; I don't go anywhere often.

She touched her pearl necklace and thought over a pleasant memory a long time ago of a surprising occurrence on an otherwise unremarkable day.

*** 

Alycea and Ed had been married for several years and were having the usual ups and downs in their marriage. She had gone to the local drug store one day to pick up a prescription for her mother. A handsome man with dark, piercing eyes that cut into her like a sharp knife and left her feeling weak kneed, stood at the counter.

This was the day she had met Marco. She said his name in a whisper. She couldn't get her breath when he spoke to her, "I'm Marco. Can I help you?"

Alycea stuttered, coughed and finally replied, "Yes!"

Marco frowned at first then his face broke into a dazzling smile. "How can I help you?"

She smiled back and felt warm all over as if he had held her in his arms and kissed her. The people behind her were getting impatient as they began to shuffle their feet in exasperation waiting for their turn at the register.

Marco stepped aside, took Alycea by the hand and led her to the storage room. He signaled for a clerk on his way to the room to take over the register.

In the back room he took Alycea into his arms and without a word spoken between them, he kissed her passionately. He reached under her dress and pulled down her panties. Before she could resist, he was inside her. She responded in kind until they both reached satisfying climaxes, more than one for her.

Alycea exchanged a few more kisses with Marco and adjusted her panties and left the store. She had to return a moment later to get the prescription she had forgotten to pick up. She saw Marco behind the counter and he winked at her. She was helped by another clerk and left the store. She thought about what she would have had to say to her mother if she had forgotten the prescription – anything but the truth.

On her way home she could still feel the tingling sensations down there from his touch. Would she see him again? It was a shocking but enjoyable experience. She shivered and thought, what did I do?

There were many more trips to the drug store after that unforgettable day but she never saw Marco again. Over the years she thought of him and wondered if it had all been a dream. She sighed and thought, if it was a dream, it was the best one ever!

She sighed and thought about how most of her pleasures were now being taken away from her. I can't eat much of anything I used to enjoy anymore. I used to love all kinds of meat but have a hard time swallowing it. I like ice cream because it goes down easily and feels cool to my throat. But at times, the cream in it makes me choke.

I used to love steak and onions but now I can't eat either one. They give me extreme gas. No one wants to be in a room with a gassy old woman! I don't move fast enough to get to the bathroom in time either if I eat these things when they cause me distress.

As for sex, that is now a thing of the past but the mind still remembers the pleasant feelings and longs for the pleasures enjoyed only by the young. The only thing I use to do is read about it in all the tawdry novels of romance. Now that has been taken away from me too because of my poor vision.

Oh, my goodness, what is there left for me? Francisco and Ed, I bet you two are up there watching and laughing at me and my many silly problems. I am ready to go any time God wants me. Isn't He ready yet? Doesn't He think I am ready? I have been ready for a long, long time, I tell you! If you can, please, one of you, put in a good word or two for me and tell Him I am ready to come up there. I will even go to confession right after my party if He wants me to. He can take me tonight. I will put out my best dress. I want my girls to know which one I want to be buried in. After all, I want to go up there looking my best.

Alycea came out of her reverie when she heard Belinha's voice calling her. "Mae, do you want to open your gifts since you didn't want to eat any of your food. Your plate is still full. Aren't you hungry? I can help you open each one and read the cards for you. Ok?"

Alycea just nodded to Belinha as she was already tearing open the first large box. Oh, will this ever end, Alycea thought. Why can't they just come over to talk to me and tell me who they all are and listen to what I have to say for a change? I really don't need all this stuff.

She looked around the room at all the children of various ages, from babies to teenagers to adults. Her granddaughter, Jasmine, caught her eye and came over to sit next to her.

"Avoa, are you feeling all right? Do you want something to drink? I can get you some of that liquor, Bailey's Irish Cream, you like at the bar." Jasmine knew what her grandmother liked and saw the sparkle in her eye as she mentioned the liquor. She went over to the bar and bought her a Bailey's in a snifter and placed it on the table in front of her grandmother.

Alycea reached over and grabbed the glass and lifted it to her lips taking at first a small sip then another before putting it back down on the table. Jasmine found herself grinning at the sight of her ninety-five year old grandmother sipping the liquor and making curious noises as she enjoyed it as if it were sex.

It was nice to see her grandmother content even if it was only for a short time.

# CHAPTER 51

## PRESENT TIME

"Avoa, I thought you were having a good time at your ninety-fifth birthday party. Did you ever use any of the presents you received, the new bedspread, sheets, blankets, and the warmer for your coffee?" Jasmine looked at her grandmother anxiously hoping that she would see her smile again.

It seemed like such a long time ago when she had genuinely smiled or laughed out loud. It seemed she had lost all joy in life when her husband, Francisco, had died.

Jasmine remembered that sad day when her mother had called to give her the bad news. It had already been five years since Francisco had died. Her mother had told her that Avoa was hysterical when she had called and didn't know what to do without him. Avoa was too far away from them being in Rhode Island and needed to come back to be with her family again.

Belinha and Jaco had gone to visit their mother along with Caterina and Dean to help her clean out the house and pack up her things to move back home. Belinha had told Jasmine that Alycea was pale and had lost some weight because she was not eating properly. Belinha had been worried about her mother being depressed. It seemed worse than when her mother had lost first, her twin brother,

Antonio, then her first husband, Ed, and then her brother, Manuel. Maybe it was because her mother had been a lot younger back then and had been living locally and closer to her family.

Alycea just smiled a weak, sad smile at her granddaughter and told her, "I don't care to live anymore. Life holds nothing more for me. There are no more surprises or things that I can do."

"Please don't say that, Avoa." Jasmine hugged her grandmother before she left and said, "I will visit you again soon and more often so that we can talk." She also promised, "I'll bring you a lobster roll, your favorite, from a local sandwich shop near my house, the next time I come to visit you."

Alycea's eyes lit up at the mention of lobster and her smile grew a little bigger. She kissed her granddaughter's cheek and said, "Thank you for sitting with me. I look forward to seeing you soon and eating the lobster roll." She smacked her lips at the thought.

But, more troubled times were ahead for Alycea.

\*\*\*

"Mom is in the hospital again, Raymond. She is anemic and her diabetes is out of control. Dr. Everest is taking care of her and said she is now resting comfortably. She is expected to be in the hospital for a few days until he can get her diabetes under control," Jasmine explained to her brother who was disturbingly quiet on the phone.

"Ray, are you okay? You seem too quiet. Is everything all right with you and Loren? Are the girls okay?" Jasmine was anxiously waiting for her brother's response and hoping for the best. Their family couldn't take anything more with their mother's declining health over the past several years.

329

"Oh, yeah, we're all fine. I just got laid off from work, that's all. Thank God we are all healthy, not like Mom. I have to find another job but the company is letting me take a severance package which will tide me over for six months until I can find another job," Ray sighed thinking about what expenses he had and how he was going to pay for his two daughters' college educations.

"Well, that is a relief. I thought you were going to say you or Loren or the girls, Coralyn and Leanna, were sick. Don't scare me like that, okay, little brother? I feel badly for you about your job but you are young enough yet to find something else. It will work out for you, don't worry. Try to go see Mom. It would make her happy and perk up her spirits, okay? I need to call Shannon now and find out more about Mom. She brought Mom to the hospital and is there with her now. I plan to go to the hospital shortly," Jasmine said goodbye to her brother and then dialed her sister.

"Shannon, how's Mom doing? What did Dr. Everest say? When is she coming home?" Jasmine took a breath and let it out slowly.

Jasmine was worried about her mother's health. It had been declining. Her mother had not been watching her diet closely, as usual. Jasmine was also worried about her dad. He was having some funny things happening to his memory lately and they had stopped him from driving a year before that. He was anxious all the time and now was worried about his wife. He needed to be driven to the hospital every day to visit her or he would get upset.

Jasmine was living close by after she had divorced her husband, Frank. She was alone now with her two children out of college and living away from her. She was happy and on her own after many stressful years of marriage. Her daughter, Brittany, had just finished college and her son, Timothy, was now married and had a little boy, Donald. Her children came to visit her and called often. She felt as if her life was just beginning now and she was at last free.

Jasmine loved being a grandmother herself now, and could understand, at times, how it felt to be alone as her grandmother was. She called her twice a week and made plans to go see her again and bring the lobster roll. She wanted to tell her grandmother face to face about her mother being in the hospital. She knew her Avoa would get upset about it. She always worried that her daughters were going to die before she did.

***

"Hi Avoa, are you hungry? I hope you are. I brought your lobster roll," Jasmine said as she walked into her grandmother's tiny apartment holding the lobster roll in a bag out in front of her as a peace offering.

"Hmm, I can almost smell it now. Thank you, Jasmine. I am a little hungry. It is almost dinner time. Can you get me a plate and a cup of coffee from my thermos over on the counter? The thermos was one of the presents from my last birthday. It has come in handy for me to keep my coffee warm all morning and even into the early evening. Cindy fills it up in the morning with fresh coffee and it keeps me all day. I usually drink about three to four cups a day. It keeps me wired."

Jasmine giggled at her grandmother's remark. "Yes, I guess it does, Avoa!"

Jasmine did as she was instructed by her grandmother and placed the lobster roll, which she cut in half, in front of her Avoa with a cup of coffee, cream and no sugar. Avoa could not have the sugar any more due to late onset diabetes.

She watched as her grandmother dug into the lobster roll, putting as much as possible into her mouth and picking up the pieces that dropped out and shoving them into her still full mouth. There were a lot of oohhs and aahhs as she chewed. It was plain to see that she was thoroughly enjoying herself.

Alycea had eaten one half of the lobster roll and sipped her coffee as she announced that she was full and would save the other half of the sandwich for the following day's lunch. She sighed with contentment as her granddaughter removed the rest of the sandwich and handed her a napkin to wipe her face and hands.

"Jasmine, don't worry about that plate, just wrap the sandwich and put it in the refrigerator, if you will, please. I really enjoyed that. It was delicious! Thank you. It has been a long time since I had one of them." She laid her head back against the pad of her rocking chair as a dreamy look suddenly came into her eyes.

"You know, Francisco used to take me for a ride to the beach on a Sunday and we would get a lobster, cole slaw, fries, steamers, and have a feast. He loved seafood too. We had so much in common, more than with Grandpa Ed and I. Oh, you know I have been most fortunate to have loved two men in my day. Well, there was another one but.....that's another story." Jasmine looked over her shoulder as she was cleaning up after her grandmother's dinner with a raised brow at the insinuation of another lover.

Her grandmother never ceases to amaze her. There was always something new she would learn about her Avoa's fascinating life.

Jasmine wondered if this was the time to tell Avoa about her mother being in the hospital. It was a shame since she seemed to be in such a good mood for a change. She had no choice, she must tell her in case her condition got worse.

She knew her grandmother would be upset upon hearing of her mother being hospitalized. Alycea always got angry over the fact that her daughter, Belinha, never took care of herself and was careless about her eating habits and her diabetes. Alycea had lived with her mother's diabetes for most of her life. She knew what her mother had gone through as did Belinha. Her daughter knew better than to neglect her health. She knew the consequences.

"Avoa, I need to tell you something. My mother is in the hospital again. Her diabetes is out of control and she has become anemic. She hasn't been watching her diet, as usual, but she should be much better and ready to come home in a few days. I didn't want you to worry but I thought you would like to know," Jasmine said this all in one breath before she chickened out.

"Oh dear, your mother is always doing that. She loves to eat everything she is not supposed to and then her diabetes goes haywire. I keep telling her not to do that. I worry about her all the time as if she were still a child. What room is she in? Can you call her for me before you leave today? I want to talk to her. It would help if you could write down the room number and phone number for me by the phone. I can call her every day until she gets home. Ok, dear?" Alycea furrowed her brows and shook her head at her daughter Belinha's, behavior.

"Of course, Avoa, I would be happy to do that for you. Now don't scold her please. She knows she was wrong and besides, she is worried about my dad too. He is having some troubles of his own right now. Go easy on her okay, Avoa? She cries so easily nowadays. I can't even ask her how she is feeling. She is always crying." Jasmine's voice as well as her facial expressions were pleading with her grandmother to be kind.

"Do you think I am heartless, Jasmine? Do you really think I would be mean to your mother now that she is not well? What kind of mother would I be? I have always done my best with both my girls. They always were completely different from each other and still are. Belinha was always the more sensitive one while Caterina was the stronger one. I loved them the same, as you know. I always loved them the same," Alycea repeated herself just to make more emphasis

333

on the facts when she felt somewhat uncertain or guilty about something. Jasmine learned this after having spent many years with her grandmother and the many observations she had made.

Jasmine's mother knew that her own mother had favored her sister over her. While Caterina had always felt like the one less loved by her grandmother, Filomena. It was sometimes a hard thing to take, especially when they were growing up. Jasmine knew that even though her mother was a grown up, she still always felt like a child in her mother's presence or whenever Belinha had to deal with Alycea.

Belinha had suffered much when her grandmother, Filomena, father, Ed, and Uncle Manny had died. They had been her staunch supporters. In her ill health now, she needed support from her loved ones, especially her mother, Alycea. Jasmine tried to be there for her mother as much as possible not trusting her grandmother to be much of a support.

Jasmine hoped that her mother would not be angry with her for telling her grandmother that she was in the hospital again. She knew one way or the other she was going to get hell. She kissed her grandmother goodbye after she dialed the hospital for her and excused herself. She didn't want to be around when her grandmother scolded her mother for not taking care of herself.

Jasmine got into her car and drove up to the hospital to see her mother, dreading the fact that she would not be happy with her at all. By this time she was sure her grandmother had said more than enough to her mother during their phone call. Jasmine vowed to stop in at the hospitality shop before going up to visit to buy a bunch of flowers and a magazine for mother to soften her wrath a little.

The flowers and magazine did a lot to defuse Jasmine's mother's ire. But she still had to hear her mother's complaints and what her Avoa had said to her, verbatim.

# CHAPTER 52

Jasmine had just met with her grandmother again to go over her notes and verify dates and events. She also had asked her grandmother if there was anything else she had wanted to add to her life story before Jasmine started typing up her notes to begin her book.

"Well, I guess I told you everything there is to know about me for now. I am not dead yet. There may be more to tell you before I die. You are up to date since you are visiting me more lately and nothing has happened in between your visits."

"I guess you're right, Avoa. I definitely intend to visit you once a week, if I can. If you need to talk to me in between, I wrote my number down on your telephone pad next to the phone. You can always call me. Ok?"

"That's fine, Jasmine. Thank you."

"Maybe the next time we meet, you can tell me about your mysterious other lover? I'll understand if you want to keep him a secret though. I am just curious. I can leave it out of my book if you wish." Jasmine looked hopefully at her grandmother of the possibility of learning a little about this mystery man.

Jasmine never did learn the identity of this mystery man in her grandmother's life. She could only wonder who he could have been and possibly make up something interesting to put into her book about him. She did secretly hope that if her grandmother had an affair it was after her grandfather's death and not before. The thought of such a thing was not pleasant to her.

As it turned out, Jasmine would have to put her grandmother's interests and work on her book on the back burner to deal with other more pressing medical problems of her dad.

Well, we all have good intentions of visiting those we love, as Jasmine had with her grandmother, but sometimes things happen to prevent us from following through with those good intentions.

Death in the family can be one of those unfortunate happenings.

***

The phone rang on her bedside table and she couldn't believe the time on the clock. It was 4:00 a.m. Who could be calling at this ungodly hour? Jasmine thought as she rolled over and grabbed the phone off its princess cradle. She knew that early calls never were good news.

"Sis, Dad is in the hospital! Mom called me on the phone and woke me up at 3:00 a.m. and I went over to her apartment and found Dad on the bathroom floor. Evidently he had passed out. I called 911 immediately.

"He's breathing but oh, my God...I don't know what to do if he dies! Can you come to the hospital as soon as you can? I don't want to be alone here. I left Mom home with Josh and the boys to look after her. She was not feeling well. She's frightened too! I called Ray and he's coming soon. I'm sorry for waking you. I just didn't know what to do. I did not want to make any life-threatening decisions on my own. You do understand, don't you, Sis?" Jasmine could hear her sister's frantic voice and deep sobbing that kept muffling her speech.

"Of course, I will be there as soon as I can. I am over a half hour away, as you know, and I need to get dressed. Why don't you try to relax a little until I get there? I will stop at the Donut Hut and get us both a strong cup of coffee. We can sip as we wait. Please call me if you hear or know anything else about Dad, okay? I will keep my cell phone on. You have my number." Jasmine tried to keep her voice calm in spite of her racing heart and the tears that were now blinding her vision.

Jasmine's husband, Giovanni, had now woken up and was listening intently to his wife's side of the disjointed conversation. He waited patiently for her to get off the phone before he asked her what had happened.

She related the dreadful details as she rushed around to get her clothes ready. Giovanni jumped out of bed with her and rushed to do the same. Within ten minutes they were on their way.

Giovanni looked over at his wife's sticken face and said, "I'll drop you off first and then go to the Donut Hut and pick up three bagels and three coffees and head back to the hospital."

When she got to the hospital, Ray, with his usual large cup of coffee in hand, was driving into a parking lot at the same time. She waited for him and got him up to speed on their father's condition as they walked toward the hospital entrance to the emergency room.

"Where's Giovanni going?"

"He's going to get some coffee and bagels at the Donut Hut."

"I'm all set. I figured I might need this. I hope Dad is doing better."

"Yeah me too, Ray. Shannon was out of her mind when she called me. I'm worried about her too."

"Shannon is strong. She will be okay. It's Dad who isn't."

"I guess you're right, Ray."

Jasmine thought it would be a good idea to call her Aunt Caterina to tell her about her father's hospitalization. Her aunt could be the one to relate the news to Avoa. She didn't feel up to speaking to her grandmother right now. She was too upset and her Avoa would only get her more upset. She would probably put the blame on her mother.

As long as they all catered to Avoa in her advancing years, she would be less cantankerous. Avoa was fortunate to have had two loving and doting husbands. It was difficult for the family to fill the void left by Ed and Francisco.

They all did the best they could but there were always others to worry about too.

***

Jasmine and Ray ran up the ramp to the emergency room entrance of the hospital. Giovanni caught up to them a few minutes later in the emergency room and held Jasmine's hand tightly to give each other strength to face whatever needed to be faced. They saw her sister, Shannon, with her head down sitting in the front row of seats in the waiting room.

"Shannon! How is he doing? Have you heard anything?" Jasmine grabbed her sister in a bear hug as they cried on each other's shoulders. Ray came around both of them and wrapped his sisters in his arms in a cocoon of support.

Shannon related what had transpired since she had been at the hospital, "The nurse came out to ask me for more information and permission to treat him since he was not coherent yet. She said she would come and get me. I could see him when they put him in his room. They will be running a lot of tests and Dr. Everest is here examining him now." Shannon sniffled as she pulled a bunch of tissues out of her pocketbook to blow her nose.

Giovanni handed out the coffees and bagels and urged his wife and Shannon to eat and drink and calm down. While they were sipping their coffees, Giovanni, ever the rock, strong and always in control of situations like this went over to the window, introduced himself, and asked the nurse, whose name tag read Mrs. Taylor, "Is there anything new about Jaco Gomes."

Mrs. Taylor looked up from her paperwork and shook her head and said, "No," in an impersonal way which was not meant to insult or hurt family members. It was just the way medical personnel could distance themselves from all the illness and heartache of their positions.

"As soon as I know anything, I will let you know." The nurse then went back to her work and answered her incessantly ringing phone.

Giovanni walked back to the women who were both wiping tears from their eyes as they anxiously and expectantly looked up at him. He just shook his head at them and said, "There is no new information but the nurse assured me she would let us know when she heard anything. The best thing to do, ladies, is to drink your coffee and eat your bagel to keep up your strength."

"You both have to be strong for your mother and father alike. Your mother is not up to dealing with this, as you know. She is not strong in will or health. You must be there for her to lean on." He sat down next to his wife and took her small hand into his and gave it a reassuring squeeze as he sipped his coffee and ate his bagel. Ray settled down on the other side of Giovanni to talk about mundane things such as golf and work just to settle his nerves.

Jasmine looked lovingly over at her husband as he was smiling and conversing with her brother and thought how much her life had changed when she first met and then married Giovanni DeAngelo. She didn't know how she had ever survived without him in her life.

She knew that her whole family loved him, especially Ray. They had a lot in common and had gone golfing on several occasions.

Jasmine felt the tears pooling in her eyes as she thought of her mother and father and how much they loved Giovanni too. Her husband had begun to call her parents Ma and Pa soon after they were married. This show of respect and affection deeply touched her parents and only brought them closer to their son-in-law.

Her first marriage had been difficult and there were many problems dealing with dialogue. They didn't have any. The second time around she had finally found someone much like her own father. Giovanni was kind, considerate and just all around wonderful to her. She felt like a queen. He lavished her not only with material things but also gave her the respect and the freedom to be herself that she relished and had desperately needed for a long time.

Their marriage was strong. Jasmine thought back to the day that she had first met, Giovanni. He was the lawyer on a case. As a paralegal she had been instructed by the lawyer she worked for to pick up the case files. This lawyer was working on the same case in tandem with Giovanni. From the first moment she saw Giovanni she had fallen hard and fast. What she hadn't known at that time was he had fallen for her in the same way. It was only six months later they were married.

She remembered the day she had introduced Giovanni to her Avoa. Avoa had gushed over Giovanni hugging and kissing him and telling him how handsome he was. She loved him from the start because she could see how happy he made her granddaughter. Giovanni had made her Avoa happy by calling her Avoa from the moment he had met her.

Jasmine's mind was brought back suddenly to the present time. A short while later after bagels and coffee had been exhausted, Dr. Everest came into the emergency waiting area and beckoned them to follow him into the treatment area. There they found their father still in a bed out in the hallway being strapped down to the gurney by two nurses and an orderly. He was definitely agitated but awake and looked confused about where he was and why he was there. He looked directly at his daughters and didn't seem to know who they were.

Shannon and Jasmine both were shocked at his appearance. He was awake but his eyes looked glassy, and that confused and frightened look on his face disturbed them. He couldn't understand why he was being strapped down to the gurney. He kept looking at them for some help and reaching out to them.

The sisters reached out at the same time to each take one of their father's hands to calm him to make it easier for the orderly to finish strapping him down to the gurney. They spoke softly to him with tears in their eyes and hoarse throats choked with emotion. They had never seen their father like this. He seemed helpless and fragile. He had always been strong and had taken such tender care of them. He had been loving, kind and funny, doing silly things to make them laugh when they were sad. He had also been a rock for his extended family, especially for Alycea all those years ago. If only Jasmine and Shannon could do something for him now. They looked at one another for an answer.

Dr. Everest explained that he was running some tests, a CAT scan, X-rays and blood was being drawn on their father. Dr. Everest thought that there was some definite swelling in his brain and that he may have suffered from a stroke.

Jaco had been acting strangely lately and had been recently diagnosed as possibly having early signs of Alzheimer's. He would subsequently have neurological surgery to remove a clot on his brain due to a stroke. He never regained consciousness or spoke again after the surgery. He subsequently died a month later when his heart just stopped.

Alycea called Jasmine and Shannon daily to get an update during this time and was concerned about her daughter, Belinha's, health even more so after her son-in-law had died.

Belinha had subsequently suffered from a stroke within a month after her husband's death and had been paralyzed on the right side and restricted to a wheelchair for the remainder of her life. She followed her husband, Jaco, three years later after becoming depressed and succumbing to an infection which had finally led to congestive heart failure and ultimately her death.

Alycea was traumatized over the loss of her daughter and son-in-law. She could not understand why she was spared to live longer than her youngest daughter. She had lost some more of the spark that was once part of her personality. She had always called and spoken to each of her daughters on a daily basis and now called Caterina, her only daughter, twice a day to make up for losing Belinha.

Caterina was beside herself with grief over losing her little sister, and having to deal with her mother on her own was even more trying and tiring for her. Her health was not good now either. She had recently suffered through triple by-pass surgery and had been having back problems for years and was in constant pain. Her husband, Dean, had his own share of problems too with hip replacement surgeries and knee problems from his years as a football player.

Alycea feared that she would lose Caterina before God took her. She prayed each night that He would take her first. She implored St.

Theresa to help her and even prayed to her mother to intercede if she could. She could not stand to lose another daughter. She had to die first but what could she do? She had a strong heart the doctors told her and the only problems were her dimming vision and her sciatica, which was the reason she could no longer walk for long distances. She now needed the aid of a walker just to get around her little apartment. Longer distances required a wheelchair.

Alycea had to be put into a wheelchair to be brought into the church for her daughter's funeral. She was distraught and exhausted from crying and had to be brought directly home after the prayers at the gravesite.

Once home after Nolando got Alycea settled in her kitchen with a cup of coffee, he went back upstairs to his family. Alycea decided to take a walk in the backyard. There was a path that went through the woods. She felt restless and was upset over losing her daughter. She wanted to get away from the confining space of her tiny kitchen. She felt like the walls were closing in on her.

She couldn't cry anymore. Her eyes were all dried out. If she could get outside, she would feel better. She needed to pray to St. Theresa to help her. Also, she wanted to talk to Francisco. She had many one-sided conversations with him since his death and always felt better afterward. She didn't want anyone to hear her talking to herself though.

She stumbled, nearly fell a few times and somehow managed to walk slowly as she followed the path holding onto trees as she moved along. She felt tired and winded but kept walking. When she was far enough away from the house, she leaned against a tree and began her conversation with her deceased husband.

Shortly afterward, her grandson, Nolando, brought down her dinner but found an empty apartment. He called out her name and looked around the yard. He followed the path into the woods and found her lying down in a pile of leaves. She was fast asleep. At first he thought she had died. He shook her awake and helped her back to her apartment. He gave her a hot cup of coffee to wake her up completely and served her dinner.

"What were you doing out there, Avoa?"

Alycea finished swallowing her food and answered, "I like to go out there. I feel close to God and Francisco."

Nolando shook his head and said, "You can't do that anymore, Avoa. You could get hurt and we wouldn't even know it. If you need to go outside, call me. Okay?"

Alycea nodded and continued eating. She would continue to go there again and again and not tell anyone.

# CHAPTER 53

A week before her grandmother's one hundredth birthday, Jasmine called her, "Hi Avoa. Are you up to having some company today? My daughter, Brittany, is coming with me to visit you. Did you have a nice visit with my son, Timothy, the other day? He told me he enjoyed talking and spending time with you. His boys are really getting big, huh?"

"Yes, I am here. I have nowhere else to go, Jasmine. What time are you coming over? I would love to see you both. I haven't seen Brittany for a while since she got married last year. Oh yes, I did really enjoy spending time with Timothy and his sons. They are getting so big. They weren't too sure of me at first since I hadn't seen them since they were babies. They were adorable. They kept calling me Avoa and kissing me."

"I am glad to hear that. They love you, Avoa, as we all do. You remember that, ok? We will be over right after work. Is there anything you would like me to pick up for you for your dinner? Do you want another lobster roll or something else?" Jasmine could almost hear her thinking about what she wanted to eat. She wasn't eating as much as she used to but she still loved her lobster.

"Oh dear, don't go to any trouble for me. I'll be happy just to see you both. But…a lobster roll sounds good. I really enjoyed the last one you brought me. I ate the rest of it the next day. That seemed like so long ago, doesn't it?" Alycea always had a way of letting her family know that she was being neglected and she never lost her assertiveness.

Jasmine had to keep the chuckle back as she spoke to her Avoa, "Not too long. That's good, Avoa. I'm glad you enjoy lobster so much."

Avoa was still the feisty woman she remembered growing up. That much had never changed. She surprisingly looked darned good too, for nearly one hundred years old. Her hair was stubbornly holding onto its dark brown to almost black color amidst the gray and white and was as thick and lustrous as ever waving here and there around her face.

The family had been planning Avoa's big birthday for weeks before and now with only a week to go, they were all hoping she would make one hundred years. They wanted to have the big celebration and get a citation from the President of the United States. They would also request citations from the Mayor and Governor of the city and state. They had requested the local paper to write an article about her and her 100 years after her party. That would be a surprise to her. Avoa would just love that. She craved attention and anything they could do to keep her happy, they did. She could be quite trying at times but they all loved her. She was, after all, the matriarch of the family. They were all here because of her.

*** 

A few days after her party the local newspaper sent a reporter and photographer to Avoa's house to do a special piece on her 100th birthday. She was in her glory. She had two young men there to listen to her every word and snap her photo. She posed and batted her eyes at them. They both got quite a kick out of her. They mentioned this to Avoa's grandson and his wife right after they finished talking with Avoa. They all got a chuckle out of that.

A week after Avoa's one hundredth birthday celebration, with citations and all the hoopla to go along with it, Jasmine's cousin, Nolando, called her to tell her that their grandmother was in the hospital due to an infection. He said that Avoa would be there for a few days before being put into a nursing home.

Jasmine shuddered at the thought of her grandmother being in a place where she had no control over herself or anything else. She would not like it and would fight them all the way. She feared that this could be her grandmother's demise. She relayed the information to her sister, Shannon, and her brother, Ray. She wanted them to be prepared for the worst.

This made Jasmine remember when her mother had to be put into a nursing home for a short time after each hospitalization. She had gotten weaker and could not be left alone in her in-law apartment after her father had died. It had been too difficult for Shannon to keep an eye on her mother all the time. She still had to work and her own family to care for. It was the most difficult thing to do for all of them. It proved to be their mother's downfall which could repeat itself now with their grandmother.

Jasmine knew how feisty her grandmother was and how difficult it had become for her cousin and his wife to care for Avoa in their home any longer. She had been living with them for ten years now. They had been wonderful to her and had done all they could to keep her in her own apartment in their home.

No one expected Avoa to survive this long - to be one hundred years old. She was the oldest living relative in the family. No one ever came close to surviving to that ripe old age.

Jasmine had lost both of her parents, with her father dying first. She didn't want to think about her Avoa dying. Jasmine knew that it was time for her but it was going to be hard on all of them to say goodbye to Avoa.

Jasmine went to see her in the hospital the day before she was released to go into the nursing home. Unfortunately her grandmother was sound asleep and did not wake up to see her there. She tried everything to wake her up, talking and shaking her lightly, but she slept on and on. She finally left after kissing her forehead and lightly patting her on her hand swollen from the IV.

The next time she saw her was in the nursing home a few days later. She looked wonderful. Her hair was all done up and she was smiling as Jasmine walked into her room. Her grandmother had talked non-stop, excited about her new surroundings which thoroughly surprised Jasmine. She hadn't expected her grandmother to be as accepting of the big change in her living quarters.

This newfound excitement lasted all of one month. She steadily went downhill after that by refusing to listen to her attendants and pushing her food away. She became at first stubborn and then increasingly more despondent with each passing day.

Jasmine thought back to the day she and Brittany had visited with Avoa in her basement apartment for the last time and how talkative and excited she had been to have company. She had eaten most of her lobster roll too, along with her usual cup of coffee. She had told them stories of her life, most of these Jasmine knew by heart while Brittany had only heard for the first time.

Brittany had told her great grandmother her good news; she was pregnant with her first child. Avoa had jumped up and down from her rocking chair as far as a one hundred year old woman possibly could, bringing her hands up to her wide open mouth and a surprised and happy look coming into her cloudy eyes. She had taken Brittany into a tight embrace saying, "Oh little Brittany, I am really happy for you. You are going to be a mother. What do you want to have? A girl would be nice, don't you think? Your brother, Timothy, has three boys. A girl would definitely be wonderful. I can't wait to hold her in my arms. I will be a great, great grandmother! Your baby will be beautiful just like you and your handsome husband, Philip." Avoa had then clapped her hands together in excitement. Feeling magnanimous, Avoa had then given Jasmine a gift, a beautiful needlepoint that her family back in Madeira had given to her years earlier. She also tried to give Brittany one too but Brittany had told Avoa she would have to pick it up another time. She didn't have any place to put it in her crowded little bungalow. They had had a wonderful visit and left with a good feeling and closer to Avoa than ever before.

Avoa had taken Jasmine aside just before they were leaving her apartment, whispered something to her, and had placed an object into her hand.

Brittany had been curious as to what that was all about. She had asked her mother about it and Jasmine had just shrugged her shoulders saying, "You know Avoa, she was just saying goodbye. She thinks that she will not live much longer. I told her not to worry that she would live to be one hundred and ten. She has been doing this each time I come, as if it were going to be the last time we see other."

"Well Mom, she is, after all, one hundred years old and the chances are she will not live much longer. She still does seem hearty though, doesn't she?" Brittany smiled just thinking back over some of the funny things her great grandmother had said about her life and sex. She always talked about it. It made Brittany blush just at the thought of her great grandmother as a sexual being. Eww, yuck!

Jasmine joined in with her daughter with a few yucks of her own. It broke them both into fits of giggles. Avoa was one in a million!

Brittany looked beautiful in her pregnancy and just glowed. She turned to look at her mother with a dazzling smile and said, "Mom, do you think Avoa was happy that I am going to have a baby? She thinks it is going to be a girl. Phil wants a boy but, you know, I think I would like a girl. I think you would too, right?" Brittany waited for her mother's response.

"Well, sweetie, I want a healthy and happy grandchild. The sex doesn't matter to me. I will love it no matter what. I dearly love all my grandsons as you know. They are precious. Each one is a joy and has a special distinctive personality. I look forward with great anticipation to see what this child will be like. We know it will be beautiful!" She looked at her daughter with love and admiration. She was proud of the beautiful, strong, and intelligent woman she had become, and felt she had done a good job of raising both her children. Her son was a handsome and successful man with three beautiful sons and a wonderful and lovely wife, Marianne. Jasmine was so blessed, she felt as if she would burst.

Joy sometimes seems too fleeting, for it would be the last time that they would laugh over Avoa and her inimitable ways. They knew her death was inevitable and they would have to face it one day. But they avoided thoughts of her death as long as they could. Over the next few months they would witness her deterioration and have to come to terms with her demise.

Once Avoa was in the nursing home, Jasmine went to see her twice a week. She noticed the drastic change in her grandmother's demeanor. Avoa Alycea always had a glassy, faraway look in her eyes as if she was being heavily medicated. She was usually half asleep when Jasmine arrived and seldom was alert enough to talk to her. She missed her feisty, outspoken, opinionated grandmother. She had even asked a few nurses to check on her Avoa because she was concerned about her condition. They just told her that her grandmother was sleeping and not to worry, after all she was one hundred years old.

This greatly disturbed Jasmine and she discussed this with her siblings, cousins and Aunt Caterina who all assured her that this was to be expected. They all thought that she would snap out of it and become once again her exuberant, feisty and talkative self. This was not to be.

Jasmine once again got an early morning call, this time from her cousin, Nolando, telling her in a choked voice, "Jasmine, I'm sorry, I have some sad news. It's Avoa. She's gone."

Avoa, Alycea Ataide Rubelo Tavares had died, fittingly, on May 11$^{th}$, Mother's Day. He explained that the nursing home had called him to say that Alycea had disappeared from her room. He had gone there to help find her. He knew where she could have gone. Evidently, she did not take her medication in the morning that would have kept her sedated. This enabled her to walk out of the home somehow without anyone seeing her.

Nolando helped search the grounds and found her an hour later in the woods sitting up against a tree. She appeared to be fast asleep but when they checked for a pulse – there was none.

It had been five months after she had reached the age of one hundred years old. She went out with a bang on her favorite day of the year, a day on which she would always be remembered by her family with great love and devotion.

She was an extraordinary woman of her time. She lived during a difficult century and survived many tragedies in her lifetime which had only made her stronger and more resilient. She lived through a recession, The Great Depression, two World Wars, Korean War, Vietnam War, and the Gulf War and saw nineteen presidents from Theodore Roosevelt to Barack Obama preside over the USA.

She passed on a wonderful legacy to her large family and would always be remembered as Avoa (Portuguese for grandmother) to everyone who knew her whether they were related to her or not. She was a grandmother to one and all.

Her booming laugh may now be silenced along with her courage and feistiness but it would forever live on in her family's hearts and minds.

She may not have been perfect but she was special, for she had paved her way to a new land, a new home, and a new life enabling the rest of her family to live in freedom and prosperity.

# CHAPTER 54

In case you are wondering about the gold coins, unfortunately for the family Avoa never mentioned them in her will and never told anyone but Atty. Stevens, her lawyer, and much later on, her granddaughter, Jasmine, about them.

Jasmine had obtained the key to the safety deposit box from her grandmother before her death, when Alycea had slipped it into her hand along with a note of explanation as Jasmine was leaving her grandmother's apartment after her latest visit.

Avoa had put a finger to her lips and whispered, 'Jasmine, this is a gift for you to show you how much I love you. Do with it whatever you want. Where I am going I will not need it. Do not tell anyone of this gift. That is all I ask. I don't want everyone fighting over it. I know you will do much good with it.'

Jasmine remembered being a little confused at first then it had dawned on her that this was the key to her grandmother's hidden fortune after reading her note. She felt guilty about not telling anyone but she promised her grandmother to keep her secret and that she would use the money wisely.

She was going to use the money if there was enough to do some home improvements, take a little trip with her husband, help her children with their mortgages and save a little for her grandchildren's future education. If her mother and father had survived, she would have taken care of them too. She would also give a little to both her brother and sister who were struggling with their children's college tuitions and mortgage payments. She knew she had to include the rest of the family by giving some to each of her cousins and let them take care of their extended families. She did not want to cause any dissension amongst everyone.

She also was going to send a generous donation to St. Theresa's Society of the Little Flower in memory of her great grandmother, Filomena, and her Avoa. Over the years St. Theresa had always kept the family together through the faith and love that was shared with her beginning with Jasmine's great grandmother, Filomena, and then her Avoa Alycea. St. Theresa became the patron saint of the family.They turned to her for prayer and guidance.

Jasmine continued to pray to St. Theresa with much love and praise for all that had been given to them through her intercessions with the Lord to this day keeping the tradition going.

***

At the reading of Alycea Ataide Rubelo Tavares' last will and testament one week after her death, her lawyer, James Stevens, was not present. Supposedly he had turned over his practice to his associate, Stephen Goss, and had left the country.

Avoa had left all her personal belongings such as jewelry and clothes to her remaining daughter with a few odds and ends and paintings and framed needlepoint to each of the grandchildren. Any money left in her bank account was to be given over to her grandson, Nolando, for taking care of her all those years. There was not much else left to give away.

Nolando and Cindy cleaned out her apartment and packed up her things and brought them over to his mother, Caterina. What Caterina didn't want was then given away to charitable organizations or just thrown away.

\*\*\*

Jasmine had gone to the bank after the reading of her Avoa's will with the intention of opening her grandmother's safety deposit box with the key that she had given her. She had figured that the coins would have more than tripled in their worth by now. She was planning on cashing them in as soon as possible and would have to pay the necessary taxes on the amount.

Jasmine's grandmother reported that after she had found the coins in her basement, Atty. Stevens had taken them to a gold dealer. There was approximately 250 ounces of gold in the metal container under Francisco's tools. At that time, it was estimated to be worth around $100,000. If gold continued to rise off the charts it would probably be worth, if currently selling at $1700 per ounce, around half a million dollars.

She picked up the box, which Jasmine thought seemed surprisingly light for its contents, turned the key in the box slowly, carefully and then opened it.

The box...was empty.

Jasmine stood looking at the empty box and shook her head. She knew where the gold had disappeared to now. She wondered if this person was enjoying his carefree life at her Avoa's expense.

She looked up and whispered, "Sorry Avoa, but thank you, just the same, for all you have done for me and our extended family. We love you. Say 'hi' to Grandpa Ed, Granny Filomena, Uncle Manny, Uncle Antonio and Francisco for me.

## THE END

# OTHER BOOKS BY J.E. SPINA

**Novels for 18+**

*Hunting Mariah* (Finalist in Authorsdb 1st Lines Contest)

*How Far Is Heaven*

*An Angel Among Us (A Short Story Collection)*

*Mariah's Revenge (Sequel to Hunting Mariah)*
 (Finalist in Authorsdb 1st Lines Contest)

*In A Second*

# ABOUT THE AUTHOR

J. E. Spina is a retired administrative secretary from a public school system in Massachusetts. She has always loved writing poetry, novels and children's stories.

This is the fifth novel that J.E. Spina has published. She also has a short story collection written under J.E. Spina.

She has published 17 children's stories and 12 middle-grade novels under Janice Spina. Janice is working on a YA fantasy series and four books in a new mystery series.

J.E. Spina lives in New Hampshire with her husband, John, and two tanks of fish. John is the illustrator of her children's books and designer of her book covers.

If you enjoyed this book, please leave a review where you purchased it and spread the word to your family and friends. J.E. Spina loves to hear from readers and welcomes reviews from wherever her books are purchased. She says, "It's like Christmas each time I receive a review!"

If you would like to be on J.E. Spina's email list to receive updates, newsletters, and special deals on books, please send a request to Jemsbooks.com and put in subject line **JEMSBOOKS MAILING LIST**.

# A NOTE FROM THE AUTHOR

This story was written over ten years ago. I dedicated this story to my grandmother, a formidable character, who paved the way along with her mother for my whole family to come to America, Land of the Free; Home of the Brave.

It is entirely through my creative license and imagination that this began to form in my head. I did use some of my grandmother's characteristics in the main character, but everything else is purely fictional except for those facts listed below.

There are some similarities between my grandmother's life and this story. Let me explain. She did have a twin brother and an older brother. She did emigrate from Madeira, Portugal, traveled to Brazil to meet her twin brother, obtained her license when she was in her forties, and ended up in a nursing home. Everything else that happened before, in between and after was created in my mind.

If you have never been to Madeira, hopefully, you will travel there one day. Madeira is a beautiful island, a green, mountainous place rich in history, breathtaking landscapes, flora and fauna and culture with talented artisans who create outstanding wine, pottery and needlepoint. The cover is an actual photo my husband and I took from our trip there in 2018.

I think most writers create stories and base their characters on people they know or have met at one time or another in their lives. It is much easier to write about someone or something you know than not. But, at the same time it is a joyous adventure to create something out of nothing and ride with it. I did a little of both. I had fun embellishing and creating scenarios that I thought would be interesting to my readers. Please note that some places in this story are actual cities/towns while others are not.

I hope you enjoyed this work of fiction. I am sure my grandmother would have loved it!

Thank you for purchasing one of Jemsbooks. I appreciate your kind support of me and my books.

If you like this book, a review would be greatly appreciated wherever you purchased it. Reviews and word of mouth are the best way to spread your thoughts about books. Please share your review with friends and family. I would love to hear from you. You can reach me at jjspina(at)comcast(dot)net.

All my books are available on Amazon and Barnes & Noble. Watch for more books coming for all ages.


With Blessings & Love,

J.E. Spina